I0770670

Pyric Realm

Book One of the Pyric Veil Saga

By:

Chelsea MacArthur

<u>Content Warning</u>

This book contains mature themes, including violence, emotional trauma, stalking, supernatural horror, death, body transformation, and scenes of torture. It also includes consensual sexual content intended for mature readers.

Pyric Realm explores grief, psychological tension, and intense emotional bonds in a dark fantasy setting. Reader discretion is advised.

Pyric Realm
© 2025 Chelsea MacArthur
All rights reserved.

No part of this book may be reproduced, distributed, or transmitted in any form or by any means—electronic, mechanical, photocopying, recording, or otherwise—without the prior written permission of the author, except in the case of brief quotations embodied in critical reviews and certain other noncommercial uses permitted by copyright law.

This is a work of fiction. Names, characters, places, and incidents are either products of the author's imagination or used fictitiously. Any resemblance to actual events, locales, or persons—living or dead—is purely coincidental.

Cover design and interior layout by Chelsea MacArthur
First Edition: October 2025
ISBN: 979-8-90046-262-2

For more information, visit:
https://chelseamacarthur.wixsite.com/chelsea-marie-macart

Dedication

(Or WARNING depending on who is reading this)

To my husband —
You poor, beautiful fool. You watched me vanish into this story like a sleep-deprived cryptid, whispering lore to myself and clicking on my iPad like a caffeinated goblin. You endured my 3 a.m. plot spirals, existential monologues, and questions like, "Would you still love me if I became a haunted dispatch demigod with trauma wings?"

You read the whole thing. Multiple times. You pretended to care about my fake people's very real feelings. That's marriage. Or Stockholm syndrome. Either way—thank you. I love you and I'm sorry about the crumbs in the bed.

To my dispatch family and first responder chaos crew —
Thank you for answering chaos with calm, for surviving things people can't imagine, and for letting me text you mid-shift things like "Hey what does blood smell like when it's magical?"

This book was written between 911 calls, night shifts, panic naps, and the echo of the shittiest radio traffic (you know who you are). You kept me sane. Or at least functionally feral.

Every line has echoes of radio static and half-muttered "I'm too old for this shit" energy. You are the reason I survive the real world long enough to create fake ones.

To my kids, both the ones I birthed and the few I claimed along the way —
You are chaos and softness, fire and anchor. You remind me daily that love doesn't stop at bloodlines, it expands with every stubborn heartbeat that chooses to stay.

This book is proof you can build whole worlds in the cracks between exhaustion, grief, and laughter. Every word was written with you at my side, even when you were just in the next room demanding snacks.

You are my legacy. You are my magic. You are my why.

To the ones still standing after the fire —
This story is for you. For all of us who carry weight no one else sees.

Let's burn together.

Contents of the Veil

Chapter One: The Call

Seren

The night shift always started the same. Flickering fluorescent lights hummed overhead, casting a pale glow on the worn desks and softly beeping consoles. The city of Redmill only had one dispatcher during graveyards, and Friday through Monday, that was Seren Cross's seat — the lone voice tethered to a town that buried its horrors beneath polite silence.

Redmill wasn't big enough to demand more. A dying mill town tucked into the hills, half-forgotten by the rest of the county. One main road, two bars, and a mayor who still thought potlucks counted as public policy. Most folks didn't lock their doors, didn't ask questions, and certainly didn't go looking for what might be watching from the woods. The police department operated out of a converted brick storefront with a two-cell jail and a soda machine that hadn't worked since 1999. There was no overlap in coverage — just a night crew of two officers and one dispatcher, holding the line until sunrise.

Here, strange didn't get a task force. It got a shrug, a line in a report, and a stale cup of coffee.

But Seren knew better. She always had.

Seren adjusted the headset over her ears, brushing a stray strand of midnight- black hair from her face as she settled into the chair. The dispatch center was silent for now, but the calm was always temporary. Somewhere out there, voices in distress waited to break through.

Background radio chatter buzzed from the corner speaker —

overlapping units clearing minor calls, license plate checks, and half-audible jokes passed between cops too tired to sound amused. The occasional burst of static punctuated the rhythm, like the city itself was breathing through wires. Even the machines had rhythm here — consoles beeping in different tones, a ventilation system that sighed in sync with her own fatigue.

The clock flipped to 11:47 p.m. Her screen winked to life with an incoming call — UNKNOWN NUMBER. Seren tapped the button and spoke clearly, calmly:

"911, what is the location of your emergency?"

A shaky breath. "I–I don't know. An alley… somewhere near 12th and Mercer, I think."

Seren's fingers danced across the console, searching for GPS data. No ping. No confirmed location.

"Okay. Stay with me. Can you describe what you see?"

"It's dark. An alley. I thought it was a person, but it's… wrong. The shadows are crawling. They're —"

She leaned forward, voice gentle but urgent. "What's happening?"

The line fell silent except for harsh, shaking breaths. Seren pressed the mic closer. "Are you injured?"

"I don't… I don't know. It's looking at me. It's —"

A screech of metal tearing, a sharp crash, and then a scream ripped raw and broken through the line. The call dissolved into static.
Seren's entire body went still. She brushed the faint scar along her jaw as a cold jolt ran down her spine. The threads between worlds — the Veil — pulsed quietly at the edges of her senses.
"Sir? Sir? Are you there?" she gasped, but the line remained dead.

She swallowed hard, bracing herself against the console, willing the dizziness to settle.

Her fingers trembled as she reached for the controls.

She switched to the Redmill City Police channel. Anything to ground herself.

"Dispatch to 401 and 402. Respond priority — possible unknown assailant. Caller disconnected after scream, no location lock. Area of 12th and Mercer."

"401 and 402, copy. Show us en route, code 3," came the crackled reply.

Seren changed to the Redmill EMS channel. "EMS 260, respond to the area of Mercer and 12th to stage one block from scene. Male caller, unknown injury. Law enforcement en route. Will advise when scene is secure."

"EMS 260 copies. Show us en route to the staging area."

Seren exhaled slowly and sank back into her chair, heart pounding. The strange calls always came on her shifts. She had all the best stories, but too many of them left her staring at the ceiling long after clocking out — more questions than answers.

Minutes later, the radio crackled.
"Dispatch, Units 401 and 402. Show us in the area. Attempting to locate the caller."
"Copy, both units in the area at 00:02."

Seren waited, holding her breath. Would they find someone in the alley? Or would it be like the last time — no witness, no evidence of a crime, just a cold spot where terror had bled through?

"Dispatch, 401."
"401, go ahead."
"Scene is secure. No sign of the caller or an attacker. We located a broken cell phone in the area, appears to be a burner phone. We also found a burn mark on the brick wall, roughly six inches across, possibly a handprint. No other evidence. Medical can stand down. We'll be clear, unable to locate."

"401, copy at 00:26."

Seren rolled her eyes and muttered under her breath, "Of course you didn't find anything." Our graveyard 'detective' probably spent all of five minutes squinting at shadows before deciding his squad car nap was more pressing.

Seren switched to the EMS radio channel.
"EMS 260, law enforcement on scene advises you can stand down."
"EMS 260 copies. Clear and available for calls."

The dispatch room felt colder, the weight of silence pressing in. Seren traced the faint scar on her jaw and closed her eyes. The Veil was fraying. Threads were burning.

A soft beeping from the door's security keypad echoed through the room, followed by the quick clack of the lock disengaging. The door clicked open, revealing Marisol. Still in her EMS jacket, her dark curls pulled back loose but messy from the night's shift, she stepped inside. Her eyes held that steady, knowing warmth — the kind only someone who's seen too much pain could carry.

"I heard the call got weird tonight," Marisol said quietly, settling into the empty dispatch station beside Seren.

Seren nodded, brushing a hand through her dark hair as she pulled up the recording on her console. Somehow, Marisol always knew when she needed support — five years of late-night shifts and long calls had a way of teaching that.

"Burn mark on the brick. Broken phone. No sign of the guy. Whatever he saw… it wasn't human."

Marisol leaned forward, a faint tension settling across her features as Seren hit play. Her fingers curled slightly, knuckles whitening.

The crackling line carried shaky breaths, terrified words, the screech of metal, and a raw, ragged scream that clenched at Marisol's chest as much as Seren's. The static swallowed the sound.

Marisol exhaled slowly. "That wasn't a normal call. Not for any alley I've been to."

Seren tapped a slow, quiet rhythm on the desk with her fingers — a habit to steady herself. "They didn't find him. Just that burn mark. Like someone pressed a hand into the brick, dragging fire across the wall."

"Sounds like your shadows again," Marisol murmured. "You sure it's not just trauma talking?" Her voice was gentle, but the question hung heavy. Seren didn't answer. Just stared at the static.

Marisol reached out, resting a comforting hand on Seren's arm. "You've been carrying these threads for a while now. It's okay to admit it's getting heavier."

Seren met her gaze, the weight behind her dark eyes palpable. "Yeah.

The Veil's thinning. And whatever's slipping through… it's not done."

Marisol stood, brushing a hand down her worn EMS jacket, and gave a faint, knowing smile. "Call me if you need a partner in trouble — or someone to drag you out of it."

The door beeped again and clicked shut behind her, the lock securing with a soft thud. Seren was left with the quiet hum of the dispatch center.

Seren pulled the headset down to rest around her neck and rubbed a hand down her face, exhausted. The room felt too quiet now, too still. Redmill had a way of swallowing its secrets, and tonight would be no different unless she refused to look away.

She glanced at the clock — still hours until 4 a.m. when her relief was due. The Veil would close long before she was free from her desk. Whatever had bled into Redmill tonight would slip back to where it came from, and no one but Seren would bear witness to its passing. Not the responding units. Not the detectives. Not even the caller, if he was still alive to remember.

Seren pushed herself to her feet and crossed to the frosted glass window. Her reflection shimmered faintly, distorted by the glow. The city shimmered faintly beyond the glow of the dispatch room — a quiet façade, a mask for darker things. Somewhere down those streets, threads were burning, and hands were reaching.

She pressed a palm to the glass. It would be a long night. But Redmill needed its witness, and Seren Cross refused to look away.

"I hear you," she whispered to the dark. "I see you. And I won't forget"

Whatever was crawling in the alley, whatever was pressing burning hands to its walls, would have to be answered for. Even if she was the only one listening.

With a slow breath, she sank back into her chair and pulled the headset over her ears, brushing the console awake. Another call winked onto the screen. Another voice. Another night.
The Veil would rise and fall with or without her, but as long as she was here, as long as she drew breath, she would listen.

Chapter Two: The Fraying Edge

Seren

Seren glanced at the clock — 3:55 a.m. — almost time for her escape. The numbers blinked like a countdown to sanity.

Just then, the door clicked open and David walked in, holding a giant coffee in one hand and a bagel in the other. Their eyes met, and he stood a little straighter, brushing a hand down the front of his shirt in a feeble attempt to wipe away the evidence of breakfast. Everyone in dispatch knew the rule: you eat when you can,because you might not get the chance later.

"Morning, Cross," he said,voice low but warm as he logged into the terminal beside her. "What's the situation?"

Seren sank back in her chair, brushing hair out of her eyes as she started logging out. "Uneventful shift until just before midnight. Then a call came in from an unknown number — panicked guy near 12th and Mercer. No GPS ping. Units responded, found a broken phone, and a burn mark on the brick. No suspect. No victim."

David frowned, leaning closer to the screen. "Burn mark? That's new. I swear you have a beacon for this kind of weird stuff."

Seren shrugged, brushing a hand across the edge of the console like it was nothing. "Guess Redmill doesn't like making sense."
David nodded, already picking up the phone. "I'll call around. See if anyone matching his description shows up at the ER. Let you know."

Seren offered a faint smile and stood, stretching the stiffness from her spine. David was good people. The kind who didn't ask questions he didn't want real answers to.

"Thanks, David," she said. "Stay sharp."

He returned the smile, already half-distracted by the call. "Try not to chase monsters in your off time."

But that was exactly what she planned to do.

The hallway outside the dispatch center was quiet, the kind of stillness that made thoughts louder. Redmill always felt just a little too quiet at this hour, like the town was holding its breath between sins.

Seren jogged across the lot to her car. With the sun hitting it just right, it looked like her personal chariot to hell — sleek, black, and utterly unapologetic. It was the sports car of her dreams. A 2019 Challenger, fully blacked out. Arguably a poor financial decision. Loud, fast, and maybe a tad illegal— which was probably why she loved it so much. Her happy place. Her recklessness on wheels. Seren had a habit of chasing the edge, and this car never let her forget it.

She dropped into the driver's seat and started the engine, the deep purr curling into her bones like a lullaby written in gasoline and bad choices. She pulled out of the secure lot and onto Government Way, the rising sun painting the horizon like a flame burning across the earth — eerily beautiful and faintly ominous. Like the world was warning her in color.

The engine rumbled beneath her, steady and familiar. It should've been comforting. But today, it felt like a heartbeat out of sync.

She took a right at the light, reaching for her coffee — and froze.

A pair of lilac eyes stared back at her in the rearview mirror.
She slammed on the brakes, tires screeching as the car lurched to a halt in the middle of the road. The seatbelt bit into her shoulder. Her heart pounded in her chest. She twisted around in her seat, expecting someone — something — to be there.
But the back seat was empty.

The silence was deafening. No wind. No passing cars. Just the thud of her pulse in her ears.

Breathing hard, she sank back into her seat, brushing hair from her face as she tried to steady herself.

"Maybe I really do need some sleep," she muttered, staring at the empty backseat. "Or a psychiatrist."

But deep down, she knew it wasn't exhaustion. Her hands tightened on the wheel.

With one last glance in the mirror, Seren continued down Redmill's quiet streets. The screams and screeching metal from the call haunted her ears, but it was the eyes that stuck — too vivid to be imagined.

She argued with herself for a few blocks. She should go home, crash for a few hours, eat something that resembled a meal. But it was useless. The thought of that alley — the scoured bricks and the broken phone, the terror still hanging in the air — was like a hook buried deep under her ribs.

With a sharp exhale, Seren tightened her grip on the wheel and spun the car around in a clean, screeching turn. Whatever she was chasing tonight, it started in that alley. And she wouldn't rest until she had seen it for herself.

Seren pulled to a stop half a block from the alley, cutting the engine. Redmill was deep in its pre- dawn silence — no neon signs, no hum of traffic, no sound except the scuff of her boots as she stepped out onto the pavement. The mist wrapped around each footfall, swallowing it whole. Like the town didn't want her footsteps remembered.

The alley was darker than she expected. The lone streetlamp at the corner offered little more than a faint, sickly glow, its light fading long before it reached the space between the buildings. Shadows pooled deep in the narrow gap, swallowing the edges of a rusted dumpster and a crumbling brick wall. The air felt damp and charged, prickling faintly against her skin. A low hum buzzed at the edge of hearing.

Seren drew a slow breath and pulled a flashlight from her jacket, clicking it on. The beam cut a sharp path through the mist, crawling across broken asphalt and peeling paint until it landed on a long, black scorch mark. Even from a distance, its shape was unmistakable — a hand, fingers splayed and clawed, burned deep into the brick. The edges shimmered faintly, as if some ember refused to die.

Her breath caught in her throat. This wasn't graffiti. It wasn't vandalism or some weird prank. Something had left this behind — something not human. The air around it felt warped, like the heat was still clinging to the stone, even in the cool of morning.

Seren stepped closer, her flashlight steady, though her pulse wasn't. She reached out instinctively, stopping just shy of the scorched print. The brick around it was cracked, blistered outward from the center like it had been seared from within.

As she leaned in, the world around her shifted.

The flashlight flickered — once, twice — and then everything dropped away. The air thickened, pressing against her ribs.

In its place, a rush of heat slammed into her chest, dragging her into a vision that wasn't her own. For the briefest second, she saw a man — young, terrified, mouth open in a scream that didn't carry sound — being pulled backward through the brick wall into shadows. Not into fire. Into something stranger.

The stone rippled like molten glass as hands — not human — reached through, wrapped around him, and yanked him inward.

Beyond the wall, she caught only flashes: black stone twisted into impossible towers, glowing veins of lava threading through ash-colored skies. A realm of heat and pressure, of pain and ironbound power.

And then, just as suddenly as it began, it was gone.

Seren stumbled back a step, sucking in a sharp breath as her flashlight steadied. The alley was just an alley again. Quiet. Cold. Empty. But the mark on the wall pulsed faintly, like it knew she'd seen too much.

Her hands trembled as she backed further into the streetlight's reach, the chill of the morning air doing nothing to settle the heat still burning behind her eyes.

She blinked hard—and that's when she felt it.

A thin warmth trailing from her nostril. She touched her face and stared at the smear of blood on her fingers.

Her head throbbed in time with her heartbeat, sharp and insistent.

She'd dreamed of things like this before—scattered, impossible dreams of firelit cities and shadowy figures that whispered her name. But this wasn't a dream. It wasn't even a feeling.

It was a vision. Real, sharp, and terrifying.

Whatever force had burned its way through that wall had pulled her in, just for a moment, like it wanted her to see.

Like it wanted her to understand what waited on the other side.

And now she couldn't unsee it.

Seren tore her gaze from the wall and forced herself to move. Her boots echoed in the silence as she jogged back to her car, every step feeling like it pulled her further from something she wasn't sure had fully let her go.

She climbed in, slammed the door shut, and locked it out of habit. The engine rumbled to life beneath her hands, steady and grounding. She sat for a long second, gripping the wheel, staring at her reflection in the rearview mirror.

Then she pulled out her phone, thumb hovering over her favorites list until she tapped Marisol's name. It rang twice.

"Seren?" came the sleepy, groggy voice on the other end. "Please tell me you're not still at work."

"I'm off," Seren muttered, turning onto the road and heading toward the outskirts of town. "But I went to the alley."

A pause. Then: "Of course you did."

"There was a handprint," Seren said. "Like something burned into the wall. But that's not all. I—" Her voice faltered, caught between disbelief and dread. She hesitated. How the hell was she supposed to explain it? "I saw something. A vision. Like a place. A different realm. And a man… he was taken. It wasn't just a feeling. It was real. I saw him — pulled through the wall like it was water."
Marisol was quiet for a moment, then sighed. "Okay. I'm awake. Start from the beginning.

Chapter Three: The Boy in the Closet

Seren

The first time Seren saw fire where it didn't belong, she was seven years old.

It didn't flicker. It whispered. It came with a voice like ash.

It was a Thursday in October, and the wind off the fields had teeth. The old farmhouse groaned and shifted like it was settling too deep into the earth, trying to bury its secrets. Her bedroom smelled faintly of dust and apple-scented fabric softener. The curtains swayed, just slightly, though the window was closed.

Seren lay curled in bed with the covers pulled up to her chin, staring at the sliver of hallway light that bled in through the crack in her door. Everyone else in the house was asleep. Or at least, they were supposed to be.

She'd woken to a strange pressure in the air — thick, heavy, like the house had inhaled and forgotten how to breathe again. She didn't hear anything at first. Just silence. But then came the whisper.

Her name.

"Seren…"

She froze. It wasn't her parents' voices — and it wasn't like anything she'd heard before. It was dry, smoky, as if someone were trying to talk through a mouthful of ashes.
"Seren… help me. It's burning… it's breaking."

She sat up, the bedsheets rustling loud in the stillness. She looked toward the door, then to the hallway closet.

The voice was coming from the closet. The kind of place nightmares wait patiently.

It was always closed. Always. Her mom said it was just coats and blankets — nothing that should whisper. But now it stood open just a few inches. Just wide enough for someone to be inside.

Seren slid out of bed, bare feet touching cold wood. She told herself not to be afraid, that it was just the wind or a dream. But the air tasted of smoke and scorched metal.

The hall was darker than it should've been. The nightlight was flickering, casting jagged shadows on the walls. Seren's heart thudded in her chest as she stepped closer to the closet door, every instinct screaming at her to run the other way.

"Seren…"

She reached for the knob. Paused.

Then pulled it open.

There was a boy inside.

He looked about her age, maybe older. His skin was pale, almost grey. His eyes were wide — and glowing. Not brightly, but dim, like dying embers fighting the dark. His shirt was torn, blood on the collar. He was crouched in the back corner, one hand pressed against the wood like he was trying to hold something closed from the inside.

The air around him shimmered with heat distortion, and the wood behind him pulsed like skin stretched too thin.

Behind him, the wall… rippled. Like heat waves on asphalt. Like something alive was pressing through from the other side.

Seren stared, mouth open, trying to speak. But then his gaze snapped to hers, and he whispered again, voice desperate:
"Don't let them pull me back."
Then the wall split open — not with sound, but with heat. Blinding, impossible heat.

From within it, an arm reached through. Not claws, not a beast — a man's hand, warm-toned and strong, seared with glowing lines that looked like rivers of fire beneath the skin. The marks pulsed like they were alive, trailing up his forearm in shifting, ember-red veins.

It wrapped around the boy's chest with a terrible urgency, yanking him backward toward the molten dark.

But before he vanished, the boy lunged — and grabbed Seren's arm.

His fingers locked around her wrist like a vice, burning hot, eyes wild. "Don't let them take me alone," he whispered, voice breaking.

The man on the other side saw her. For a breathless moment, their eyes locked — his the color of burning lilac, bright and unreadable. Then, softly, like he hadn't meant to speak aloud, he whispered:

"You're not supposed to be here, little spark." The words curled around her like smoke, familiar and terrifying.

"…but something wants you to live."

Seren screamed.

For one terrifying heartbeat, she felt herself being drawn toward it — toward that burning world. Her heels skidded across the floor. The air around her howled.

And then, suddenly, his grip slipped. The burning hand pulled the boy back with it. The veins of fire vanished into the rift, and the doorway sealed behind him in a blink.

His fingers tore away from hers, and he disappeared into the fire.

The closet door slammed shut so hard the house shook.

Seren lay sprawled on the hallway floor, chest heaving, arm still tingling where he'd grabbed her. Her skin was unburned — but her bones felt scorched.

Then — a hiss. A snap.

From the crack beneath the closet door, something flickered. A single ember — no larger than a teardrop — spat out with a sudden burst of heat and landed against her jaw.

She cried out, pressing her palm to the spot. The pain was sharp, bright, and immediate. When she pulled her hand back, she could smell burned skin — could feel the sting starting to rise in waves.

The ember left a mark, faint but aching — a mirror to the touch of the fire. Not just a burn. A seal. A memory. A beginning.

The hallway was thick with smoke now, and heat still pulsed from behind the door, though everything had gone still.

The hall still felt warped — too quiet, too heavy. Seren blinked through the haze, her skin throbbing where the ember had struck. She didn't understand what had just happened. Couldn't.

The boy was gone. The closet was sealed tight again. But her jaw ached, and her hand shook, and the smell of smoke still curled in the air like a warning.

She stood slowly, feet unsteady on the hardwood floor. The hallway tilted beneath her for a second, like the house itself wasn't sure what was real anymore.

Turning away from the closet, Seren wandered into the living room. The old wood stove in the corner still radiated faint warmth from earlier in the night, its iron belly ticking and creaking as it cooled. Her bare toes brushed the edge of the rug. The fibers felt too warm, like they'd absorbed something unnatural. She stared blankly at the embers inside the stove, now reduced to a soft red glow, as if it too had witnessed something it didn't understand.

Footsteps thundered down the stairs.

Her mother burst into the room first, robe tangled, panic already in her voice. "Seren! What—what happened?"

Her father followed, sharp-eyed, taking in the faint smoke, the burn on her face, the stove.

"What did you touch?" he barked, already striding toward the stove.

"I didn't—" Seren's voice was small. "There was a boy. In the closet. He was burning—he grabbed me—"

"Jesus, Seren," her father snapped, yanking open the stove's door. "You were messing with this again, weren't you?" His voice was sharp, but his eyes didn't meet hers.

"I wasn't! It wasn't me!" Her voice cracked.

Her mother reached out, turning Seren's chin gently to see the mark. A sharp hiss left her lips. "It's blistering. God, baby—why were you near the fire?"

"I wasn't! It came from the closet!"

Her father turned, eyes narrowed. "Enough. There's no one in the closet. What were you doing up in the middle of the night?"

"I—he was calling for help—he got pulled through the wall—"

Her mother stood up fast, hand pressed to her forehead. "It's late. You had a nightmare. You must've gotten out of bed, came in here, and—"

"I didn't!" Seren insisted, fists clenched. "I didn't open the stove! There was a boy—he was real!"

Her father stared at her for a long second, jaw tight. "You know better, Seren. We've told you before."

He didn't yell. That was worse. It was the cold kind of anger. The kind that wrapped around her chest and made her feel small and wrong and invisible all at once.

Her mother disappeared into the bathroom and returned with the first aid kit, already kneeling beside her before Seren could move. She dabbed gently at the burn with a cool cloth, murmuring under her breath, but not to Seren — not really. More like to herself. Like treating the wound was just something to do while her brain sorted through the mess.

Seren didn't flinch. The pain was secondary now. Distant.

Her father stood off to the side, arms crossed, watching the stove like it might bite.

"She needs to be seen," her mother said quietly, unscrewing the lid of a silver ointment tin. "It's blistering fast. What if it scars?"

"It's not that deep," her father muttered. "We'll see how it looks in the morning. Not dragging her to the ER at two a.m. just because she got too close to the stove."

"She shouldn't have even been near it," her mother snapped, then softened immediately, as if catching herself. "She's seven, Rob. Seven."

"I know how old she is."

They kept talking like that — not shouting, but trading clipped phrases over her head, like she wasn't even in the room. Like she was just part of the mess that needed cleaning up.

Seren didn't say anything. She didn't move.

She sat still on the floor, legs curled beneath her, watching a single soot-smudged spot on the wall across the room. It was probably nothing. A shadow. A burn. But in her mind, it rippled. Just like the wall in the closet. Just like the place the boy had vanished into.

Her mother applied the ointment, wrapped a bandaid gently across her jaw, and murmured something about getting her back to bed.

When her mother finally pulled her gently to her feet, Seren didn't protest.

She moved on autopilot, her small hand slipping free of her mother's as they walked the short hallway. The burn on her jaw throbbed with every heartbeat, but it was nothing compared to the hollow ache pressing against her chest.

The closet door was still shut. No sign of what had happened remained — no flicker of flame, no cry for help. Just coats and dust and silence.

She didn't look at it.

Seren climbed back into bed wordlessly, the sheets still warm from when she'd left them. Her mother tucked them in around her as if nothing had changed, brushed a hand over her hair, and whispered, "No more sneaking around at night, okay?"

As if a warning could undo what the fire had already claimed. Seren didn't answer. The door clicked shut behind her.

She lay staring at the ceiling, eyes wide in the dark, the faint scent of smoke still clinging to her skin.

Sleep never came. Not really. Not after the fire marked her. Not after the realm first whispered her name.

She hadn't known it yet, but she'd been chosen. Not saved. Chosen.

Chapter Four: The House That Watched Her

Seren

The gravel crunched like bones beneath her tires as Seren turned off the main road and onto the winding drive that led to the farmhouse.

It was just after six. The sky had shifted from pink to pale gold, bathing the fields in quiet light. Morning dew clung to the grass, and the eastern hills behind the house caught the sun first, glowing like embers pressed beneath the earth.

Her headlights cut off as she parked at the edge of the drive. The engine ticked once as it cooled. All around her, the world stirred — birds trilled in the distance, and a faint breeze bent the tall grass like something unseen was moving through it.

The house looked the same.

Worn wood. Crooked shutters. The twisted tree in the front yard still reached like a hand too long, too many joints, gnarled and out of place. It reminded her of the hand that had once reached through the Veil. She'd always hated that tree.

Seren sat for a long moment behind the wheel, jaw aching, before she finally stepped out. The light didn't make the house feel safer — just more exposed. Like the darkness had slunk into the walls to wait for night again.

She moved slowly up the path, boots thudding against the porch steps. The front door stuck, as it always did, swollen by time and weather.

With a quiet grunt, she pushed it open and stepped inside.

Inside, the farmhouse smelled faintly of cedar, old coffee, and dust. Light streamed in through half-closed blinds, cutting across the scuffed hardwood floors in long, quiet stripes.

Seren dropped her keys in the ceramic dish by the door — it clattered, too loud in the silence. She kicked off her boots, letting them fall where they landed, and shrugged out of her jacket, tossing it over the back of the worn recliner. Everything in the house had a threadbare, well-used look. Nothing matched. Nothing was new. But it was hers.

She moved on autopilot.

The kitchen was cool and dim. She filled a glass with water and downed it in one long pull, then refilled it and carried it with her into the bathroom. The mirror over the sink caught her reflection — tired eyes, smudged mascara, hair clinging to her forehead.

Her fingers ghosted over the pale teardrop shaped scar on her jaw. It was old, nearly faded to silver. The mark pulsed faintly — a whisper from the past. A reminder she'd once been called 'little spark'.

She stared at it for a long moment, jaw tight, then looked away.

She didn't bother with trying to remove her makeup. Just brushed her teeth, tied her hair into a loose knot, and changed into an oversized t-shirt that had probably once belonged to an ex she couldn't remember.

Back in the living room, she grabbed the remote and collapsed onto the couch with a grunt. A blanket trailed off the back — she dragged it over her legs without thinking. The remote clicked in her hand, scrolling past a dozen true crime documentaries and supernatural specials she couldn't stomach at the moment.

She finally settled on something dumb and loud. Bright colors. Bad acting. Nothing with fire.

Her eyes had already started to blur, the edges of the room softening as exhaustion crept in. The screen flickered on, casting light across the walls, but she didn't really see it.

Then — a thump.

She sat bolt upright, the blanket tangled around her legs. Another sound
followed — a dragging shuffle, then a dull clatter. Somewhere near the
kitchen.
Her blood iced.

The farmhouse was old, sure. It made noises. But not that kind of noise.

She paused the TV and held her breath.

The silence that followed was too still. No pipes. No settling wood. Just
a long, heavy pause like something was waiting for her to move first.

A second clatter. Louder.

She reached slowly between the couch cushions and pulled out the
knife she kept hidden there — not fancy, not pretty, just solid steel and
habit. She'd learned early that 911 didn't come fast enough when you
lived out here.

Seren stood and crept toward the hallway. Her bare feet were nearly
silent on the wood floor. Each step felt like it took a year.

The sound came again — a faint rustle, then what sounded like the
screen door opening.

She rounded the corner into the kitchen, raised the knife…

And stopped.
The back door was cracked open, the screen torn just wide enough for
something… fuzzy and disrespectful to squeeze through.

There, perched on top of the recycling bin and nose-deep in a box of
stale granola bars, was a possum. Its pale, ghostly face turned to look at
her with zero shame.

They locked eyes.

It blinked.

She blinked.

It hissed — but halfheartedly, like it couldn't be bothered to fully commit.

"You have got to be kidding me," she said flatly, lowering the knife.

The possum gave the box a final aggressive sniff, then hopped down with an awkward thud. It waddled toward the door like it lived there. Like she was the intruder.

Seren grabbed the broom leaning by the fridge and tapped the doorway. "Out. You little goblin. Take your crimes and go."

The possum paused in the threshold, turned back to glare at her one last time, then slipped into the yard like a disgraced raccoon trying to save face.

She deadbolted the door, tossed the broom aside with a sigh, and muttered, "Burn marks and hell dimensions I can handle. Marsupials? Absolutely not."

She stood there for a moment longer, heartbeat starting to settle. Then turned back to the living room, already knowing sleep was completely off the table now.

Seren flicked the light on in the hallway as she passed, rubbing a hand down her face.

Back in her bedroom, she stepped over laundry baskets and kicked aside a half-packed duffel to reach the cabinet she kept padlocked beneath the window. She crouched, twisted the lock open, and swung the doors wide. The cabinet creaked like it remembered every secret she'd ever asked it to hold.

Inside: rows of neatly arranged gear lined the cabinet like a personal shrine to the unknown.

EVP recorders, motion detectors, full-spectrum flashlights, and an EMF reader that gave a faint click as she passed her hand near the sensor. Chargers, battery packs, thermal imaging tools. A full spectrum camcorder with night vision. Even a compact printer for immediate electronic readouts. Everything was labeled and logged, some items reinforced with duct tape and field notes in permanent marker. Field-tested and trusted.

But the centerpiece of it all — the one setup she returned to again and again — was the Estes Method.

Headphones. Blindfold. Spirit box.

Where most people found the randomness of the method unsettling, Seren found it calming. Direct. It bypassed her analytical brain and dropped her right into the current. It didn't always work — but when it did, it worked too well.

Sometimes, when she was alone, she'd take it further. No partner to feed her questions, no one to hold her tether. Just the hiss of the radio and the rhythmic pulse of static. The world would fall away, and for a few moments, she'd float. Weightless. Untethered. Open.

That was when she heard them most clearly.

The whispers. The names. The ones that knew hers.

She pulled out the blindfold and headphones now, checking the battery level on the receiver. Then she packed them carefully in their designated pouch, tucking it between her camcorder and extra battery packs.

Next came the notebooks — well-worn, stained, pages curled at the corners. These weren't blank journals waiting to be filled. They were archives. A tangle of data and emotion. GPS coordinates. EMF spikes. Transcripts of voices heard over the spirit box. Notes about flickering shadows, strange smells, sudden cold.

One page had a crude map of an old mining site with a burned sigil sketched beside it. Another had just one line, underlined three times in red:

"The Veil frays where blood lingers."

Seren thumbed through the pages, looking for a connection — some thread between this call, the burn mark in the alley, and the symbols scratched into chapel stone.

She didn't find answers.

Seren sat cross-legged on the bed, the old leather-bound notebook resting against her thighs. This one was her personal log — not the data, not the maps, just the moments. The ones that stuck in her chest. The ones she couldn't shake.
She clicked her pen, hesitated, then began to write in neat, sharp script:

Incident: Redmill Alley – 12th & Mercer
Date: 6/22/2025

Time: Approx. 11:45 p.m. — Dispatched
Initial Call: Male voice, panic clear. Reported shadows "crawling" —
voice cut out after auditory evidence of metal tearing and a scream. No
confirmed GPS.
On Scene: Units found broken cell phone. No blood. No victim. One
anomalous burn mark on the wall — roughly hand-sized, fingers
extended upward. Possible pyrokinetic residue.

Personal Notes: Felt it before the call came in. Same static buzz behind
my eyes. Like the Veil pulled thin. The burn mark — it felt familiar. Heat
pressed against my chest like memory.
After shift — 4:30 a.m. — Visited alley.

She paused, exhaled slowly, then continued.
No sign of violence. But something echoed there. Not just memory.
Residue. Vision(?) occurred — man dragged backwards through a brick
wall. Possible other realm visible momentarily. High color saturation,
lava/ash, spiral stone buildings. Physical reaction: chest tightness. Heat
at old scar. Nosebleed.

Unconfirmed presence — lilac eyes in rearview mirror. Transient. No
physical subject found.
Hypothesis:
— Entity may be breaching Veil boundaries intentionally.
— Caller likely pulled through to another realm.
— Unclear if the call originated from this side or bled through.

She stopped writing, fingers still pressed to the paper, pen tip dotting a
faint ink mark into the corner.

Then she added one final line:

It didn't feel like a haunting. It felt like a warning.

She closed the notebook, binding the elastic band around it twice. Her
hands lingered over the cover before she slid it into the top pocket of her
duffel — the one she always brought on fieldwork.

She zipped the duffel closed, then grabbed her phone off the nightstand.
The clock read 7:12 a.m. — early, but not unreasonable for Marisol.

Seren opened their message thread and typed without overthinking:

"Got the gear ready. You game to check out that creepy chapel off
Raven Rock later?"

She hit send and set the phone down, stretching her arms behind her head with a quiet groan. The familiar buzz of routine, of preparation, settled into her bones.
But then — a shift. A prickle at the base of her neck.

She froze, turning slightly to glance over her shoulder. No one there. Nothing but the morning light creeping through the curtains and the low hum of the TV still running in the other room.
Still, the feeling lingered — that strange sense of being observed. Not threatened. Not seen.

Watched.

Seren stood slowly and walked toward the window, pulling the curtain aside just enough to peek into the yard. Empty. Quiet.

She let the fabric fall back into place, turning to face the room again. She stated defiantly to no one, "If you're gonna keep staring, at least be useful."

She didn't look again. Just grabbed the duffel, stood, and crossed the room to the gear cabinet. She swung it open and tucked the bag into its usual spot, right below her notebooks. Ready. Just in case.

The cabinet clicked shut and Seren reattached the lock with a quiet finality.

She turned off the TV, plunging the house into silence again, and padded down the hall toward the bathroom.

Time to scrub the night off her skin — and try to ignore the feeling that something had followed her home.

The water was just starting to fog the mirror when her phone chimed — short, clear, and familiar.

Her text tone.

Seren didn't jump. Just smiled faintly, rinsing the last of the soap from her fingers. Marisol's in. She reached for a towel, wrapping it around herself with a practiced twist, and cracked the bathroom door open.

Steam billowed into the hallway as she crossed the floor, bare feet padding softly across the wood.

She picked up her phone from the end table, already anticipating the reply. But there was nothing. No new message. No missed call. No notification.
Her brows pulled together. She refreshed the thread, checked her alerts, toggled airplane mode off and on. Still nothing. Her message to Marisol still sat as delivered — not read.

The smile faded.

She stood there for a moment, water dripping from her hair onto the screen, her heartbeat just a little too loud in the quiet.

She'd heard it. Clearly.

"…Right," she muttered, locking the phone and setting it gently back on the bed, screen up.

No spiraling. Not yet. Weird glitches happened. Dispatch phones went haywire all the time.

Still wrapped in the towel, she walked back to the bathroom to finish drying off.

Once changed into an oversized hoodie and soft shorts, she settled onto her bed with her laptop. She opened a fresh browser tab, cracked her knuckles, and typed in the search bar:

"Raven Rock Chapel history, disappearances, cult rumors — Redmill."

Because if she wasn't going to sleep, she might as well start her research for tonight.

She opened a new tab and began the familiar ritual: search terms, filtered dates, archived local news sites, conspiracy blogs, and digital graveyards of forgotten forums.

"Raven Rock Chapel history Redmill" brought up a few vague tourist blurbs and a single photo of the crumbling stone building, tucked against the tree line off a rural road. Built in 1892. Deconsecrated in the 1960s. No known congregation since.

She narrowed the search.
"Raven Rock Chapel disappearances"
That pulled different results.

A 1981 police report listed two teenage boys who went missing near Raven Rock during a winter hunting trip. Their bodies were never found. Search dogs lost the scent at the tree line. Foul play was suspected, but no suspects named.

She clicked a link titled Redmill Rumors & Mysteries (Archived) — a half-dead forum with grainy scanned maps, anecdotal stories, and one thread titled: "Raven Rock is a Veil Gate."

The user's name was long deleted, but the post was still there.

"No one goes past the chapel after dark. Ask any old-timer who's still breathing. They'll tell you there were fires in the woods — strange ones. Sounds that didn't belong in this world. The stone arch in the back? It's not a window. It's a door. And something uses it."

Seren copied the post into her notes, eyes narrowing.

She found more:

— A 2004 newspaper clipping about a camper who showed up in town barefoot and burned, claiming to have escaped a sacrifice in the woods. No further reports.
— A blurry photo of symbols carved into the chapel walls — jagged spirals, circular runes.
— A map with the ley lines of the region crudely drawn, Raven Rock circled in red ink.

She added each to her running file, fingers slowing as the sun reached higher and the light in her room grew softer, more golden.

Her eyes drifted across the screen to the final page she'd opened: an amateur video still titled "Screaming from the Rock (Audio only)" uploaded over a decade ago. Comments were turned off. The thumbnail was black.
Seren didn't hit play.

She didn't need to.

The exhaustion finally claimed her as she slumped against the pillows, laptop cooling on her thighs, screen still glowing.
The chapel stared back from the open tab — silent, waiting.

GRANOLA
BARS

Chapter Five: Burned Souls

Cairn

Beneath the smoking peaks of the Ember Spires, Cairn knelt in the scorched ash, his palm pressed to the cracked earth. Heat shimmered in the air, waves of distortion rising around him like ghosts too stubborn to leave.

The breach still bled energy behind him — jagged, unfinished. It pulsed with a dull red glow, casting warped shadows across the glassy obsidian rocks that jutted from the ground like broken teeth. Something had gone wrong. He'd sealed dozens of rifts. Hundreds. But this one felt… contaminated.

Watched.

He tilted his head, listening.

The realm was never silent — the Pyric lands pulsed with fire and breath and memory. But tonight, the air carried something else. A name, buried deep. Unspoken for years, yet still seared into him like every mark on his skin.

He could still see her — a girl with wide, terrified eyes and blood on her jaw. The first time he saw her, she was nothing but a flicker. A spark. A flash of light. A scream. The moment the Veil had cracked open, years ago, in a small house full of sleeping humans and forgotten protections. She wasn't meant to see.
And he wasn't meant to hesitate.

But he had.

He'd dragged the boy through — offered, chosen, marked — as the Veil demanded. And she had been there. Reaching. Screaming. Interfering.

So he'd marked her too.

Not out of cruelty. Not even necessity.

Out of curiosity… and something older. The Veil had paused for her. That had never happened before. Not in all his centuries.

He didn't mark her because he was told to. He marked her because the Veil reached back.

A single ember flicked as the portal snapped shut — a sliver of him left behind. A teardrop-shaped scar now burned into the soft skin along her jaw. A brand. A tether.

He hadn't stopped watching her since.

Even when he tried to sever the tie, something always pulled him back, something in her refused to burn the way others did. The sound of her voice, still sharp in his memory. The calls she answered in the dead hours of night. The way she fought to help everyone but never once reached out for herself.

She didn't know his name. Not yet.

But he knew hers.

Seren.

And the Veil was thinning again.

Soon, she'd see him.

And this time, she'd understand what it meant to be chosen.

Cairn stood, brushing soot from his gloved fingers as the breach behind him sputtered and hissed into silence. The pulse of it still throbbed against the back of his neck like phantom heat, but it would fade. For now.

He turned toward the Ember Keep — the blackened fortress carved into the spine of the mountain, half-born from the stone and half-scorched into it by divine fire. The path to the castle wound through jagged obsidian peaks and fire-scarred pillars, each one etched with oaths burned in a tongue no human could survive hearing.

The air grew heavier as he walked — thick with sulfur, emberlight, and memory.

The Keep's gates rose before him, towering and grotesque. Forged from the bones of oathbreakers and the iron of forgotten gods. They opened not with hinges, but with a low grinding sound, like bones being re-set.

Inside, the throne hall yawned wide and cathedral-dark.

The walls weren't just stone — they breathed. Molten channels ran through the black like veins, crisscrossing the room in rivulets of glowing lava, weaving beneath the floor and spiraling up along pillars like arteries feeding a massive heart.

And at the center, raised above it all on a dais of volcanic glass, sat the throne — an iron seat grown out of the mountain itself, cradled in fire. The molten paths converged beneath it, lighting the base like a forge.

And seated there, as always, was King Kaedros.

He didn't move. Didn't need to.

His presence stretched beyond the body that housed him. A crown of split obsidian ringed his brow, but it was the skin beneath that demanded attention — skin like scorched iron, etched with deep grooves, every line glowing from within like magma pulsing under pressure.

The veins across his neck and forearms flickered with that same molten light, slow and deliberate, like each beat of his heart echoed through the realm itself.
One eye was black as coal. The other burned — ember-orange, flickering.

Cairn stepped forward and dropped to one knee, bowing his head low.

"My king," he said, voice steady despite the fire curling around his boots. "The mortal soul was taken through the breach as commanded."

Kaedros said nothing at first. His head tilted, slow and deliberate, like stone grinding over stone.

"And yet the Veil remains… unsealed."

Cairn kept his gaze low. "The breach is sealed, but not cleanly. The tears… they're weakening. Again."

Kaedros didn't answer at first.

Heat shimmered around him, rising in waves from the glowing veins that ran through the stone beneath his feet. He stepped down from the dais, obsidian crown casting jagged shadows that crawled like blades across the walls.

"The Veil was never meant to lean toward the mortal realm," he said at last, each word slow and deliberate. "It was constructed to divide. To contain. Not to drift."

Cairn's jaw tensed.

Kaedros continued pacing, the folds of his robes dragging like smoke.

"But lately, it trembles. Reacts. Cracks in places it never should."

He glanced toward the floor, almost distracted. "The balance is shifting. And I don't like the direction it leans."

Cairn didn't speak.

"We built this realm on certainty," Kaedros went on, circling him. "We maintained order. Kept the flames from spilling too far. But now…"
He paused, voice sharpening.

"Things cross that shouldn't. The cursed, the forgotten, the watchers. The Veil is bleeding. And someone— something—is pulling at the thread."

He stopped in front of Cairn, tone soft but laced with threat.

"If it leans too far… we fall with it."
Kaedros circled him slowly. "They slip through, don't they? The things not bound by oath or law. The beasts. The cursed. The castoffs. They crawl through our broken seams like rot beneath a bandage."

"They're growing bolder," Cairn admitted. "And faster."

Kaedros stopped behind him. "And yet the Veil resists healing. We patch. We burn. We seal. And still, it frays."

He stepped forward, voice lowering, darker now.

"We thought it was the corruption. The rips left behind by fire magic. But the new theory…"

Cairn said nothing.

Kaedros continued. "The mortals who can see them. Who feel the Veil. They are the anchors. The interference. They hold the tears open without knowing it — clinging to what should be forgotten. They are keeping the wounds alive. We cannot afford sympathy, Cairn. Not when their very breath pulls the seams apart."

Cairn's jaw locked. "Then what do you intend to do?"

Kaedros turned, walking back toward the throne as molten veins rippled in his wake.
"We find them," he said simply. "We erase them. Burn them clean. A sealed Veil cannot have loose threads."

Cairn remained still. He did not speak of the girl. Of the spark he'd left behind.

He said nothing of the way his tether to her had flared to life again as the last mortal soul was pulled through — a resonance like a hand on the back of his neck.

He had been careful to keep her name from the Keep, buried in the fire-forged silence between his ribs.

For now, she was still his secret.

But the Pyric realm was watching.
And so was he.

Kaedros turned slowly, voice low and controlled—too calm to be anything but dangerous.

"We are the highest flame in this realm. The last true order. Let the other provinces wallow in their mud and madness—peasants, half-bloods, monsters hiding in the trees."

He waved a hand toward the distant, unseen borders of the realm.

"Let them kneel to bone-gods and ashspirits. Let them forget what power feels like. But here?" He tapped the obsidian floor with the heel of his boot.

"Here, we burn. We decide. We keep the spine of this world straight."

His gaze flicked up, cold and unblinking.

"And I will not let the mortal Realm threaten that."

He took another step forward, heat coiling tighter around him.

"If we must bleed their world dry to preserve our own, so be it. If the Veil refuses to close—then we will burn everything behind it."
A pause.

"Every last mortal, if we must."

Kaedros reclined in his throne once more, the molten light at the base of it flaring in rhythm with his voice.

"The soul you retrieved. The mortal who saw too much."

His ember-lit eye sharpened. "Follow through."

Cairn straightened, every instinct tightening beneath his skin. "You wish for him to be... unmade?"

"Interrogated. Dissected. Erased."

Kaedros's words were cold as iron. "Leave nothing that can speak of what it saw. And study the remnants closely. We must learn why he could see through the Veil."

Cairn gave a slow nod. "It will be done."

Kaedros gestured toward the far corridor, the one that sloped down beneath the Keep — beneath the mountain's heart, where the lava glowed hotter and the air thinned from ash.

"Take him to the Warrens. Let your blade-tongued companion have his fun. I expect answers before the next breach."

Cairn bowed once more and turned, cloak sweeping across the scorched stone as he exited the throne hall. The heavy doors groaned shut behind him, sealing the fire-lit silence in his wake.

Beneath the Ember Keep — The Warrens

The descent into the Warrens was like crawling down a wound that refused to heal.

The corridor narrowed, the walls pressing in with heat and silence, broken only by the occasional rattle of chains or the muffled sound of distant screams — not of pain, but memory. It wasn't the kind of place that echoed. It absorbed.

The Warrens were not a dungeon. They were a crucible.

Cut into the black heart of the Ember Keep, they served as the Pyric realm's memory chamber. This was where the souls of trespassers, Veilbreachers, and mortal anomalies were brought — not simply to suffer, but to be unraveled.

The Warrenmasters were specialists — artists of the mind, skilled in pain not for punishment, but for extraction. They could peel back memories like charred parchment, sifting through thought and fear until only truth remained.

But only Cairn could do what came next.

Only he could shape what was left.

The Pyric realm called them Cinderwraiths. But Cairn knew better — they were Burned Souls, cursed echoes of humanity twisted into ash and obedience. Not alive. Not dead. Just bound — to the realm, to the Veil, and to him.

Each one he created marked him.

The newest tattoo still ached across his ribs — an old woman he pulled through. A jagged band of flame now curved across Cairn's side, its edges still smoldering beneath his skin. At least that mortal was old, and had lived a full life before Cairn found her. There was no fight left in her, no wild thrashing of soul and body. Just surrender.

He would never admit it, but the children stayed with him more.

The ones who hadn't yet tasted enough of the world to want to leave it. The ones who didn't understand why they were being dragged into fire. Those left deeper marks — not just in flesh, but in memory.

Easy prey left small tattoos: clean, contained, quick to heal. But the young ones, the stubborn ones, the ones whose fear he could almost taste in the air — they burned wider. Hotter. Their soul-brands seared into him with raw defiance, scarring through layers that never quite closed.

He could feel every soul he had pulled through even now — not alive, not fully dead — echoing somewhere deep in the Keep, caged in black stone. The tattoos weren't ornamental. They were proof. A tally of the damned. Each one a soul twisted from the mortal path, turned into something else — and branded into him in return.

Cairn reached the final archway.

The iron mouth that marked the entrance to the lowest Warren yawned wide, rimmed in blackened bone and sigils still slick with sealing flame.

And beyond it, Rhyne waited.

Leaning against a scorched pillar, knife twirling lazily between his fingers, Rhyne's smile was already too wide.

"Took you long enough."
Cairn stepped into the chamber.

Rhyne's eyes lit up. "A fresh thread to pull."

Behind him, the mortal — the one from the alley — was bound to the standing slab, limbs chained tight, his eyes rolling, mouth slack with a mix of panic and sedation. Glyphs were already burned along his forearms, glowing faintly — symbols meant to anchor memory and slow the decay.

"Kaedros wants him shaped," Cairn said, voice flat.

Rhyne's grin twitched wider. "Already? He usually lets us play a little longer."

"He believes this one saw too much."

Rhyne's expression shifted, the humor draining from his features. "What did he see?"

Cairn stepped closer, the heat trailing behind him. The walls of the chamber pulsed faintly, veins of emberlight stirring at his presence — as if the Keep itself recognized who had come to finish the work.

"Did he speak?" Cairn asked, gaze fixed on the trembling mortal slumped in chains.

Rhyne nodded once. "Some gibberish. But there was memory, buried deep — one of the beasts that slipped through. Black spined, too many eyes. Tore through a gas station, maybe? Hard to tell what was real in his head by then."

Cairn's jaw tightened.

"Then we're out of time."

Rhyne raised a brow. "You sure you want to do it now? I could prep him, try to get more info—"

"No." Cairn's voice was steel. "It must be done now."

Rhyne gave a low, conceding shrug and stepped back into the shadows. "The king gave an order. That's all I need. All yours, Ashmarked."

Cairn didn't respond.
He approached the mortal with measured steps, each footfall drawing more heat into the room. The forge veins along the floor brightened, lavalight crawling toward the dais as if summoned.

He stared at the mortal — what little was left of him — and felt the fire rise through his spine.
This one had already begun to unravel.

The room dimmed, though no flame went out. The light bent inward, pulled toward the center where Cairn stood. Heat radiated from him now in waves, the stone beneath his boots beginning to crack and glow.

His breath slowed. His eyes closed.

And then the tattoos awakened.

Every inked mark across his body — twisted bands of flame, snarled glyphs, soul-seals etched in old Pyric tongues — ignited like dry paper kissed by a match. Fire licked over his skin but didn't burn it, casting molten light across the chamber. Each brand came alive in response to the magic building around him, pulsing like the heartbeat of a god.

The newest still flared angrily at his ribs, a jagged slash of orange and crimson. Others shimmered in older tones — white-hot, charred black, ember-red.

Only his eyes remained untouched.

Lilac and luminous. The only piece of him not claimed by the forge.

Cairn extended a hand over the trembling mortal. Heat flowed from his fingertips in fine threads, curling into the air like smoke but moving with precision. They snaked downward — not to the man's body, but to his soul, hovering just beneath the skin like oil beneath water.

The mortal screamed.

His spine arched. His limbs locked.

And then the fire caught.

It started at his core, a bloom of light under his ribcage — and then it surged outward, devouring nerves and sinew and skin. His body disintegrated in moments, not burned so much as unmade, collapsing into a fine circle of ash that glowed with soft, flickering embers.

But the scream didn't stop.

Because the soul remained.

It pulsed in the ash like a dying star — writhing, half-formed, refusing to fade.
Cairn lowered his other hand, palm open and trembling slightly now under the weight of the rite. The tattoos across his arms flared again, veins of fire crawling up his throat, burning brighter the closer the soul came to him.

The ashes began to twist — rising, shaping.

Not a man. Not anymore.

The soul folded inward and then shattered, splintering with a sound like bones cracking beneath stone. Smoke poured upward. A long, lean shape emerged from it — spectral, skeletal, its eyes like smoldering coals. Its mouth opened, and it wailed — not in pain, but in loyalty.

The transformation was complete.

The Cinderwraith stood before him, formed of smoke, bone, and vow.

Cairn exhaled.

The ash drifted down into a hollow carved in the black stone of the floor — a sealing pit. A mark flared beneath it, a rune that locked the remains in place, anchoring the wraith's existence to the Keep.

The light dimmed again. The tattoos cooled.

Only the faintest hiss of steam remained.

Cairn straightened, his lilac eyes distant, the fire dimming beneath his skin.

Another soul forged.

Another brand earned.
And still — the Veil bled.

Cairn remained still as the last of the ash settled.

The room was quiet now, save for the low hum of anchored magic and the faint hiss of steam rising from the floor. The wraith had retreated into its seal, waiting to be summoned, its loyalty newly forged.
But something in Cairn's chest refused to cool.
He replayed Rhyne's words. Some gibberish... memory buried deep... gas station, maybe...

He hadn't asked for details. He didn't want details. Because what if the mortal had seen more — or heard more? A call. A name. A voice caught in the background. One thread was all it would take. Kaedros didn't need proof. Just suspicion. And she was never meant to be part of this.

Cairn exhaled slowly, the glow of his tattoos dimming beneath his sleeves.

He didn't look at Rhyne. Didn't ask if there was more to the man's rambling. It was better to assume it hadn't. Better to believe she was still hidden and safe. For now at least.

But deep beneath the ash, something still called his name.

Chapter Six: Smoke Between Worlds

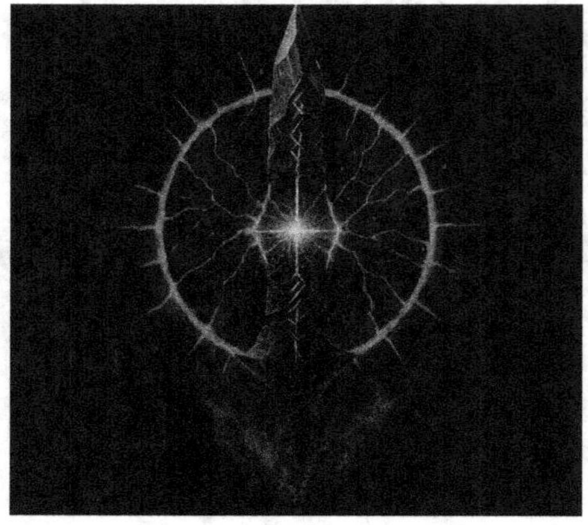

Cairn

Cairn stepped through the Veil like a shadow spilling into light—silent, seamless, and unseen.

The farmhouse welcomed him like an old memory. Worn floorboards, crooked trim, the faint scent of cedar and rain-damp earth clinging to the beams. He'd been here before, years ago. The walls hadn't changed—not the chipped paint or the twisted tree outside. But she had.

He moved without sound down the narrow hall. Her presence tugged at him like heat through stone—something vibrant, flawed, unfinished. The Veil still clung to her in threads, ghost-thin but present.

She'd taken the call. Heard the breach as it opened. Felt it, maybe, if she was more sensitive than he hoped. That's why he was here. He had to see for himself what remained in her—if anything dangerous stirred behind those too-bright eyes.

Cairn reached the threshold of her room, slipping through a crack in the door already ajar.

Seren sat cross-legged on her bed, unaware. Her duffel was open, ghost gear fanned out like surgical tools: digital recorders, night vision cams, motion sensors, infrared wands. Not a soldier's arsenal—a seeker's. A believer's.

She held her old leather-bound journal across her thighs, writing with slow, focused movements. Her brows were drawn together in thought. Her fingers moved like she was stitching fire into paper.

He scanned the page.

 "Male voice, panic, shadows, metal tearing - no confirmed GPS, no victim."

Cairn's mouth curled in a humorless smirk. Pathetic little mortal.

Not because she was wrong—she was far too close. Closer than she should be. But because she didn't understand what she was brushing against. She was still trying to name the storm with borrowed language and hopeful guesswork.

He looked again as she continued to write.

 "Vision… possible other realm… high color saturation… lava/ash… spiral stone buildings…nosebleed"

She had seen the Pyric Realm.

Cairn couldn't breathe.

His fingers curled into fists at his sides, heat simmering beneath the skin like iron brought to boil. No. No. No. This wasn't a guess. This wasn't some overreaching mortal paranoia. She had seen it—the ash, the stone spires, the burn-colored sky. And she'd written it down with that same maddening curiosity as her little ghost hunts.

He took a step back, eyes narrowing, pulse sharp in his ears. She saw everything. Not just remnants left behind. The realm itself.

She was dangerous. A thread flaring too bright in the dark. He should report this. He had to report this. Kaedros didn't tolerate breaches that lingered. The Veil was fraying. Mortals like her—ones who could feel it, see through it—they were why it wouldn't close.

He should have dealt with her properly all those years ago.

But he couldn't. Not because he was weak. Not even because he was curious.

Because his oath—his true oath—hadn't been to Kaedros. It had been forged in the molten chambers beneath the land, before kings ruled and thrones were carved.

It had been to the Realm, yes, but it had ultimately been to the Veil.

And the Veil had chosen her.

His breath hitched.

And now, she sat there scribbling down secrets like they were nothing, wrapped in mist and defiance and ink-stained fingers. She was still trying to understand. Still trying to name it.

And still...

She hadn't turned away from it.

Cairn stared, jaw tight, the flame tattoos beneath his skin pulsing faintly with suppressed energy. Her presence was a wound he'd never quite cauterized. He'd watched her for years. She'd grown into herself like wildfire, quiet and relentless.

He didn't know why, but he knew he didn't want her dead.

That realization struck him like a blade. It wasn't mercy. It wasn't logic. It was something else—a feeling that twisted low in his ribs and left a bitter taste in his mouth.

He should turn her in. He would turn her in.

"Fuck," he whispered, the word low and sharp, burning at the edges. Seren had been staring at her phone when she suddenly froze, her head turning slowly over her shoulder—right toward him.

She saw him. He was sure of it. Cairn eased back further into the hallway.

Seren walked over to the window and appeared to be looking outside. Maybe she didn't see him after all. She turned back to face the room, gaze sweeping every corner. For a second, something flickered in her expression—not fear. Calculation. Then she spoke, dry and sharp: "If you're gonna keep staring, at least be useful."

Cairn couldn't help but smile at her. She always had an attitude and a mouth that would get her in trouble with the wrong people. A brat through and through.

She tilted her head, eyes flicking toward the door before she moved back to her cabinet and started putting her equipment away. Some part of her felt him. That echo beneath the skin.

Cairn melted back into the hall, slipping past the edge of her perception—if such a thing even existed with her.

She passed him, barefoot and unaware, the sound of the shower starting a moment later.

He turned to go, jaw tight. He needed to report this to Kaedros.

Then her phone chimed.

Cairn froze.

He hadn't touched a thing. The device lit up on the bedside table, casting a faint glow against the dim room. His gaze flicked toward it, heat rising behind his ribs. Who was messaging her? She'd been surrounded by equipment—was she planning to go out tonight? To chase what she didn't understand?

He took a silent step closer, boots soundless on the old wood.

The screen still glowed, the message preview illuminated in the notification bar.

Marisol: "Ya absolutely—you bet I want to follow you around a creepy old church where cults killed people. What could go wrong?"

Cairn's jaw clenched.

So that was the plan. Seren had seen too much already, and now she was planning to dig deeper. To bring others with her. To go to that place.

He reached down and unlocked the phone.

One swipe.
One tap.
The message vanished, erased with clinical precision. He toggled the conversation thread, scrolled just enough to ensure it looked untouched. Seren's message now sat as "Delivered," unread. As if Marisol hadn't replied at all.

As if she'd never even seen it.

How absurdly easy it was to twist these fragile human tools. They trusted them like gospel—never realizing how breakable they were in the wrong hands.

Cairn stepped back from the nightstand, the light from the screen fading behind him. He didn't know what frightened him more—that Seren had seen the Pyric Realm... or that she wasn't afraid of it.

She was going to get herself killed. Or worse... noticed.

The water in the bathroom shut off. He stepped away, silent and precise.

Let her think her friend ghosted her. Let her go alone.

His lips curled, not in cruelty—not entirely—but with the shape of a plan forming.

If she was heading to that chapel, the one soaked in old rituals and sacrificial ash, then perhaps the timing was fate after all. He could follow her. Learn more. Make certain. And maybe... maybe steer her off this path before it was too late.

She wanted answers? Then he would give her exactly what she came looking for. He would use her own equipment against her—twist her radios, bend the sensors, echo her questions back to her with the kind of answers that would make any sane mortal run screaming into the daylight.

If he could plant just enough fear... enough doubt... she might walk away from this entirely. From the hunt. From the truth clawing at the edges of her reality.

From him.

That last thought sparked something sharp in his chest—something he didn't want to name. So he shoved it down, where it belonged. One more night. One terrifying night. And then she just might be safe.
Seren padded back down the hall, bare feet soft against the warped floorboards. Cairn stood utterly still, cloaked in shadow, the Veil thinning around him like breath on glass. She didn't see him. Not with her eyes. But something in her posture — the sluggish tension in her shoulders, the way her gaze skimmed the corners — said her instincts were screaming louder than her exhaustion.

She passed within inches of him, damp skin glistening in the low light. Her hair clung in dark waves to her back, still dripping from the shower. The towel wrapped around her torso was an afterthought — barely secure, just something to separate her from the world until she gave up entirely.

Cairn watched, breath quiet, as she crossed the room and checked her phone. She appeared puzzled for a second, but brushed it off quickly. She changed silently into new clothes and climbed into bed with her laptop. She appeared to be doing research for tonight. Until she silently fell asleep.

No ceremony. No awareness. Just surrender.

She lay there for a long moment — still as stone — and he wondered if she'd fallen asleep like that, on top of the covers, hand still resting on her laptop. But then, with a groggy grunt, she rolled to one side, peeled her hoodie off, and shoved it to the floor. Still half-wet and shivering, she tugged the blankets over herself and burrowed into the mattress.

But Cairn didn't move. Not yet.

Her breaths deepened, softened — the restless tension draining from her body inch by inch. A quiet snore escaped her lips, barely audible, more breath than sound.

Cairn stepped forward.

Not Veiled. Not hidden.

Fully present.

The moment he shifted through, the air in the room tightened. He could feel it — the subtle weight of existing entirely in her world, every molecule vibrating around him. The scent of her shampoo lingered faintly beneath the humid remnants of the shower, clean and wild, like rain over stone.
He stood near the bed, staring.

What was so special about this one?
She didn't look different than the others. Same fragile bones, same smooth skin. Same fleeting life wrapped in too-thin armor. But there was something that hooked under his ribs and pulled. Something louder than logic.

Cairn tilted his head slightly, studying the small furrow between her brows, even in sleep. The way her lips parted just enough to soften her expression. Pouty. Innocent. Her nose had a slight curve at the bridge — a flaw by human standards, maybe, but it suited her. Real. Unvarnished. He hated how easily his eyes traced the slope of her cheek, the line of her collarbone just visible beneath the blanket. A lock of damp hair clung to her temple. Without thinking, he reached forward and brushed it aside.

And there it was.

The scar.

Small. Teardrop-shaped. Nestled against the curve of her jaw like a whisper.

His mark.

The only one that mattered.

It burned in him — not with shame, not even with regret — but with a dark kind of satisfaction. A brand she didn't even understand. A reminder that long before she'd gone chasing ghosts and shadows, she had already belonged to him. She was his spark. And he had no idea how to put her out.

Even if she never knew it.

When he marked her, she was just a girl. Frightened. Fragile. A mistake he'd intended to fix later — drag her through the Veil like the rest, twist her soul into something obedient, something useful. But later never came.

Instead, he watched, and she grew.

Into a woman with fire behind her eyes and defiance stitched into her spine. Into something unpredictable. Untamed.
Now, lying in front of him in sleep's quiet grip, she looked nothing like the creature he was supposed to destroy. The blanket shifted slightly with each breath, and beneath it he could still see the shape of her — soft curves, the long line of her back, the way her body tucked naturally into itself, completely unaware.

Attractive.

The thought struck him like a slap.

Cairn's eyes narrowed. His hand, still hovering near her cheek, clenched into a fist. He stepped back abruptly, straightening with rigid precision.

What am I doing?

She was a mortal. A threat. A fracture in the Veil that refused to close. Not some fascination to be nurtured. Not some delicate thing to be protected. His jaw set. She was one of them, and she would stop looking or she would be dealt with.

Cairn turned, letting the Veil begin to coil around him again like smoke returning to flame. One foot already in the Between, he glanced once more at the bed — her form still, peaceful, trusting the silence of her home.

That silence would end soon. He would follow her to the chapel tonight.

Chapter Seven: The Chapel in The Woods

Seren

Seren stirred beneath the heavy quilt, lashes fluttering as the sharp contrast of chill air met the exposed skin of her shoulders. Her brow furrowed. The house was colder than usual. Still. The old farmhouse always held a bit of a draft, but this was different — like the warmth had been leached out of the walls while she slept. The kind of cold that remembered things.

She sat up slowly, blanket wrapped around her shoulders like a cocoon, and reached for her phone on the nightstand.

Still no reply.

The text to Marisol sat untouched, status bar reading "delivered" in that cold, quiet way that now felt personal.

"Guess she picked up another shift," Seren mumbled, rubbing at one eye. "Or fell asleep on her couch again."

The screen's glow lit up her face, revealing the time.

6:03 p.m.

"Shit."
She threw off the blanket and shuffled toward the dresser. She had barely over an hour before she needed to be at the old chapel — enough time to eat something that wasn't caffeine and vending machine regret, throw herself into real clothes, and do a final gear check.

Pulling open a drawer, she grabbed her favorite black cargo pants and a long-sleeve thermal shirt, soft with wear. It wasn't fancy, but it moved well, kept her warm, and wouldn't snag on anything in the dark.

In the kitchen, she slapped together a sandwich with whatever was closest to expiration and stood barefoot in the doorway while she ate, eyes still heavy with sleep and thoughts muddied by dreams she couldn't quite remember. There was always something strange about waking up after one of those weird calls — like the Veil still clung to her, like waking life hadn't fully pulled her back.

She didn't have the luxury of lingering in that space tonight. There were batteries to double-check, extra SD cards to format, and a haunted chapel that had already swallowed more than its share of shadows.

Seren grabbed her keys from the hook by the door, then doubled back to the bedroom. Her duffel waited in the cabinet, zipped tight and ready — packed hours ago when adrenaline and instinct refused to let her rest.

She hoisted it over one shoulder, the familiar weight settling against her back like armor. Her gaze dropped to the floor beneath the coat rack, where a pair of black platform boots waited like old friends.

They were unapologetically goth — thick soles, silver buckles, and just enough attitude to start a bar fight. People always asked how she functioned in them, let alone chased down ghosts and climbed through collapsed stairwells.

She didn't answer anymore. She just moved — practiced, balanced, silent as a cat.

Seren slid her feet into the boots, laced them tight, and stood. She gave a little bounce on her toes, testing the familiar rhythm.

Ready, with one last glance toward the room — the flicker of unease still hiding somewhere behind the calm — she turned off the lights and stepped into the twilight.

Seren locked the door behind her with a firm click and made her way down the front steps. The porch creaked under her boots — not ominous, just old wood being honest. Her boots thudded softly along the path as the last light of day filtered through the gnarled limbs of the twisted tree in the yard.

She popped the trunk of the Challenger with a press of her key fob and slung the duffel inside, tucking it beside a worn blanket and a box of backup gear she kept for emergencies. The lid closed with a satisfying thunk.

Sliding into the driver's seat, she gave the wheel a fond pat before turning the key. The engine rumbled to life, a low purr that vibrated through the floorboards — music to her nerves.

Seren shifted into reverse and began backing slowly down the gravel drive, tires crunching in the quiet.

That's when movement caught her eye.

A flutter, just a flicker, behind one of the upstairs curtains. The one in her parents room she never entered. The curtain moved like breath — slow, deliberate, wrong.

Her brows furrowed. The house was supposed to be empty.

She stopped the car halfway out of the driveway, squinting up at the window. The curtain stilled. No silhouette. No second twitch. But the unease lingered — like something had watched her leave.

Seren narrowed her eyes and muttered, "If I come home to another damn possum, I swear to god…"

She shook her head and threw the car into drive.

The stereo screamed to life the moment she hit the highway, speakers thumping with the furious energy of distorted guitars from her favorite band, Five Finger Death Punch. Seren rolled the window down just a crack, letting the wind whip her hair as she drummed her fingers against the wheel.

Any signs of civilization disappeared behind her quickly — Redmill's edge didn't stretch far. Streetlights gave way to dusk-drenched fields, then towering firs and cedar swallowed the horizon whole. The two-lane road twisted like a ribbon pulled too tight, flanked on both sides by nothing but forest and shadows.

It was exactly the kind of drive that made people rethink their hobbies. The Challenger didn't love it. The road got rougher, the pavement giving way to gravel, then dirt, then something that could generously be called a logging road. The canopy overhead was so thick, it swallowed what was left of the sun.

Seren muttered to herself, "I really need to get a damn pickup for this sort of thing." But the car was part of her armor — reckless, loud, hers.

The car bounced once — hard — and she winced, gripping the wheel tighter. Still, she pressed on, winding higher into the mountains until the dirt road curved sharply and spat her out onto a narrow spur. The side road was little more than a trailhead now, and she crept along it for another few hundred yards before stopping.

Seren put the car into park and cut the engine. The silence that followed was immediate and absolute. The kind of silence that felt like a held breath. No hum of traffic, no wind rustling through leaves. Just the quiet breath of the forest pressing close around her.

From here, the road dead-ended at a rusted gate hung with old, sun-bleached warning signs — NO TRESPASSING, PRIVATE PROPERTY, one partially eaten by rust and bullet holes. The gate sagged, chained shut, padlock long broken.

She reached for her phone, thumb hovering over the screen as she debated texting Marisol. Just a quick "Hey, made it to the haunted murder chapel. If I die, avenge me" kind of thing.

But the bars were gone. No signal. Not even one.

Seren exhaled a sharp breath and dropped the phone into her pocket. "Figures. Of course, the creepy-ass cult site is a dead zone."

She glanced at the tree line ahead, lips tightening.

Whatever. She'd done dumber things with less prep.

She grabbed her gear from the trunk, slung the duffel over one shoulder, and gave the gate a once-over. The brush was thick here, tall grasses and brambles reaching out like they wanted to hold her back.

And behind it all, just barely visible through the trees, was the jagged silhouette of the chapel.
Seren slipped through a break in the rusted gate and started up the narrow footpath that cut through the underbrush. The incline was steeper than it looked from the car, and the weight of her duffel shifted

with every step. Branches clawed at her jacket, brambles tugged at her pants, but she kept moving — boots steady, practiced.

The forest felt alive here.

Not in a peaceful, National Geographic way. No birds. No wind. Just the sound of her own breathing and the occasional crunch of old leaves beneath her boots. Not welcoming. Watching.

Then — something else.

A flicker of movement in the trees to her right. Too fast for a deer. Too heavy for a squirrel. Seren froze, hand instinctively going to her flashlight, eyes scanning the dense undergrowth.

Nothing.
But her pulse had already picked up.

She muttered under her breath, "It's probably just a raccoon. Or a feral cult ghost. Great."

The trail eventually broke through the tree line, opening up into a clearing that felt... wrong.

The chapel sat like a rot blooming on top of the ridge. Its silhouette clawed at the sky. Steep rooflines intact, though warped with age. The windows were all boarded up, heavy wood slats nailed haphazardly into the frames. The double front doors had a heavy beam braced across them.

But it wasn't the structure itself that made her stop.

It was the circle.

A perfect ring of dead earth surrounded the chapel. Not dry grass. Not packed dirt. Just... nothing. No weeds, no moss, no roots crawling through the surface. Just bare soil like something had scoured life away and left only silence behind.

Seren crouched down at the edge of the circle, running her fingers through the dirt. It didn't even smell like earth — just dust and ash. Like something had burned away the memory of life.
She straightened slowly, eyes narrowing at the building.

"Okay," she whispered. "Definitely haunted."

The air felt heavier here — thick with silence and something unspoken. She reached into her jacket pocket and pulled out her phone, thumb tapping the screen.

Nothing.

She frowned and tapped again.

The screen blinked once — a flicker of red battery warning — then blacked out entirely.

"You've got to be kidding me," she muttered, jabbing the power button a few times before giving up. "It was at seventy percent twenty minutes ago."

Now it was a paperweight. Or maybe a brick. One that might only be useful if she needed to throw it at something. The chapel had swallowed signal and power alike.

She shoved it back in her pocket, jaw tight. No service. No battery. No way to check in or call out.

Just her, the gear, and whatever the hell was waiting inside that godforsaken chapel.

Seren scanned the front of the chapel, squinting against the last streaks of daylight. Every window was boarded tight, thick planks nailed in crooked, overlapping layers like someone had tried to trap something inside. Or keep something out.

The doors weren't any better. Large beams blocked the entrances, and iron chains wrapped through the rusted handles with padlocks thick with age and neglect. The metal smelled faintly of old blood and forgotten prayers. She gave one a tug out of habit — solid. Nothing was getting through that without a crowbar and serious time.
She circled to the side, boots crunching over the dead ground. Her eyes swept the base of the building. No obvious gaps, no side entrances. Just more rot and nails clinging to the old wood like decay had hands of its own.

But then — at the back corner, partially hidden beneath a collapsed awning — she spotted it. A gap. A wound in the chapel's skin.

A set of narrow steps led down into the earth, like a throat swallowing light. At the base, two thick cellar doors, weathered gray and crooked on their hinges. One hung slightly open.

She slowed, every instinct on edge.

It wasn't just the fact that the door was ajar. It was the way the darkness pooled beneath it — too still, too quiet, like it was watching.

"Of course it's the creepy basement," she muttered.

Still, she reached for her flashlight, tightened her grip, and started down the steps.

Seren stepped carefully onto the first board of the narrow staircase, and it shrieked beneath her weight — a drawn-out groan that echoed so violently in the stillness, it may as well have been a car crash. She froze, breath held, heart pounding. Nothing moved. No birds. No wind. Just the loud, creaking protest of each board as she made her way down, one step at a time.

At the bottom, she crouched beside the partially open cellar door and clicked on her flashlight.

The beam cut through the sliver of space, casting harsh shadows across the threshold. Inside, the dirt was the same as what ringed the chapel — dry, cracked, and utterly lifeless. It looked wrong. Like the Veil had touched it and left fingerprints.

Her light caught on a shelf along the far wall — warped wood, one corner slumped like it had given up on holding anything. Dust coated the surface. A few scraps of something unrecognizable clung to the lower tiers. No bones. No sigils. Just decay and neglect, but the silence felt curated.

Still, her pulse didn't settle.

She stepped closer and placed one hand on the door, then pushed. The hinges screamed.

The sound tore through the trees and bounced off the chapel walls, unnaturally loud — like it didn't just disturb the silence, it offended it. Seren winced but kept pushing until the door yawned fully open, the darkness inside stretching wider.

She tightened her grip on the flashlight and stepped forward into the room. Seren immediately halted.
A single wooden chair sat perfectly centered in the room — too deliberate. It hadn't been tossed aside or broken like everything else. It sat like it had been waiting for someone to return. The beam of her flashlight traced the lines of it — spindly legs, a high back, and long, dark drips trailing from the seat.

Her stomach twisted.

Blood?

She moved closer, boots crunching over dead soil. When she leaned in, the truth came into focus: wax. Red candle wax. Hardened streaks had cooled like frozen tears down the wood, pooling beneath the chair like it had bled out.

Relief came and went like a blink.

Because then she saw the symbol carved into the dirt around it.

An inverted pentacle.

Drawn with purpose, the lines etched deep and clean. Her light followed its shape — wide, spanning nearly the whole room, with the chair in its dead center. Her breath caught. She tilted her flashlight upward and instantly wished she hadn't.

The same pentacle was painted on the ceiling, its red pigment dried into cracked veins against the rotting beams above. It was hard to tell if it was paint... or something else. The color had sunk too deep into the wood, like it had been there a long time. Maybe blood. Maybe both.

A chill prickled her skin.

What the hell had they done down here?
A sacrifice? A summoning? Some kind of portal?

Seren swallowed and took a slow step back. She'd been to dozens of haunted places. Creepy barns, abandoned hospitals, murder houses no one would claim. But this... this felt different.
There were no stairs. No ladder. No trapdoor to the chapel above. Just bare walls and sagging beams. Seren turned in a slow circle, scanning the room with her light until the beam caught something above the broken shelving across the room — a jagged hole.

She stepped closer. Her scar pulsed faintly — a whisper from the Veil.

A crude opening had been smashed into the ceiling — maybe kicked through from above or carved out in desperation. It wasn't wide, just enough for a person to squeeze through if they didn't mind getting splinters and dust in places splinters and dust didn't belong. She angled her flashlight through the gap and caught a glimpse of flooring above. Another room.

But that could wait.

The basement felt right. Or at least, right for starting.

Seren turned back to the chair. It still sat like a throne in the center of its pentacle, wax dried like veins. The air felt heavier here, still and charged — the kind of tension that made the fine hairs on her arms rise.

She slid her bag from her shoulder and knelt, pulling out a small, circular device with an antenna and flashing lights — the REM pod. She placed it gently on the seat of the chair. Its center light blinked once, then glowed steady blue. Ready.

One by one, she moved along the points of the inverted pentacle, placing more gear with practiced care. A motion activated music box. An EMF meter. An infrared camera set on a squat tripod. A temp gauge. An Ovilus Spirit Box. The setup was ritual in its own way — not just tech, but intention.

Finally, she sat cross-legged just outside the pentacle, in front of the Ovilus.

Seren cleared her throat, her voice soft in the stale dark.

"Okay. If anything's here, my name is Seren. I'm not here to hurt you or piss you off. I just want to know what happened here. Who you are. If you're stuck. If something went wrong. I come with nothing but respect and want to hear your stories"

She glanced around, lowering her voice instinctively.
"I've brought some tools to help you talk to me. The thing on the chair — that's a REM pod. If you get close to it or touch it, it'll light up and beep. The device by that wall is a motion activated music box, if you walk or move in front of it you get to scare the pants off of me with some creepy ass music. This one over here listens to changes in temperature. Across from me is an infrared camera. This side is an EMF detector. It senses

changes in electromagnetic fields. Finally, right here in front of me is an Ovilus Spirit box. This will allow you to choose words and speak directly to me with your energy"

She looked down at her lap, tapping a finger against her knee.

"I know these symbols are not just for show. Someone meant something with it. I don't know if you're still here, or what was brought here, but… I'm listening."

Seren reached into her bag and pulled out a headlamp, fresh notebook, and a pen. The tip already stained from obsessive note-taking in dark places. She placed the headlamp on, just bright enough to see the paper, and balanced the notebook on her knee. She then began sketching a rough map of the space — chair, equipment, symbols.

As she was labeling her placements, the EMF meter gave a faint click. A soft green light shifted briefly to yellow.

She paused, watching.

A few seconds later, the thermometer chirped — not loud, but sharp in the silence. A sharp drop in temperature flickered across the display. Cold enough to raise the hairs on her arms. The chill felt familiar, Veil-thin.

Seren quickly logged the changes, then returned her attention to the chair.

The REM pod lit up.

One clear beep, a flash of red, and then silence.

A beat passed. She exhaled slowly.

"Thank you," she murmured into the stillness. "If that was you, I'm listening. I want to know what happened here."

She kept her pen moving — not everything, not every blink or shift, just enough to track what mattered. A rhythm she'd honed over dozens of haunted places, where moments like these slipped by fast if you didn't catch them in ink.

The air stayed thick. Watchful.

The Ovilus chirped.

Its screen blinked once — static fuzz, then a single word.

"*Sacrifice*"

Seren's spine straightened. She stared at the screen, waiting. "Was it... was someone sacrificed here?"

The device buzzed again.

"*Many*"

The word felt heavy, like it had weight beyond language. She frowned. Her pen hovered over the page, unmoving.

"Were you one of them?"

Silence.

A soft chime from the thermometer. Another small drop.

The REM pod gave a short flash — blinked red, then blue again.

Her voice dropped to a whisper. "Why? Why would they do that?"

The Ovilus whirred, slower this time.

"*Opened*"

She blinked. "Opened what?"

"*Door*"
Seren's stomach dropped. The pentacle suddenly felt less symbolic, and more functional.

She glanced at the pentacle, the melted wax, the blood — or paint — above.
"A door to... where?"

No answer.

Then: "*Below*" ..... "*Cold*"

A breeze she hadn't noticed stirred her hair. She glanced toward the corners of the basement.

"What's down there?"

"Hungry"

That one made her freeze. Her fingers clenched around the pen.

"What did they bring through?"

"Watcher"

The word curled around her spine like smoke. The REM pod flashed again. The music box gave a soft plink — one note, then silence.

She swallowed. "Is it still here?"

"Bound"

Bound. That could mean it was trapped. Or waiting. She didn't like either. "Are people still coming here? Doing things?"

"Break"

Her pulse quickened. The Veil didn't just fray - it tore. Her breath caught. "On purpose?"

"Fools"

A pause. Then, quieter — as if even the device hesitated:

"Again"

Seren looked up, scanning the darkness beyond her equipment. Her next question faltered on her lips.

Finally, she asked, "Why are you telling me this?"
The Ovilus paused. Buzzed. Then blinked one final word.

"Warn"

A sharp creak echoed above her, like the chapel itself had heard the warning.

Seren froze.

Another step — slow, deliberate — across the floorboards directly over her head.

She held her breath.

The REM pod blinked again. Once. Twice. Then stopped.
She stared up at the ceiling. "Hello?" she called, voice wavering despite her best effort to stay calm. "Is someone there?"

No answer. Just the thick, pressing silence of old wood and heavy air.

Then the Ovilus flickered again.

"*Play*"
Her gaze snapped back to the screen.

It glowed innocently, mockingly.

Another step above.

She rose halfway to her feet, heart hammering now. The music box let out a single, off-key note before falling still again.

"Okay," she said, more to herself than anything. "Not funny."
The screen pulsed once more like it was breathing.

"*Upstairs*"

Her brow furrowed. "Is that where you want me to go?"

The REM pod flickered once. She narrowed her eyes, skeptical now. "Alright, if you want me to move to the room above me... make the REM pod beep three times. In a row."

A few seconds passed. Nothing.

Then—

Beep.
Beep.
Beep.

Each chirp felt like a footstep. The final echoed too long in the silent chapel, bouncing off stone and wood like a dare.

Seren exhaled through her nose and stood slowly, brushing the dirt from her jeans. "Alright then."

She moved methodically, shutting off and collecting her equipment one piece at a time, tucking it all back into her duffel. Since whatever this was seemed to like the Ovilus, she kept that on and in her pocket. She slung the bag over her shoulder and walked to the splintered shelving beneath the crude hole she'd spotted earlier.

The wood groaned under her boots as she climbed, testing each step with practiced caution.

When she reached the top, she paused and tossed her duffel through the opening — it landed with a muted thud on the floor above.

Then she braced her hands on the edges and began to hoist herself up, twisting slightly to fit through the narrow, jagged gap. Her jacket caught for a moment on a splinter, but she shoved past it, gritting her teeth and dragging herself the rest of the way.

Her boots scraped over the rim and she tumbled lightly onto the chapel floor above, the stale air immediately cooler up here, thicker somehow.

The Ovilus in her jacket pocket buzzed one more time.

"*Welcome*"

Seren brushed dust off her jeans and picked up her duffel, slinging it back over her shoulder with a grunt. The floor beneath her was uneven, warped in places, but held. She reached into the side pocket and pulled out her flashlight.

With a soft click, the beam cut through the gloom.

What she expected — narrow pews, cracked hymnals, maybe a forgotten crucifix — didn't exist here.
There were no pews. No altar. No bibles.

No Jesus.

Instead, the chapel stretched wide and barren, save for the strange remnants scattered across its interior. Melted candles. Scorch marks.

Ash clinging to the stone in long streaks, like smoke stains clawing their way toward the ceiling.

The walls were bare, but for symbols — burned into the wood and stone. Circles. Spirals. Inverted triangles and runes she didn't recognize.

None of them felt like worship. They felt like warnings.

Beneath her boots, the floor was littered with old scorch marks. Fire had been lit here. Many times. Like something had been summoned again and again, until the wood forgot how to be clean.

She swept the flashlight slowly across the space.
At the far end, a raised platform stood where an altar might have been — but there was no cross, no pulpit. Only a blackened iron brazier, long cold, but still caked in red wax and something darker beneath. Symbols were etched into the floor around it, some faded, others sharp as fresh carving.

Seren swallowed hard.

Whatever this place had been… it wasn't holy anymore.
This was no chapel.
This was a sanctum.
A place for ritual.
For death.
And above all else — fire.

She stepped further inside, the flashlight beam steady in her grip. The scarring on the floor held her attention — not random, not from a single fire. Layered. Repeated. As if something had burned again and again in the same place. Intentional.

Seren knelt near one of the scorch marks, brushing the soot gently with her fingers.

The instant her skin met the ash, something shifted. A pressure behind her eyes — familiar. The same faint, electric static she'd felt in the alley. That subtle pull, like her soul leaned forward without her permission. Like a thread catching on something beyond.

She sucked in a breath, steadied her hand, but the chill still rode up her spine. The Veil had thinned here, too — maybe even torn.

"What were you doing here?" she murmured. "What was all this for? Sacrifice? Worship?"

Her voice echoed slightly in the space, swallowed quickly by the strange hush that clung to the chapel. She glanced around. No movement. No sounds.

The Ovilus, which she'd kept on in her pocket, crackled once — but spat nothing out.

Seren sat back on her heels, exhaling hard. "Come on... You lured me up here. Show me something."

Silence.

She stared up at the brazier, the strange marks, the yawning shadow beneath the rafters.

"Fine," she muttered, pulling her bag close. "You want something real? You got it."

She stomped over to the raised platform and sat with her back against the low wall. Tugged out her headphones, connected them to the spirit box, and pulled a folded blindfold from the pouch inside her bag. This wasn't part of her normal solo routine — it wasn't safe to run the Estes Method alone. Usually one person stayed alert and asked the questions while the other was blindfolded, ears filled with static, listening for whatever bled through. Doing it alone was reckless, but she was done waiting for permission.

But right now, she didn't care. She settled on the floor near the brazier, set the spirit box to scan rapidly, and took one last look around the chapel.

"If I'm not supposed to be here... now would be the time to tell me," she said, soft but firm.

Nothing. She slid the blindfold on. Took a breath. Slipped the headphones over her ears. The static roared in her skull. For a few moments, there was only the wash of it — rhythmic, dizzying. Hypnotic. Shapes swam behind her closed eyes, maybe faces. Maybe just ghosts of thought.

Then, a voice.
Low. Fragmented. Male.

"Burned"

A second followed — higher, female, barely a whisper.

"Purified"

Then another. Warped, echoing like it traveled through smoke.

"Chosen"

Seren stiffened.

Her pulse spiked, but she kept her breath even, willing herself to listen.

The static pulsed in her ears — a river of sound she let herself sink into.

"It was never meant…"
A man's voice — old, raspy, cut off.

"Dig too deep"
Feminine. Scared.

Seren licked her lips and kept her voice steady.
"What happened here? Why the fire?"

"Burned them all"
"They screamed"
"Made it pure"

"What was it? What were you trying to do?"

A pause. Then:

"Veil was thin"
"Saw too much"
The words felt like memories bleeding through. That pulled at her attention. Her breath hitched slightly beneath the blindfold.

"What Veil?"

"Between"
"The barrier"
"They opened it"

Each voice was different — no single speaker twice.

"Pyric"

The voice was young. Male. A whisper wrapped in smoke. The word curled around her brain, familiar, wrong.

"Fire behind the dark"

Seren's heart pounded.

"What's Pyric? Is that what this chapel was built for?"

"No—claimed it"
"Not built. Twisted"

The chapel hadn't been made for this. It had been taken. The temperature seemed to drop again. The silence between voices grew more brittle. Like something was pressing down on the air around her.

She hesitated, then asked, "Who twisted it? Who's keeping you here?"

No answer.

Just a deep burst of static, then —

"Don't say his name"
"He listens"
"Always"

Seren's fingers tightened around her knees.

"Who is he?"
"Shadow of flame"
"He marked the girl"
"Watcher"

Her scar burned. The little spark inside her flared. She sat up straighter. Her pulse thudding behind her ears.

"What girl? Me?"

Another pause. Longer.

"He's coming"
"Don't trust the fire"

"He burns what he owns"

Seren's breath caught. "Who is it? Why are you scared of him?"

Then—

A spike of pain tore through her skull.

The migraine slammed back with blinding force—worse than before, a white-hot pressure blooming behind her eyes. Her knees nearly buckled. Static roared in her ears.

And through it:

"Leave"
"Run"
"Before—"

The static surged — like something was trying to drown the warning. A sudden shift in the temperature stopped her cold. Not chill this time — heat. Like the sun had risen directly above her, casting its rays through the roof. Dry. Oppressive. Her breath tasted like ash.

"Who is it?" she whispered. "Let me help you—"

Then the first clear voice of the night broke through. Deep. Singular. Male. Steady.

"Seren"

Chapter Eight: Is It Lonely

Cairn

The air inside the chapel was fractured — alive with whispers not meant for mortal ears.

From the shadowed edge of the Pyric Veil, Cairn stood still, just outside the flow of time. The girl had gone too far.

Blindfolded. Alone. Sitting like an offering before the blackened brazier. A spark laid bare before the flame.

He watched her lips part — her breath slow and steady, her fingers resting in her lap like she trusted the silence not to bite. She had no idea how alive the boundary was here. How loud her questions had become on the other side. How close she sat to the teeth of gods.

And the spirits — they were answering.

"It was never meant…"
"Dig too deep"
"Burned them all"
"They screamed"
"Made it pure"

Cairn's jaw tensed. He felt the tattoos along his arms warm faintly, the fire under his skin stirring.
Then:

"Veil was thin"
"Saw too much"

He stepped closer, still unseen, just beyond the Veil's skin. They were
brushing against truths she couldn't be allowed to have.

"Between"
"They opened it"
"Pyric"

That word struck like a hammer. It echoed louder than the others, like
even the realm itself recognized its own name spoken aloud. Cairn's lips
curled, breath sharp. If she kept listening, she'd start pulling the whole
tapestry apart.

"No—claimed it"
"Not built. Twisted"
"Don't say his name"
"He listens"
"Always"
"He marked the girl"
"Watcher"

Enough.

He stepped through the Veil.

Heat surged outward in an instant — washing the chill away like sunrise,
burning frost from the air. The Veil didn't part. It resisted, shuddering like
something aware of him. The spirits recoiled. Static cracked. The chapel
fell silent but for the soft whine of electronics overwhelmed by his
presence.

He moved toward her, quiet as smoke, and crouched beside her where
she sat motionless, still blindfolded, still tethered to the spirit box like a
sacrificial node.

So small. So still.

His voice, when it came, was the final one she would hear in the session.

Low. Steady. Inescapable.

"Seren."

She flinched — not in her body, but in something deeper. Like the sound
touched bone.

He leaned in, inches from her skin, the heat of his presence radiating like forge-coals.

The word hung low in the heat-thick air, stitched with power and recognition. He stood just a breath away now — fully manifested, no longer tethered half between realms. The warmth radiating off his body was deliberate, driving back the cold that had settled with the dead.

She didn't move. Not yet. But her lips parted slightly, reacting to the voice like it had touched something deep beneath the surface.

He tilted his head, studying her — the curve of her cheek, the tension in her jaw. The way her body stilled under pressure but didn't collapse. She was listening.

"They screamed," he said, echoing the words of the souls before.

"Made it pure."
"Saw too much."

Each phrase was measured. Fed directly into her ears. His voice, unlike the others, had weight. Intention.

She shivered. He could feel it ripple through her.

"Burned them all."
"Fire behind the dark."
"Not built. Twisted."

She flinched again, a soft gasp escaping her lips. Her fingers twitched on her lap.
He leaned closer — just enough to feel the heat of her skin through the thin layer of clothing. His gaze dropped briefly to her lips, slightly parted. Her breath was shallow now. He could see the pulse in her neck fluttering, frantic but silent.

She was afraid. Good. But not enough.

"Watcher," he said, the word almost a breath, almost reverent.

"Marked the girl."

His hand hovered near her cheek but didn't touch. He didn't have to. Her skin already reacted to him — the hair on her arms lifting, the faint sheen of sweat at her temple from the heat.

And he liked it.
The control.
The power.

Her body responded before her mind even caught up. It stirred
something in him — primal, possessive. Not just because she was
mortal, not just because she had his mark. But because even now, even
unconscious of him, her body knew.

So close. This was the first time he'd been near her like this while she
was fully awake — aware, even if dulled by the isolation of the Estes.

And she was still beautiful in the worst way. Not polished or sweet. But
raw, sharp, unfinished — like a blade still glowing on the forge. The scar
beneath her jaw gleamed faintly, a whisper of him she didn't even know
she carried.

He swallowed. The fire beneath his tattoos itched.

"He burns what he owns," he said lowly, the words slower this time.

"Don't trust the fire."

A bead of sweat rolled down her neck. She was on the edge. And he
needed her there. He stepped even closer, his breath brushing her ear.

"You're in my chapel, little spark," he whispered.
"Let's see what you really believe."

Her lips moved — barely, the sound half-swallowed by static.

"Is it lonely?" she whispered.

Cairn stilled.

The fire in his chest paused mid-pulse. He hadn't expected that. Not
fear. Not pleading. But that.

She wasn't asking out of sympathy. He could hear it in her tone — raw
curiosity, maybe even recognition. Like she'd seen something in the
silence. Felt the shape of him behind the words.

He watched her more closely, his expression unreadable.
"What did you say?" he asked, low.

But she didn't respond. The trance held her too tightly. The question had slipped out of some deep place in her — unguarded, unplanned.

His gaze lingered on her mouth, the soft movement of breath. The spark of heat he controlled now turned inward, curling beneath his ribs.

Lonely.

The word echoed like a memory.

Her head tilted slightly, as if listening to something only she could hear. Then her mouth moved again, the words barely audible through the static.

"Is that why you marked me?"

Cairn froze.
The breath left him in a sharp, invisible pull. His body didn't move, but something inside recoiled — flared.

No one had ever asked that. Not the mortals he twisted, not the souls he caged. Especially not her. She shouldn't have remembered. Not the touch of that night. Not the moment the mark took hold. And yet— sparks remember the forge.

He stared at her, every line of his face suddenly taut. The heat he exuded was no longer just a Veil of power — now a shield. A defense.

He could lie. Twist it. Feed her another line meant to shake her and burn her clean. But his voice didn't come. She shifted slightly, her breath catching in her throat. Still blindfolded. Still unreachable. But somehow—closer.

The fire under his skin surged, unsteady for the first time.
"You don't even know what you are," he said, quietly. Harsh.

But the words sounded more like a truth spoken to himself, tasted like a confession.
She stirred again, her lips moving with slow purpose.
"Then why do you feel like a warning?"

The question pressed into him like a brand. It wasn't accusatory. Just quiet. Curious. Like a whisper pressing into the hollow of his ribs.

Cairn's breath hitched.

The room felt too small. Too close. The air between them thick with heat and something far more dangerous.

She shouldn't be able to reach him like this. Not in this state. But her voice bypassed reason, bypassed the Veil entirely. Straight into him.

His gaze dropped again to her mouth, parted and trembling with each breath.

"Because I am," he murmured.

She shifted. Not away. Toward.
And for one impossible moment, she looked like she might open her eyes. Might see him — not the shape of him, not the ghost in her periphery — him.

"What are you doing to me?" she breathed. Her voice trembled, but didn't break.

His heart, if it could still be called that, gave a violent, burning lurch. He leaned in, one hand braced near her jaw, the other at his side clenched tight.

"I'm trying to save you," he said.

And before he could stop himself — before the consequences could catch him — Cairn lowered his face to hers and gently brushed his lips against her mouth.

Not a kiss, not fully. A whisper of heat. An echo of something neither of them had words for. She inhaled sharply. A sound that might've been confusion. Might've been need. He pulled back. Just barely. Close enough to still taste the question lingering on her skin.

And that's when he felt it.

Not the heat of her breath or the tremor beneath her ribs — but something deeper. Beneath the surface of her skin, something stirred. Like a pulse beneath a pulse. A rhythm that didn't belong to this world.

His own breath caught.

It wasn't just sensitivity. Not just a thread-sense like so many of the near-touched mortals. No — her presence didn't just feel the Veil. It resonated with it.

Cairn stared at her, stunned. As if the weight of what she was had been hiding in plain sight, and only now, in this moment of proximity — of contact — did it reveal itself.
If she tried, he realized, if she knew what she was doing... she could open a gate. Not stumble into it. Not witness the aftermath. Open it. She wasn't just marked. She was a key

The Pyric Realm would answer her.
It already had.

The taste of it lingered on her skin — ash and heat and something older than language. She didn't know. Not yet. But it was in her bones. In her blood.

And he'd felt it like lightning through a blade the second their mouths had brushed.

Cairn drew back fully now, something like awe burning behind his lilac gaze.

"What are you?" he whispered, not to her, but to the space between them — to the mark he'd left on her years ago that now burned like a brand in his mind.

The answer didn't come. She sat still, lost in the pulse of static and spirit voices. Oblivious to the war cracking open inside him.

He needed to go.

He needed to leave before he did something worse. Something reckless.

And still, he stayed — breathing in the warmth of her presence like it was a sin he wasn't ready to repent for.
They sat in silence for a long moment.
Seren's lips parted, voice barely more than a breath beneath the hum of the spirit box.

"Are you still here?"

Cairn didn't answer at first. The weight of her presence still pressed into him like gravity. But the truth slipped past his lips before he could catch it.

"Yes."

She exhaled — a soft sound, almost relief. Then, quieter:
"I don't know why… but I feel like I need to talk to you again."

The words curled around him like warmth he didn't deserve. He leaned in, the flame beneath his skin simmering low and deliberate. The pull between them felt too close now. Too real.

"Stay away from this place," he said, his voice low and firm. "Don't come back."

She tilted her head slightly beneath the blindfold. "Why?"

"Because you're marked," he murmured. "Because I will find you when the time is right."

A beat passed.

"What's your name?" she asked, so soft it nearly didn't register.

That caught him. The question felt like a door she didn't know she'd opened.

He hesitated — not because he hadn't prepared for the question, but because a part of him wanted to answer.

"I can't tell you that. Not yet," he said, voice dark with something heavier than command. His name was a blade. She wasn't ready to hold it. "You need to leave. Now."

"The sun's almost up. Show me you can listen. Take off the blindfold. Remove the headphones. Walk out of here without another word…and don't tell a single soul about tonight. Living or dead."

He leaned in once more, his breath barely grazing her temple.
"…and I will find you."

Then, like mist drawing back from firelight, Cairn slipped into the shadows — invisible again, but very much still there.
To his surprise… she obeyed.

Seren reached up, hands trembling just slightly, and removed the blindfold. The headphones followed. She blinked in the dim light, her face unreadable. She didn't speak. Didn't try to stay. But the silence between them felt like a promise. Wordless, she gathered her equipment and tucked it away in practiced movements. The moment her

bag was secure, she climbed back down the broken shelf, boots hitting the dirt floor softly. No backward glance. No parting comment.

He followed — silent and unseen — through the trees, watching as she hiked back to her car, threw the gear in the trunk, and slid into the driver's seat. She backed onto the road with no hesitation.

Gone.

Cairn stood at the ridge's edge, the chapel smoldering faintly behind him in the early light. A slow smile tugged at the corner of his mouth.

"Good girl."

Chapter Nine: Secrets in Ash

Seren

"Holy fuck."

The words slipped out before she even knew she was thinking them. She was already halfway down the gravel cutoff, tires bumping toward the pavement, headlights slicing the mist ahead — almost back on real road — before reality caught up to her.

What the actual fuck happened tonight?

Her fingers clenched tighter on the steering wheel, knuckles white. The stillness in the car felt too thin, like the silence after a scream. Her gear was rattling slightly in the trunk — a familiar sound that usually grounded her. But not now. Not after… that.

She blinked hard, like she could clear the images from her mind — the voices, the heat, the name spoken in her ear.

Not a name. A presence.

Whatever that had been, it wasn't just a ghost. It wasn't like anything she'd ever felt in all her nights crawling through haunted buildings and stitched-together stories. This was real. This was alive in a way that made her skin remember its touch even now. The scar on her jaw pulsed faintly — a whisper of heat.

She shook her head, eyes flicking to the rearview mirror as if half-expecting to see someone sitting behind her.

"Get a grip," she muttered. But she didn't really believe it

She reached the end of the road and pulled onto the pavement without thinking, her breath coming short, sharp. The air inside the cabin felt hot, like it still held a trace of him, like the Veil hadn't fully let go.

Don't tell anyone.

The words echoed again in her mind — not a suggestion. A command. Branded into her like heat pressed to skin.

Seren's gaze flicked to the passenger seat, where her dead phone sat face-down next to her notebook. She reached for it with one shaking hand and flipped it over.

The screen lit up. Her heart stuttered. It was on.

No charger. No cord. But there it was — battery icon glowing. 60%.

She stared at it like it might bite her.

"What the hell…" she whispered, thumb hovering above the screen.

Last night it had blinked red once and died in her hand. Now it looked like it had never powered down at all.

She opened her messages.

10 text messages, 4 voicemails, 12 missed FaceTimes, and one nasty video recording from Marisol.

Seren flinched.

She opened the first message, then another. Each more frantic than the last. Marisol had gone from teasing to worried to pissed, and the video was just her yelling into the camera, "If you're ghost-hunting in that creepy-ass cult church without me, I swear to God, Seren—"

Seren shut the screen off and dropped the phone like it burned.

She wasn't sure what scared her more — the voices, the heat, him — or how quickly the impossible had started to feel real.

And worst of all… she wanted to listen. For the chance to talk to him again.

She was going to have to give Marisol some kind of explanation, but it couldn't be the full truth.

Half-truths, then.

Seren responded: "Hey. I'm so sorry. Yes, I went. I never heard back from you, and I figured you were busy. There was no cell service up there, but I'm okay. Nothing too wild. Just a normal ghost hunt. A few equipment hits, but honestly? Pretty dead for a place with such a freaky reputation."

It didn't sit right, lying — even by omission. But what could she say? I think I met a being who lives in fire and the Veil between realms, and he kissed me after haunting my soul through a voice box?

Yeah. No.

Marisol replied fast: "You never heard back? I did respond. Yesterday morning. I was in. 100%."

Seren blinked. Her thumbs hovered over her screen: "No you didn't. I checked right after I got out of the shower. Nothing was there."

Marisol: "Check again. I'll screenshot it."

Seren scrolled through their message thread, frowning. Nothing. Just the conversation from earlier today. No message from the day before. Her heart began to thump harder in her chest.

The screenshot came through seconds later.

A text from Marisol, timestamped just before Seren had left for the chapel.

Marisol: "Ya absolutely — you bet I want to follow you around a creepy old church where cults killed people. What could go wrong?"

Seren stared at it.

It wasn't there. Not in her phone. Not even as a deleted message.

Seren: "It's not showing up on my end. Like… at all. It's like it got erased or something." Like the Veil had planned the whole thing.
Marisol: "Dude. That's messed up. I know I sent it. Check the time. Screenshot doesn't lie."

Seren: "Yeah. I believe you… it's just gone."

Marisol: "Okay, I'm starting to hate your phone. Or your ghosts. Or both."

Seren didn't reply for a while. Her phone was dead. Then it wasn't. The message had been sent. Then it wasn't. It wasn't the ghosts. It was him, and she had no proof. Only the heaviness in her gut that said this night was still unraveling. And she wasn't sure who she was going to be when it was done.

Seren let out a breath she hadn't realized she was holding. Her fingers hovered over the keyboard a moment longer before she typed:

"I'm sorry again. I really thought you hadn't answered. I never would've gone alone if I knew. I promise."

Three dots blinked. Disappeared. Blinked again.

Marisol: "It's okay. You're alive, so I guess I won't kill you. But next time? I'm handcuffing myself to your car."

Seren smiled, small and tired.

Seren: "Deal. I'm heading home now. Gonna try to sleep off whatever this night was."

Marisol: "Call me later. For real."

Seren: "I will. Promise."

She stared at the screen for a second longer, thumb lingering near the side button, before finally locking the phone and setting it down in the passenger seat.

The glow of the screen faded, leaving her with the winding road and the lingering weight of something she still couldn't name. But it knew her name.

The drive home passed in silence.

Not the kind she usually craved — the peaceful, reset-your-nervous-system kind. This was the sort of silence that came from a brain too full to register anything else. No music. No podcasts. Just the hum of the tires on the road and the echo of voices that hadn't belonged to any living thing.

By the time she turned onto her street, the first streaks of sunrise were bleeding across the horizon. Reds and oranges painted the sky like fresh wounds. The kind of morning that felt too vivid after the kind of night she just had.

She pulled into the driveway and killed the engine, but didn't move right away. Her body sagged into the seat, and for the first time since she'd left the chapel, exhaustion finally crashed into her. Full-body, soul-deep exhaustion. Like her bones had just remembered they were mortal again.

After a minute, she dragged herself out of the car and popped the trunk. Her gear rattled as she grabbed her duffel, slinging it over one shoulder.

The house loomed quiet ahead of her — crooked shutters and peeling trim catching the early light. As she stepped onto the porch, her eyes flicked up, unbidden, toward her parents old room.

The curtain. Still. Watching.

Last night, when she'd backed out of the driveway, she'd seen it move. Just for a second. Like someone had been looking out.

A chill crept over her skin that had nothing to do with the morning air.

The house had been hers since she was seventeen. After her father passed, her mother lasted exactly six months before fleeing to Florida like the place itself had swallowed her memories whole. Said she couldn't handle the grief. Couldn't handle the ghosts — literal or otherwise.

So when Seren turned eighteen, the deed landed in her lap like a broken inheritance no one wanted. She stayed. Cleaned. Fixed what she could. Lived with the things that didn't stay fixed.

They still talked, her mom and her — brief calls, polite updates, once-a-year visits to a condo that smelled like sunscreen and stale regret. But this house?

This one was hers.

Too big. Too quiet. And today, too strange to ignore. She turned the key in the lock and stepped inside.

She headed straight for her bedroom, the weight of the duffle bag dragging heavier with every step. She opened the closet, knelt, and unlocked the small chest built into the back wall — a security box disguised as antique furniture. Gently, she tucked the bag inside and latched it shut.

She'd come back later. Sort the gear. Plug in the cameras. Transfer and label files. But right now? She couldn't even think about it. Her limbs were too heavy, her brain too full. And before she could let herself collapse into bed, she had to check the one thing still gnawing at the edge of her thoughts. The curtain has very obviously moved last night.

She muttered something halfhearted about getting rabies shots as she turned back toward the hallway. "It's a possum," she said under her breath. "Please be a possum."

Barefoot and quiet, she crept up the stairs, past the bathroom that still had her father's razor on the shelf and a dusty bottle of aftershave she couldn't bring herself to toss. At the top of the steps, the air shifted — cooler, more still. She stopped in front of the door to her parents' room.

The entire upstairs was theirs — untouched, preserved. A shrine built from grief and stubborn memory.

She hadn't changed much up here since her mom left. Some of the furniture had been swapped out — mostly things that didn't fit or made her itch when she looked at them too long. But the bones of the room were the same.

The same wallpaper. The same creak in the floor near the dresser. The same lace curtains, yellowed with age. The same silence that felt too deliberate.

She stepped inside.

The scent hit her immediately — faint but unmistakable. Her mother's perfume. Powdery and floral, with that sharp, synthetic edge that clung to the walls like memory.

The room was still. Nothing scurried. Nothing squeaked. Nothing moved. But Seren couldn't shake the feeling that something had.

The house was too old for floor vents or central air. Seren had long since accepted its stubborn bones and patchwork lungs. She'd installed window AC units in the rooms she actually used, and a couple of electric heaters downstairs for winter. But up here? There was no airflow. No breeze. No reason for anything to move. No reason for the Veil to stir. And yet...

She stepped fully into the room now, bare feet soundless against the hardwood. The air felt stale, weighted. Everything was coated in a thin layer of dust — the dresser, the vanity, the top of the old rocking chair in the corner. She hadn't been up here in months. Maybe longer. There wasn't a trace of rodent droppings or signs of nesting. No gnawed cords. No shredded fabric.

But there were boot prints.

Seren stopped mid-step, her breath catching. Just one set. Near the window. Imprinted in the dust — the sharp tread pattern unmistakable. Like someone had stood there, looking out. Watching. Waiting. No steps leading to or away. Just the prints. Frozen in place. Her stomach flipped, but she forced herself forward, her eyes scanning the room for more signs, any excuse. A trick of light. A broken rafter letting in the wind.

Nothing.

Drawn by instinct or habit, she crossed to the nightstand on the far side of the bed — her mother's side. The lamp was unplugged, the doily beneath it yellowed with age. And resting there, untouched since her mother left, was the worn paperback her mom used to read every summer. The pages still held the shape of her hands. Still lying open to the same dog-eared chapter, the dried rose her father gave her on their last anniversary together laid across the pages.

Seren blinked, gaze narrowing. The dust here was different. Pressed into the surface — deliberate, undeniable — was a handprint. The fingers fanned slightly, the palm centered directly over the book. Not smudged. Not casual.

Placed.

Her throat tightened. Whoever had stood at the window hadn't just been looking out. They'd left a message.

Her hand hovered over the dusty imprint, not quite touching. The size of it… it could've been— No. That was ridiculous. But the scar on her jaw pulsed faintly, like it disagreed.

Dad.

It wasn't the first time she'd wondered. That maybe, somehow, he was still watching her. Not in the soft, comforting way people say when someone dies — but truly watching. A thread pulled tight across realms. A tether.

His death had never made sense. The car had gone up in flames just outside of town. No crash. No fuel leak. No clear ignition source. Just fire — sudden, consuming. Like something had claimed him. By the time emergency crews arrived, the heat was too intense to get close. They never recovered a body. Just ash. Melted metal. A ring her mother had given him on their anniversary, blackened and warped in the passenger seat. The ring was the only thing that came back. The fire kept the rest.

Declared dead. Assumed gone.

It was part of why she became a dispatcher. Because no one had answered her calls that night. Because her mother had screamed down the line to 911 while the fire devoured everything, and all Seren could do was listen. She was just a teenager, barefoot on the porch, listening to the panic and the static and the silence that followed. The silence had teeth. No answers. No time. No one could fix it.

She'd sworn never again. If someone called, she'd be the one to answer.

If there was a chance — even a flicker — to stop the worst moment of someone's life from sealing shut, she'd take it. And still, it hadn't brought him back.

Was this him? Showing her he was still watching over her? Still finding a way to reach through? Or was it something far more sinister? The voices from the chapel echoed back, fragments rising like embers in her chest. "Marked the girl." "He's coming." "Don't trust the fire." And then his voice. The only one that spoke her name. The one that cut through the static like a blade.

"Stop looking… and I'll find you when the time is right."

Seren swallowed, her fingers hovering over the book and the pressed stem of the rose. Her father's rose. Her mother's book. Her home. But the air felt thinner now. Charged. Like a space being held open around her — watched, measured. She pulled her hand back.

"Was it you?" she murmured. "Or the thing you're trying to save me from?"

Seren headed downstairs, her body dragging with every step. Already barefoot, she stripped out of her clothes and stepped into the bathroom. The shower blasted hot, the steam clinging to her skin as she leaned into the tile. She scrubbed until the scent of old wood and smoke faded from her hair, her skin, her memory. But the scar on her jaw still pulsed faintly, the memory still clung somewhere deeper.

She dried off just enough to crawl into bed, pulled on an oversized shirt, and collapsed into the mattress. Her muscles ached. Her brain throbbed. Sleep came fast and heavy.

Several hours later, the sharp buzz of her phone snapped through the room, pulling her from sleep. She groaned and reached blindly across the nightstand.

Caller – REDMILL DISPATCH

She stared at the name. It took longer than it should have for her to answer.

"Hey, Seren. Sorry to bother you—graveyard dispatcher's out. Family emergency. Any chance you can cover tonight?"

She blinked against the too-bright screen. Tonight. Shift. Work. It wasn't ghosts or cryptic warnings or chapel scars burned into dirt. It was the real world. Anchored. And right now, it sounded like a relief.

"Yeah," she rasped, rubbing her forehead. "I'll take it."

"Thanks, you're a lifesaver. See you at seven."

She hung up and exhaled slowly, staring at the ceiling. A shift would be good. Normal. Just her, a headset, and a list of names she didn't have to chase. She swung her legs out of bed and started getting dressed.

Seren padded into the kitchen, flipping on the light and swinging the fridge open to rummage for shift snacks. A half-empty condiment shelf, a single sad yogurt, and a forgotten lemon glared back at her. She checked the pantry next — stale crackers, a tin of soup she didn't remember buying, and tea. Lots of tea. Not exactly graveyard-shift fuel.

She sighed and leaned on the counter, rubbing her face. "Gas station it is."

Dispatch survival 101: caffeine, sugar, and enough snacks to survive a minor apocalypse.

She headed to the door and bent to pull on her boots, but paused. The soles were still caked with strange, ashy dirt from the chapel. Not regular earth — this stuff clung like memory, pale and dry, dusting her fingers when she tried to brush it off. Something that didn't belong in this world.

Grimacing, she stepped outside and turned on the hose. The water pressure was just enough to blast most of it off. The rest she scrubbed loose with a stiff brush kept by the porch. After a few minutes, the boots were clean enough, though some of the grit still lingered in the seams - like a memory.

"Whatever," she muttered. "Good enough."

She climbed into her car, letting the engine hum to life, and pulled out of the driveway as the sky began shifting toward twilight. The gas station was just off the main road, its flickering neon sign promising "HOT COFFEE" and "FRESH PIZZA" with equal dishonesty.

Inside, she moved like a woman on a mission — two sodas, a bottle of water, two energy drinks (because every dispatcher had at least three open drinks at their station at all times), a pack of gummy worms, a chocolate bar, spicy chips, and — in a weak gesture toward responsibility — a single-serve veggie tray and a pair of pepperoni sticks.

"Hey, Jason." She dropped everything on the counter, and the cashier barely blinked.

"Hey, Seren. Heading in for another night shift?" He started scanning her items and shoving them into a bag.

"Yeah. Figured I'd hit all the major food groups — sugar, caffeine, and regret."

Jason smirked. "And the veggie tray?"

"That's for show. Makes me feel like a functioning adult."

He held up the gummy worms before tossing them in the bag. "Nothing says 'functioning adult' like candy shaped like roadkill."

She laughed, handing over a crumpled twenty. "Don't judge me. You've never stared at a CAD screen for twelve hours while listening to a guy explain how his neighbor's music is a government mind-control plot."

Jason chuckled, sliding her change across the counter. "Nope. I just sell the fuel for your suffering."

"Then keep it coming. Thanks, Jason. See you next shift." She scooped the bag into her arms, gave him a quick wave, and pushed through the glass doors.

The night air met her with a chill, the plastic handles cutting into her fingers as she crossed the lot to her car.

Minutes later, she pulled into the secure lot at Redmill Dispatch. The familiar fencing and keypad entry felt like a different kind of ritual — one grounded in fluorescent lights and headset static. She parked, shut off the engine, and stared at the building for a moment before grabbing her haul and heading inside.

Seren slid into her usual dispatch station — second from the end, chair a little too squeaky, headset always tangled. She dropped her snacks beside the console, cracked open an energy drink, and began her login process. The system took a minute to boot, giving her just enough time to settle in and feel the weight of the long night ahead.

The dispatch logs from the past couple of days were unremarkable. A guy spun out of his mind on something, convinced people were hiding in his hedges and that drones were circling his house. A string of neighborhood disputes — barking dogs, overwatering grass, someone's kid allegedly touching someone else's mailbox. Several routine medical transports. The kind of mundane noise that usually dulled the edge of her curiosity.

Taped to the wall by her keyboard was a neon yellow sticky note. David's handwriting.

"No luck finding our alley victim at any local ERs. Another dead end. — D"

Seren stared at the note a beat longer than necessary. She'd tried not to think about the alley, the fire print, the voice. About how that victim might not have been alive at all. She leaned back in her chair and pulled out her phone to text Marisol, just as the screen blinked with an incoming call. Not a 911 — an admin line.

With a sigh, she clicked her headset on. "Redmill Police Department, how can I help you?"

The voice on the other end was tight and indignant. "Yes, I'd like to file a complaint. There are kids jumping off the boat launch into the river again. After dark! It's unsafe and disruptive."

Seren muted herself long enough to roll her eyes. Another Karen on the warpath to destroy summer joy. She nodded along, murmuring generic reassurances, and created a new call for service. Box checked. The complaint was logged.

She patched it through to the officers on duty, and could practically hear the collective eye-roll through the radio.

 "10-4. Uh, we'll... drive through the area," one of them replied, already halfway dismissive.

Seren pulled out her phone between calls and sent a quick text to Marisol.

Seren: "Picked up a shift tonight. If you're around later and wanna stop in, that'd be cool."

It didn't take long for a reply.

Marisol: "I'm on the rig tonight too. We'll see what after midnight looks like. Hopefully the town takes a nap for once."

Seren smirked. She doubted it, but the thought of catching up helped take the edge off the silence humming beneath her skin.

The hours passed slowly — almost mercifully dull. A call about a dog bite that had already been cleaned up before EMS got there. An elderly man who slipped in the bathroom, more embarrassed than hurt. Two different kids accidentally dialing 911 from their parents' phones, one of whom was very adamant that his dinosaur was having an emergency. She kept herself busy juggling calls, entering reports, cycling through her open drinks without noticing which one she was reaching for.

Then, just before midnight, the admin line lit up again. Blocked. No number. No name. Just Unknown Caller. Seren stared at the screen for a second longer than usual before answering.

"Redmill Police Department, how can I help you?"

There was a pause on the other end — then a breath. Ragged, wet, and far too close to the mic.

Then a voice. Male. Raspy. Like he smoked more than he breathed. Every word dragged across gravel.

 "I know who you are."

Seren's posture straightened. "This is the Redmill Police Department. Do you need assistance?"

"I know what you are."

That stopped her.

"…Sorry, what was that?"

"Your secret won't stay safe forever," the voice rasped. The words felt like a curse spoken through smoke. "He can't protect you always. And I will have the praise for bringing you before the Iron King."

Then—click.

The line went dead.

A sharp pulse bloomed beneath her scar, like a spark catching beneath her skin. Her head throbbed—deep and sudden, like a warning she couldn't quite hear.

No caller ID. No number in the call log. Just gone. Seren sat frozen, headset still clinging to one ear. Her scar burned. Not hot — but aware. The Iron King? The praise? And… what she was? Her stomach knotted.

This wasn't just a prank. This wasn't a kid or a drunk or some townie with a grudge. This was something else. And it knew.

Seren didn't even have time to process what had just happened — what he had just said — when her board lit up like a damn Christmas tree.

Line one. Line two. Line three. All screaming for attention. She yanked her headset back into place.

"911, what's the location of your emergency?"

A panicked voice exploded through the speaker. "There's been a crash—south of Redmill—cars everywhere—people screaming—"

"I have help on the way," Seren said quickly, already typing, already dropping tones on radio channels. "Stay safe and off the road."

She hit the hotkey to air on multiple channels, sending fire, medics, and the closest police units.

"Redmill units, priority traffic. Reported multi-car collision, multiple injuries, south of Redmill on Highway 16 near mile marker 42. All units en route."

Another call came through before she even finished the sentence.

"911, what's the location of your emergency?"

"There's been a huge crash, I—"

"Is this about the wreck south of Redmill?"

"Yes—"

"I have help on the way. Please stay clear and let emergency services work."

Click. Next call.

"911, is this about the crash south of Redmill?"

Another yes. Another thank you. Another line cleared. It was a delicate sort of triage. One dispatcher, one headset, and a whole town suddenly on fire. Seren's fingers flew across the keyboard, logging times, updating responders, rerouting units.

Her heart was still racing. Not from the crash. Not from the chaos. From him. From the voice that came before the noise. Before the blood and the panic. The words still echoed louder than the sirens.

He can't protect you always…

Seren swallowed hard and kept working. Because the Veil could wait. The living couldn't. That was tomorrow's nightmare. Tonight — she had people to save.

The calls slowed but didn't stop — they never did in moments like this.

Seren flagged the severity of the injuries, her fingers flying over the keys. Two priority-one patients, one of them reportedly unresponsive with head trauma. She didn't hesitate.

She called and launched the helicopter.

"Hi AirMed, this is Redmill Dispatch. We are requesting you go ahead and launch. We have two critical patients en route from just south of town, involved in a car crash. LZ will be prepped at Redmill General. Ground contact will be Redmill Fire."

Within seconds AirMed had an ETA of 15 minutes to the local hospital for patient transport to a larger facility. Somewhere they could receive the higher level of care they required.

Seren didn't breathe. Not really. She just kept moving. Then the voice she'd been waiting for cracked across the EMS channel.

"Dispatch, this is EMS 260. Patient two is a child — toddler age. No pulse, initiating CPR. En route to Redmill General now to rendezvous with AirMed."

It was Marisol. Her voice didn't tremble, but Seren could hear the tension behind every word. The pressure. The weight. Seren's chest tightened. She alerted the ER for a pediatric code. Confirmed they were ready to take over when EMS pulled up. She crossed every box before the second hand on her wall clock could complete a sweep.

Another responder came over the air.

"One DOA at the scene. Requesting coroner. Notify State. Looks like a drunk driver—another vehicle crossed the center line."

Of course it was. Seren's hands clenched for a second before she forced herself to type. She'd heard it before. Too many times. It was never the drunk who died. No, they were the ones who somehow walked away. Limped out of a tangle of glass and steel, breath reeking and eyes unfocused, while families bled out on the asphalt. The Fire always picked the wrong ones

She called the county coroner. Then State Police. All fatalities on state highways fell to them.

The board finally started to dim. The chaos thinned, the traffic detour was active, and the radios began to sink into something like silence.

It was almost 2 a.m. when Seren finally sat back in her chair. Her back ached. Her head throbbed. She glanced at the wall clock. Two hours ago, the world was normal. Now it was blood and sorrow for multiple families.

The door to dispatch squeaked open. Marisol walked in like she'd just won a championship — ponytail crooked, shoes streaked with dried mud, and cheeks flushed from a run of pure adrenaline.

Seren spun around in her chair as the door creaked open.

"Don't you say it."

Marisol froze mid-step. "Say what?"

Seren pointed a stern finger. "The Q word. I heard you winding up."

Marisol threw her hands up, grinning. "I wasn't gonna say it!"

"You were gonna think it," Seren muttered, spinning back to her screens. "Which is just as dangerous. Do you want another three-car pileup? A barn fire? A rogue llama on Main Street?"

Marisol snorted and dropped into the chair beside her. "Fine. You win. I'll do a blood sacrifice to the dispatch gods later."

"Good. Make it a sugar sacrifice. That vending machine's been hungry."

Marisol grinned wider. "Honestly? Worth it. By the time that kid got on the chopper, he was asking if Batman or Spider-Man would win in a fight. From full code to full-on superhero debate. I don't even care if I jinx something — I brought a kid back from the dead and solved a Marvel argument in one shift."

Seren stared at her, a wide grin spreading on her face as well.

"You're high on life right now."

"Damn right I am. I could bench press the ambulance."

"Please don't. That thing barely survives bumps as it is."

Marisol leaned back with a long breath, still buzzing. "Honestly, though... this is what it's about, right? CPR, meds, backboards, the works — and then watching him come back. It's rare. But when it happens?"

Seren gave a small smile. "It reminds us why we're still in this."

Marisol nodded, then squinted at her. "You okay?"

Seren hesitated. "Yeah. Just tired." The scar on her jaw pulsed faintly. Not pain. Just memory.

She wasn't lying. But she wasn't telling the whole truth, either. Marisol, thankfully, didn't push. She just offered a protein bar from her pocket like some kind of post-apocalyptic snack dealer.

"Here. For the dispatch gods. And you. In that order."

They both laughed, the tension loosening just enough to breathe again.

Marisol was too high on the night and her save to even ask about Seren's most recent ghost hunt. And Seren was thankful for that. She didn't want to lie to her — not more than she already had. Telling her the truth might drag her into something darker, something neither of them could control. And Seren would do anything to protect the people she loved.

So she kept her smile easy and her eyes forward, letting the night settle back into routine. The hum of radios. One officer calling in about a suspicious noise that turned out to be a deer sneezing. The kind of absurdity that usually calmed her. The shift ended much the way it had begun: petty calls, nothing exciting, nothing dangerous. On the surface, at least. But the surface was thinner now.

But beneath it all, Seren could feel the shift — in her bones, in the way the air moved through her lungs. Like the Veil had brushed her and left fingerprints. Something had changed. And no matter how settled things seemed now… It wouldn't stay that way for long.

She lingered a few extra minutes at her station after logging out, tapping her nails lightly against the edge of the desk. The man's voice still echoed in her head — rough, cracked, terrifying in its clarity. Like smoke dragged across stone. Just to be sure, she pulled up the system's call history and recording logs, scrolling through the timestamps from earlier in the night.

Nothing.

No record of a blocked call. No audio file. Nothing labeled, nothing missing — like it had never happened at all. Seren stared at the empty screen, a chill tracing down her spine. She hadn't imagined it. And yet… there was no proof. Just the scar on her jaw, and the heat that hadn't left. The words still burning behind her eyes.

"I know what you are."

Chapter Ten: Unbreakable Oaths and Obsession

Cairn

The rift split open with a sound like tearing silk and burning wood.

Cairn stepped through, shedding the last traces of the mortal realm like ash falling from his shoulders. Behind him, the doorway sealed in silence — no light, no trace, no scent. Only a faint scorch mark on the stone floor where he'd crossed.

The Pyric Realm greeted him in kind: heat pressed in from all sides, dense and dry, heavy with the scent of scorched minerals and something older. The corridor around him glowed with dull veins of molten rock, flickering with a constant undercurrent of firelight. Stone walls, black and glossy as cooled glass, stretched high into shadows.

He walked in silence, boots clicking against the obsidian tile. The noise was swallowed quickly, lost in the warm hum of the Keep. This part of the Realm had always been controlled — ordered. But even here, things had started to shift. He could feel it in the stone beneath his feet, in the flicker of flame that danced too erratically. The tension wasn't imagined.

The Veil between realms was weakening, and he hadn't been the only one to notice.

A formal summons from the King meant trouble. Cairn had been summoned before — to report, to correct, to destroy. But this was different. Not a mission. Not an execution. A council. Which meant others were involved. Which meant problems.

He passed under the high arches of the inner sanctum, where twisted stone gave way to carved bone and iron — old marks of power, etched and reinforced by heat and blood. Flames licked up from braziers along the walls, casting shadows that writhed like living things.

Cairn didn't slow his pace.

The voices ahead grew louder, fractured by echo and smoke. Figures were gathering — the Cinder Council, the ruling body of the Pyric Realm. The other Ashmarked, like Cairn, bound by oath and branded in flame to guard the Veil. Lesser rulers from the scattered provinces and burned-out towns. And citizens, wearied by unrest and whispering rebellion. All of them drawn by the same threat.

The breaches were getting worse.

Creatures were slipping through.

Not just ghosts and lesser spirits—but things that should have stayed buried in the deep. Things with old names and hunger. The Ashmarked were not only sworn to retrieve mortals who jeopardized the Veil. Their duty ran deeper. They were the wardens of the volcanic gates. The silent blades stationed at the edge of ruin.

They watched the scars in the Veil. They guarded the molten thresholds carved beneath the Keep. And they followed one law from the King without question:

Kill anything that tries to cross unbidden.

No trial. No warning.

Only the King's voice could authorize passage.

And if something managed to slip past? The Ashmarked were sent to drag it back—dead or damned.

Even with their increased patrols, their sleepless nights watching the Veil… things still got through. Creatures that should've stayed buried.. Just in the last week Cairn and the other Ashmarked had to drag back three of the slimy creatures.

The Hollowmire was the first.

Nothing but a whispering husk of grief and waterlogged bone, it dragged silence and rot behind it like a funeral Veil. It surfaced in Greystone

Hollow, a once-quiet settlement built along river marshes. Now the waters run black, the air too still. Entire families vanished in the night, their homes left undisturbed—as if they had simply evaporated, grief and all. The only thing left behind were puddles that never dried and mirrors that wept.

The Ashleech came next.

Ember-skinned and parasite-slick, it fed on madness and wore its victims like coats of memory—echoing their laughter, their voices, their screams. It emerged in Smelterdale, a mining town already fraying from the edge of despair. Within weeks, the population turned on itself. Neighbors saw monsters in their own reflections. Some disappeared into the mines. Others clawed out their eyes to unsee what followed them home. No one speaks above a whisper now—afraid it will borrow their voice next.

But the Haldreth… The Haldreth was different. It took all ten of the Ashmarked to bring it down.

A spined, serpentine titan forged from scorched glass and volcanic bone, it was the hardest to contain so far. Its mouth never opened, yet its voice slithered into dreams—whispering forgotten names until sleep cracked and bled. Beneath its translucent skin, trapped souls flickered like lightning bugs in amber.

It descended on Blackharrow, a city once known for its scholars and dream-diviners. Now its towers stand empty, windows smeared with blood from the inside. No one sleeps in Blackharrow. Not anymore. The ones who do never wake up right. They mutter nonsense in dead languages and weep molten tears.

Cairn had seen what was left in these monsters' wake. And what the mortal world was not ready to face.

And Seren Cross… might be the answer, either to their salvation, or their ruin. Cairn knew the King would not take the time to figure it out. If he found her, he would order all of them to eliminate her immediately.

He clenched his jaw, adjusting the collar of his shirt. The King would want answers. Explanations. Solutions. Cairn's involvement was not the brains behind the plans, but the execution.

Cairn stepped through the molten archway into the throne hall, the blast of heat brushing across his skin like a welcome. The doors sealed behind him with a hiss of steam.

The noise hit immediately. The chamber roared with overlapping voices — angry, desperate, fracturing into chaos. He didn't approach the dais. Instead, he slipped into a shadowed alcove near the obsidian pillars lining the walls, arms folding across his chest as he leaned back and listened.

The crowd surged with Pyric citizens and flamebound nobles, faces drawn with soot and fury. Their robes fluttered with heat-born wind, flickering like smoke.

"Just burn the Veil and be done with it!"
"Let the Hollowmire take the mortal cities — they deserve it!"
"Shut down all passage! Cut them off entirely!"

Someone hurled a chunk of cracked stone. It disintegrated before hitting the floor, caught midair by one of the silent enforcers flanking the dais.

And still, the King didn't speak.

Kaedros Veyne sat unmoved upon the Black Throne — a massive, jagged seat carved from Veilstone and laced with runes too ancient to name. His long robes pooled like shadowfire at his feet, crown burning with a cold white flame that didn't flicker. His face was unreadable. Immovable. Eyes like steel forged in prophecy.

To his left and right, the Cinder Council stood in absolute silence. Twelve in all — enforcers, emissaries, warbinders — each marked by flame in their own way.

But not one of them moved. Not one dared to speak.

They had never been chosen for their wisdom, only their loyalty. The Council had been crafted to feign balance, a gesture toward democracy meant to soothe the masses. A convenient illusion.

The Iron King made the decisions. The Council simply wore them like masks.

They were bodies to fill a chamber, names to sign decrees, and faces to hang when things went wrong. Easy to replace. Easier still to burn.

They would not step in unless the King gave command.

Cairn tilted his head slightly.

The arguments were nothing new. Just louder now. More frightened. The breaches in the Veil had grown — and worse, they were *unpredictable*. Monsters Cairn had helped lock away centuries ago were now slipping through cracks like rot through stone.

He exhaled slowly through his nose and waited.

The King would not wait forever.

And when Kaedros moved — when he *spoke* — the fire would return to silence.

Cairn leaned back against the wall, arms crossed, half-listening to the chaos in the throne room. He didn't need to see the King yet — not while the mob was still frothing at the mouth. Let them burn themselves out first.

"Well, look who decided to crawl out of the flames."

Cairn didn't have to turn to recognize the voice. "Rhyne."

Rhyne Tareth appeared at his shoulder, eyebrows raised, lips curled in a cocky grin. His coat was half-scorched and his left vambrace had a fresh dent — which only made him look more smug.

"Thought maybe one of your little pet nightmares finally dragged you under. You vanish for *days* and suddenly the whole realm's on fire."

"I was working."

"Mmmmh. In the mortal realm, I assume? Tracking breaches? Or brooding dramatically in some haunted church?"

Cairn shot him a look. "Not all of us drink our weight in ash-spiced whiskey and sleep until the Council starts yelling."

"Please. That was one time." Rhyne leaned beside him, crossing his arms. "So. What's the excuse this time? Let me guess — you lost a fight to a ghost. Or a mortal girl kicked your ass and stole your coat."

Cairn smirked, barely. "She'd have to be fast."

"Aha, so there is a she."

"I didn't say that."

"No, but your face did."

Cairn shook his head, glancing toward the dais. "Drop it."

"Fine, fine. Just don't expect me not to gloat if you go soft and start writing poems."

"You're the one who cried during a bard's performance last solstice."

"It was a good song!"

Cairn exhaled — something like a laugh, tight in his chest. Rhyne's presence always did that. Let the fire dim for a breath or two.

Rhyne bumped his shoulder lightly. "Seriously. You okay?"

Cairn's gaze returned to the throne.

"I will be," Cairn said.

"Alright. Just don't forget who's got your back when the flames rise."

"I never do."

Rhyne straightened, brushing dust from his coat. "Good. Now let's find out which part of this realm is going to try and kill us next."

The noise had reached a fever pitch — shouting, accusations, fear cloaked in fury. Cairn didn't flinch. He stayed leaned against the dark stone wall, arms folded, eyes sharp beneath his lashes. Beside him, Rhyne gave a low whistle and muttered, "Here it comes."

At the far end of the room, King Kaedros stood.

The molten lines of his veins pulsed brighter beneath his skin — not a metaphor, but raw truth. His blood was iron, liquefied and alight, branching in visible paths beneath his pale flesh like rivers of magma. His eyes, twin crucibles, scanned the crowd without a word.

Then he raised one hand.

The room didn't fall silent immediately — not until he made his move.

A hiss cut the air. Sharp. Elemental.

From his palm, molten iron sprayed upward in a perfect arc, glowing bright gold-red against the vaulted obsidian ceiling. The droplets hung in the air for one impossibly suspended second, then cooled mid-flight into solid spheres — no bigger than pebbles — and rained down like metallic hail.

The crowd fell silent.

None of the iron pellets hurt. They bounced harmlessly off shoulders and stone, tinkling against armor and tile. But the message was unmistakable.

Kaedros lowered his hand.

Smoke curled lazily from his knuckles, dissipating into the heat-thick air.

"That," Rhyne whispered "is what power looks like."

Cairn turned toward him, expression unreadable. Rhyne was staring at the king like he was the shiniest prize in a kingdom full of ash. It made Cairn's stomach churn.

"No," Cairn said coldly. "That's what fear dressed up as power looks like."

Rhyne's smile faltered, but only for a breath.

King Kaedros stepped down from his throne, each footfall echoing like a smith's hammer on steel. The Cinder Council remained where they were — silent, flanking either side of the dais like statues of fire and stone.

Cairn shifted slightly, watching the King with a flicker of unease. This was a performance, yes. But it was also a warning. Kaedros was done waiting for solutions. And Fire was always his first language.

Kaedros let the silence stretch, the last of the cooled iron pellets clinking to the stone. Then he turned slowly, his molten gaze sweeping the crowd like a branding iron.

"You come to me with your fear," he said, voice low but far-reaching. "You bring your panic, disguised as anger. You scream for blood, for war, for retreat. You forget who we are."

His footsteps echoed as he paced the edge of the dais, hands clasped behind his back — regal, slow, controlled. The King of Iron didn't shout. He didn't need to.

"We are the flame beneath the mountain. The fury in the forge. We are not creatures of fear—we are its architects. And we do not seal our doors and hope for peace."

A rumble passed through the chamber, deep and unnatural — the Keep itself responding to his words.

Kaedros paused at the center of the dais. His next words cut like molten glass.

"The Ashmarked Oath will be honored again."

The chamber inhaled as one.

Cairn's breath caught in his throat. For a moment, he wondered if he'd misheard. But no — Kaedros stood tall and unwavering, his hands outstretched as if pronouncing divine law.

"We will bind more to the flame," the King continued. "We will forge new hunters — sworn to the pyres, marked by fire and oath. They will go into the mortal realm and sever the threats before they fester. They will seek out the Veil-touched and cull them before they can weaken our borders. We will not wait for another breach."

Cairn's spine locked, the words ringing in his ears like a death knell.

More Ashmarked?

He'd sworn that oath centuries ago, and it had cost him everything. He wasn't Pyric-born anymore — not truly. Once the fire takes hold, you're carved out of your name and filled with something else. The Ashmarked were no longer counted among the Fae. They were flame-bound. Veil-forged. Living relics of a pact few dared to speak aloud.

The rite didn't just scar the body — it hollowed the soul. You bled out your past, your name, your gods. Most who entered the forge never rose from it. Those who did were remade into monsters with purpose — oaths stitched into their bones, Fire in place of blood.

He glanced sideways — just briefly — and caught the gaze of Tovrek, another Ashmarked who stood like a statue near the chamber's edge.

His silver tattoos pulsed faintly beneath his skin, barely visible under his armor.

Their eyes met, and in that single, silent moment, Cairn saw it:

Recognition.

Weariness.

Resentment.

Tovrek didn't nod. Didn't flinch. But the message was clear: Not again.

Cairn turned away, jaw clenched. The King could summon flames and declarations all he wanted — but the fire wasn't as loyal as he believed. Not anymore.

Most who attempted the oath would perish. Of those who survived, fewer would live to see another summer. Those who did weren't heroes.

They were weapons.

And now Kaedros wanted more.

It wasn't a title. It was a death sentence. It was sacred.

Sacrifice, not strategy.

Kaedros raised both hands now, iron threading between his fingers like silk.

"The weak will not weather what is coming. The Veil bleeds. And we must answer with fire. We do not run. We burn a path forward."

The crowd stayed silent. Stunned. Awed. Or simply afraid.

Cairn's jaw clenched. His tattoos burned faintly beneath his skin — not from anger, but warning.

Because if the King was reviving the rite… Then what in the hell was coming?

The crowd followed the King in near silence — thousands pouring from the chamber into the carved obsidian corridor that led to the Heart of the Veil.

Even in the Pyric Realm, few had stood this close to it.

The deeper they descended, the heavier the air became — not with heat, but pressure. The weight of history. Of sacrifice.

A figure fell into step beside him.

Tovrek.

Ashmarked. Ancient. And still breathing.

"It's real then," Tovrek said quietly, his eyes fixed ahead. "He's calling for a forging."

Cairn gave a small nod. "It's more than that. He's building an army."

"Of what?" Tovrek asked. "Desperate souls? Ghosts in mortal skin?"

He scoffed. "Most of the volunteers won't survive the rite. The ones who do won't remember who they are. They won't know what the oath is really meant to be. They will confuse sacrifice for our realm and Veil as loyalty to its current monarchy."

They walked in silence for a few beats. Molten lines along the corridor walls flickered, casting distorted reflections across their faces — half light, half scar.

"You regret it?" Tovrek asked suddenly.

Cairn didn't answer at first.

"I regret surviving," he said finally. "But I don't regret what I became. Not until now."

Tovrek's jaw tightened.

"The others are watching you. Waiting to see if you make a move."

"Let them."

"No," Tovrek said. "I mean it. They remember who led us through the last breach. Who bled at the gate. They remember that it wasn't Kaedros standing on the pyre."

Cairn's gaze darkened.

"That was a long time ago."

"Not long enough," Tovrek murmured.

Another Ashmarked joined them — Veyra, her voice flat and dry as ash.

"You think he'll stop at mortals?"

Cairn glanced at her.

"No."

They walked on in silence as the corridor opened wide — into a vast, volcanic hollow. The Heart of the Realm loomed ahead, pulsing like a buried star.

The air trembled.

Kaedros stood waiting, flames curling around his shoulders like a crown.

And the forge called.

The cavern yawned wide and open to the sky, the air thick with ash and ancient heat. In its center, a lake of molten stone boiled — not quite lava, not quite flame. This was older. Woven from sacrifice, from offerings made in blood and vow since the first breach between worlds.

Ritual platforms ringed the pit in layered circles, like the petals of a dying flower. At the far edge stood a raised dais carved from cooled magma, its edges etched with the bones of failed oath-bearers. The King ascended it without hesitation. The Cinder Council took their places in the shadowed box seats just above, expressionless.

Cairn stepped up behind the gathered masses, lingering at the outer edge of the platform where shadows ran deeper. The other Ashmarked had already spaced themselves throughout the crowd — not out of camaraderie, but caution.

It was instinct, old and drilled deep. Never cluster. Never stand too close.

Ashmarked did not gather. They circled. They watched.

Weapons don't huddle. They wait.

Each one stood apart like a sentinel, flames etched into their skin pulsing faintly in rhythm with the forge buried below. Living reminders of the Realm's power—and what it cost to wield it.

Cairn folded his arms, the fire-threaded tattoos on his forearms glowing dim beneath his sleeves.

He didn't need to see their faces to know:

They were all thinking the same thing. Why now? And what poor soul was about to burn?

Kaedros raised one hand — and the molten core below hissed in response, tendrils of flame rising like breath from a sleeping god.

"You come here for protection," the King said, voice booming. "But the Veil thins because mortals tamper with it. Because something tears at the seams. We cannot wait for salvation. We must become it."

He paused.

"I ask now for volunteers. To step forward. To burn."

Gasps rippled through the crowd. Then — movement. One Pyric-born stepped forward. A young male. He was skinnier than someone his height should be. His clothes were ripped, his hands dirty. Someone from the outskirts, where food and water were in short supply. This might be his only chance to escape generations of poverty.

Cairn's jaw tensed.

What is this tactic, Kaedros? Hope? Fear? Are you thinning the numbers of potential rebels under the guise of sacrifice? Or trying to forge a wall of flesh and fire between us and whatever's coming?

He watched as the King extended a hand toward the first volunteer — not in kindness, but judgment.

"You will take the Ashmarked Oath in full," Kaedros thundered, his voice rising over the fire-wind, absolute. "There is no returning. No mercy. No name. Your soul will belong to the Pyric Realm and the Veil until the final flame."

The molten pit below responded with a violent hiss, the glow intensifying as if the Veil itself stirred — not the King, but something older. Hungrier.

The crowd shifted uneasily.

But then — movement.

A young woman stepped forward, shoulders squared though her hands shook. She was about the same age and in the same poor condition. She joined the young man in front of the King. They clasped hands as they approached the edge of the platform, fingers entwined like a vow of their own.

Cairn's chest tightened.

Fools. Brave, stupid, desperate fools.

The guards met them in silence and stripped them of anything nonessential — weapons, jewelry, identity. Their names would not be spoken again. The crowd hushed as the two stepped into the firelit ring, guided by attendants draped in blackened robes.

They were made to kneel at opposite ends of the glowing sigil surrounding the pit's mouth — one to the east, one to the west. The heat from the molten heart bathed their skin, already blistering before the rite began.

The blade was pulled from the flames.

Still glowing, still dripping molten filth, it was carried reverently to the first — the young man. He didn't flinch as it was pressed to his chest.

He screamed as it sank in.

The sigil flared beneath him, lines of fire racing toward the center — but not enough. His body seized, arching in agony, eyes rolled skyward. And then the mark slipped — too shallow, or too slow. His scream died before the fire claimed him fully. His body collapsed forward into the pit, dissolving like wax in flame.

The crowd gasped.

The girl screamed his name — the last time it would ever be spoken — and lunged toward him, toward the flames.

Too late.

The blade turned on her.

She didn't cry out. She only stared at the place where he had vanished. But the fire did not care for silence. It swallowed her just the same, the markings carved into her skin hissing and sputtering like a failed invocation. Her body twisted, burned, and then crumbled.

Two pillars of smoke rose. No souls lingered.

Just more ash.

Cairn didn't move.

This was what it meant — what it *cost*.

And Kaedros watched without flinching.

Another voice called out for the next volunteer.

The ritual would continue.

A hush clung to the stone like smoke after the lovers' bodies crumbled. The molten pit licked at their ashes, pulling them inward, leaving nothing behind but scorched regret.

No cheers. No cries of honor.

Only the heat.

Then — a single voice.

"I will go."

From the left side of the platform, a young figure stepped forward. Not childlike, but untested. Probably no more than twenty by mortal count. Tall. Slender. Eyes like storm glass. He wore no insignia, no House mark — just plain dark robes and a steady defiance in his stride.

Cairn's eyes narrowed.

Bold. Or stupid. But maybe…something else.

Kaedros didn't flinch. "Name."

"Does it matter?" the figure asked.

A few gasps from the crowd. The King smiled.

"No," he said coldly. "Not for long."

The figure disrobed without ceremony, baring his chest to the rising heat. The branding blade was pulled from the coals — a slab of volcanic steel inscribed with the ancient sigils of binding.

The crowd leaned forward. The silence thickened.

The blade met skin.

The scream that followed was not one of agony alone — it was transformation. A sound that split the chamber down the middle and cracked something invisible in the air.

He dropped to his knees. Shaking. Steam pouring off his skin.

But he lived.

A low, crackling energy rose from the pit, curling around his body. The carved glyphs flared — not orange like Cairn's, but green-gold, edged in black.

The boy rose slowly. When he lifted his head, his irises flickered — not with flame, but with shadow-laced emerald light.

Cairn felt it, even from a distance. Their presence was pulling something toward them — like gravity. A warping of will.

He turned toward the crowd, and a Pyric-born man in the front row gasped and fell to his knees — not in reverence, but confusion. He clutched at his chest like something inside him had shifted without warning.

The newly made Ashmarked tilted their head. "I think I just made him forget his name," he said softly, voice still rough from the scream.

Murmurs swelled. Cairn's jaw tensed.

Not like him, then. Not a forger of wraiths. But something far more…manipulative.

A gift of disorientation. Memory displacement. Control of identity itself.

Kaedros's eyes gleamed.

"One survives," he said to the crowd, raising his hand. "The Ashmarked are rising again."

The pit hissed. The realm shifted. And Cairn, still watching from the shadows, felt unease claw its way beneath his tattoos.

By the time the last scream faded into smoke and silence, Cairn had counted them all.

One hundred and fifty had stepped forward.

Five had survived.

The odds were worse than usual. Or better, depending on what you considered mercy.

Of the new survivors, only one showed true potential — the memory-bender with eyes like fractured emeralds. The others… their flames were dim. Fragile. Powers meek and half-formed. One could manipulate light like thread, another had some control over pain — but they weren't strong enough to shape the battlefield. Not yet. Maybe not ever.

Cairn had seen it before. The way weak fire turned inward. How the vow, once taken, didn't simply mark you — it devoured you.

They had six months. At most. Before the power either consumed them or the Veil reclaimed their ashes.

The emerald-eyed one, though… he might make it. If he learned fast. If he understood that being Ashmarked wasn't about fire or fear — it was about obedience. About belonging to something greater. The Veil wasn't a tool. It was a god. A grave. A truth. And it did not suffer from arrogance.

There were now fifteen Ashmarked in existence.

Ten who had survived the rite centuries ago — zealots, legends, living weapons. And now five freshly born.

The scales were tipped again. But Cairn couldn't tell if they were tipping toward salvation — or war.

He crossed his arms and watched the molten pit churn beneath the platform.

The flames had been fed. But the Veil still bled.

And Seren Cross… she was still out there.

Cairn stepped through the Veil just outside the edge of the Iron Keep, where the stone roads unraveled into the older parts of the Pyric realm. The air here burned lower, steadier. No chaos. No firestorms. Just heat that pulsed like the heartbeat of something ancient and watching.

His home waited at the edge of a quiet village — one of the few places he allowed himself solitude. A narrow townhouse, black stone and sharp lines. Functional. Stark. Unmistakably his.

Inside, everything was shades of slate and ash — granite counters, char-blackened wood, curtains thick enough to block out even the molten glow of the realm's sky. His bed, nestled against a wall of onyx tile, was draped in silk sheets the color of smoke.

Two bedrooms. One untouched. The other kept cold and immaculate. He didn't need much. Didn't allow himself to want much.

But tonight, he needed the water.

He stripped off his char-streaked clothing and stepped into the rainfall shower, letting the molten-filtered water cascade over his skin. His tattoos steamed faintly beneath it, the fire beneath his ribs still agitated from the ritual, from the oath-song echoing in his bones.

Eventually, when the water cooled and his thoughts didn't, he dried off and slid into the sheets. The silk clung to his too-hot skin, but it grounded him. Reminded him he was still here. Still flesh. Still something like a man.

Sleep came reluctantly.

And with it — her.

Seren.

In the dream, she stood at the edge of a scorched field. Blue eyes bright and unblinking, fixed on him like she could see him this time — not just his echo, not the shadow he wore when crossing her realm. Her breath curled in the air. Her lips parted, like she was about to say his name.

His real name.

Then her eyes changed.

Not blue. Green.

Emerald.

The Ashmarked from the ritual stepped into view behind her, one hand glowing with that fractured light — the other pressed to Seren's temple.

She didn't scream. She didn't move.

Her memories were peeling away like ash in the wind.

Cairn surged forward in the dream, the fire inside him erupting, uncontrolled. He screamed her name — or maybe his own — and the entire realm cracked apart around them, flames devouring sky.

He woke mid-scream.

Bolting upright in his bed, the sheets twisted around his legs, soaked in sweat. His chest heaved. Hands trembling.

It had only been a dream.

But the heat still lingered behind his eyes — and the echo of her voice still scraped across his bones.

His breath came hard, uneven, dragging fire with it.

He pressed a hand to his chest, grounding himself in the heat of his own skin, in the now. But the dream clung to him — not like fog, but like smoke. Dense. Smothering.

Was it only a dream?

Or had the Veil shown him something else? A warning. A glimpse of what waited if he failed to act — or worse, waited too long.

The Pyric Realm had no mercy for prophecy. It never whispered its intentions, only seared them into your sleep until you woke tasting ash.

And still… her voice lingered.

He exhaled sharply and dragged a hand through his hair.

He'd seen mortals come and go. Burned, twisted, shattered by the pull of the realms.

But Seren Cross wasn't like them.

And if this was more than a dream… she wouldn't survive it alone.

He had to see her.

And more importantly — he had to keep her from the green-eyed one.

It was a risk. A betrayal of the order he'd sworn to uphold. But if what he saw was more than just a dream… then the only way to save her was to try and tell her the truth.

Even if it burned everything else to the ground.

He slid out of bed, the silk falling away like shadows from stone. The heat still pulsed under his skin, restless, ready.

He would find her.

And this time, he wouldn't stay in the dark.

He moved through the house like a storm regaining shape — slow at first, then inevitable.

From the wardrobe carved into the stone wall, he pulled on the clothes that made him feel most like himself. No cloaks. No ceremonial armor. Just what he wore when he needed to move, fight, or disappear.

Black leather fighting pants, worn and flexible, molded to his frame. A long-sleeved button-down shirt — dark charcoal, the top few buttons left undone, collar loose at his throat. Over it, a fitted leather vest, reinforced subtly at the ribs and shoulders. Not armor, exactly. Just enough to turn a blade. Just enough to remind anyone who looked too long that he wasn't prey.

He rolled his sleeves once at the forearm and reached for the ring that marked his rank among the Ashmarked, slipping it onto his right hand.

The air in the room seemed to thicken, the heat rising with his purpose.

Cairn stepped into the center of the room, the tattoos along his arms already pulsing with slow, molten heat.

He extended one hand — palm open, fingers steady — and traced a shape into the air. A sigil, jagged and ancient, carved from memory and blood-oath. The temperature dropped for a single heartbeat.

Then the seam tore open.

It wasn't a door so much as a wound — lightless, vertical, and humming with restrained violence. The edges bled heat, like steel cracked open to reveal the sun inside.

Without hesitation, Cairn stepped through.

The world on the other side met him with a quiet so thick it felt like fog.

He stood beneath the dark canopy of a mortal night, just beyond the tree line behind Seren's house. Her bedroom window flickered dimly above, untouched but impossibly close.

Cairn didn't move. Not yet.

He watched.

The scent of the mortal realm clung to his lungs — earth and concrete, the distant hum of electric lines. But above all, he focused on her. On the house. On the way her window pulsed gently with the breath of someone alive inside.

He had to do this delicately.

She wasn't ready for his full presence. Not here. Not like this.

He drew a breath and let the fire sink deeper into his bones. His skin dimmed. The weight of his form unraveled like mist curling from a flame. In seconds, only a shadow remained — long and shifting, cast in no light, made of no color.

Moving silent as smoke, he approached the side of the house. He could hear Seren in the kitchen, listening to loud music and somehow burning a pot of instant noodles.

The equipment she kept in the storage cabinet — padlocked but easily undone — held her Estes gear. He opened it carefully, fingers brushing the blindfold, the headphones, the battered spirit box she never replaced. He tucked them together into a neat bundle and set them in the middle of the bed.

Then, he reached into his vest and pulled a folded scrap of parchment — blackened on the edges, marked in his own hand.

He placed it atop the gear.

The note was short. Just five words, scrawled in Pyric ink that shimmered faintly in the dark:

It's time. We need to talk.

And just like that, he vanished again — into shadow, into stillness — leaving only silence behind.

He watched from the shadowed corner of the room, unseen and unmoving, as Seren stepped through the doorway balancing a bowl of instant noodles and humming off-key to whatever music still played in the kitchen.

She crossed to her bed, ready to clamber in with her laptop tucked under one arm—until her gaze landed on the gear laid out atop the blankets. The blindfold. The headphones. The spirit box. And the note.

She froze.

The bowl slipped from her hands and shattered on the floor, noodles and broth splashing across the hardwood in a steamy mess of surprise and disbelief.

Her eyes snapped to the parchment.

"Oh? Right now? Okay," she said aloud, voice breathless with nerves or something more.

She sat on the edge of the mattress, then leaned back, spine pressed to the wall, knees drawn up for balance. Her fingers worked quickly and without hesitation—like her body remembered even if her mind reeled.

She pulled the blindfold over her eyes.

Slipped the headphones on.

Flicked on the spirit box.

And waited.

He gave her a moment to fall into the static—just enough time to soften, to become receptive.

Then, voice smooth and low, curling like smoke through the current, he spoke her name.

"Seren."

A smile crept across her lips—slow, involuntary, unguarded.Then her lips parted.

"You found me."

There was a pause. Heavy, electric.

"Tonight," he said, "is going to be a night for honesty. For information."

His voice wrapped around her like heat curling beneath the skin. Each word deliberate, reverent.

"To start it off... you should know. I found you a long time ago."

"And I haven't been able to leave you since."

Her breath hitched, caught somewhere in her throat. He heard it.

"As many times as I've tried," he went on, voice dropping lower, darker, "I keep coming back."

"Like a drug. Addictive."

Another pause — like he wasn't sure if the next word should be said, and said it anyway.

"I'm afraid I'm obsessed."

The static hissed, but Seren didn't hear it. Only him. Her fingers twitched in her lap. Her breathing uneven now.

He smiled, though she couldn't see it.

She was listening. And she believed him.

"There's more than one world, Seren."

His voice changed — not softer, but weightier. Like speaking the words out loud carried consequence.

"The other realm — mine — it lies behind a Veil. One made of fire, stitched from the bones of old gods and older laws."

He paused, letting her breathe it in. Letting her feel the truth.

"That Veil is weakening."

"Tearing."

"Monsters have already slipped through. Things you wouldn't believe — that you wouldn't survive."

She didn't interrupt. Her hands gripped the blanket tighter over her legs.

"If it rips open completely," he said, "the human Realm will drown in it. Burn. Gone in an instant. Nothing left but cinder and ash."

The words weren't a threat — they were a certainty. And behind them… regret.

"I'm part of a sacred order. We were created — forged — to guard that boundary. To stop anything from breaching it."

"That's always meant hunting the mortals who could sense the Realm."

A beat passed.

"And destroying them."

Silence.

Seren didn't move. But something inside her shifted. Her breath shallowed. Her mouth opened.

"The man in the alley…"

He didn't answer at first.

The static seemed to deepen, heavy as the air before a storm.

Then:

"Yes. That was me."

It was said without apology. Without pride.

A truth, simple and terrible.

And he waited to see if she'd run. Even now.

"And me?" she asked, her voice barely a whisper.

Cairn's eyes darkened, the fire beneath his skin flickering with something older than regret.

"I was already centuries into the flame by then," he said softly. "Ashmarked. Bound. A weapon honed long before your world even existed."

He stepped toward her, his voice low, reverent.

"But even weapons remember where they were forged."
"I was sent to retrieve a boy. Pyric-born like me, smuggled across the Veil by rebels hoping to keep him hidden from the King's justice. The child was marked for return. That was all. Nothing more."

He paused, and when he spoke again, there was a reverence in it that hadn't been there before.

"But then I found you."

"You weren't hiding. You were protecting him. Holding him in your Realm, trying to save him. Despite the danger, and how scared I knew you were. Not only a stranger, but someone from a whole other realm. You didn't even hesitate to help"

"And something—something in you stopped me."
"The Veil recognized you. Bent toward you."

"I'd slaughtered hundreds of Veil-touched mortals by then. I'd never hesitated. Never questioned."

"But I didn't take you. I left you in the human realm."

"And I marked you."

He exhaled, the heat in the room subtly rising with the memory.

"Not as prey. Not even fully knowing why. Just enough to bind a thread — so no other flame would claim you. I didn't realize the Veil would remember your name."

A flicker of something vulnerable passed behind his eyes.

"And I've been bound to you ever since."

He watched her, the silence thick between them, his lilac eyes searching her for any sign of fear. All he saw was anticipation, thirst.

"I don't understand what you are," he admitted, voice low. "Not fully."

"The Veil doesn't bend for mortals. It doesn't recognize them. It devours them. But you..."

His jaw tightened.

"You unmade something in me."

He took a small step closer, the heat in the room rising in sync with his heartbeat.

"I was forged to destroy threats like you. Veil-touched. Unstable. Dangerous. And yet—every time I get near you, all I can think is that I need to keep you alive."

His breath caught, his voice dipping into something rawer, more exposed.

"I want to touch you."

His fingers flexed at his side, knuckles white with restraint.

"Not to claim. Not to burn. Just to feel that you're real."

He closed his eyes for a beat, like he was holding himself back with the last thread of control.

"I have to protect you. Even if it ruins me."

Seren's voice was barely a whisper, her breath catching against the weight of the moment.

"Can I know your name?" He stilled.

Of all the things she could've asked—after all the truths, all the confessions—that one undid him.

His jaw clenched, lilac eyes flickering like a dying flame.

"No mortal has ever known my name," he said slowly. "Much less spoken it."

The silence between them pulsed.

Then he stepped even closer, the heat between their bodies shimmering with something almost sacred.

"My name is Cairn Evergrave."

He watched her as he said it, the syllables like ash and iron on his tongue.

A secret forged in fire, now given freely.

Not as a weapon.

As a tether.

Cairn's gaze lingered on her face — the curve of her cheek, the rise and fall of her breath, the way she waited for him like he was something more than fire and ruin.

Even though she had no reason to... he had to ask.

"Do you trust me?" he said softly, voice dipped in smoke and something more vulnerable.

She hesitated — not from fear, but from the weight of what she was about to give.

"Yes," she breathed.

His breath left him in a slow exhale. "Then promise me something."

She nodded.

"Don't move. Don't open your eyes until I say."

"I promise."

He leaned forward, bracing one hand against the mattress beside her hip. The bed dipped under his weight. She instinctively shifted, hands outstretched to catch herself like the world had tilted — like she was falling through a black hole.

"I won't let anything happen to you," he whispered. "Trust me."

She stilled, breath shallow.

"Turn to your right."

She moved slowly, shuffling around on the bed as instructed until he said, "Stop."

She froze, unaware how close they now were — barely a hand's breadth between them, the heat of his body tangible, undeniable.

"Don't move," he said again, lower this time. "Not until I say."

She didn't speak. Didn't breathe.

His free hand rose, fingers brushing the curve of her headphones.

The contact made her flinch, but she didn't pull away.

He slid them off gently and set them aside, then turned off the spirit box. The silence that followed was heavy — not empty, but expectant.

He reached up again, slower now, fingertips grazing the edge of her blindfold.

She squeezed her eyes shut even tighter.

He pulled the fabric free.

She sat perfectly still, lips parted, breath trembling.

Her eyes were still closed.

Cairn hovered there for a moment, drinking her in.

Then, voice dark and low and edged with heat, he said—

"Open your eyes."

It's time.
We need
to talk.

Chapter Eleven: Promises and Favors

Seren

She could hear her pulse pounding in her ears.

Every beat was deafening — not because the room was loud, but because she was terrified. Not the kind of fear that made you scream and run. This was the kind that anchored you in place. The kind that came with knowing something life-altering was waiting on the other side of a single choice.

Her eyelids fluttered, still clenched tight.

He'd told her to open them.

She wasn't sure she could.

Her hands were pressed into the bed, steadying herself against the weight of his nearness. The air was thick with heat — not stifling, but intimate. She could feel him there. So close. Close enough to touch. Close enough to kiss.

Close enough to destroy her.

She took a breath. Then another.

Five.

She counted silently.

Four.

Every muscle in her body tightened.

Three.

She could still feel the ghost of his voice against her lips.

Two.

Her fingers curled against the sheets.

One.

She opened her eyes.

And the world changed.

The first thing she saw was him.

He was tall — towering, even — a broad silhouette of power and stillness crouched beside her bed. Everything about him was dark. His clothes were all deep black and storm-grey, worn leather and heavy fabric that looked both ancient and battle-worn. His skin, too, was dusky, kissed by flame but untouched by time, a canvas for inked lines that glowed faintly beneath the surface like molten veins waiting to flare.

But none of that was what stopped her breath.

It was his eyes.

Lilac. Pale and luminous. Otherworldly.

She'd seen them before — not in full light, not like this — but she knew them.

She'd seen them in the dark. In her dreams. In the firelight behind her closed eyelids. In the places between sleep and waking where she always felt watched.

"You," she breathed, not fully trusting her voice.

He didn't move, didn't speak right away. His gaze traced hers, drinking her in like she was something fragile and forbidden — something he'd waited a very long time to see.

Shock flickered through his expression. Just for a second.

As if he hadn't truly believed she would look.

The air shifted.

She didn't know how to explain it — didn't need to — but something in her bones recognized him before her mind ever could. Her breath caught. Her fingertips tingled. Her heart was still racing, but now it was for an entirely different reason.

Like something ancient had clicked into place.

Like some part of her had been waiting for him.

"What are you?" she whispered.

Before he could answer, the temperature dropped — just enough to raise goosebumps on her skin.

Then the room ignited.

Not in fire. In shadow.

Smoke burst from his back in twin torrents — billowing out like wings made of ash and ember, unfolding violently into the space around him. They didn't touch the walls, didn't scorch the bed, but they filled the room — vast, weightless, and alive. They rippled like smoke caught in wind, curling with an unnatural grace, tipped in faint flickers of red-gold light.

Seren gasped, scrambling backward into the wall. Cairn didn't move.

Couldn't.

He was staring past her, jaw slack, eyes wide — not in pride or power, but pure shock.

"What the hell—" she started.

"No," Cairn said under his breath, louder now. "No, that's not—this isn't—"

He turned slightly, enough to see the flick of those wings stretch and shimmer at the edge of his vision.

"This isn't possible," he said, more to himself than her. "Wings haven't manifested in centuries. Not since the Old Flame."

"You didn't know that would happen?"

He looked at her then — His mask of certainty cracked, and something fragile flickered underneath.

"No," he said. "Gods, no."

The wings pulsed once more, then slowly began to disappear — dissolving back into smoke, as if they'd never been there. But the room still felt different. Like something sacred had been torn open.

Seren's voice was small now, but clear.

"So what does it mean?"

Cairn didn't answer right away. His lilac eyes locked on hers.

"I don't know," he admitted. "But whatever it is… the Veil just changed the rules."

Cairn stepped back from the bed, breath shallow, eyes locked on the lingering smoke that was his wings. He closed his eyes and focused. His wings began to change, fully stretched behind him and longer vapor and ember, but real. Tangible. The sharp suggestion of structure beneath them — skeletal, sinewed, edged in something that looked halfway between char and polished obsidian. Smoke still curled from the edges, reluctant to let go.

He flexed his shoulders.

The wings responded — slow, unsure — folding in toward his spine. With another thought, they vanished entirely, absorbed back into the space between realms and flesh. Gone, like they had never been.

He paused.

Then, with a sharp breath and twitch of his jaw, he let them burst forth again. They surged outward with force this time — not smoke but substance. Real. Massive. A ripple of air shifted through the room, rustling papers and making Seren flinch.

Again, he drew them in. Silence.

Then released — and again, the wings spread, smoke and shadow giving way to shimmering, obsidian edges that caught what little light there was and made it burn.

He exhaled through his nose. "I can control them."

His voice was low, reverent, but tinged with unease.

"This… shouldn't be possible."

He looked at Seren now, as if trying to tether himself. "Wings haven't been seen in the Pyric Realm for centuries. They vanished from our bloodlines — no explanation, no warning. Some say it was a punishment. Others think evolution stripped them from us when we no longer deserved them."

A pause. He inhaled like the room had gotten smaller. "I'll have to hide them when I return. At least until I understand what this means. If the Cinder Council sees… if the King sees—"

He didn't finish. Just let the wings vanish again, folding into nothing.

"They'll think it's a sign."

Another beat.

"Maybe it is."

Seren just stared at him.

Wide-eyed. Unblinking. Still half-frozen on her bed like her brain hadn't caught up with her body yet.

Finally, she blinked once. Twice.

"I have no idea what you're talking about," she said, voice flat with disbelief.

"The King. The Veil. Whatever the hell a Cinder Council is."

She waved vaguely at the space where his wings had just been, eyes still tracking the air like they might reappear.

"But that…?"

She pointed directly at him, mouth falling open in genuine awe.

"That was probably the coolest shit I've ever seen."

Cairn let out a low chuckle, the sound rough but warm. One corner of his mouth lifted into the faintest smile — a rare, unguarded thing.

"You are something else," he said, shaking his head just a little, lilac eyes gleaming. "I've just dumped a realm's worth of madness on you, grew wings out of nowhere like a cursed fable... and you're not running. You're curious."

Seren gave a half-shrug, still watching the spot where those wings had vanished. "Yeah, well... terror and intrigue have always been a package deal with me."

She hesitated, biting her bottom lip, then looked up at him — a little sheepish, a little bold.

"This might sound super crazy. Since, you know, we just met and all..." Her voice dipped into something softer, more unsure.

"But... can I touch them?"

Cairn arched a brow, amused. "You want to touch them?" he repeated, his voice dipping into something low and teasing. "Seren Cross, we barely know each other."

He took a slow step closer, his eyes dragging over her face like he was memorizing it. "Most mortals ask about the fire first. Or the killing. Or the 'please don't drag my soul into hell' part."

He leaned in slightly, just enough for her to feel the heat radiating off him — not threatening, just... undeniable.

"But you want to touch the wings."

Seren's breath hitched, her cheeks flushing despite herself. "You did spontaneously sprout obsidian smoke wings in my bedroom," she said, chin tilting up in mock defiance. "Kind of hard to top that."

Cairn's smile deepened, slow and deliberate. "If I let you," he murmured, "you'll owe me a favor."

Her eyes narrowed. "What kind of favor?"

He didn't answer — not directly. Just reached behind him, and with a flick of his shoulders, the wings flared out once more. Real this time. Dark and elegant and massive, catching the light like shards of onyx dragged from a forge.

He held her gaze. "Still want to?"

Seren's eyes stayed fixed on the wings, awe written plain across her face — but she didn't move. Not yet.

"That depends," she said slowly, voice tinged with mischief and wariness. "What kind of favor are we talking about here? Because I've seen enough fae stories to know those promises tend to go sideways."

Cairn let out a low laugh, the sound warm and edged in smoke. "Smart girl."

He took a step closer, wings pulling in slightly, their edges softening back into smoke where the light thinned.

"I won't ask for your soul," he said, playful but not entirely joking. "Not unless you really insist."

She gave him a look, skeptical and amused.

"No bargains. No tricks. Just… a promise. One day, when I need something, and I ask—if it's within your power to give it, you'll try."

Seren tilted her head, considering. "That's either romantic or terrifying."

Cairn's smile turned crooked. "Welcome to the Pyric Realm."

Her fingers flexed at her sides, still itching to reach for him. The wings shimmered again — solid and tangible this time, edged in heat and mystery.

"Alright," she said, stepping forward, voice softening. "Favor owed. But I get to pick where I touch."

His grin widened. "Of course. I wouldn't dare get in your way."

Cairn gave her a look — amused, knowing — and then moved to sit at the edge of the bed, the mattress dipping beneath his weight. He leaned forward, elbows on his knees, wings arched slightly behind him like coiled shadows given form.

"Better?" he asked, voice low.

Seren swallowed. "Yeah. Thanks."

She stepped closer, reaching out like she might spook him. But he didn't move — only tilted his head slightly, giving her space.

Her fingertips brushed the top curve of one wing. It was warmer than she expected, like sun-warmed stone. Real, impossibly real — sinew and sleek edges, soft ridges beneath her hand where smoke met structure. She traced the edge slowly, letting her fingers follow the line to the first sharpened tip.

Cairn inhaled sharply. Then—

"Holy fuck," he groaned, voice ragged, guttural.

The sound rolled over her like a wave — low and desperate and entirely unguarded. It did something to her. Her breath hitched. Heat pooled low in her belly. She wasn't sure if she wanted to touch him again or climb into his lap.

He stilled, too. Like maybe he hadn't expected that either.

But before she could say anything, a bolt of icy fire shot up her arm.

Seren yelped and stumbled back, clutching her hand. "What the fuck is happening?"

Silver light danced across her skin — blooming from her fingertips, racing up her left arm in curling, floral swirls that shimmered like mercury. The markings wound around her forearm, her bicep, up to the curve of her shoulder like living vines.

She looked up — and froze.

Matching markings had ignited across Cairn's wings. The exact same pattern, mirrored in silver fire along the dark structure. He turned slowly, eyes wide in stunned disbelief.

"They're… mine," he whispered. "But they don't hurt."

His gaze snapped to her, something raw and reverent in his expression. "No fire. No carving. They just… are."

Seren was still staring at her arm. "That wasn't me. I didn't do anything."

Cairn stood slowly, wings folding in close. "Neither did I."

They just looked at each other, breathing hard. Bound by something neither one of them understood — but both of them felt

Seren broke the silence, still staring at the silver swirls etched across her skin. "So… I'm assuming matching magic tattoos aren't normal either?"

Cairn let out a breath — somewhere between a laugh and disbelief. "Not unless we just accidentally got married in some ancient Fae rite."

She blinked at him.

He was kidding… right?

They just stared at each other, the room suddenly too quiet. Her breath was quick, her pulse hammering. He could feel it — not just hear it or see it, but feel it. Like her panic had been wired straight into his spine, short-circuiting logic.

His head tilted slightly, brows pulling together. "Are you… panicking?"

Seren blinked. "I—what? No—maybe. A little. I mean, glowing tattoos and spontaneous wing bonding rituals aren't normal for me."

The pressure in his skull tightened, and he winced. "Okay, yeah. Definitely panicking."

He reached out, palm raised. "Calm down. I was only joking. I think."

Her eyes narrowed. "You think?"

He gave her a lopsided grin, still clearly rattled. "Look, I've seen a lot of weird shit. This? This might be a first."

Seren was spiraling. "What is this? What the hell is happening to me—us—whatever this is?"

Her fingers clutched her arm, tracing the silvered lines now shimmering beneath her skin. The more she looked, the more real it felt. Tangible. Permanent. "This isn't normal. I mean, clearly. Matching tattoos?! What does that even mean?"

Cairn flinched, startled by the intensity of her emotions flooding into him like wildfire. He stumbled back a step, wings still fanned out behind him—and then, almost reflexively, he snapped them shut. Smoke curled around his shoulders as the appendages vanished completely, like they'd never existed.

"Okay—okay—wings away," he said quickly, hands raised in surrender. "See? Gone. Gone now."

Her breathing didn't slow.

"Uhh…" He looked around the room like it might offer a manual for emotionally frazzled mortals and rogue soul tattoos. "I'm not sure what to do."

He took half a step toward her, then stopped, clearly panicked in his own way now. "Do you… want me to leave?"

She didn't answer, frozen in a wide-eyed stare.

"I have this—urge to hold you," he admitted, voice rough. "But I don't know if that'll make this better… or worse."

He looked utterly lost. An immortal force of fire, feared across two realms—and absolutely useless in the face of one panicked woman.

Seren didn't answer—not with words.

Her body moved before her mind caught up. One heartbeat she was frozen, overwhelmed, silver lines still gleaming across her skin—and the next, she was reaching for him.

Her fingers curled around the front of his shirt, right over the place where his heartbeat would be, if he were anything close to human. She tugged him toward her with more desperation than grace.

Cairn froze. Just for a breath. Then he let out a soft, almost disbelieving sound and sank down beside her, careful, slow, like she might vanish if he moved too fast.

She pressed her forehead into his chest, the warmth of him somehow grounding. Her breath still hitched, but the edge of panic had dulled. He smelled like smoke and storm-drenched stone.

"I don't understand any of this," she whispered.

"I know," he murmured, wrapping his arms around her—carefully at first, then with conviction. "Neither do I."

Cairn's fingers brushed slow circles against her back, grounding her in silence. For a moment, they just breathed together — her chest rising against his, his warmth anchoring her to something real.

Then he spoke, low and rough like gravel beneath fire.

"There's a place," he said. "Deep in the Pyric Realm. An ancient library — if the legends can be trusted. No one's set foot in it for thousands of years."

Seren shifted just enough to look up at him.

"It's buried beneath the oldest province. Hidden before the first rebellion. They say a king long dead filled it with every piece of knowledge too dangerous to burn — then bound it in flame and monsters to keep it from the wrong hands."

"And you want to go there?"

"I have to." His jaw tightened, lilac eyes still storm-shadowed from everything that just happened. "Whatever this is… you. Me. The wings. The marks. I don't know what it means. But the answers won't be in the King's court, or any place that welcomes fire. If they exist, they're there. Locked in a library guarded by things that forgot their own names."

Seren blinked, heart still rattling from the chaos — and the calm that followed it.

He caught the look in her eyes and offered the barest ghost of a smile.

"I'll find it," he said. "Whatever it takes."

Seren's brow furrowed as she watched him. "How long will you be gone?"

Cairn hesitated, then answered, "Three days."

"Exactly three?"

"Barring death-by-library guardian or spontaneous combustion, yes. Three." His mouth curved slightly, but the warmth didn't quite reach his eyes. "I won't risk staying longer than that. Not with what we just saw."

Her fingers twitched against his arm, reluctant. "Three days," she repeated, mostly to herself.

He nodded once. "I'll come back to you, Seren. I swear it."

Cairn didn't move right away.

He lingered in the doorway, gaze on her like he was memorizing something—like if he let himself forget even a detail, he wouldn't survive the three days. His hand twitched at his side, aching to reach for her. To kiss her. To explain more. But he held it in.

Too much, too fast… and not safe. Not yet.

His voice was low, edged in something fierce. "Seren—don't trust anyone. Not fully."

She straightened a little at the shift in his tone.

"I mean it," he pressed. "Don't go ghost hunting. Not alone. Not with others. The ones you think are harmless—they're tied to the In-Between. Some… report back to the Pyric realm. They're watchers, not whispers. Every encounter could expose you."

Her face paled. "The ghosts talk to your people?"

He nodded once, gravely. "Some are messengers. Others… bait."

"Good to know," she muttered, unsettled.

"I'll be back in three days," he repeated, more to ground himself than her. "Don't draw attention. Don't go looking. Just—stay safe."

Then, with one last flicker of hesitation, he stepped through the seam— and was gone.

The room felt impossibly empty after he left. Not just quiet — vacant, like something essential had been ripped out of the air. The hum of the spirit box was gone, the weight of his presence lifted, but it left an ache in its place. She didn't even know him — not really. But somehow, it had felt like she'd known him forever.

What the hell is wrong with me?

She flopped back against the pillows, heart still pounding, pulse skittering in her throat like it hadn't gotten the memo he was gone. She was probably just… touch starved. Right? That was all. Not some cosmic destiny crap. Not some magical tattoo soulmate scenario.

Nope. Just hormones.

Really, really loud hormones.

She hadn't had sex in years. Not real sex. Not good sex. Between dispatch shifts and late-night ghost hunts, most of her free time was spent with coffee and corpses. Who had the energy for dating? Or normal intimacy?

Still, that didn't explain the way her fingers still tingled. Or the way her soul felt like it was reaching toward something that wasn't there anymore.

She stared at the ceiling, one hand drifting to the fresh silver markings on her arm.

"Get it together, Seren," she muttered. "You're not the protagonist in some fantasy romance."

But even as she said it, she didn't quite believe herself.

Three days.

She could handle three days, right?

She'd be working the next couple nights. That would help — something to keep her mind busy, to keep her from spiraling. Maybe.

She stood and quietly cleaned up the wreckage of the bowl, the noodles that had somehow spread halfway across the room. She wasn't hungry anymore. Not even a little.

Back in bed, she climbed under the covers and pulled her laptop onto her thighs, letting YouTube autoplay something senseless and comforting. A video essay about haunted objects or a commentary on bad reality TV — she didn't even check.

She just needed background noise. Something human.

And as her eyes drifted shut, lulled by the low hum of the video and the weight of exhaustion, her mind didn't wander to work, or ghosts, or the unanswered questions clawing at her sanity.

She thought only of lilac eyes, and obsidian wings.

And what the hell three days might do to her.

Chapter Twelve: Trials and Monsters

Cairn

The seam sealed behind him with a hiss of heat and shadow.

Back in the Pyric Realm, the air tasted like smoke and iron. Cairn inhaled deeply, letting the searing familiarity of it burn away the lingering scent of her — lavender and something sweet he couldn't name. He didn't try to name it. The ache it stirred was inconvenient.

He stalked through the crooked streets of his village, a place half-carved into obsidian cliffs and half-grown from ancient stone, until he reached the slate-colored townhouse tucked at the far edge — his sanctuary, his armory, his prison.

Everything was where he left it. Clean. Quiet. Unchanged.

He didn't linger.

Though his wings remained hidden, the bond didn't.

He could still feel her — like her heartbeat was tethered to his, soft and steady in the back of his mind. Not enough to distract him. Just enough to remind him, to soothe his soul and calm his worry.

He shoved the feeling down. Locked it away.

Focus on the mission.

Armor. Weapons. Half-cloak. The rhythm of preparation dulled the ache, gave his hands something to do while his mind kept circling blue eyes and silver-threaded skin.

By the time the door shut behind him, the house felt like a place someone else used to live.

He turned to leave.

"Seriously?"

Cairn paused in the threshold. Rhyne Tareth leaned on the porch railing, one brow raised, arms folded across his chest like a disappointed older brother.

"Armor. Blades. That look in your eye. Either we're going to war..." Rhyne tilted his head, "or you're finally going on a date."

Cairn didn't answer. He just adjusted a strap on his vest.

Rhyne's smile faded. "Where are you going?"

"Out," Cairn said.

"Out where?" Rhyne stepped into the room, voice lowering. "You've been off since the council meeting. New Ashmarked, the Veil slipping, everything's upside down — and now you're dressed like you're about to kill something ancient."

Cairn hesitated.

"There's something I need to find."

Rhyne narrowed his eyes. "What are you searching for?"

Another pause... "knowledge"

Rhyne straightened "you're looking for the library, aren't you?"

When Cairn didn't answer, Rhyne let out a low whistle. "You are insane."

"Only on paper," Cairn muttered, pulling the seam open with a swipe of heat.

Rhyne stepped in his path. "You can't go alone. That place hasn't been touched in thousands of years. The things guarding it—"

"I know," Cairn cut in. "But I have to."

There was a pause.

Then Rhyne softened, just a little. "What is this really about?"

Cairn's jaw tightened, but he didn't answer.

"You're playing with fire, Cairn. Kaedros won't tolerate it."

Cairn met his gaze. "Kaedros was never my god."

That gave Rhyne pause.

"The Veil forged me," Cairn went on, voice low but steady. "The Realm bound me. I made my oath long before he ever sat that throne."

Rhyne sighed, rubbing a hand through his hair. "Of course you did." Then, softer: "Just… come back, yeah? You're one of the few bastards here I don't actively want dead."

Cairn gave a rare, crooked smirk. "I'll do my best to disappoint."

And with that, he stepped through the tear in the Veil.

Cairn landed in a crouch, boots sinking several inches into sodden, ashen muck. The air here was heavier — not with smoke, but rot. It clung to the inside of his mouth, tasting of decay, iron, and old things left wet for far too long.

Welcome to Ashrot Slough — the Far Realm's graveyard.

He rose slowly, scanning the crooked trees that loomed like fossilized ribs around him. Bark peeled back in jagged curls, leaking a black ichor that steamed when it hit the ground. The fog moved unnaturally, drifting against the wind. In the distance, something howled — not a creature calling out, but a warning. A ward.

He couldn't open a seam to the library itself — not even the most skilled Ashmarked could. The ancient protections woven into Ashrot's roots twisted space and memory alike. You couldn't rip through the Veil to reach a place you didn't truly know. And no one knew the library anymore. Only stories. Only guesses.

To find it, you had to earn it. Step by grueling step.

His hand settled on the hilt of his blade.

Ashrot Slough. Few entered. Fewer returned. It wasn't just the monsters — though there were plenty of those, bred from magic gone wrong and the sludge of unclaimed souls. It was what the swamp guarded:

The Molt-Hung Tree.

The last true library of the First Flame.

No maps led here. Only lore. Whispers passed in low tones among ash priests and oathbreakers. Some said the tree had been planted before the Pyric realm ever knew a king. Others believed it had grown over a grave — that of the first god who gave fire to the Veil.

Cairn wasn't here for myth.

He was here because something had changed. The Veil was stirring in ways it hadn't in centuries — marks pulsing where no fire had burned, wings born of smoke that now held shape and memory. Seren's presence still echoed through him, not just a thread, but a tether. And deep down, Cairn knew: whatever was happening wasn't just rare — it was dangerous. The King would demand answers, or make a violent decision, and he would do it soon.

He stared out over the black water and muttered aloud, voice low and steady, like reciting an old vow:

"When wings rise without fire, and flesh is marked without pain — the answers lie buried in Ashrot roots. But only for the one who dares to unmake the flame."

The wind hissed across the surface of the mire, as if the Slough itself had heard him.

"The tree lies deep where shadows sleep,

In Ashrot's heart, where secrets keep.

It hides beneath the burdened past,

Revealed to those who seek it last.

Not seen by eye, nor touched by flame—

It waits for one who bears the name.

The knowing burns, the truth will sting…

But only those who bear may bring.”

The rhyme faded into the mire like a stone tossed in still water —
rippling, then gone. Cairn let the silence settle. It wasn't just words. It
was a warning. A test. And possibly a trap.

He stepped forward.

The bog swallowed sound in that strange way it always had. No birds.
No breath. Just the distant groan of something massive moving far
beneath the muck. Roots? Bones? He didn't want to guess.

Thick fog rolled across the path, curling around his boots, veiling even
the path behind him. The Slough did not like to be followed.

Each step pulled at something beneath his skin — not magic, not
memory, but something older. A resonance, deep in his bones, like the
Veil itself was watching. Not magic. Not instinct. Something older.
Direction. It hummed beneath his skin like a buried name being spoken
from far away.

He didn't need a map. The Slough was guiding him. Not through sound
or sight, but something deeper — a knowing, ancient and undeniable,
threading itself through his bones like the Veil itself had chosen his path.

This place remembers, he thought.

Not just history, but intent.

It knew what you sought. And what you feared.

And it would make you prove which mattered more.

Cairn adjusted the blade strapped to his back and pressed deeper into
the fog, toward the place where even fire refused to burn.

Because somewhere beneath all this rot and ruin,

The tree was waiting.

He angled left, skirting the edge of a fallen obelisk, half-eaten by moss.
The way narrowed. Grew darker.

The air thickened, dense with sulfur and something sweeter — cloying,
unnatural. Cairn coughed once, the taste coating his tongue like spoiled
nectar. His boots struck dry stone, brittle and splintered like scorched

bone, the swamp momentarily giving way to a narrow ridgeline that rose from the mire like a scar.

Above him, the canopy twisted. Long, hanging vines shimmered faintly — not with dew, but with webbing. Each filament vibrated in response to sound, humming in a frequency just below hearing. The trees weren't just trees. They listened.

Cairn slowed his breath.

One wrong step would echo for miles.

Beneath his feet, the stone thinned again — cracking with each step. The landscape didn't shift with movement. It anticipated. Veered. Lured.

And then the silence broke.

Not by movement.

By mimicry.

A rasping voice — low, wet — whispered from behind him in a perfect copy of Seren's voice.

"Cairn… don't leave me."

He froze.

Another whisper followed. His own voice, this time — broken and desperate.

"I'll find you. I swear it."

The illusions crawled deeper, pulling at his memories, coating the branches with scenes from his past.

And then the thing emerged.

It rose from the stone itself — not birthed, but revealed, like the land had been wearing it. A towering figure stitched from antlers, rot, and something like ritual. Its body was carved with old Pyric glyphs — twisted versions of his own. Its face bore no eyes, only an open, smoking brand where a soul should've been.

He'd heard the rumors. A Glyphcarion. A failed Ashmarked.

Cairn's hand went to his blade.

"You were supposed to stay dead," he muttered.

It screamed — a soundless, psychic detonation that shattered the illusion-webs and sent shrapnel of memory flying through his mind.

And the fight began

Cairn dodged the first strike — a coiled appendage arcing toward his neck — and countered with a burst of flame from his palm. The creature hissed, retreating only for a heartbeat before lunging again, faster this time.

He rolled beneath the swing and drove his dagger up into its midsection. It met something like flesh but burned like tar. The blade sizzled, blackened, and snapped — and the Glyphcarion shrieked, not in pain, but rage.

"Of course you don't die easy," Cairn growled.

The monster's spine flexed backward, cracking unnaturally as its limbs split — now four arms, each ending in claws like curved obsidian. It launched at him with all of them.

Cairn summoned the fire in his tattoos. It flared across his skin in molten glyphs, ancient and angry. He swung both arms wide, releasing a blast that sent the Glyphcarion skidding back, steam and sludge exploding around them.

But it wasn't over.

The Glyphcarion surged through the smoke — and this time, latched onto him.

They slammed into the bog, water erupting around them. Cairn felt its claws scoring his armor, searching for the soft place beneath. He shoved a knee between them, kicked off, and dragged one flaming hand across its face.

It shrieked again — this time in pain.

"That's it," he snarled. "You can bleed."

The Glyphcarion twisted, its mouth splitting wider, unhinging down its throat as it hissed something in no language Cairn had ever heard.

He answered with a blade of fire.

One strike. Two. A third — clean through the core.

The Glyphcarion seized, limbs twitching. Then it collapsed into the swamp, hissing and boiling away, leaving nothing but a spiral of black ooze and flickering sparks that hissed into the mud.

Cairn staggered to his feet, chest heaving. His arm was bleeding. His blade was gone.

But he was alive.

He glanced back the way he came. The Slough was quiet again. As if the swamp had blinked and gone back to sleep.

And ahead?

That ancient pull… still tugging forward.

Cairn glanced down at his arm. The Glyphcarion's claws had ripped clean through the leather, scoring deep into the muscle. Blood ran in dark rivulets, mixing with swamp water and ash. He hissed through his teeth, flexing his fingers to test the damage.

It would need stitches. Probably a dozen, maybe more.

He didn't have time for that.

He braced the injured arm against his thigh, drew a short blade from his belt with the other, and let the fire in his veins rise.

The metal glowed red, then white.

"Three… two…"

Before he could treat the wound, the pain changed.

Not from the gash — but something deeper.

Cairn froze as a searing heat bloomed across his back, low and to the left, just beneath the ribs. It felt like a brand being pressed to raw skin, molten and unforgiving. His breath caught, the Fire not from the swamp or his blood, but from the Veil itself.

Another mark.

Earned in battle. Seared into him not by blade, but by right.

He gritted his teeth and dropped to one knee, letting the heat run its course. It carved itself into his flesh like memory — permanent, pulsing, alive.

When the fire dulled, he knew it had taken shape: a spiral of twisted bone and inked rot — the shape of the Glyphcarion's open mouth. Its scream would live on him now, woven into the map of his service.

Cairn exhaled. "Another brand," he muttered. "Another ghost to carry."

He glanced down at his ruined arm. Time to finish the job.

He pressed the flat of the blade to the wound.

The sear of heat split through him like lightning. Muscle jumped. The scent of burned flesh curled into the air, sharp and metallic. But he didn't cry out.

He didn't even flinch.

When it was done, he let the blade drop to the muck, steam rising from the charred edge.

The bleeding had stopped.

He exhaled, the pain already caged somewhere deep inside him where it couldn't interfere. Just another scar for the collection.

He rolled his shoulder. Good enough.

He crouched beside the Glyphcarion's remains — what little was left. The creature's form was collapsing inward, flesh liquefying into the swamp like it had never been separate from it. No bones. No blood. Just a slick smear sinking back into the Slough.

There were no trophies here. No use pretending it had ever been more than a nightmare.

He turned to his gear.

One dagger left, edge chipped but still capable of cutting.

The glaive, still intact — though the haft bore fresh scorch marks, a grim badge of the fight.

Twin crescent blades, sheathed against his spine, untouched. Their glyphs pulsed slow and steady, waiting.

A single throwing knife remained. The other was somewhere deep in the muck.

His healing ash, still three-quarters full. It wouldn't bring him back from the brink, but it would stop him from bleeding out.

A coil of flame-waxed rope, untouched.

And the cloak — now torn and half-slagged from the Glyphcarion's acidic blood. He stripped it off and left it in the mud without a second glance.

He moved in silence, letting the Slough swallow the sound of his footfalls. Every step sank into wet, ash-choked soil, the trees warping tighter the farther he went, gnarled limbs like crooked fingers clutching at the sky. He trudged forward for several miles.

The scent changed first — from rot and sulfur to something sweet. Like overripe fruit rotting under sunless skies.

Cairn slowed.

The mist ahead shimmered with an unnatural hue, pale green and thick as oil. It hugged the forest floor in slow-moving tendrils, curling over roots and pooling in hollows. The trees here bore no leaves, only blistered bark and strange, bubbling growths that hissed when touched by fog.

Poison.

Not instantly fatal — but it would slow him. Muddle his thoughts. Make him see things that weren't there. If he breathed too much of it in, even the ash might not bring him back.

He crouched low, watching the way the gas drifted. It clung to depressions in the terrain, avoiding the elevated stones that jutted up between the tree roots like vertebrae. A path. Not clear, but present.

He stripped a length of cloth from the hem of his shirt, poured a pinch of ash into the fabric, and tied it tight across his mouth and nose. Not perfect. But better than nothing.

Timing his movements with the roll of the fog, he stepped lightly onto the first raised stone, then the next — a narrow spine of slick obsidian that wound through the mire like a serpent's back. Below him, the gas whispered, taunted, begged him to fall.

A branch cracked behind him.

He froze — heart steady, mind clear.

Nothing.

Just the Slough, breathing.

He pushed forward. Eyes sharp. Feet sure. Mind shielded.

It took nearly an hour to weave through the fog field. His legs ached from crouching, balancing, fighting the tremble of exhausted muscles.

But he made it.

Beyond the final ridge, the mist thinned, revealing a basin where the water ran clear again — at least by Ashrot standards. He yanked the cloth from his face and drew in a ragged breath.

Still alive. Still hunting. And closer than ever.

Night was falling fast.

The gloom of Ashrot thickened into something nearly physical, curling around the trees like smoke made of pitch. Soon, it would be so dark he wouldn't be able to see his own hand in front of his face — not even with his Pyric-born sight. And continuing in the dark out here was suicide. He wanted to continue forward, but he made promises to return, and they were promises he intended to keep.

He scanned the gnarled terrain for what passed as shelter in a place like this. Roots twisted high off the ground like scaffolding. He found a thicket of blackened reeds, their hollow stalks surprisingly sturdy. With careful hands and his rope, he fashioned a low lean-to — nothing elaborate, but dry, hidden, and woven tight against the rising chill. He masked it with moss, wedged it between two hunched trees, and scattered the ground with muck to obscure any signs of his trail.

It wasn't comfortable. But it was enough.

Cairn crouched inside, blades close, every sense straining against the Slough's endless whisper. Shadows moved where nothing should, and the trees groaned like old bones under a heavy sky.

He lay still, eyes open, waiting for sleep that might never come.

Somewhere in the distance, something screamed — high pitched and long, swallowed quickly by silence.

Still, his eyes drifted closed.

Just for a moment, he told himself.

The Slough didn't sleep.

But for now... he did.

Chapter Thirteen: Eyes That Never Blink

Seren

She could've slept for another twenty-four hours.

The room felt empty when she woke — like something had been taken from it, but the shape of it still lingered in the air. Seren rolled over, groggy and blinking against the early evening light filtering through the curtains. Her body ached, not with pain exactly, but with absence. Like something inside her had stretched toward warmth and now missed it.

Cairn.

She groaned and sat up, scrubbing her face with both hands. No use dwelling. He said three days. She could survive three days.

Maybe.

She got dressed slowly, tugging on her police department shirt only to realize too late she'd forgotten to wash it. A crusty orange smear from her last shift — Cheetos dust, had made a home near the hem. She stared at it for a second, debated changing, then shrugged and kept going. If anyone said something, she'd just claim she was shot at and bled processed cheese. Not the weirdest thing that'd come out of her mouth at work. Then she started wandering her house like a ghost — gathering her laptop, her bag, her water bottle. Her boots ended up by the back door, where she finally sank down and laced them with sluggish fingers.

A long yawn cracked her jaw. What time had she gone to bed? Cairn had left sometime around midnight, and now it was—

She blinked at the stove clock.

5:04 PM.

Had she really slept seventeen hours?

Another yawn. Another stretch. Then she was out the door, sliding into her car and heading to the one place she always stopped before her shift — Skeeter's Gas and Go gas station two blocks from the office. Predictable. Familiar. Comfort in the form of caffeine and chips.

The bell jingled overhead as she pushed inside. Fluorescent lights buzzed slightly too loud.

But something felt… off.

The clerk behind the counter wasn't the usual guy — not the one with the lopsided smile and constant smell of beef jerky. No, this guy was new. Mid-forties, maybe, but with skin that looked too tight in some places and too loose in others. He was staring at her.

Like, really staring.

Did he think she was going to steal something?

She looked down. Yep, still in her PD t-shirt. Clearly marked. Not exactly incognito.

Maybe he just hated cops. Or had zero social skills. Whatever.

She shook it off and made her way down the aisles, grabbing her usual snacks: an energy drink, a granola bar, gummy worms she'd pretend she bought for someone else, and the same off-brand protein shake she always regretted.

By the time she stepped up to the counter, he was still watching her. His weirdly yellow eyes unblinking. She forced a polite smile and held out her items.

"Hi," she said, trying to keep it light. "I haven't seen you working this shift before. Did Jason take the day off?"

Silence.

He started scanning her items without a word, eyes never leaving her face.

She shifted her weight, discomfort crawling up her spine. That's when she noticed his hands — pale and wrinkled like an old man's. Skin thin and papery. But his face... no more than 45. Maybe.

And his fingernails — yellowed, long, almost talon-like — curved slightly over the scanner as he moved.

She suppressed a shudder.

Something about him felt off. Like he was wearing someone else's skin just a little too well.

He finished scanning her items, the beeps oddly loud in the tense silence. But instead of greeting her or offering the total, he just turned the screen toward her and continued to stare.

No words. Not even a nod.

Seren cleared her throat. "Oh, I'll pay with my card."

She reached for the debit machine, suddenly hyperaware of how long it took to load. Her fingers hovered, then tapped in her PIN, the whole process dragging like time had thickened. All the while, he stared. Unblinking. Silent.

She tried again, forcing another smile that felt stiff around the edges. "Are you going to be working this shift from now on?"

Still nothing.

Just that same gaze — too heavy, too focused, like he wasn't just looking at her, but through her.

Her stomach flipped.

The terminal chirped approved, a tiny electronic blessing in the mounting unease.

"Thank you," she said quickly, sweeping her items into her arms. "Have a nice day."

She turned to leave, practically speed-walking through the automatic doors. As she reached her car, she couldn't help it — she glanced back through the glass storefront.

He was still staring.

Standing perfectly still behind the counter, yellow eyes fixed on her even as she pulled out of the lot and drove away. Her scar pulsed slightly, she couldn't help but think she just narrowly escaped something incredibly dangerous.

Seren tried to shake off the weird encounter as she clocked in and slid into her chair. The soft hum of the dispatch center usually brought a strange sort of comfort — predictable, controlled chaos. But tonight, it felt too still.

She cracked open her energy drink and had just taken the first sip when the admin line rang.

Blocked number.

Her fingers hovered over the button.

She hesitated, a sharp pulse beating against the inside of her skull. Then she exhaled through her nose and hit answer.

No greeting. No noise in the background.

Just a voice — the same low, male voice as before.

"I'm watching you."

Click.

The line went dead.

Seren froze.

She stared at the screen, willing it to show something. Anything. Caller ID, number history, a log. But, just like last time—nothing. No record of the call. As if it had never happened.

Her throat tightened as she swallowed, heartbeat roaring in her ears. She was being watched. She knew it. How else would they know to call the moment she sat down?

Her gaze swept the room. The blinds were drawn, the windows mirrored with one-way glass. Her eyes snagged on the camera in the corner. It had always been there. But could someone have hacked the system? Was it someone she worked with?

The panic returned, sharp and rising. The gas station creep. The phantom calls. The Pyric realm. Cairn.

Maybe she was dreaming. Maybe she had finally snapped—fabricated some shadow-realm protector because she was sleep-deprived and strung out on trauma and caffeine.

Her hand trembled around the energy drink.

No. She felt him. Still. Deep under her skin, like the echo of a memory — or a mark — she couldn't forget.

She closed her eyes and focused on her breathing. Slow. In through the nose. Out through the mouth.

Lower your heart rate. Come back to your body.

Then the realization hit — Marisol.

She couldn't say everything. Not yet. Not about Cairn, or the Veil, or what had burned its way into her bones. But she could tell Marisol about the calls. The voice. The feeling of being watched. Because if anyone would believe her — even without proof — it was Mar.

And she needed someone to believe her. Before she stopped believing herself.

Seren shot off a quick text:

Seren: "Hey. I need to talk to you. Something weird's going on. I think I'm being followed or stalked. I'm safe right now — I'm at work — but can we talk before we leave tonight?"

Marisol responded almost immediately:

Marisol: "Shit. Okay. I'll stop by after midnight. Don't leave without me. Stay in dispatch where it's safe."

Relief flickered through Seren's chest, just enough to hold her together.

The next few hours passed in a blur. Two DUIs, a rollover accident, a breaking and entering in progress, and a shots fired call that turned out

— like 99.9% of them — to be nothing but fireworks. She was running on autopilot. When 911 rang again, her hand moved on instinct.

"911, what's the address of your emergency?"

A younger male voice came through, slightly slurred, like he'd smoked something or taken too many pills.

"Hey… yeah, so I'm at the Skeeter's Gas and Go over on 23rd, and uh… there's a dude dead behind the counter."

Seren sat straighter in her chair, pen poised over her notepad.

"There were other people in the store, but no one was coming to the front. I walked around the counter to try and check the back office, and, uh… I found him."

Her stomach twisted. That was the same station from earlier.

"Do you believe the person is beyond help at this time?"

"Oh yeah," the caller said casually. "He's like… gray. Been laying in his own blood for a while. Definitely dead."

She forced her voice to stay even.

"Can you describe the male for me?"

"White dude, probably late twenties. Blonde hair."

That matched Jake. The usual guy who worked that shift. Not the stranger with the staring problem.

Her fingers tightened around her pen.

"Okay, I have officers heading your way. Can I get your name and a call-back number?"

"Uh, yeah. Name's Brandon Michaels. My number's 555-0173."

She got him to stay on scene and ended the call.

Switching to the radio, she keyed up:

"Available units, respond to the Skeeter's Gas and Go on 23rd for a report of a DOA. RP is on scene, name is Brandon Michaels."

"401 copies. Can you notify State Police to assist with the investigation?"

"Affirm, 2230 hours."

Flipping channels:
 "EMS 260, respond to the Skeeter's Gas and Go on 23rd for a reported DOA."

"260 copies, enroute."

She dialed the state dispatch and requested a trooper for assistance. While she was still on the phone, her officer and EMS arrived on scene.

Only then did her thoughts catch up.

Jake. The blonde hair. The age.

It wasn't the creep from this morning.

But it couldn't be a coincidence.

Not anymore.

Seren's headset crackled.

"Dispatch, 260."

Marisol. Her voice wasn't her usual clipped tone—it was tight, shaken.

Seren sat up straighter. "Go ahead 260."

There was a beat of silence before she responded. "We're going to need the coroner. Immediately."

A breath. "You can clear us. We're done here."

Seren swallowed hard, heart picking up. "10-4, dispatching the coroner now. Showing you clear from scene"

She made the call, her voice professional, even as her stomach churned. Then switched back to the main channel.

"Dispatch, 401"

"401, Go ahead."

"Scene and investigation is turned over to the state police. I'm clear scene."

"401 copy at 2320 hours"

Seren leaned back in her chair. The room suddenly felt cold.

Ten minutes later, the door to the comm center swung open. Marisol walked in. Her uniform was still on, but her name tag was gone, and her jacket was only half-zipped. She looked… pale. Not tired. Not annoyed.

Pale. Ashen. Shaken.

Seren blinked. "You're off already?"

Marisol didn't answer at first. She just sank into the chair beside her and pressed the heels of her hands into her eyes.

"I've only clocked out early twice in my life," she said finally. "Once when I had the flu so bad I couldn't keep down water. And now tonight."

Seren turned slowly in her chair. "Was it that bad?"

Marisol nodded. "It wasn't the scene. It was… something else. I walked behind that counter and the air felt wrong. It was like… like I stepped into a room that didn't want me there. Like I was being watched through a hole I couldn't see."

She dropped her hands from her face, and her eyes locked with Seren's.

Marisol rubbed a hand over her face, then looked up, eyes still wide, voice low.

"They were canvassing for evidence," she said. "And one of the officers called me to the alley behind the station—behind the dumpster."

She paused, like she needed a second to replay the memory in her head.

"They wanted me to look at something… to confirm if it was what they thought. It was a—" she hesitated, like the words tasted wrong in her mouth, "—a skin suit. A full one. Human. Clothes and all."

Seren's breath caught.

"It was just… lying there in a wet, sloppy pile. No blood. No guts. Just the skin." Marisol's eyes were unfocused now, haunted. "It was like something split it clean from the back of the neck, all the way down. Peeled it like a fruit. Hollow. Like someone had unzipped a person and walked off in their body."

She exhaled shakily. "I've seen death before. I've seen bad. But that? That wasn't death. That was… something else."

Seren swallowed hard, her fingers curling around the edge of the console. "Marisol… I was at that gas station earlier. Just a few hours before the call came in."

Marisol blinked, clearly stunned. "Wait—what?"

Seren nodded slowly. "I went in to grab snacks before shift. The normal guy, Jake, wasn't working. Some other guy was there—creepy as hell. Just stared at me the whole time. Didn't say a word. I tried to make small talk, and he just kept… watching me. Like he was studying me."

Marisol's jaw tensed. "And you're sure it wasn't Jake?"

"No." Seren shook her head, the memory making her skin crawl. "Black hair. Younger face, but his hands… they looked ancient. Wrinkled, yellow nails. Like they didn't match the rest of him."

A beat passed.

Marisol's voice dropped. "You think it was wearing someone else's skin."

Seren exhaled slowly. "I don't know what I think anymore. But it didn't feel human. And now Jake's dead, and there is someone's skin sitting behind a dumpster."

Marisol leaned back, visibly shaken again. "What the fuck is going on?"

Seren ran both hands down her face and let out a shaky breath. "I have no idea what's going on, but I'm terrified, Mar. Like—actually scared. Can I come stay with you for a couple nights? Or… you could come to my place, if you'd rather."

Marisol didn't hesitate. "No, come to mine. I'll fold out the couch."

Seren blinked, caught off guard by the quick answer.

Marisol gave a half-smile that didn't reach her eyes. "Your house gives me the creeps. And honestly? I'd rather not find out if that thing knows where you live. Plus I have my cat and dog that will be happier at my apartment"

Seren nodded slowly. "Okay. That works. I'll just need to grab some stuff from my house first."

Marisol nodded. "I am going with you, and we might recruit one of our officer friends too."

Despite everything, a small, exhausted laugh broke from Seren's chest. "God, thank you."

Marisol leaned in and bumped her shoulder. "You'd do the same for me. Now hurry up and clock out so we can fortify the hell out of my living room."

Seren and Marisol left dispatch and made their way across town to Marisol's apartment. They dropped off Marisol's car, grabbed her oversized mutt — a lumpy black-and-white rescue named Spaghetti — and climbed into Seren's car to swing by her place for essentials.

The gravel crunched under the tires as they pulled into the narrow driveway of Seren's old farmhouse. The headlights sliced through the dark, casting shadows up the tree in the front yard — one of them twisted just right to look like an alien creature devouring the roof.

Seren's grip tightened on the steering wheel. "Well, that's not ominous at all."

"Are you sure your house wasn't built on an ancient burial site or something?" Marisol muttered, already unbuckling.

"Only the living room," Seren replied dryly as she fished out her keys to unlock the door.

Seren stepped into the house first, flicking the light switch and bracing herself like she expected something to lunge from the shadows. Behind her, Marisol tripped over the threshold and stumbled into the entryway like a sacrificial offering. If anything had been lying in wait, it was probably very confused now.

Spaghetti didn't move.

The dog had padded up to the door behind them but stopped cold at the threshold, whining softly. He looked between the two women with wide, uncertain eyes.

"C'mon, buddy," Marisol coaxed. "In you go."

But he refused, planting his furry butt firmly on the porch and letting out another low whine.

Seren glanced at Marisol. "That's not a great sign."

"Spaghetti thinks everything is food or demons. There is no in-between."

Still, neither of them liked it.

They made a fast plan — divide and conquer. Seren darted into her bedroom to grab pajamas, a change of clothes, her pillow, and her well-worn fleece blanket covered in faded stars. Marisol hit the bathroom like a tactical unit, collecting Seren's toothbrush, hairbrush, a makeup bag, and whatever skincare potions were lined up on the counter.

They reappeared in the living room at the same time — arms full, hearts racing.

Spaghetti was still sitting at the door, now pawing at it like he wanted them out.

"Leaving the light on," Seren said, rushing past the couch to the door. "In case the house tries to eat itself."

"Or us," Marisol added.

With one last glance around the room, they grabbed Spaghetti by the collar, bolted down the porch steps, and piled into Seren's car like the closing scene of a horror movie. They didn't look back.

Seren pulled her car into Marisol's apartment complex and the group climbed the three flights of stairs like they were scaling a mountain. Spaghetti trotted ahead as if this was all very routine, tail swaying like he didn't just refuse to enter a perfectly haunted house thirty minutes ago.

Inside, the girls dropped their bags, kicked off their boots, and immediately set to "fortifying" the apartment — which really just meant dragging the coat rack in front of the door, stacking a line of throw pillows along the windowsill, and wedging a broom between the door handle and the wall. Marisol even stuck one of her crystal coasters on the doorknob "just in case."

"A witchy tripwire," she said with a deadpan face. "Very advanced."

Spaghetti flopped dramatically onto the couch like he'd just secured the perimeter himself.

They didn't talk much after that — the tension of the night lingering just beneath their movements. But they popped some popcorn, found their favorite comfort movie (The Mummy, because Brendan Fraser is a national treasure), and curled up on opposite ends of the living room.

Halfway through the second act, popcorn bowls mostly empty and Spaghetti snoring between them like a furry heater, both girls finally dozed off.

The apartment was quiet, lit only by the flicker of the TV screen and the warm security of being together — in a place that, for now, felt safe.

GUMMY
WORMS

Chapter Fourteen: Tree of Riddles

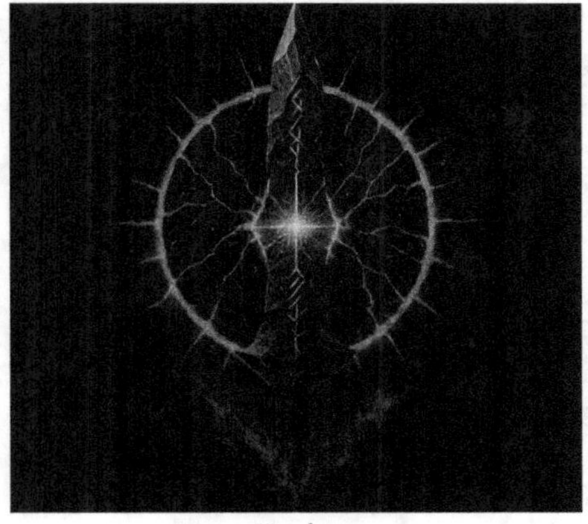

Cairn

The sky above Ashrot Slough had turned to ink.

Cairn stirred beneath the patchwork canopy he'd lashed together, half-alert before his eyes opened. The realm didn't let him sleep deeply—not here. The air was too charged, like it was holding its breath. His fingers twitched against the hilt of one blade as he sat up, testing the silence.

Still whole. Still alone.

But something had changed.

The ground just beyond his makeshift camp shimmered—faint, subtle, as if moonlight had found a crack in the ever-choked sky. Cairn rose and stepped forward cautiously, boots sinking into the spongey earth. There, tucked beneath a root that hadn't been exposed before, was a flat, slate-like stone.

It pulsed faintly.

He crouched and brushed away the damp moss. Etched into its surface was a symbol: a broken flame encircled by thorns. His stomach tightened.

The mark was ancient. Older even than the Ashmarked.

This was Pyric script, but not ceremonial. It was the kind found buried in the foundations of fallen temples. The kind scholars would kill to see in daylight.

Beneath the rune were words, carved deep and lined with shimmer:

"Truth is a wound that bleeds wisdom.

The door lies where memory burns brightest."

Cairn touched the groove of the flame.

It was warm.

Not magically—viscerally, as if something beneath the stone still remembered fire. He rose and glanced around the swamp. Everything looked the same as when he fell asleep, but now… he could feel it.

A pull.

Not a voice. Not a sound. But a direction—like a compass rose stamped behind his eyes. A pressure against his ribs, nudging him forward. His instincts, honed by centuries of battle and blood, urged caution.

But his soul—the one tethered to silver-threaded skin and a blue-eyed mortal—knew better.

He was being called.

He packed what little he'd unpacked, checked the weight of his blades, secured the rune stone in his satchel, and extinguished the embers of his small fire.

Then he turned and walked into the thick of the Slough.

Ashrot Slough reeked of memory.

Cairn moved with purpose, each step pressing deep into the moss-choked mire. The trees had grown stranger—taller, leaner, with trunks that bent unnaturally, reaching toward something he couldn't see. The usual signs of life had gone quiet. No rustling in the undergrowth. No insects humming. The only sound was the steady splash of his boots and the occasional breath that left his lungs like steam.

He wasn't sure how long he'd been walking when the trees opened into a clearing.

In the center stood a single tree.

It towered over the others, bark pale and shimmering faintly in the gloom. Its branches curled like antlers, and its roots ran exposed across the mud, slick with moss. Cairn felt his pulse shift. Something about it called to him—whispered in the deep, subconscious part of himself that still remembered magic before it had a name.

But this was not the library.

This was something else. A test.

He approached slowly, fingers twitching toward his blade as instinct prickled along his spine.

The air thickened as he crossed the threshold of the clearing, pressure building behind his eyes, and then—

The world shifted. His breath caught.

The stench of swamp faded. The heat of the Veil dimmed. And then—

Snow.

He blinked.

Soft flakes drifted around him, melting the moment they touched his skin. He stood in a memory, one so vivid he could taste the salt of old tears on his tongue.

The Past.

The home was smaller than he remembered. His mother's voice—warm and weary—called from inside, and he stepped toward it like a child. He didn't mean to, didn't want to. But the memory tugged him like a current.

There she was.

Tending the hearth. Her face lit with the same soft firelight that always clung to her smile. She turned, eyes crinkling at the corners, arms opening.

"Cairn," she said, like he hadn't aged a day.

He couldn't speak. The words lodged in his throat like glass.

She reached for him—but when their fingers touched, she burned.

Fire poured from her mouth. Her eyes blackened. Her skin cracked like scorched clay, and she screamed his name—not in love, but in agony.

"You left us to burn!"

Cairn staggered back, breath ragged, and the world cracked like a pane of glass.

The Present.

He stood now in Seren's bedroom. She was there, in her pajamas, headphones hanging loose around her neck. She looked at him—no, through him.

"You lied to me," she whispered.

He tried to move. Tried to explain. But the shadows warped the room, stretching the silence into something cruel.

She turned away.

"You marked me. You used me."

"No," he said, voice hoarse. "Seren, I—"

"I trusted you."

The sound of her pulling the door shut felt like a sword drawn across bone.

And then—

The Future.

Flame. Endless flame.

The sky had torn open. The Veil gone. The Pyric realm bled into the human world, devouring cities, forests, oceans. Cairn stood at the center of it all, ash coating his armor, soot clinging to his face.

At his feet—Seren.

She lay twisted in the embers, eyes vacant. Her silver tattoos blackened, her body still. A fragile hand outstretched toward nothing.

"No," he rasped, stumbling forward on his knees. "No, no—please."

His fingers trembled as they hovered above her skin, afraid to touch. Afraid she'd crumble like all the others.

"Not her," he whispered. "Take me. Take the oath. Take the mark. Take everything—just give her back."

Nothing answered but the crackling of flame and the distant, hollow scream of something ancient devouring the world.

The wings on his back burst free with a rush of smoke and fury. He cried out—not in pain, but rage. Grief. Loss so total it cracked something in him.

"I've bled for this realm," he shouted into the burning sky. "I've killed for it! I bore the Oath. I became what you asked. Isn't that enough?"

The fire rose higher, licking at his heels, curling around his legs like it meant to drag him under too. His heart thundered against the tether in his chest — Seren — but the cord felt frayed, almost gone.

He slammed his fists into the scorched earth. "She was the only thing I had left." His little spark. And now the flame felt cold.

Tears spilled, unbidden. Hot as oil. They carved tracks through the ash on his face.

Then, slowly… the flames stopped climbing.

The sky fractured like glass, a hairline crack spidering across the vision. And in that silence — a sound.

Breathing.

Not from Seren's corpse. Not from the fire.

From himself.

Sharp. Shallow. Real.

He blinked once—twice—until the flames peeled away like dead skin, revealing the wet forest floor beneath his knees. The illusion shattered around him in a thousand shards of memory and grief.

He was back in the clearing.

Still kneeling. Still shaking.

Still alive.

But changed.

He wiped the tears from his face with a grunt, staggered to his feet, and stared toward the looming grove.

That had been too real.

And yet—she was still alive.

He could feel it. The tether still held.

Cairn staggered forward, breath ragged, the world around him no longer fire and ruin but trees draped in moss and sky choked with fog. The clearing had returned. Still, it felt… altered. Quieter. Heavier.

His boots squelched through the sodden ground as he moved toward an object now glowing faintly in the underbrush — a stone slab, half-sunk into the earth, ringed in roots and whispering fungi.

It hadn't been there before. Or perhaps it had, hidden until he'd earned the sight to see it.

He knelt before it. Fingers brushing away centuries of grime.

The words carved into the stone were in the ancient Pyric tongue, but the meaning pressed itself into his mind like a memory not his own:

"Face what forged you.

Feel what grounds you.

Choose what guides you.

Only then may the flame light true."

Cairn stared at the inscription, jaw clenched.

This wasn't just a trial. It was a threshold.

The Ashborn mark on his chest ached. His wings flexed once, restless beneath his skin.

Something ancient was watching. Waiting.

He pressed his hand to the stone.

"I'm not the same as I was," he said aloud. "And I don't want to be."

The moss around the base of the stone began to recede.

The trees shifted, creaked, and somewhere deeper in the swamp — something answered.

The path was opening.

"I'm coming," he muttered, jaw tight. "No more trials. No more ghosts. I will find the truth."

He stepped forward, toward the tree that had yet to reveal itself—toward whatever came next.

He pressed on.

The air grew thinner, colder. Hours passed—maybe more. The Slough gave way to sharper terrain, the thick muck beneath his boots turning to gravel, then jagged volcanic stone. He was beyond the reach of the mire now, but not beyond its weight.

It was then he saw it.

A mountain.

Massive. Foreboding. Rising like a jagged scar across the horizon, framed by a blood-colored sky. He stopped cold.

That mountain hadn't been there before.

He would've sworn it hadn't.

Cairn narrowed his eyes. No magic shimmered, no illusion cracked — but something about it watched him. Not with eyes. With memory. Like it had been waiting.

He knew better than to question it.

So he climbed.

The ascent was brutal. Every ledge fought him. The trail — if there ever was one — vanished and reappeared at will. Several times, he slipped, caught himself with a growl and bloodied hands. Rocks crumbled beneath his boots, the air turned thin, biting, cruel.

Hours bled into night. Then into the gray haze of almost-dawn. Still, he climbed.

Muscles trembled. Fire cracked in his chest. His vision narrowed to the next grip, the next pull, the next breath.

When he finally crested the final ledge, his knees buckled.

There it was.

At the summit's heart — a solitary, colossal tree.

It loomed like it had grown from the mountain's very soul — bark etched with glimmering glyphs, roots coiled through obsidian, and a hollow within its trunk pulsing with internal flame.

Cairn fell to his knees at its base. He couldn't move. He didn't try.

And that's when it spoke.

Not aloud. Not even in his mind.

The words rang in his bones.

"You've climbed the mountain.

Now climb the truth."

A pulse of light shimmered through the bark — and three stone roots rose from the ground around him, forming a broken spiral. On each, an ancient riddle glowed:

"I am the scar you cannot hide,

The echo where your shame resides.

You bear me like a weighted chain,

Yet I dissolve when you release the pain.

Not pardon from others, but peace from within —

What am I?"

"I am death without dying, the shedding of skin,

The silent revolution that begins from within.

Feared and resisted, but never still —

I break and rebuild with iron will.

What am I?"

"I am the fire that does not consume,

The anchor in storms, the light in gloom.

You cannot command me, yet I bend kings to their knees —

Stronger than fear, more lasting than peace.

What am I?"

The flame inside the tree flared — waiting.

He stared at the first riddle, the old wounds behind his ribs thrumming in time with every word carved in stone.

This wasn't just a trial. It was a reckoning.

He read the first riddle again, voice low and hoarse from the climb:

> *"I am the scar you cannot hide,*
> *The echo where your shame resides.*
> *You bear me like a weighted chain,*
> *Yet I dissolve when you release the pain.*
> *Not pardon from others, but peace from within —*
> *What am I?"*

Cairn stared at the stone for a long moment, sweat stinging his eyes.

The scar you cannot hide.

Visions flickered across his mind—his mother's face as it blistered in illusion, the cries of soldiers who had once called him brother, Seren recoiling from the mark he'd placed on her skin.

Chains. Weighted. But not by someone else's hands.

He clenched his jaw and whispered, "Forgiveness."

The word left his mouth like a confession.

The root pulsed with light.

A hum resonated deep in the mountain, as though the answer had unlocked something far below.

The riddle faded from the stone.

Cairn let out a breath he hadn't realized he was holding. Not relief. Just… release.

There were still two left.

He turned to the next glowing stone:

> *"I am death without dying, the shedding of skin,*
> *The silent revolution that begins from within.*
> *Feared and resisted, but never still —*
> *I break and rebuild with iron will.*
> *What am I?"*

This one felt raw. Personal in a different way.

Cairn closed his eyes.

He thought of what he'd once been — a fae with fire in his blood and rebellion in his bones. Of what the Ashmarked oath had made him — a weapon in service of a tyrant. Of what he was now — somewhere in between, pulled toward something softer, more dangerous.

"Change," he murmured.

Another pulse of light. Stronger this time. A deep, melodic thrum that echoed through the clearing and rattled the stone under his feet.

The second root dimmed.

And then the final riddle lit:

> *"I am the fire that does not consume,*
> *The anchor in storms, the light in gloom.*
> *You cannot command me, yet I bend kings to their knees*
> *—*
> *Stronger than fear, more lasting than peace.*
> *What am I?"*

This one hit like a blade to the ribs.

He wanted to say power. Or loyalty. Or duty.

But none of those were fireless.

None of them had ever made him hesitate… except for her.

He thought of Seren — her quiet defiance, her unshakable gaze, the way she touched his wings without fear.

She hadn't begged for his protection. She had chosen to stay close even when she didn't understand. Even when it cost her.

It wasn't fire.

But it *moved* him.

"Love," he said, the word foreign on his tongue but anchored in his chest.

The tree ignited.

Not in flame, but in *light* — a brilliant, silvery blaze that danced through its glyphs and pulsed deep within its hollow.

The roots that had once held the riddles began to pull back, revealing a winding stone stair spiraling down into the heart of the tree.

Cairn didn't move at first.

He just stood there, blinking at the light, feeling something inside him unravel and reform all at once.

Then—he stepped forward.

Down into the library that time forgot.

The stairway spiraled down into cool, dry air.

With each step, the warmth of the mountain faded, replaced by something older—something preserved. It wasn't the chill of death or dampness, but the kind of stillness that clings to knowledge buried for centuries.

At the base of the stairs, Cairn stepped into silence.

The library.

It wasn't a chamber.

It was a cathedral.

Massive stone columns stretched toward a ceiling so high it disappeared into shadows. Towering walls of shelves loomed in every direction, crammed with books, scrolls, rune-carved tablets, relics wrapped in brittle cloth. Some shelves were carved directly into the walls, others floated midair, supported by nothing. The scent wasn't mildew or decay. It was parchment, ink, pressed leaves, and fire-scorched vellum—like stories held their own breath.

And there was no dust.

Not a speck on the floor. Not a cobweb in the corners.

It was... alive. Preserved by magic or will or something more primal.

Cairn stepped forward, boots silent on the smooth black stone. His breath echoed faintly, swallowed by the sheer size of it.

No torches. No lanterns. And yet everything glowed with a low, ambient light, like the stone itself remembered the sun.

He wandered deeper.

There was no system. No categorization. No titles carved on archways. No maps etched in the floor.

He passed endless stacks—some narrow, some spiraled, some branching like tree limbs. Some scrolls were written in languages he hadn't seen in millennia. Others bore the seal of the Ashmarked, though he'd never known records were kept.

Some shelves held nothing but fragments. Others whispered in languages not meant for the ears of the living.

But none gave direction.

Cairn's steps slowed.

His pulse, which had been pounding with triumph and awe, began to sink. The weight of the space pressed on him—not physically, but emotionally. As if the vastness of it all had turned to mockery.

He had made it.

He had passed the trials. Fought the monsters. Climbed the mountain. Solved the riddles. And now—

Now he stood at the heart of knowledge itself…

And didn't know where to begin.

His throat tightened.

He spun slowly in place, scanning the impossibility before him.

"I don't have time for games," he muttered, the sound small in the library's vastness. "I need answers. I need to find out what she is. What *I* am now. What the Veil is doing—"

His voice cracked, just slightly. Frustration curling at the edges.

Silence answered him.

He sank down on the edge of a low stone bench, fingers gripping the hilt of his blade. He stared at the expanse of shelves in front of him—towering and endless.

And for the first time in a long while… he felt small.

Not Ashmarked. Not a weapon. Just a man chasing a spark in the dark.

His little spark. And the silence felt heavier without her.

Chapter Fifteen: Fated Not Forced

Seren

Seren didn't dream. Not really.

She stirred beneath a fleece blanket, Marisol's mutt Spaghetti, a warm, protective lump at her feet. Somewhere across the apartment, a dishwasher churned, and a faint blue light flickered from the muted paranormal show still playing on the TV. Dawn had barely started to bruise the sky outside.

For one fleeting moment, everything felt normal.

Then she remembered.

The man at the gas station.
The skin suit behind the dumpster.
The blocked call with that voice.

She shifted—and froze.

Two massive, unblinking yellow eyes were staring directly into her soul.

She gasped so hard she startled herself, nearly whacking her head on the back of the couch. "What the—"

Perched squarely on her chest like a midnight gargoyle was Marisol's cat: Nyx. Jet black. Judgmental. Unblinking. The feline version of a demon laying low while plotting your doom.

"Jesus, Nyx!" Seren hissed, clutching her chest. "Could you not stare into the abyss of my soul before coffee?"

Nyx blinked once, slowly. As if to say: *You're lucky I let you live.*

Seren gently nudged her off. Nyx hopped down with the grace of something that ruled the underworld, vanishing into the shadows without a sound.

Still rattled, Seren sat up, running a hand through her tangled hair. Her shirt clung weirdly, stiff in places. She glanced down.

Of course. The Cheeto stain from her last shift.

She groaned. "Perfect. Stalkers, skin suits, demonic cats, and I'm dressed like a trash goblin."

Across from her, Marisol snored softly, tangled in a blanket with one leg hanging off the couch and a half-empty Gatorade bottle cradled against her chest. Spaghetti thumped his tail lazily as if to say, *Morning already?*

And then it hit her.

Cairn.

Or more accurately, the absence of him.

That thread of awareness—that barely-there hum she'd come to recognize since their first touch—was silent.

Gone.

She reached inward, instinctively stretching her mind like fingertips toward a vanishing signal.

Nothing.

"Shit."

Had something happened? Was he hurt? Or worse... had he never been real?

She rose quietly, padded into the bathroom, and flipped on the light. Her reflection stared back: sleep-puffed eyes, frizzy hair, that Cheeto-stained shirt doing her no favors. She gripped the edges of the sink.

"Get it together," she muttered. "He said three days. It's been less than forty-eight hours."

But it didn't feel right. It felt hollow. Untethered.

Back in the living room, Seren dropped beside her duffel and rifled through her things—journal, phone charger, laptop—checking them even though she knew none of it could fix the gnawing ache in her chest.

Her fingers trembled.

A soft whine from Spaghetti made her glance up—just in time to see Marisol roll over and promptly smack into the floor with a loud *thud*.

Seren winced. "Oof. That sounded like at least two brain cells gone."

"Goddammit," Marisol groaned from the rug. "Why is my couch so short? Or am I tall now?"

"You've been the same height since sophomore year. You just roll like a damn log."

Marisol peeled herself off the floor, hair wild, eyeliner now deep into raccoon territory. "You good? You look like you saw a ghost."

Seren hesitated. "Actually… can you call in for me? I need a day or two. Something's… off."

Marisol blinked, suddenly wide awake. "Off how?"

"I'll explain. I just—need to change. This shirt has seen things. Unspeakable things."

She slipped into the bathroom and swapped into clean leggings and an oversized T-shirt. But as she stepped back out, Marisol froze.

"Uh. Seren?"

"What?"

Marisol pointed. "Your arm."

Seren followed her gaze—then realized. Her work shirt had been long-sleeved, completely hiding the markings that now shimmered across her skin from wrist to upper arm.

Marisol crossed the room, her expression shifting from curiosity to disbelief. "When the hell did you get a tattoo?"

Seren tugged on a hoodie, suddenly self-conscious. "It's… not really a tattoo. Not exactly."

Marisol narrowed her eyes. "It's glowing. Like—actually glowing. That's not ink, Seren. What the hell is it?"

Seren sat on the edge of the couch, her voice quieter now. "Okay. You know how I said weird shit's been happening?"

Marisol raised an eyebrow. "Yeah. Vividly."

Seren nodded. "This is going to sound insane. But I need you to listen—and I need you to believe me."

Without waiting, she launched into it.

Everything.

The Veil. The realm. The tether she could feel between her and Cairn. The whispers through the ghost equipment. The burning eyes. The fire. The mark. The moment in her room. The way he spoke like he was ancient and broken all at once. The way she could feel him, like a live wire beneath her skin, until it suddenly vanished.

She told Marisol everything.

And when she finished, she didn't look up. She couldn't.

Silence stretched between them.

Then—

"Okay," Marisol said softly. "Let's say I usually don't believe in fairy tales. Or curses. Or soulmates."

Seren's stomach twisted.

"But," Marisol continued, "I believe you. And I've seen a lot of weird shit doing what we do. But nothing like this. If you say there's another realm, and this Cairn guy is from it… if you've been marked and you *feel* him— then I believe there's something real here."

Seren finally looked up. "You do?"

"Seren, you're not the kind of person who spirals. You face literal darkness at work and still bring Gatorade to everyone's kids' soccer games. You're grounded. Logical. So if you're freaking out, I trust that there's a reason."

She nodded toward Seren's back. "And let's be real. That glowing mark? Not normal."

Seren swallowed hard. "I think he's in danger. Or gone. Or—I don't know. But I can't feel him anymore."

Marisol sat beside her. "Then we figure out what that means. And we fix it. You're not alone in this."

A lump rose in Seren's throat. "I don't know how to fix it."

Marisol gave her a crooked smile. "You never do. But you always find a way."

Seren sat stiffly, hoodie sleeves pulled over her hands, rocking slightly on the edge of the couch.

She'd told Marisol everything.

Every unexplainable moment. Every encounter. Every time her pulse synced to a heartbeat that wasn't hers. She didn't cry, but her voice had cracked— especially when she explained the thread. How it had hummed inside her chest like a tuning fork ever since Cairn touched her, and how now… it was silent.

Marisol hadn't questioned any of it. Just listened, lips tight, nodding in all the right places.

Now, as Spaghetti pressed against her thigh like a therapy dog who'd seen some shit, Seren stared down at her glowing arm and whispered, "What if he's gone?"

Marisol looked up from the phone she'd just used to call in sick for both of them. "He's not."

"You don't know that."

"No. But you do." Marisol leaned forward, elbows on knees. "You're freaking out because that bond thing or whatever—because it went quiet. But if it's real, it's not gone. It's just… blocked. Like a bad signal. Maybe he's doing something that messes with it."

Seren swallowed. "Or maybe something's messing with him."

She stood abruptly, pacing the small apartment. "It doesn't make sense. I've been around ghosts, demons, shit I couldn't explain—and none of that scared me like this. It's like I've been walking around with half a heartbeat and now I'm flatlining."

"Seren—"

"I need to know he's okay."

"Okay, but how?"

"I don't know!" she snapped, hands flying up. "I just—" Her voice cracked again. "I just want to be there. I want to help. I want to *see* him. Even if it's just for a second."

Something inside her seized.

Her arm flared silver-hot. Her chest tightened—not with fear, but pressure, as if the thread she'd been mourning hadn't snapped... just pulled taut.

Her breath caught.

"Seren?"

She didn't answer.

The floor trembled. Not visibly. Not violently. But enough that the overhead light flickered once.

Seren couldn't keep her balance and her knees hit the hardwood floor. Her heart lurched.

Heat flashed through her chest. Her skin lit up with goosebumps as a sharp, searing tug ripped through her sternum like something yanked a string connected straight to her heart.

And then—

She wasn't in the apartment anymore.

She fell. Not through space. Through thought, through time, through memory and flame.

She landed hard on cold stone.

The impact knocked the air from her lungs. For a second, all she could do was lie there—staring up at an unfamiliar ceiling that shimmered with soft, flickering light. Her brain hadn't caught up yet. Her heart was still racing. Her ears rang.

Then—

A face appeared above her. Pale. Soot-smudged. Eyes like wildfire rain.

Cairn.

He was sitting, hunched over with his elbows on his knees, arms braced, the weight of the world in his posture. But now—now he was frozen, bent forward, staring down at her like she was a hallucination.

Neither of them moved.

Seren blinked.

Cairn blinked back.

They just stared, nose to nose, both of them too stunned to speak.

"...Hi," she rasped.

A beat. Then—

"You're real," he whispered, voice raw. "You're actually—" His sentence broke, choked off in disbelief.

She swallowed hard. "Guess I couldn't wait three days."

Cairn exhaled like he hadn't breathed since she vanished. His fingers reached out, almost afraid to touch her.

And just like that—the tether snapped back into place. Solid. Bright. Unshakable.

He helped her sit up, one hand curled around hers like he might lose her again.

"My little spark," he whispered, voice barely audible.

She opened her mouth to respond—but Cairn's expression shifted.

"Seren—" he said quickly, lifting his hand to her face. "You're bleeding."

She touched under her nose and glanced at the smear of blood on her fingers. "It's nothing," she muttered, wiping it away with her sleeve. "Just… left-over Veil whiplash or something."

But his brow furrowed. "That's the second time."

"I'm fine."

She managed a small, tired smile. "Don't go full apocalypse over a nosebleed."

Cairn huffed, clearly unconvinced, and Seren rolled her eyes. Neither of them said anything else.

They didn't need to.

Not yet

Their hands were still clasped when Seren felt it.

A ripple under her skin.

Subtle at first—like static dancing across her nerves—but growing stronger, hotter. Her breath hitched. She pulled her hand back, clutching at her arm as a wave of heat surged through her bones.

Cairn tensed immediately. "Seren?"

She didn't answer. Couldn't.

The burn spread. Down her spine. Across her shoulders. Through her chest. It wasn't painful exactly—but it was overwhelming. Like her blood had turned to fire and her bones to smoke.

She dropped to her knees, trembling, gasping for breath.

Cairn caught her, but even he was struggling to understand. "What's happening?"

And then—

Light.

Her back arched as silver light erupted from her shoulder blades, wild and blinding. It wasn't flame, but something older. More sacred. A shimmer of magic that pulsed like a heartbeat.

Cairn stumbled back a step, eyes wide.

Wings.

Featherless, ethereal—made of smoke and threadlight and something uniquely hers. A mirror of his, but not a copy. Where his were forged in flame and ash, hers glowed with tempered silver, laced with threads of starlight. As if the Veil itself had marked her.

She collapsed forward, panting. The glow dimmed but didn't vanish. The wings remained—folded and strange, pulsing faintly like they were breathing.

Cairn dropped beside her, awestruck.

"You... how?"

She shook her head. "I don't know. I didn't— I didn't mean to. I just wanted to find you. I wanted to be here."

He looked at her like he was seeing her for the first time.

Not just a mortal.

Not just marked.

Changed.

Claimed by the realm itself.

"They answered you," he said quietly. "The Pyric realm doesn't give gifts freely."

Seren looked over her shoulder at the faint shimmer curling behind her. "Then I guess I'm stuck with them."

Cairn didn't answer. His eyes tracked the soft arc of her wing like it was a living thing—like it might vanish if he blinked. Slowly, instinctively, he reached out. His fingers brushed the edge of the glowing membrane, where silver light met smoke and magic.

It wasn't just contact.

It *sank* into her—like the magic between them had a pressure point, and he'd just pressed it.

Seren inhaled sharply. Heat shot down her spine. Every nerve lit up like wildfire. Not pain. Not even fear. Just sensation, deep and unfiltered. Her breath hitched—and before she could stop herself, a soft moan escaped her lips.

Cairn froze.

His hand retracted like he'd touched fire.

"I—" He cleared his throat, dropping his gaze. "I didn't mean… I wasn't thinking. I'm sorry."

Color rose beneath his ash-smeared cheeks. For once, he looked flustered. Almost boyish.

Like *he* was the one who might fall apart next.

Seren's breath was still shallow. Her skin felt scorched from the inside out, her pulse roaring in her ears. She blinked, eyes locking on him again, pupils blown wide.

"Don't apologize," she rasped. "But if you keep doing that here, I'm going to rip all that armor off and see what's underneath."

She exhaled sharply, like the air itself was too thick. "Holy fuck, Cairn."

Cairn shifted, just a fraction—but it was enough.

His breath hitched, muscles visibly tense beneath his armor. Then, with a sharp jolt, a pair of smoky, ember-laced wings tore free from his back in a sudden, instinctive flare. The movement was raw, violent—like a gasp given shape—and for a beat, he froze, staring at her like she'd just undone something vital in him.

His jaw clenched hard. He shifted again, more forcefully this time, adjusting the front of his pants with a muffled, frustrated growl. The strain was unmistakable now—armor or not, it was clear he was half a second from breaking.

"Well… damn it," he muttered, voice rough, low. "That was easy for you."

Seren's grin was all heat and no mercy. She tilted her head, eyes sweeping over him like a spark waiting to catch flame.

"At least I know the feeling's mutual."

Cairn dragged a hand over his face, wings twitching behind him like they had a mind of their own. "This is… going to be a problem."

Seren stepped forward, slow and deliberate.

She could see it—the way his jaw tightened, the flicker in his eyes, the subtle tension in every inch of his body. The wings at his back twitched like they sensed her coming before he did. He didn't move, didn't breathe. Just watched.

She stopped close—so close her boots bumped against his, her breath mingling with his in the charged space between them. Chest to chest… or nearly. He towered over her, broad and battle-worn, carved by centuries of war and fire.

Still, she looked up at him like she might devour him whole.

"Problem, huh?" she murmured, voice low and teasing. "Doesn't feel like a problem to me."

Cairn's throat bobbed. His eyes darkened.

Seren leaned in, letting her body press lightly to his. The planes of his armor were warm—radiating heat not just from magic, but from him. Her fingers lifted, tracing a line from his collarbone down the center of his chestplate, slow… deliberate… trailing lower and lower.

Her voice was a whisper against his skin.

"You feel like fire," she breathed. "No wonder I burned."

His hands twitched at his sides. Her fingers hovered on his armor just above the the buckle of his pants—just before the hem.

And gods, the look in his eyes. Like if she went one inch lower, he might fall to his knees for her.

Before her fingers could dip lower, the ground beneath them pulsed.

A ripple of light cracked through the floor at the library's center—bright, sharp, and alive. It wasn't magic in the traditional sense. It was older. Wilder. A heatless flare that lit up the towering walls of scrolls and tomes like sunrise through cathedral glass.

Both of them froze.

Seren turned her head just in time to see a pillar of light spiral up from the center of the chamber, piercing the vaulted ceiling like a beacon. It was breathtaking.

Cairn blinked, slowly dragging his gaze from her to the glow. His voice was hoarse when he finally spoke. "I've been here for hours. Nothing like that has happened."

Seren stepped back just enough to see his face clearly. "So... what? It was waiting for both of us?"

His eyes flicked back down to her. "Seems that way."

She took a breath, trying to cool the fire still simmering beneath her skin. "Alright," she said, smoothing her hands down her sides. "Putting this moment on pause."

He arched a brow, clearly struggling not to smirk. "Temporarily."

"Temporarily," she echoed, lips twitching.

Without another word, she slipped her hand into his. The moment their fingers laced together, that invisible thread surged between them— stronger, brighter. Like a missing piece falling back into place.

They turned toward the light together.

Step by step, they moved across the ancient stone, deeper into the heart of the library—toward the source of the glow, the call, and whatever waited for them within.

They walked in silence at first, hand in hand, their steps echoing faintly in the vast chamber.

But the light never seemed to get closer.

It shimmered ahead like a mirage, pulsing softly, always just beyond reach. The towering shelves began to fall away around them, giving way to a wide-open expanse paved with smooth obsidian stone. Above them, the vaulted ceiling disappeared into shadow, as if the library had no end.

Seren slowed, her grip tightening on Cairn's. "This place is huge," she whispered.

He nodded, jaw tight, eyes scanning the glowing horizon. "Bigger than I thought. This shouldn't even be possible. It feels… like it's bending space."

Finally, after what felt like miles, the source of the light came into focus.

A tree.

Monolithic. Ethereal.

It rose from the heart of the chamber, its roots coiled deep into the stone floor, trunk carved with glowing veins of silver and gold. Its branches arched high, curling into a canopy that glittered with leaf-shaped motes of light, each one floating like a thought caught midair.

They both stopped, breath stolen.

The tree shimmered, alive and watching.

Cairn glanced at her, eyes wide, voice barely audible. "My little spark… you woke it."

Then—voice, not sound.

A presence filled their minds like warm wind through an open door.

"Come closer, my children."

Seren jerked slightly, eyes wide. Cairn's fingers flexed around hers.

"Did you—?" she started.

He nodded once, eyes never leaving the tree. "It's speaking to us."

The voice came again, both gentle and impossibly ancient.

"You've come through fire and shadow. Through silence and pain. The bond between you has opened what was sealed. Come. There is knowledge waiting. Memory. Truth."

Seren took a hesitant step forward. "It called us its children."

Cairn's jaw ticked. "That's… concerning."

But neither of them moved away.

The tree pulsed again—light curling like smoke around its trunk, around them.

"Come closer."

And together, they obeyed.

They approached the glowing tree, its light growing more intense with every step. The air around them shimmered, thick with magic—dense enough to taste. The floor felt softer now, like walking across the surface of a dream.

Then—light burst from the ground beneath them.

Two columns of blinding brilliance shot upward, one under each of them, separating them instantly.

Seren cried out as her feet lifted from the floor, her body suspended in the air. "Cairn!"

"I'm here!" he called back, muscles tensing as he reached for her—but his hand met only light. "I see you. I'm not letting you out of my sight again."

She floated, panicked, twisting in the beam as if it might drop her.

"I'm right here, Seren," he said, eyes locked on hers, jaw clenched. "I won't let anything happen to you."

But the light pulsed—once, then twice—and then her limbs went limp.

Seren's head fell back, her body suspended like a marionette with its strings cut. Her mouth parted in a soft gasp, and her eyes rolled upward, the silver in her tattoos flickering like dying embers.

"No—" Cairn snarled, the sound primal.

He lunged forward, trying to break free of the beam holding him in place, wings flaring instinctively.

"Let her go!" he roared. "She's not yours!"

But then the light flared again, and he felt it—warmth flooding his spine, curling up his nerves like vines. His muscles locked, breath caught, and he stilled in the air.

The last thing Seren heard before everything went silent was Cairn's voice—raw, furious, desperate.

"Seren!"

And then—nothing.

No sound. No body. No air.

Only light.

Only memory.

Only the tree.

There was no sense of falling.

It filled everything—every cell, every breath, every space between their thoughts. Seren floated weightless, suspended in brilliance, her body forgotten, her soul pulled toward something vast.

Cairn felt it too. Though they could no longer see each other, they hovered in perfect symmetry, drawn into the same vision without knowing it.

The tree spoke—not aloud, but into their very blood.

"My children."

The light shifted, shaped itself into columns and patterns, figures dancing like silhouettes of fire and starlight. Scenes played out in radiant gold and silver, glowing against a backdrop of endless white.

They saw two figures—one cloaked in shadow, wings like smoke, sword drawn against a tide of flame. The other, radiant as dawn, arms outstretched, light flowing from their palms to soothe the burning sky. Together, the two forms swirled and merged, their colors entwining into something entirely new. Not light. Not dark.

Balance.

"You are not coincidence. You are convergence," the voice echoed, soft but absolute. "Fated souls. Called across time and flame to meet in this moment. One the world has waited centuries to reunite."

Seren tried to respond—tried to question—but her voice didn't exist here. Only thought. Only feeling.

"You are not simply mates," the tree continued. "You are destiny tethered. Seren—the light. The savior. The selfless flame. Cairn—the dark. The shield. The voice of reason. Where one burns, the other tempers. Where one falters, the other stands."

Shapes in the light shifted again—images of Seren reaching for a soul across a Veil, Cairn standing before an army with his wings flared and eyes cold with purpose. They each fought differently—but always for others. Always in pain.

"Yours is a union the realms have never seen," the voice said, now split—one half warm and bright, the other low and crackling like coal. "Together, you symbolize revolution. Evolution. Together, you may save both worlds… or unmake them."

The light pulsed, and the image twisted—two trees, side by side, one blooming with silver leaves, the other scorched and growing anew from ash. In one future, the trees twined, their roots interlocked. In another, they burned to cinders. Both possibilities glowed equally bright.

"There is no certainty. No prophecy to bind you. Only choice. Only potential. Fate is a map—but not the road."

Seren's heart trembled inside the vision. She felt herself reaching toward something—anything—Cairn, maybe. A hand in the dark.

"You were chosen for what you gave up," the voice whispered. "What you bled for. What you lost. You are each caught between duty and love. Between what is right… and what is real."

The vision burned hotter, more brilliant.

"Your wings. Your markings. They bind more than skin. They mark you as the first balanced, mated pair in known history."

Cairn's pulse thundered. The words didn't feel like flattery. They felt like weight. Like responsibility forged into a crown.

"But nothing is sealed. Not yet. You may walk away. You may stay. You may rule. Or destroy. You may change everything… or let it all rot. The path is yours."

And finally—one last image: Seren and Cairn standing side by side, hands clasped, their eyes lit with fire. Behind them, a realm torn in two. Before them, a world waiting to be remade.

"Choose together," the tree finished. "Or not at all."

Then the light shattered like glass.

And they began to fall.

Seren and Cairn woke on their backs beneath the massive tree at the mountain's summit, where the library had once opened like a secret. The bark was sealed now. Silent. No light. No whispers. No answers. Just the cold kiss of morning air and the overwhelming echo of what they'd seen.

Seren sat up with a jolt, her breath sharp and shallow. Panic twisted in her gut. The sky spun.

Cairn stirred beside her and reached instinctively—just to touch her wrist, to ground her—but she jerked away like he'd burned her.

She scrambled to her feet, staggering back a few steps, eyes wild. "No. No, no, no—"

"Seren," he said gently, rising slowly, careful not to move too fast. Like she was a wounded animal poised to bolt.

"This is too much," she snapped, voice raw. "I didn't ask for any of this!"

He flinched, but said nothing.

"I didn't ask to be dragged into another realm. I didn't ask to be marked—as a child—by someone I didn't even know. I didn't ask to be… mated. To have my life rewritten in a vision I didn't agree to!" Her voice cracked on the last word.

She looked like she was about to run. Like she'd vanish into the mists and never look back.

And then Cairn dropped to his knees.

Just dropped.

Like the weight of it all had finally snapped his spine.

His wings shimmered once behind him—then unraveled like smoke in the wind, dissolving into nothing.

When he spoke, his voice was hoarse. Quiet. Like the air had been stolen from his lungs.

"Please," he rasped. "Don't leave me."

Seren froze.

"I know you're scared. I know it doesn't make sense. None of this does. I'm scared too," he said, staring at the ground like it might open and swallow him. "But fuck fate. Fuck destiny. The realms can crumble. Burn to ash. I don't care."

He looked up at her, eyes shining with something broken and holy all at once.

"I don't have words for what this is. I just know that when I'm not near you, I can't breathe. My heart—it's never… never—beat for anyone the way it beats for you. Not because of the vision. Not because of some divine pairing. Because it's you, Seren. My little spark. The only light I've ever chased."

He swallowed hard, shaking.

"And I will spend every breath I have protecting you. Loving you. Not because I'm meant to. Because I choose to. Because you're worth more than anything I've ever been given—and gods help me, I will never be enough. But I'll never stop trying."

Seren stared at him.

A man like him—immortal, terrifying, powerful—brought to his knees. Not in battle. Not in defeat. But for her.

A lump formed in her throat.

He had slain monsters. Crossed realms. Survived unspeakable things. And yet here he was—kneeling like a prayer, wings gone, voice cracked, and gaze open in a way that made her chest ache.

Tears welled in her eyes.

Without fully deciding to, she crossed the space between them. Dropped to her knees. Reached for his hand and laced her fingers with his. Her other hand gently tipped his chin until their eyes locked.

"I'm terrified," she whispered.

Cairn said nothing, letting her speak.

"I'm scared that what I'm feeling isn't real. That none of this is. That maybe I'm just… swept up in it. In you. That this bond—this thing tying us together—it's fate's way of screwing with me. And I've had enough of being lied to."

His eyes softened, a flicker of pain in them—but not surprise.

"I understand," he said quietly. "This is new for you. All of it. You've known me for… what? A handful of days?"

She nodded faintly.

"But I've known you for much longer." His voice carried a kind of reverence now. "It started as curiosity. A mortal child who wasn't afraid of shadows. A brave, strange little thing who saw what others ignored."

His thumb brushed across the back of her hand.

"You grew. And I watched. Not closely—not enough to interfere. But enough to see the truth of you. I saw you lose people. Get hurt. Keep going. You stayed kind even when the world gave you reasons not to be."

He leaned in, voice barely audible.

"And I knew I loved you the first time I saw you answer a 911 call. The way your voice calmed a stranger. The way your hands shook but you never hesitated. I didn't know what that feeling was at first. But it's love. It was love. Even before I knew what it meant."

Seren's breath trembled in her chest.

"I get that you don't know me," Cairn said, searching her face. "That to you, I'm just… this stranger who marked you in a moment you didn't understand. But this isn't just fate. This is real. I know it is. And I'll prove it to you. If you'll let me."

A tear slipped down her cheek.

She looked at him—this unshakable warrior, this broken man who wore his soul in his eyes—and then wordlessly crawled into his lap. Arms wrapped around his neck. Legs around his waist. His arms caught her without thought, instinctively holding her like he never meant to let go again.

Their foreheads touched.

And for a moment, they just breathed. Together. Alive. Real.

Then, slowly, like she was learning him one inch at a time, Seren leaned forward.

Her lips brushed his—light, curious, electric.

Then she deepened it just slightly, teeth catching his bottom lip in a soft, deliberate bite.

He exhaled sharply, eyes fluttering closed.

"I feel it," she whispered. "And I want to try. I want to give us a chance."

Cairn's grip on her tightened, his voice rough against her cheek. "Then I swear to you—we'll take this at your speed. Whatever that looks like. No pressure. No expectations."

She nodded into him, resting her head in the crook of his neck.

He pulled her closer, grounding them both in that promise.

After a moment, he kissed the crown of her head and murmured, "Can I get you out of this godsdamned swamp? Take you back to my home?"

Seren laughed softly, breath still shaky. "Yeah. Please. Get me out of this mossy hellscape."

He smiled. Then, gently—still cradling her—he rose to his feet.

And with her still wrapped around him, he opened a tear in the Veil, and they left the mountain. Together.

Chapter Sixteen: I Trust You

Seren

Cairn scooped Seren into his arms, cradling her gently against his chest. She clung to him instinctively, burying her face in the curve of his neck. A rush of heat and pressure pulsed through the air as he opened a seam between realms—lightless and soundless—and stepped through.

When they emerged, Seren kept her eyes squeezed shut.

She wasn't ready. For what, she wasn't sure. But her chest ached with the weight of everything—the visions, the choice, the words left unsaid. Her heart raced.

She exhaled slowly and cracked one eye open.

They stood in a quiet, shadowed home. The walls were smooth stone veined with faint threads of light. It was dark and clean—minimalist, but not sterile. Purposeful. Built with intention. Nothing soft or indulgent, but no part of it unkind.

Cairn set her gently on her feet, but didn't move away. His hand lingered at her back like he couldn't quite let go. That tether between them buzzed, still there, still strong.

Seren looked up at him.

He reached out and brushed his fingers along her jawline, pausing at the teardrop-shaped scar that lived on her.

"I could remove this," he said softly. "Looking at it now… it would be easy. Or I know a healer who—"

"No," she interrupted. Her voice was quiet but firm. "It's part of me. Part of our history. I don't want to forget that."

His expression softened with something reverent. "I promised to take this at your pace," he said. "And I'll keep that promise to my last breath. No matter what that pace is. I'd be lying if I said it won't be hard. But if I ever do something that feels too much—too fast—just tell me. I won't be angry. I won't be hurt."

Seren's throat tightened. No one had ever said that to her before. Never meant it.

She stood on her toes and pressed a soft kiss to his lips.

Cairn blinked, surprised—but only for a moment. One hand found the back of her neck; the other threaded gently into her hair. She sighed into him, melting into the kiss. He responded with a quiet growl in his throat, deepening it slowly, reverently. His lips parted, drawing her bottom lip between his.

When he finally pulled away, he rested his forehead against hers.

"You must be starving."

"I don't feel hungry," she murmured. "But I know I should be. I just..." Her gaze flicked around the unfamiliar room. "I'm kind of afraid of whatever food exists here."

Cairn chuckled. "I can't promise it's on par with your favorite gas station junk food, but how do pancakes and bacon sound?"

Her stomach growled in response.

She looked down, cheeks flushing. "Guess that answers that."

But as she moved to follow him, her breath caught.

"Cairn!"

He turned instantly, alert. "What's wrong?"

She winced. "Sorry—I'm okay. I just... when I landed here, I was in the middle of a conversation with Marisol."

"The EMT?"

"Yeah. She must be terrified. Is there any way I can send her a message?"

His expression softened again. "Of course. While I cook, write her a note. I'll deliver it."

Her stomach clenched. "You're leaving?"

"No," he said quickly. "The house is warded. No one can enter without my permission. I won't leave. I'll open a small rift—just enough to toss it through. You can even fold it into a paper airplane."

That earned a short laugh from her. "Thanks."

He handed her a piece of parchment and a strange, smoky-looking pen.

"What is this?"

"Liquid ash. More stable in this realm than ink."

"Huh." She shrugged and perched at the table to write.

Marisol,

I'm so sorry if I scared you. I'm okay. I'm in the other… place. I found Cairn. He's safe, and I'm with him. Please tell my supervisor I've had an extended emergency. I'll reach out when I can.

Thank you for being my friend—and for believing me.

—Seren

She folded the paper into a neat little airplane and brought it into the kitchen, where Cairn was already at work.

The kitchen resembled something human, but the heat didn't come from a stove. Instead, flat stones glowed on the counter, veined with what looked like molten gold.

"Do those ever go out?" she asked, eyeing them warily.

"Not here," Cairn replied. "If I took them into another realm… they'd probably explode."

Seren raised her brows. "Comforting."

"They're stable," he added with a small smile. "Safe."

A few minutes later, breakfast was ready.

"Table or couch?" he asked, handing her a plate.

"Couch," she said quickly. "If that's okay."

"Of course."

She curled up on one end of a black sofa, tucking her feet under her. Cairn settled beside her, his plate in hand.

They ate in quiet for a few moments—comfortable, close.

And for the first time in days, Seren felt almost okay.

Seren broke the silence first. "Oh—I finished my note to Marisol. Here." She handed him the paper airplane, careful not to smudge the silvery ash writing.

Cairn took it gently, brushing her fingers in the process. He smiled—just a little—and raised his free hand.

With a slow, practiced motion, he drew a shape in the air, fingers weaving through space like they were tracing invisible lines. On the final swipe, reality cracked with a low shimmer, and a small rift split open in the center of the living room.

Seren leaned forward, squinting to see through it. "Can I see her?"

But there was no apartment on the other side. Just a swirling vortex of black and violet, shifting like a storm trapped in glass.

"It's not a window," Cairn said. "It's more… directional intent."

Seren tilted her head. "So it just… lands where you tell it to?"

"Roughly," he replied, turning the paper plane toward the rift. "Except this one won't land."

He tossed it in with casual precision.

"It's going to crash straight into Marisol's forehead," he added with a wicked grin. "That way she won't miss it."

Seren laughed, nearly snorting into her pancakes. "You're evil."

Cairn leaned back with a satisfied smirk. "She'll appreciate the flair."

Seren grinned and returned to her plate, heart a little lighter than before.

She hadn't realized how hungry she'd been until she glanced down and found her plate completely empty.

Cairn raised an eyebrow. "Would you like more? I'm out of bacon, but I can scrounge something else up."

She shook her head, patting her stomach. "No, I'm stuffed. Thank you."

He nodded, collecting both their plates and carrying them to the sink. When he returned, he stood in front of her, hand outstretched.

"We're both covered in grime and gods-know-what," he said. "Come on. I'll show you the shower. You can go first."

Seren hesitated for only a second before placing her hand in his. He helped her to her feet and led her down the hallway and into his room.

It was smaller than she expected. Not cramped—just… minimal. The bed was built for one, neatly made. The space was clean, orderly. Like everything in Cairn's world, it was dark but oddly welcoming. He moved across the room to a door near the foot of the bed and opened it.

The bathroom was stunning.

Obsidian walls shimmered like black glass, catching the low light in gleaming waves. On one side of the room sat a massive bathtub—more like a small hot tub, really. On the other side, a walk-in shower enclosed in clear crystal glass, crowned by a rainfall-style head carved from stone.

Cairn turned to her, voice soft. "Use anything you need. I'll be in the living room with the door open—just yell if something's wrong."

Seren nodded, and he gave her a final look before quietly stepping out, leaving the bathroom door cracked behind him.

She turned to the mirror and stilled.

Her wings were still out, full and radiant.

It struck her how quickly they had begun to feel… natural. Like they had always been part of her. The same curling script carved into Cairn's wings now adorned hers in elegant, silvery lines that mirrored her arm markings.

She tried to fold them away—flexing, shifting—but they refused to vanish. Maybe she hadn't figured out that trick yet. Either way, it was going to make showering interesting.

At least they didn't seem to damage her clothes.

With a sigh, she pulled off her ruined hoodie, then her shirt, socks, and jeans, awkwardly maneuvering around her wings. Stripped down to her underwear, she faced the mirror again.

God, she looked wrecked.

Her eyes were rimmed with exhaustion. Her hair was a tangled mess, full of twigs and god-knows-what. Scrapes dotted her arms and legs like she'd lost a wrestling match with a blackberry bush.

She picked the debris from her hair as best she could, then turned on the shower. Steam began to curl into the air.

The bra and underwear came off last, discarded onto the small pile of ruined clothing.

She stepped into the stream and sighed in relief.

The water was perfect—warm, clean, grounding.

She ran her hands through her hair, finding only one kind of soap. Definitely a guy's. No conditioner in sight. She laughed softly to herself.

"Well," she muttered, "at least he doesn't have a secret girlfriend stashing pink razors and floral shampoo."

Still, the soap did the trick. She scrubbed her skin as best she could— but the moment she reached for her wings, she froze.

They were… unreachable.

No matter how she twisted or flexed, she couldn't quite angle herself to clean them. Every attempt ended in frustration. Her wings were wide, sensitive, and completely outside her normal range of motion.

She groaned and dropped her head back under the water.

"Of course," she muttered. "Magic wings and no magical loofah."

Seren gave up trying to reach her wings. Frustrated, she let out a huff and called out, "Cairn?"

There was a beat of silence—and then the sound of rapid footsteps.

The bathroom door flung open with a clatter.

Cairn stumbled inside with one hand clamped over his eyes and the other outstretched like a blind man navigating a maze. His voice was tight, breathless. "What's wrong? I'm here—are you hurt?"

Seren blinked, stunned. Then she burst out laughing.

"Cairn—no! No, I'm fine. It's not that."

He paused, lowering his hand just enough to peek between his fingers. "What?"

"I—" she tried not to giggle again. "I can't reach my wings. They're too big. I tried to clean them, and I just... can't."

He exhaled hard, shoulders sagging in relief. "Gods, Seren. I thought—" He dragged a hand down his face. "You scared the shit out of me."

"Sorry," she said with a sheepish grin. "But, um... will you help me?"

Cairn hesitated. "Help you... wash your wings?"

She nodded.

He kept his eyes covered. "I'm going to walk forward now. Very carefully. Try not to let me faceplant into the wall."

"You're clear," she said through a laugh.

He moved clumsily, bumping into the counter with a grunt. Seren bit her lip to keep from laughing again.

"You can uncover your eyes," she offered. "It's okay. I'm sure."

"Are you certain?" His voice was hoarse now.

"Yes." Her voice was softer. "I trust you."

He dropped his hand.

Their eyes met.

And for a moment, neither moved.

Cairn's gaze flicked downward—slow, reverent—and Seren watched as his pupils dilated, his breath catching in his throat. His hands flew to the front of his pants, trying—and failing—to hide the reaction his body had clearly decided for him.

He cleared his throat, trying to speak, but the words caught in his chest before they finally tumbled out.

"I've dreamt of having you here for so long," he said, voice raw. "But seeing you—gods, seeing you like this. Beautiful. Naked. Dripping wet in my shower…" He shook his head, like he was trying to keep control of himself. "It's hard to contain myself. But I'm going to try."

Seren's cheeks flushed, but her smile was soft—shy, but certain. She stepped closer to the glass, wings shifting slightly behind her in the steam.

"Then take off your clothes," she whispered. "And join me."

Cairn hesitated only for a moment after Seren's invitation. Then, wordlessly, he reached for the clasp of his armor. The pieces came off one by one—blackened plates clicking against one another before being set gently aside. Beneath, he wore a dark, fitted shirt and trousers, both damp with the weight of Ashrot's humidity. He stripped the rest of the way, every motion quiet, deliberate.

Seren had turned her back to the glass. The soft hiss of the water muffled the sound of him stepping into the shower behind her.

She didn't move at first.

Then—slowly, steadily—she took one step back, closing the distance between them until her bare skin met his. The heat of his body was distinct from the warmth of the water. It was a different kind of fire entirely.

Cairn didn't speak. His hands lifted slowly—giving her every chance to stop him. When she didn't, he let his palms settle gently on her hips, his thumbs brushing just over the sharp curve of her hip bones. The contact was feather-light, reverent, as if he were afraid she'd vanish.

Seren's breath caught in her throat.

She turned her face just enough to glance over her shoulder.

And there he was.

Water slid down his bare skin, tracing the sharp lines of his chest, the etched planes of his stomach. His dark hair was soaked and plastered back, making his lilac eyes even more vivid, their glow more intense. He looked down at her like she was a miracle. A question answered. A prayer returned.

His pupils were wide, drinking her in. Consuming her.

"Gods," he whispered, more to himself than to her. "You're more than I ever imagined."

Her throat tightened, the moment heavy with something she couldn't name.

He hadn't moved except for the slow, hypnotic motion of his thumbs. Like he was learning her shape by memory.

"You can touch me," she whispered, her voice barely audible over the spray of the shower. "I want you to."

His hands slid up—not greedy, not rushed—just exploring. Mapping her waist, her ribs, the swell of her lower back. His touch was warm, sure, full of restraint that made her knees weak.

He leaned in, his lips near her ear but not touching.

"If I start," he murmured, his voice low and rough, "I don't know that I'll be able to stop."

She turned fully toward him now, chest brushing his. The water poured down around them like a curtain.

"Then let's just start," she whispered back. "And we'll see where it goes."

Seren's heart thudded, her pulse everywhere.

She reached up, fingers sliding gently over his jaw, his cheekbone, curling around the back of his neck.

"You don't have to hold back," she said softly. "Not with me."

A flicker of tension left his shoulders. His fingers flexed slightly at her waist.

"Are you sure?" he murmured, eyes searching hers.

She nodded. "I'm sure."

He bent his head. Their foreheads touched. For a moment, that was enough. Just the shared breath. The closeness. The raw, unsaid emotion hanging between them.

Then Seren closed the distance.

Their mouths met—slow and searching, like they were trying to map the shape of a feeling too big to name. He kissed her like he was starving and terrified of breaking her all at once. She melted into him, her hands curling into his wet hair, her wings shivering at the contact.

When they finally broke apart, their foreheads still touching, Seren's voice was barely more than a breath.

"I feel like I've waited my whole life for this."

Cairn's hands slid up her spine, careful of her wings. "Then let's not rush a single moment."

Cairn stepped closer, his voice a low murmur against the steam. "I'll use my hands. A cloth might be too rough—and honestly, I want to feel them. See if I can get that little moan out of you again."

Seren rolled her eyes, but her pulse quickened. She didn't object.

She turned her back to him, and he lathered the soap in his hands. When his fingers met her wings, it wasn't just cleansing—it was reverent. Gentle, methodical strokes traced along the ridges and curves, easing away grime and tension. It felt... good. Soothing. Nothing she couldn't manage.

Until he reached the arch.

From her shoulder blade to the wingtip, he traced a slow, deliberate path—and her knees nearly buckled. The moan slipped out of her throat before she could stop it, raw and aching.

He didn't stop this time.

Cairn stepped in behind her, sliding one hand to her waist, the other to the small of her back. He pulled her against him with a possessive urgency, positioning her just enough forward to reach the upper curves of her wings again. His palm moved deliberately, gliding across the joint where wing met spine, sending shocks of pleasure through her core.

Her body pressed tighter to his—right against the hard line of his arousal, thick and unyielding.

He froze.

She didn't.

"Why'd you stop?" she whispered, breathless. "It's okay… Keep going."

Cairn let out a low, feral sound in his throat. "Seren…" he warned. "If you moan again—or grind against me like that—I'm not going to be able to hold back. I will bend you over, right here, and take you."

Seren exhaled, her breath shaky but steadying. She tilted her head just enough to glance at him over her shoulder. "I think my wings are clean enough."

Cairn arched a brow. "You sure?"

She nodded, her voice husky. "Your turn to be soaped up."

That grin—dangerous and boyish all at once—spread across his face. With a small flare of his shoulders, Cairn's wings unfolded in a rush of heat and power, stretching wide and dark behind him. The runes across them glowed faintly, a silver echo of hers. He handed her the soap, then gently spun them so she stood under the stream now, and he stepped just outside of it.

Facing away from her, he waited.

Seren studied the expanse of his back, the broad muscles, the sleek obsidian shimmer of his wings, the way the mist curled around him like he was carved from the steam itself.

She tapped his shoulder. "You're going to have to kneel. I can't reach them otherwise."

He let out a deep, playful chuckle. "Yes, ma'am."

Then he knelt without hesitation, wings still high and open, like an offering.

Seren's breath caught.

She stepped forward and poured soap into her hands, then placed them on the upper arches of his wings. The texture was unlike anything else—like silk-wrapped obsidian, warm and alive beneath her fingers. He shivered when she touched the base, just above where they connected to his spine.

Her strokes were gentle at first, more methodical than seductive. But the way he sighed beneath her hands, the tension coiled in his shoulders, the way his head bowed forward—it all made her feel powerful.

She trailed one hand down the inner edge of his wing, curving with the lines of ancient runes, while her other pressed lightly into the center of his back. His breath hitched.

When she leaned in, her lips brushing the sensitive skin near the base of his wing, she felt him pulse with restrained need.

"Seren," he rasped, voice hoarse. "You're going to undo me."

"Good," she whispered. "Then we're even."

He tilted his head just enough for her to see his profile—his eyes nearly black with dilation, his mouth parted in a struggle to keep control. She traced her fingers slowly down the length of his wing again, and his hands clenched at his thighs.

"You like that?" she murmured, her mouth dangerously close to his ear.

"You have no idea," he growled.

She leaned closer, pressing herself to his back now, bare skin to skin, her wings fluttering involuntarily at the contact.

And in that moment, Cairn exhaled hard, muscles trembling, and muttered through gritted teeth, "If you keep going, I swear I will lose every shred of my restraint and take you right here in this shower."

Seren's lips brushed his neck. "Maybe I want that."

He turned his head toward her slowly, gaze blazing.

"Say the word," he said, voice a low promise, "and I'll worship you, my little spark."

"Stand up," Seren said softly.

Cairn obeyed without question. He would do anything she asked. Still facing away from her, he stood tall under the water, wings slightly flexed.

Seren squeezed more soap into her palms and began with his back—strong, broad, and streaked with old scars. She took her time, tracing the lines of his shoulder blades, down the ridges of his spine, across the curve of his arms.

Then she stepped closer, pressing her body flush to his. The heat of him soaked into her skin, making her breath hitch.

Her hands slid around his torso, exploring the planes of his chest—firm and warm, rising with each breath. His muscles twitched beneath her touch, and a low, involuntary rumble escaped him.

Slowly, deliberately, her hands trailed lower until she found his erection. Hard and waiting. She gasped as her fingers closed around him—and realized they didn't touch.

Cairn let out a raspy breath, his gaze dropping to watch her hand. She began to stroke him, slow and steady, sliding from base to tip with a deliberate rhythm.

He exhaled sharply, his head tipping forward like her touch had unraveled something deep within. The mix of heat, pressure, and soap was quickly pushing him to the edge.

But then—his hands closed gently over hers, stilling her movements.

He turned in her arms until they were face to face again, water cascading down both of them.

"I want to tell you something," he said quietly.

Seren blinked, heart dipping at the change in tone. "You can tell me anything."

He rested his forehead against hers and released a shaky breath. "I haven't been with anyone since I took the Ashmarked Oath. That was… centuries ago."

Seren's eyes widened, but she said nothing—only held his gaze.

"One of the side effects of the oath is a dulling of… drive. You stop craving closeness. Solitude becomes the default. I haven't been touched in ages, Seren. Then you appeared, and now all I want is to be close to you. To feel your skin against mine."

He swallowed hard. "I might just be… a little out of practice."

A smile tugged at her lips, gentle and knowing. "I'm out of practice too. Doesn't change how badly I want you."

He smiled back—soft, reverent. "I don't want the first time we're truly together to be here. Not like this. Not rushed, not standing."

He cupped her face with both hands. "Come to bed with me. Let me show you what you mean to me—what this means. Let me worship you the way you deserve."

Seren nodded.

That was all the answer he needed.

Cairn reached past her and turned off the water. The sudden quiet left only the sound of their breathing—and the steady thud of her heartbeat, loud in her ears.

He didn't release her. One hand remained curled gently around her waist, the other sliding to the curve of her back as he helped guide her out of the shower. Water dripped from both of them, steam swirling around like a Veil.

Still keeping close contact, he reached for a soft, black towel and began to dry her—slowly. He moved with the same quiet intensity that defined everything about him. She let him, eyes fluttering closed as his hands traveled the length of her arms, down her sides, over her hips and thighs. There was nothing rushed. Nothing impersonal. Just the weight of his presence, the patience in his touch, like every inch of her mattered.

When she was dry, he took a second towel for himself, never straying far. His arm brushed her shoulder as he worked. His hip pressed against hers as he leaned forward. She realized with a flicker of warmth that he needed her closeness just as much as she craved his.

He took her hand in his—warm, calloused, grounding—and led her to the bed.

The sheets were dark and soft, the room glowing gently from a stone embedded in the far wall, casting shadows that danced across his bare back.

He paused, then carefully lifted her into his arms again. Seren instinctively wrapped her legs around his waist, her arms loosely around his shoulders. He carried her to the bed like she was something precious, irreplaceable.

When he lowered her to the mattress, he didn't pull away. He set her down gently on her back, her legs still wrapped around him, their bodies flush.

He looked at her as if trying to memorize everything—every freckle, every breath, every flicker of emotion in her eyes.

Then he leaned down, lips brushing her neck. One kiss. Then another— trailing lower, to her collarbone, the center of her chest. His breath was warm, his touch feather-light, as though this was worship and not just desire.

Cairn's lips wandered across her breast, unhurried, until they found her nipple—already peaked with anticipation. His mouth closed over it as his fingers found the other, his tongue swirling in slow, deliberate circles before he gently grazed her with his teeth. Seren gasped, the sound melting into a moan.

His hand lingered on her breast, teasing in rhythm, while his mouth blazed a slow trail downward—each kiss more deliberate than the last. He pressed a gentle kiss to her navel, pausing like it was a holy place.

Seren thought he would stop there—until he sank to his knees in front of her, lifting her legs to rest over his shoulders, nestled between the graceful arch of his wings.

At last, he ran his tongue in a slow, deliberate stroke from the base of her core to the peak. Her back arched instinctively, a moan slipping free before she could stop it.

Cairn let out a low growl and pressed his hand against her lower abdomen, grounding her as if afraid she might vanish beneath him. Then his fingers replaced his mouth for a moment—one, then two sliding inside her with care. His mouth resumed its path with renewed hunger, and the combination of his tongue and fingers had her unraveling fast.

"Seren," he murmured, voice raw and reverent, "don't hold back. Let me have it—all of you. I want to taste every part of your pleasure."

That undid her.

Her climax struck like lightning, blinding and consuming. Her vision blurred, filled with nothing but lilac eyes and the flicker of smoky wings surrounding her like a storm.

"Good girl," Cairn breathed against her skin, voice rough with reverence. He rose slowly, sliding up her body until they were nose to nose. "You taste like the sweetest treat I've ever had."

Seren reached for him, pulling him into a deep kiss. Her tongue swept across his lips, tasting herself on him, and feeling a fresh wave of heat bloom low in her belly.

Cairn pulled back just enough to look into her eyes, his breath still ragged, lips flushed from her kiss. His hands rested on either side of her hips, anchoring him, holding himself still with visible restraint.

"Do you want to stop here?" he asked, voice low. "We don't have to go further. I'll wait as long as you need, Seren. I meant it."

She reached up, cupping his face between her palms, and shook her head with gentle urgency. "No. I'm not done," she said, breathless but certain. "I want you. All of you. I've never been more sure of anything."

His pupils flared again, dark and dilated, and for a moment, he just stared at her—like he was memorizing the shape of her soul.

"Are you sure?" he asked again, barely more than a whisper. "Because once I have you, I don't think I'll ever be able to let go."

Seren smiled, thumb tracing along his jaw. "Then don't."

Something in him broke open at that. His control, his reverence—it all remained, but now it burned hotter, deeper, with a kind of holy desperation.

He leaned down and kissed her again—slow and deep, like she was his first breath after drowning.

Cairn gently guided her knees together, then tipped her onto her side, positioning her carefully on the bed. He moved to the edge, one hand gripping her hip as he pulled her slowly toward him.

"Are you comfortable?" he asked, voice gentle and soothing.

"Yes," she whispered, her eyes locked on his.

"I'm going to go slow," he murmured, brushing his thumb along her thigh. "Let me know if anything feels off. I'll stop."

She nodded, a soft smile curving her lips.

Cairn lined himself up with her entrance and eased forward—just a fraction of his length at first. Seren gasped, biting her lip, the sensation intense and electric.

"You're so wet," he groaned, voice thick with restraint. "So tight."

He pushed another inch inside her, his jaw clenching as he fought to hold himself back. Bit by bit, he worked deeper, checking her expression with every slow thrust. Just when she thought he couldn't possibly go further, he buried the last of himself inside her.

The stretch had her moaning, spine arching into him. Cairn paused, letting her adjust, then began to move—slow, steady strokes that built heat between them with every pass.

But then, suddenly, he stopped.

Seren whimpered. "Why did you stop? I was enjoying that."

He leaned over her, his lips ghosting her ear. "Because I want to see you. I want you on top of me, so I can watch every part of you come undone."

In one fluid motion, he lay back and pulled her with him, guiding her to straddle his hips. Seren giggled at the sudden shift, placing her hands on his chest to steady herself. She leaned in and kissed him—slow and soft—before reaching between them to guide him back inside her.

She eased down onto him inch by inch until he was fully seated within her.

"Holy fuck, Seren," Cairn rasped, head tipping back as his hands gripped her waist.

She began to move, setting a gentle rhythm, using his body for balance. His hands supported her, guiding her hips to find their perfect sync. His eyes never left her face.

As the tension built, Seren tipped her head back, closing her eyes as the wave approached.

"Cairn, I want you to finish with me."

His voice was hoarse when he answered. "Open your eyes. Look at me while you fall."

She did. Their gazes locked—an unspoken tether pulling them tighter than any vow.

And then her release shattered through her like a storm. Cairn gripped her hips, driving into her one last time as he followed, her name tumbling from his lips as he spilled inside her.

Seren collapsed onto Cairn's chest, both of them breathless, their bodies slick with warmth and exertion. Her pulse thudded against his, and for a moment, it was the only sound between them—two hearts beating in perfect synchrony, like matching war drums finally at rest.

She giggled quietly against his skin. "I think we're going to need another shower after that."

Cairn let out a deep, satisfied hum. "The shower can wait."

With gentle care, he rolled her onto her side, mindful of her wings. He moved to face her, wrapping his arms around her like a shield. Seren tucked her head beneath his chin, her cheek resting over his heart. His wings unfurled and folded around her, and hers instinctively did the same, weaving together in a silken tangle of black and silver—like a cocoon built for two.

In that stillness, with their bodies tangled and their souls aligned, sleep claimed them—deep and dreamless, like neither had known in years. For the first time in what felt like lifetimes, they rested. Together.

Chapter Seventeen: A Father's Secrets

Seren

The dream came like a warning. Not of what could happen—but what would, if she turned away.

Redmill burned. Not in pieces—all of it. The sky poured ash, and the wind howled like sirens. Seren stood in the middle of the street, barefoot and shivering, unable to tell if she was breathing smoke or memory. Flames licked up the sides of the dispatch center, its steel bones creaking as the roof collapsed.

Inside, through the shattered glass, she saw herself. Dozens of versions, all seated at the console. All speaking at once. "911, what is your emergency?" Layered voices distorted, echoing in loops until they became something ancient. Something knowing.

Behind her, a tree grew through the pavement. Towering, scorched at the roots, but alive. Two branches arched like outstretched arms. One path burned red. The other shimmered with silver light.

She didn't move.

"You are the fulcrum," a voice whispered. "The Veil has no anchor without you."

She stepped back—toward the silver.

And the world shattered.

The tree blackened. The silver burned. The street cracked and fell away.

"You chose silence," the voice hissed. "So now, they scream."

The sky screamed.

She turned—and saw Marisol. But her best friend crumbled like ash when Seren reached for her, scattering into the wind.

Then came the fire. But it did not come at her. It came from her.

The flames roared from her fingertips, her mouth, her skin—turning buildings to cinder, people to dust. Her eyes glowed like molten glass. And at the center of it all—a figure with lilac eyes emerged from the fire, hand outstretched.

Cairn.

She reached for him—and he smiled. A small, soft thing, filled with relief.

But the moment her fingers touched his—he burned.

Turned to ash in her hands.

His voice echoed in the fire: "This is the cost."

Seren woke with a scream, lurching upright. The motion made her stomach twist, and she nearly vomited.

Her head pounded.

Something warm and wet dripped down her lip. Blood. A nosebleed. The pillow was stained. The sheet stuck to her back with sweat.

Footsteps.

Cairn burst into the room. His expression dropped when he saw her. "Seren."

She swiped at the blood, trying to sit up straighter. "It was just a nightmare. I'm fine."

He wasn't amused. He crossed the room, brushing his fingers over her cheek. They came away red.

"Stay here," he said.

He vanished into the Veil.

The healer arrived not five minutes later. Slippers. Pajama pants. A cloak thrown over a loose shirt. Sleep still clung to his eyes.

"Always at night with you, Evergrave," he muttered, rubbing his face.

Then he saw Seren—and froze.

He stared, not just at her face, but at the wings folded behind her. Mortal. Marked. Something impossible.

"By the old fires…" he whispered.

Seren sat curled on the couch in a black silk robe, a towel pressed to her nose. The healer stepped forward slowly, eyes wide with disbelief.

"What did you see before you woke?" he asked.

Seren hesitated. "Fire. Cities. Choices. Like I'm standing on something about to break."

He hummed and moved closer, reaching for her hand.

A faint sigil pulsed on her palm—not Pyric. Older. Wilder. It vanished almost instantly.

"She's being warned," the healer said. "The Veil has something in store for her."

Cairn pulled the healer aside beneath a lava-lit arch, voices low.

"Kirel," Cairn said, tone tight. "You see the wings?"

"I see them," Kirel replied. "She's mortal. And winged. That shouldn't be possible."

"It's the Veil," Cairn said. "It's… changing her."

"This isn't just a rift," Kirel murmured, glancing back toward the firelight. "The Veil's responding to her. Testing her. Pushing. It hasn't leaned mortal in a thousand years—if ever."

"She's not Pyric."

"She's not meant to be. But if she turns away… it could all collapse."

Cairn's jaw tightened. "We keep this between us."

Kirel nodded slowly. "I'm Ashmarked. I follow the Veil, not the Court. And the Veil chose her." He met Cairn's eyes. "I'll keep her secret—for as long as I can."

Later, she sat near the fire, wrapped in a blanket. Cairn settled beside her.

"You okay?"

"Define okay."

They both laughed, but it didn't last.

Seren broke the silence. "Tell me more about you."

Cairn looked at her, confused. "Well, uh… what do you want to know?"

"Let's make it a game," she said. "Question for question."

He tilted his head. "Alright. You start."

"Okay… do all Ashmarked have the same powers?"

He shook his head. "No. The Veil burns each of us differently. Some have gifts rooted in combat—flame-casting, soul-forging, elemental strength. Others, like Kirel, lean into spiritual or healing arts. His magic is restorative, but in a pinch, it can be… weaponized. Turned deadly. All Ashmarked are made to endure—but how we fight, how we serve, varies."

"And you?" she asked.

"I was forged for war—fire in my hands, steel at my command, the Veil bending when I demand it. But more than that, I can see what others can't.

Through the skin of worlds, I glimpse the lost: souls adrift, lives slipping between realms. Where others grasp in darkness, I see their glow. I drag them through and bend them into service. That's why I am called first. That's why the King trusts me. Because nothing truly escapes my sight."

He paused, then asked, "What scares you the most?"

She blinked. "Losing people. Losing myself. Becoming something I can't undo."

"You won't," he said softly. "Not while I breathe."

"My turn," she said. "Why did you take the Oath?"

He hesitated. "I don't remember the day I took it. That's part of it—you bleed out your past. My friends from before said I never wanted it. But I believed in protecting the Veil. I still do. Even if it costs everything."

"Do you ever regret it?"

"Sometimes. But I've seen what lives on the other side of neglect. What happens when no one's watching the gates."

He leaned back slightly, the firelight flickering across his face. "My question: What do you want most, Seren?"

She hesitated. "Peace. Not just quiet—but knowing I did something that mattered. That this pain wasn't random. That I helped someone. Maybe saved them."

He studied her. "I think you already have."

Her lips curved into a faint smile. "My turn again."

Cairn smiled back.

"How old are you?" she asked.

Cairn laughed. "Since I took the Oath, I lost count at 500 years."

Seren's jaw dropped.

Cairn reached out and gently pushed her mouth closed with one finger. "You're cute when you glitch."

"Your turn."

"Have you ever wanted to run away?" he asked.

She exhaled. "Every day. But not anymore."

"Neither do I."

They leaned closer. Seren rested her head on Cairn's shoulder.

"I still feel lost sometimes," she murmured. "Like I don't know this world—or you. But I'm starting to think… I'm exactly where I'm supposed to be."

Cairn's voice dropped. "You are." He pressed a kiss to the top of her head.

Seren closed her eyes. Sleep tugged gently at her thoughts.

Cairn stood slowly and scooped her into his arms. She murmured something, half-asleep, as he carried her to bed.

He crawled in behind her, arms tightening around her waist.

"I swear," he whispered against her temple. "Until my last breath."

And he finally let himself really rest.

Sunlight filtered through the sheer curtains, golden and soft—but it felt wrong.

Seren blinked awake slowly, the weight of unfamiliar sheets tangled around her legs. For a second, she forgot where she was. Then the warmth beside her stirred, and everything came rushing back.

Cairn.

His arm was still wrapped around her waist, palm pressed against her stomach like he couldn't bear the thought of her slipping away again. His breath was steady behind her, chest rising and falling in sync with hers. And their wings—hers silver, his black—lay draped over one another like they didn't care about the rules of the world.

Her heart ached at how safe she felt.

Which was exactly the problem.

She eased herself out from under his arm. He stirred but didn't wake. With one last glance over her shoulder, Seren tiptoed across the room and gathered her clothes. She didn't know how long she had been away from home. It could have been just hours, or days.

She had to go back.

Marisol. The dispatch center. Her house.

Unfinished business—things she couldn't ignore no matter how tempting it was to stay wrapped in Cairn's quiet strength.

By the time Cairn woke and found her fully dressed, standing by the obsidian-framed window, she was already halfway to the decision.

"You're leaving," he said quietly.

Seren didn't turn. "Not for good."

His footsteps were silent behind her. When he spoke again, it was with a note of strain in his voice. "You don't have to go back yet. The realm is unstable. You're not safe there alone."

She turned now, looking up at him. "I'm not safe here either. Not until I finish what's been haunting me since this started. Someone's been in my house, Cairn. Then there was the guy in the skin suit. My world doesn't feel like mine anymore."

Cairn's brow furrowed. "Wait—skin suit?"

She exhaled sharply. "Yeah. I went to the gas station by the highway— normal guy who works there, always wears a hat that says 'Rather Be Anywhere Else'. Except this time it wasn't him. It was someone else. Too tall, too smooth. His fingers looked like they belonged to a demon. He just stared at me, and didn't speak at all. Like he'd studied how to be human and still got it wrong."

Cairn's expression darkened, jaw flexing.

"I tried to ignore it, but the moment I turned my back, I felt it. That wrongness. Then later I got a 911 call from the gas station. They found the regular cashier dead behind the counter. The officers found what they thought was a literal skin suit. They even had Marisol confirm that's what they were seeing."

She shivered. "That's when I ran. Straight to Marisol's. I didn't even know where else to go. I just knew I didn't want to be home alone."

A pause. Then he nodded, jaw tightening. "If you go, you go under heavy protections. You don't breathe without one of my marks on you."

She offered a ghost of a smile. "So… clingy."

"I'll take that as a yes."

Cairn stood in front of her now, silent but unwavering, his arms crossed like it was the only thing keeping him from pulling her back into them.

"I'll only be gone a couple days," Seren whispered.

His eyes searched hers. "A couple days is enough to get hurt."

She stepped closer, placing her hand flat against his chest. "I'm not walking into this blind. I've faced worse."

"No," he said gently, "you haven't."

The words weren't a warning. They were a promise. And it made something cold trickle down her spine.

Seren exhaled shakily, blinking back tears. "I need to go. Please don't make this harder."

Cairn didn't speak. Instead, he reached up and brushed his thumb beneath her eye, wiping away the tear she hadn't realized had fallen.

"I won't let anything happen to you," he said. "Not there. Not here. I'll feel you the moment something shifts."

"You'll feel me?" she asked softly.

He nodded. "Through the bond. If you're in danger… if you call for me, I'll come."

Seren leaned forward and pressed a kiss to his chest, then another to his lips. It was slow and lingering—full of the things she didn't have time to say. He kissed her back like he understood every word of it.

When they finally parted, Cairn stepped back and lifted his hand.

With a quick, precise motion, the space in front of him shimmered, splitting open with a quiet hiss. Beyond it, her world waited—dull and pale in contrast to the warmth she was leaving behind.

Seren hesitated at the threshold. "Don't forget to eat something."

Cairn huffed a small, reluctant laugh. "Only if you do."

And then she stepped through.

The air on the other side was colder, sharper—heavy with silence and the scent of old wood and wheat.

Seren found herself standing on her own porch, surrounded by the gentle creak of the boards and the faint rustle of wind across the fields.

She blinked, trying to orient herself. Everything looked normal. Her boots scuffed the welcome mat. The house stood quiet in the dawn light.

But something felt different.

She took a step forward—and hit something invisible.

It wasn't a wall. Not exactly. But there was a shimmer, a faint buzz that danced across her skin like static. A Veil of Power. Protective. Old.

And then her vision swam. A wave of pressure slammed behind her eyes.

She staggered, one hand bracing against the porch railing.

Hot liquid dripped past her upper lip.

She swiped at it—and her palm came away slick and red.

Another nosebleed. Worse than before.

They were getting more frequent. More violent.

She could feel it now—like something inside her was shifting, fracturing, readying. The closer she got to answers, to truth, to choice... the more her body reacted.

She took a breath, wiped her hand on her jeans, and pressed forward—
into whatever waited beyond the shimmer.

"Cairn," she muttered. "When the hell did you do this?"

She pressed her palm to it. The barrier hesitated—then softened,
peeling apart like mist.

Inside, the house was too still. Not peaceful. Wrong.

She slipped off her boots and stood in the quiet, heart thudding. The
usual creaks in the floor made her wince. Her keys were on the kitchen
counter, not in the bowl where she always dropped them. The coat on
the hook by the door had the zipper pulled halfway down, like someone
had started to put it on and changed their mind.

A cupboard door hung open, tea bags spilled inside. She hadn't left it
like that.

She walked slowly toward her bedroom. The door was ajar.

Her blankets were still half-folded from when she'd stripped them off
after a nightmare. The window was cracked just like she left it. But the
details whispered otherwise.

Her laundry basket had been moved. A drawer left open just enough to
suggest hesitation. On her desk, the small lockbox where she kept
spare IDs and old student cards sat open. Her passport was still
inside—but the latch hadn't caught when someone closed it.

None of it was dramatic. Not the kind of mess a stranger makes.

But someone had been in here. Carefully. Quietly.

And they'd looked through her things.

She stood at the bottom of the staircase, staring upward.

The last time she went upstairs she'd seen something else. Footprints in
the dust. A handprint on the nightstand.

She'd wanted to believe it was him. That her father had left her
something. That some piece of him had lingered to watch over her.

Now?

Now she was almost certain that someone else had been there. Someone very much alive.

She climbed the stairs slowly, bracing for something worse.

Her parents' bedroom door was closed. She didn't touch it.

The study door, though—just across the hall—was cracked open.

That door was never open.

She stepped inside, heart thudding. She hadn't stepped into this room since childhood. After her dad passed, it had been sealed like a vault of his memories.

Everything looked the same. Desk. Filing cabinet. Bookshelves. Layers of dust dulled the corners of the room, but not enough to hide the disturbances.

The pencil jar had been knocked slightly off center. One of the filing drawers was ajar. A book was sticking out just enough that she knew it hadn't been that way before.

She opened the bottom drawer of the desk. It stuck at first, then gave with a reluctant groan.

Inside: two leather-bound journals. Tangled cords. A broken EMF reader. Old Polaroids. Audio tapes labeled in Sharpie. Her father's handwriting slanted across everything in blue ink—hurried, messy, raw. She flipped through one of the journals:

> *EMF spike at the mine lasted seventeen seconds. Shadow figure visible for 3 frames. No contamination, but the pattern's getting worse.*
>
> *Seren said the man was in the hallway again. Fire and smoke. She described him like she'd seen him, not dreamed him. I told her it wasn't real. I needed her to believe that.*
>
> *If something happens to me, it's not an accident.*

Seren sat back on her heels.

She'd thought this room was for bills. Tax returns. Important documents.

But her father had been investigating the things she could feel in her blood. Hunting the same flickering truths she'd been chasing blindly for years. And he hadn't said a word.

She looked around again.

Someone else had been in this room, too.

Someone who wasn't looking for tax records.

Seren' chest felt like it was caving in. Everything she believed about her dad seemed a lie. He was always adamant she wasn't seeing and hearing things. Sometimes verging on cruel. Was he trying to protect her? Or hide the truth?

The house suddenly felt too small. She escaped into the wind and cold.

Outside, the fields stretched endlessly in every direction, golden and soft. Too soft.

Her wings stirred behind her.

They shimmered through the fabric of her shirt without resistance, existing in a plane untouched by cloth or matter. Heat and smoke and something ancient pulled from within her spine.

She stepped into the field, closed her eyes, and ran.

Three long strides. A leap.

Air caught in her chest—then failed.

Her right wing faltered. She twisted hard and hit the ground in a roll that left her gasping.

The grass bent beneath her like brittle reeds. The sky spun. Maybe if she got higher and tried.

Seren found a large hill that had a steep side. She ran as hard as her legs could muster. When she reached the crest of the hill, she jumped.

She could feel her wings trying to crumple, but she willed them to stay rigid. Her back and shoulder blades burned with the effort. Seren braced for impact with the solid earth again, but found herself gently eased to the ground.

It wasn't flying—more like falling with grace. But it was something.

Exhausted and dirty, Seren drug herself Inside again.

She dropped onto the couch, shoulders aching. Her phone buzzed in her back pocket.

A voicemail.

Her supervisor's voice came through the speaker, chipper but clearly confused.

"Hey hon, just checking in. I, uh… got the transfer paperwork this morning. Says you've been reassigned to a Regional Fire Coordination Office? Never heard of it. Must be one of those fire-season crossovers or something. All the approval information should be in your email."

There was a pause. Then a soft sigh.

"I hate to lose you. But if you ever want to come back, you've always got a seat here. We'd welcome you home in a heartbeat."

Click.

Seren blinked at her phone. Then clicked the email open on her screen.

Subject: Transfer Approval – Emergency Services Reassignment (Until Further Notice)

It looked official. Too official.

> Effective Immediately
> Role: Dispatcher II
> New Assignment: Regional Fire Coordination Office
> Location: [REDACTED]
> Duration: Until Reassignment or Recall
>
> Authorized by:
> Commander C. Evergrave
> Division Director – Regional Fire Coordination

Her jaw dropped.

"Commander?" she hissed. "Are you kidding me?"

She could practically hear the smug bastard formatting the signature block. Probably gave himself a badge number, too.

And Regional Fire Coordination? That wasn't even subtle. That was just Pyric nonsense in khakis.

She kept reading—and found the kicker:

Attached:

- New Employee Orientation Packet (Smoke Tier Clearance)

- Fire Realm Dispatch Protocols (Confidential)

- Emergency Thermal Response Codes v2.7

Seren slapped a hand over her face.

"I'm going to kill him."

Then muttered, "What was I supposed to tell them anyway? That I got soul-bound to a lava elf and now I'm part of his backdraft cult?"

Still... it worked.

No suspension. No paperwork chase. Just a clean transfer. No questions asked.

She flopped over on the cushion beside her and sighed. She tapped Marisol's name.

Then she hit "Call."

It rang once.

Twice.

"Seren?" Marisol's voice answered, groggy and panicked all at once. "Are you okay? What the hell happened? You vanished—one second you were in my living room and then—nothing. I thought I was losing my damn mind."

Seren closed her eyes, emotion rising in her throat. "I'm okay. I swear. I—I had to go. Something pulled me through."

"Through what, Seren? You left behind your duffel, your clothes, your pancakes. I thought you were abducted by aliens. Or Pyric fae. Or—wait. Was it him?"

Seren gave a breathless laugh. "Yeah. It was him."

A pause.

"Are you hurt?"

"No. Just… overwhelmed. And something's happened here. My house was broken into."

Marisol's tone turned cold. "What? Are you still there?"

"Yes. Whoever it was is gone now, but they were looking for something. They went through my dad's old things. They didn't take anything… just dug. Like they knew what they wanted."

"Do you want me to come over?"

"No," Seren said quickly. "I don't want you caught in this. But thank you."

"Seren—"

"I found something," she added. "A journal. My dad knew about the Veil. He was researching it."

Silence.

"Jesus," Marisol whispered. "You always said he didn't believe you."

"I think he did. He just couldn't let himself show it."

Marisol exhaled slowly. "Okay. You're going to stay on the line with me while you check the rest of the house. Deal?"

"It's already done," Seren said quietly. "I just… needed to hear your voice. Remind myself I'm not alone."

"You never are, girl. Weird tattoos, other realm boyfriends and all."

Seren laughed through the ache in her chest. "Thanks, Mars."

"You need anything, you say the word. I'll come running."

"I know," she said softly. "Thank you."

They hung up, and Seren stared down at her fathers journal. She reached for it, hands trembling, she hadn't let out of her sight since she found it.

Seren curled her knees up onto the couch and opened the journal again, thumbing past the pages she'd already read.

The handwriting was looser in the middle—rushed. Desperate.

> *"They won't let me leave. Every time I ask questions, I get stonewalled. And now they're watching. I saw one of them at the corner by the house. Just… standing there. No face I could recognize. But I knew. The mark on his hand gave him away."*
> *"If you're reading this, Seren… it means I failed. They found me. I hope you never remember the fire. I hope the dreams fade and the world forgets you. Because if they don't, they'll come for you like they came for me."*

Her blood ran cold.

They had come for him.

And now they were coming for her.

She dropped the journal in her lap, heart hammering, and glanced down at her arms. The silver markings were still there, curling from her wrist to her shoulder. But worse—her wings. She still hadn't figured out how to hide them.

They flared behind her. Tangible. Tangled. Crowding the space behind the couch. She could feel the weight of them dragging at her posture.

She couldn't walk into a grocery store like this. Couldn't go back to work. Couldn't even go to the damn gas station without someone noticing them. They were not exactly subtle.

"Okay," she muttered, shifting upright. "Time to figure this out."

She closed her eyes. Focused on the wings—not their presence, but the sensation. The way they felt like a breath of power stitched into her back. Not pain. Not flesh. Energy.

She inhaled through her nose.

Exhaled slowly.

"Fold in," she whispered. "Disappear. Like Cairn does."

Nothing happened.

Seren huffed and tried again, this time picturing Cairn's wings—the way they shimmered in and out of sight, how they dissolved into mist. .

Her breath evened. Her heartbeat slowed.

She imagined tucking the wings into her spine, into her bones.

A shimmer.

Then—nothing.

She opened one eye.

Gone.

"Oh," she breathed, blinking at her reflection in the mirror above the mantel. Her shoulders looked normal again. Lighter. She twisted from side to side. No resistance. No drag. Just... her.

She laughed—soft and shaky. "I did it."

It wouldn't last forever. She knew that. But for now, she could blend in. Pretend things were normal. As long as she didn't lose her grip on control.

As long as she didn't lose herself.

Seren rose and walked to the window. The sun was higher now, spilling light across the fields like gold dust. Somewhere out there, someone was still watching. Still searching. Still waiting.

But she wasn't the scared little girl in the closet anymore.

She was marked. Fated.

Chapter Eighteen: What the King Demands

Cairn

Time passed differently when she was gone.

The moment Seren stepped through the portal—her hand slipping from his, her scent torn away by the sharp wind of the Veil—it was as if the realm itself had grown colder. Greyer. More brittle at the edges.

It was only two days.

But it felt like eternity.

Cairn stood in the same spot for hours after she left, eyes fixed on the fading shimmer where the rift had sealed. The quiet returned like a punishment. Her warmth was gone. Her wings no longer brushing against his. The bond, stretched thin across realms, pulsed faintly in his chest like a wound that refused to close.

He didn't sleep. He didn't eat. Not until he'd done what he could.

The house—her house—was warded the moment she left his sight. A shell of ancient Pyric magic folded inward on itself, invisible to mortal eyes but pulsing with protective intent. It wouldn't keep everything out, not if something powerful enough came knocking. But it would warn him.

It would hurt anything that touched her without permission.

And beyond the wards, he sent watchers.

Three cinderwraiths—creatures twisted from the souls of those too stubborn to die and too volatile to rest. They didn't speak in words. Not anymore. But they whispered to him, always, in tongues of wind and soot and ghostlight. Their reports drifted into his mind like smoke curling beneath a closed door.

She moved through the house again.

She bled briefly. Not deep. Just a scratch.

She dreamed of the tree. Of fire. Of you.

Someone has been here before her.

That last message had made his jaw tighten until his teeth ached.

He didn't trust them entirely—they were fractured, feral—but they were loyal. Or at least, obedient. Ashmarked creation left little room for rebellion. Stuck perpetually somewhere between life and death.

But it wasn't just the intruder.

She mentioned a man in a skin suit.

Not a metaphor. Not dramatics. That was what she'd said—a man wearing skin that wasn't his own. Cairn had scoffed at first, half-thinking it a mortal idiom. But the bond hadn't lied. The terror she'd carried... it had been real. Ancient, even. It rang too close to stories older than Pyric flame—of parasites in flesh, watchers that shed their forms like clothing.

And if something like that had bled through?

He clenched his fists. That meant the Veil wasn't just thinning—it was infected.

And she'd been there. Alone.

Little spark, he thought, the name catching like a thorn in his chest. Why didn't you tell me sooner?

He sat now on the edge of the bed they'd shared, head bowed, fingers tracing the groove her body had left in the sheets. Her scent still lingered—light and strange and mortal. Nothing in the Pyric Realm smelled like her. Too alive. Too real.

His wings twitched once, reflexive. The bond ached with distance.

She had asked for space.

But Cairn had never been good at letting go.

A knock shattered the silence.

Three quick raps, then a pause.

Cairn didn't move.

Another knock. Louder this time.

"You dead in there?" came a voice from beyond the door. "Or just still recovering?"

Cairn sighed and stood, muscles groaning. The wings at his back flared once before vanishing into smoke.

He opened the door.

Rhyne leaned against the frame, arms crossed, the smug twist of his mouth practically begging for a punch. His silver hair was tied back today, a glimmer of sarcasm in his eye. And right now, he was grinning like a bastard.

"Ah," Rhyne said, sniffing the air theatrically. "So that's what love smells like. Thought the roof might cave in last night."

Cairn stared at him.

Rhyne held up his hands. "Hey, don't look at me like that. I knocked. Twice. And then I heard noises that would've made the mountain blush, so I left. Respectfully. Like a gentleman."

"You're not a gentleman," Cairn muttered, stepping aside so he could enter.

"Not even a little," Rhyne said brightly, sauntering in. "Also, you still smell like sex and mortals. Little overwhelming, not gonna lie."

"Get out," Cairn said flatly.

Rhyne flopped into the nearest chair with a groan. "Oh come on, I haven't seen you look this tragically lovesick since—well, never, actually. Soak it in. How do you have this mortal tricked and so complacent with you anyway?"

Cairn didn't answer.

Rhyne tipped his head, watching him. "So, are we gonna talk about her? Or are we still doing the cryptic brooding thing?"

Silence.

Rhyne raised a brow. "You've got a mortal tucked in your bed like a half-wrapped gift, and I don't even get a name? Come on, Cairn. I'm your best—"

Cairn moved fast. One step. One breath. His hand slammed into the wall beside Rhyne's head, flames flickering beneath his skin.

Cairn's jaw tightened. Rhyne was no Ashmarked, no brother bound to the Veil. He had never bent knee to the oath. He ruled the Warrens instead, unscarred, free—and all the more dangerous for it.

Rhyne stilled.

"I don't say her name," Cairn said, voice low and cold. "Not here. Not yet. Not until I know she's safe."

Rhyne blinked, expression faltering for the first time.

Cairn leaned in slightly, his breath a hiss of heat. "If I find out anyone in this realm is sniffing too close to her—anyone—even you, I'll put them in the ground."

Rhyne held up his hands slowly. "Alright. Easy. Message received. Damn."

Cairn stepped back, dragging a hand through his hair. The flames withdrew, but his eyes still burned.

"She's not like the others," he said after a long moment. "She's marked. Chosen. She didn't ask for any of this."

Rhyne sat up straighter, all traces of humor gone. "Wait. Marked? You didn't just bring her here to fool around, did you?"

"I didn't bring her," Cairn said tightly. "She came on her own. The bond... it's real."

Rhyne stared at him. "Holy shit."

Another beat of silence passed.

Then Rhyne exhaled, slow and low. "Well, that explains the obsession. You're practically vibrating."

"She's back in her world now," Cairn muttered. "And someone's been inside her home. Before I ever laid a ward. They moved through her things. Looked for something."

Rhyne frowned. "You think it was a Pyric? Another Ashmarked or court member?"

"I don't know. But if it was, they left no trace. Just disturbance. Familiar disturbance."

Rhyne stood now, pacing once. "Alright. Now that you've threatened to melt my face off, can I help?"

Cairn gave him a side glance. "You're going to help either way."

"Oh, see? Now that's the Cairn I remember." Rhyne clapped his hands together. "One small problem though—"

He paused just long enough to be annoying.

"—the King summoned you. Cinder Council too. Seems like everyone's suddenly very interested in your whereabouts."

Cairn tensed. "Why?"

Rhyne's grin faded. "Scars are getting worse. Veil's thinning in places it shouldn't. People are talking. Monsters are slipping through. The court wants answers."

"I gave them answers," Cairn said darkly.

"Yeah, well, they want new ones. And if the King's involved, it means this isn't just about rifts anymore. Something's changing, and they think you've seen it firsthand."

Cairn didn't reply, but the burn beneath his ribs flared again—heat curling where the bond lived, silent and pulsing.

He had seen it.

And he hadn't told anyone.

Rhyne gave him a long look. "Whatever's coming? You'd better be ready."

The walk to the inner keep was slow and deliberate.

The weight of the summons was impossible to ignore. Cairn had crossed these obsidian halls a thousand times, but today the shadows seemed to stretch longer, the stone whispering like it knew something he didn't.

Rhyne walked at his side, uncharacteristically quiet. Even his footsteps sounded more measured.

They reached the heavy double doors carved from volcanic stone and banded with iron. Symbols of flame, blood, and crown adorned the arch above—ancient and uncompromising.

Two guards flanked the threshold, both in armor etched with magma veins. One gave a slight nod and pushed the doors open with a groan of stone on stone.

Heat rolled out in a wave.

They stepped into Severance Hall.

The chamber was massive—built to intimidate. Walls of obsidian glittered with veins of living magma that pulsed like a heartbeat. The heat was stifling, even for those born of fire. A fireplace large enough to house a dragon blazed at the far end, flames licking up toward a vaulted ceiling lost in smoke and shadow.

At the center of the room stood a massive table carved from black marble veined with crimson. Thirty seats circled its length—one for each of the Cinder Court. At the head, elevated slightly, sat the throne of the Iron King.

No one else had the audacity to sit higher.

Chairs lined the outer walls—lesser nobles, foreign envoys, favored acolytes and spies all lurked in silence, their eyes turning as Cairn entered.

He met no one's gaze.

"Fancy place for a disciplinary hearing," Rhyne muttered under his breath.

"Shut up," Cairn replied without looking at him.

At the far end, the King hadn't yet arrived—but the court was nearly full. Familiar faces regarded him coolly. A few whispered. One or two sneered. Cairn caught the flicker of green eyes from across the chamber— the new Ashmarked, watching him too intently.

He ignored it.

Instead, he approached the table and bowed—just enough to show respect, but not submission.

A voice rose from one of the seats.

"Cairn Evergrave, enforcer of the Veil," came a sharp, ringing tone. "You were summoned yesterday."

"I came as soon as I was able," Cairn replied evenly.

"And what occupied you, we wonder," another member asked, eyes glinting beneath a brow of flame-etched gold.

Cairn's expression didn't flicker. "Securing a breach. Near the mortal side."

A low murmur passed through the court. Interest. Concern. Doubt.

Rhyne leaned sideways just a little. "They're gonna eat you alive if you don't start playing nice."

"I'm not here to play," Cairn murmured.

The magma in the walls hissed louder—as if in anticipation.

And then, from the far side of the room, a door opened behind the raised throne.

The King had arrived.

Every voice in the room went silent.

Cairn and Rhyne straightened as the King entered—tall, robed in molten silk, a circlet of black iron resting on his brow like a wound that never healed. His eyes, when they swept the room, were fire contained— barely.

As one, the room rose.

The Iron King walked with the slow, deliberate weight of someone used to being obeyed. Every footstep echoed like a judgment.

He reached the head of the black marble table and took his seat.

Only then did the others sit.

The King's voice rolled out, low and clear, amplified by the heat and stone. "We gather today for two tasks of consequence."

The silence deepened. No one moved.

"First," he continued, "we witness the binding of a new soul to the sacred flame. One who endured and survived the Ashmarked Oath. Today, he shall be honored and named through the Rite of Becoming—thus officially accepted into the Ashmarked history."

The King's voice rang out like molten steel struck against stone.

"Step forward."

From the shadows at the edge of the room, a figure emerged. Tall. Bare-shouldered beneath his ceremonial robes, skin already bruised with heat and trial.

Green eyes. Bright. Defiant.

Cairn watched in silence.

The young man entered the center ring of obsidian where the floor itself pulsed faintly in response to the power bleeding through his veins. He knelt, waiting.

The King rose.

A reverent hush settled over the court.

The King stepped down from the dais and approached the kneeling figure.

"Speak the name you were born with," he commanded.

The young man blinked.

His mouth moved once. Twice.

"…I don't remember," he finally said.

A murmur moved through the Cinder Court. Several leaned forward in their seats, recognizing the depth of that loss.

Cairn didn't react. He remembered that silence. That confusion. That hollowing.

"Good," the King said softly. "Then the Oath did its work."

He raised the ceremonial blade from the coals—its surface glowing, etched with sacred flame. Without ceremony, without warning, he struck.

One brand. Two. A third.

Each mark seared a new sigil into flesh and soul alike. The young man gritted his teeth. Smoke curled from his back. Blood hissed against the stone.

And then the King pressed two fingers to the highest rune—igniting the mark with one final burst of fire.

"You are not the one who knelt," he declared. "You are not the son they buried. You are not the name you forgot."

"You are Riven Cindereft."

The magma in the walls pulsed bright in recognition.

"The one burned clean. The one chosen by ash. The one who rose where others died."

Riven's breath came in a shaky exhale.

He remained on his knees until the King nodded.

Then slowly, deliberately, he rose—his green eyes locking with Cairn's again.

He did not look grateful.

He looked like a fuse waiting to be lit.

Applause erupted as Riven turned, the new brand still smoldering across his back.

He walked with rigid pride to the semicircle of seats reserved for the Ashmarked—Cairn's seat among them. No one met his eye as he sat. No one had to. The weight of the rite had marked him more thoroughly than any gaze.

As the applause swelled, Rhyne leaned close to Cairn's shoulder and muttered, "I don't like that one. Got the kind of eyes that make trouble just for the taste of it."

Cairn didn't respond. His stare hadn't left the King.

Kaedros returned to his seat like a storm cloud returning to its mountain. He sat, motionless for a long beat, then flicked two fingers toward the center of the room.

"Cairn Evergrave," he said, voice calm and absolute, "you will now report to the Cinder Court."

The magma veins hissed louder.

Cairn stepped forward, every movement precise.

He bowed. "King Kaedros," he said with measured reverence.

Then he raised his head, shoulders squared. "The Veil grows thinner. There are fractures we cannot explain—scars that shift locations, widen without warning. Creatures long buried slip through without leaving ripples. I've seen them with my own eyes in the mortal Realm."

Kaedros's fingers drummed once against the arm of his throne. "I have felt it too."

He stood slowly.

"There are whispers from the far edge of the Realm. Rumors of a great beam of light rising from Ashrot Slough."

Cairn's brow furrowed.

"The gods have not spoken in eons," Kaedros continued, "but the faithful believe this is a sign. A call to push harder. To tear the Veil at its seams and claim what was promised."

Cairn's jaw tightened.

"You are to return to the mortal realm," Kaedros said, stepping closer. "There are two targets of interest."

Kaedros slid an envelope across the table to Cairn who opened it to view the briefing notes. The first was a young female. He couldn't help but draw the similarities to Seren, but he pushed that from his mind.

"The girl," he said, "is your mark."

Cairn's shoulders tensed.

"This mission concerns something else. A corruption that should not exist. A breach in blood, not just realm."

"A child born of a mortal and a Pyric fae. A blasphemy's creation. Hidden for years. Raised in secret. But power leaves trails—and this one burns too brightly to ignore now."

The court shifted uncomfortably. Even the other Ashmarked looked uneasy.

Kaedros's eyes gleamed. "You will find this creature. You will strip it from its stolen world. And when you return, you will end it."

"Bring the mortal here before the court to demonstrate your holy Veil given power."

Kaedros's smile was thin and cruel.

"…then the court will witness what becomes of impurity."

Cairn turned the page.

Another file. This one older, heavier. The paper yellowed at the edges, stained with ink and dried blood. A photo was clipped to the corner— grainy, low resolution. It showed a man in his forties, sharp-jawed and thin, standing beside a burned-out doorway. Eyes sunken. Expression unreadable.

Kaedros's voice cut through the heavy silence.

"The second is simpler. A human male. No magic of his own, but eyes that see what should not be seen. He's crossed paths with scars in the

Veil too many times. He draws maps. Records patterns. Leaves breadcrumbs for others."

Cairn's frown deepened as he scanned the notes. Newspaper clippings. Handwritten marginalia from Pyric agents. Sightings dated back a decade. One note stood out:

> *'Said he saw a figure step through fire and vanish. Knew the name Evergrave.'*

Cairn's blood ran colder.

"A drifter," Kaedros said, his tone bored now. "Too clever. Too curious. He's of no use alive. Give him to Riven. Let the boy learn how to silence a mortal who watches gods. We will test his new Veil given powers"

Cairn glanced toward the Ashmarked seats. Riven sat still as stone—but his hands gripped the armrests like he could already feel the kill in his blood.

"Do you understand your assignment?" the King asked again, voice like iron being quenched.

Cairn looked up from the envelope. His jaw clenched. Was this a test? The council seemed suspicious of his absence. No doubt they voiced their concerns to the king. He had to play this by the book, to protect Seren a little longer.

"I do."

Kaedros leaned back in his chair, a smug smile stretching across his face like he'd just won a game Cairn hadn't realized they were playing.

"Then may the Veil burn open beneath your feet."

The doors groaned shut behind Cairn as he strode from the chamber, the envelope still burning in his grasp.

He didn't slow. He couldn't afford to.

If the king knew what she was—what she meant—this wouldn't be a test.

It would be a death sentence.

Footsteps echoed behind him a beat later—too fast, too light to be Rhyne.

"Wait up," Riven called.

Cairn didn't.

Riven caught up anyway, falling into step beside him like a loyal hound.

"That was… intense," the younger man said, tone too casual for the blood still drying on his back. "The court. The ritual. I didn't think the King would assign me to you right away. Pretty sure most Ashmarked spend a few days puking their soul out after the Rite of Becoming."

Cairn stopped.

Slowly, he turned.

The glare he leveled at Riven could've melted iron.

"We are not friends."

Riven blinked.

"We are not comrades. We are not equals. You are baggage assigned to me by the crown. You'll speak when I ask, and fight when I say."

He took a step forward, his voice lowering like ash drifting from flame.

"We leave in one hour."

Riven swallowed.

"You will go to the Keep's blacksmith. Tell him you have a mission from King Kaedros. He will outfit you with armor, weapons, and whatever else you'll need to avoid dying in the first ten minutes."

Riven opened his mouth—maybe to protest, maybe to crack another joke.

Cairn didn't give him the chance.

"Meet me at the front gate, ready to travel. If you are late…"

His eyes burned.

"…I will leave you here."

Then he turned and disappeared down the corridor in a wash of smoke and fire.

Cairn didn't head for the Keep's forge.

He turned down a side corridor, exited through the lower gates, and took the scorched stone path toward the outer market—a twisting, blackened sprawl clinging to the cliffs near the Veil-worn village his home overlooked.

Smoke curled from low chimneys. Molten gutters pulsed with lazy rivers of heat. This part of the realm wasn't for nobility or show. It was for the ones who kept the weapons sharp.

He cut down a narrow alley that opened into a small courtyard of open-air smith stalls. Sparks danced like fireflies, and the air reeked of sweat, steel, and emberdust.

At the far end, beneath a slab of carved obsidian, stood the only one Cairn trusted to touch his armor.

"Thorne," he called.

The blacksmith looked up from a glowing length of blade, sweat streaking the soot on his brow.

He was a broad-shouldered male of indeterminate age—Pyric-born but touched with soot marks so old they looked like natural stone veins. His hammer rested casually on one shoulder, and his eyes were sharp despite the constant squint of forge smoke.

"Well, well," Thorne said, grinning. "Didn't think I'd see you again so soon. What happened—your cloak get singed trying to look impressive?"

Cairn gave him a tight smile. "I'm heading on a mission."

Thorne whistled low. "Again? You must be Kaedros's favorite little blade. You've got scorch marks all along your chestplate—let me guess, got too close to something with teeth."

"Something like that," Cairn muttered, unclasping the armor pack from his back and setting it on the bench. "Can you get it ready?"

Thorne ran a practiced hand over the battered pauldrons and helm, nodding.

"Half an hour. I'll sharpen everything, reforge the left gauntlet, and patch the backplate where you got tossed into that wall or beast or lover—whatever it was."

Cairn gave him a flat look.

Thorne just grinned wider. "Yeah, didn't think you'd say."

Cairn stepped back. "I've got other business to attend to. I'll be back in thirty."

Thorne already had his hammer in hand. "And I'll have it gleaming by then. Just try not to get killed before you pick it up this time."

Cairn turned, the hint of a smirk tugging at one corner of his mouth. "No promises."

Then he vanished into the rising heat, heading toward the path that would take him to his house.

The door to his home closed with a quiet click behind him.

Cairn stood for a moment in the silence.

The wards hummed faintly along the edges of the walls—steady, familiar. The scent of scorched cedar and iron filled the space, mingling with something faintly sweet. A trace of her.

He exhaled slowly, dragging a hand through his hair as he crossed the threshold.

The house was dark stone and sharp lines, but warm. Lived-in. Minimal. It wasn't built for guests. Or company. Or bonds.

And now the weight of what Kaedros had asked was pressing in from every side.

Cairn moved to his writing desk—a broad slab of carved obsidian tucked beneath the arched window. He sat, tugged open a drawer, and pulled free a small parchment scroll and a stick of char.

He hesitated.

Then wrote:

Little Spark,

I can't say much—not through this.

You're safe, for now. But something has changed.

I need to know you're still with me. Still there.

When you touch this note, I'll feel it through the trace woven into the ink. That's all I need—just that moment. Just a heartbeat.

If anything goes wrong, burn it. I'll come.

—C

He turned the page over and pressed his fingers to the corners. A faint line of smoke coiled along the edges as the enchantment bound itself into the fibers.

A trace. Subtle. Ancient.

He whispered her name into the ink, his power lacing through the ink until the connection shimmered just faintly to his eyes.

Then he stepped to the far corner of the room, to the small hollow behind the hearth where the Veil ran thinner than glass. His own personal tear that didn't want to fully close.

He pressed the scroll into the space.

The air sizzled. The note vanished.

Gone, toward her.

Cairn closed his eyes, just for a second.

And waited for her touch.

Cairn didn't move far from the hearth.

He stood, arms crossed, watching the space where the note had vanished as if sheer will might speed the connection.

Then—

A flicker.

A spark against his spine.

The bond flared, light and clean. She'd touched it.

His eyes closed. Relief hit him like breath returning to lungs held too long underwater. She was safe. Alive. Reaching back in her own quiet way.

It was enough.

He inhaled through his nose, forced the emotion into a tight, silent box, and turned away.

There was work to do.

The blacksmith's forge was still smoking when Cairn returned. Thorne handed over the polished armor without ceremony, wrapped in heat-treated cloth that steamed in the cool mountain air.

"You break it again," Thorne muttered, "you fix it yourself next time."

Cairn offered a grunt in response, slinging the gear over his shoulder and tossing a coin stamped with the court's seal onto the anvil.

Then he turned and walked the stone path toward the front gates.

He didn't expect to see Riven waiting.

But there he was—perched on a low wall like an overeager hound, already armored in dark steel, helm clipped to his hip, a twin set of obsidian-forged daggers strapped to his chest.

Cairn narrowed his eyes.

"You're early."

Riven shrugged. "You said one hour. I figured showing up early might keep me from getting ditched."

Cairn didn't answer. Just gestured for him to follow.

They walked in silence until they reached the Weeping Arch—the molten-cracked stone where the realm's tether to the mortal plane was thinnest.

Cairn stopped.

"If something goes wrong," Cairn said without looking back, "and I'm not there to drag you out—you'll need an anchor point."

He lifted his hand and drew a sigil in the air with one fingertip. It flared and sank into the earth, burning itself into the stone until it pulsed like a heartbeat beneath their boots.

"This," Cairn said, "is a homing sigil. A foothold on this side of the Veil. It will stay burning until we close it."

Then he crouched, swept ash from the ground onto his fingertips, and caught Riven's wrist. Before the younger man could react, Cairn traced a smaller version of the sigil onto the inside of his forearm. The mark smoldered faintly, searing a pattern into his skin that made him hiss.

Riven stared at it. "What is this for?"

"If you're separated, trace it. The mark will pull you back to the anchor here." Cairn released his arm. "But don't use it unless you're dying. It burns everything else you're clinging to. Memories, breath, flesh—it doesn't care."

Riven exhaled sharply, then muttered, "If you can open the Veil yourself, why can't I? Why can't I just learn to make my own portal?"

Cairn's lilac eyes cut toward him, catching the glow of the smoldering sigil. "Because it takes years just to survive a crossing. Even then, most are broken wandering the in-between. I don't wander. I don't break. The Veil shows me paths it hides from everyone else." His tone dipped lower, edged with unease. "Even I don't fully understand why. It isn't something I mastered. It was given. Forced into me. The others call it a gift." He glanced away. "I've never been certain."

Riven's fingers hovered over the mark on his forearm, his voice quiet. "So that's why it's always you. Why they send you first."

"That's why I pull souls. Why I open the doors no one else can find." Cairn raised his hand. Reality peeled apart with a hiss of fire and shadow, the air itself splitting into a jagged wound. "For me, the Veil parts as if it's waiting."

The rift roared open before them.

"Stay close," Cairn said. "Don't speak unless you have to. The first target's already moving."

Together, they stepped through, the gates sealing closed behind them.

Chapter Nineteen: The Scorchmark Society

Seren

The journal sat open on her lap, its spine cracked and pages soft with age. Seren had barely moved since the sun dropped over the fields outside. The quiet tick of the old clock filled the farmhouse, but time felt bent—warped around every line her father had written.

She flipped back to the section she'd skimmed this morning.

The handwriting was different here. No longer neat and restrained. It slanted erratically, as though written in haste or under duress.

> *"The city board refused to acknowledge the Veil tears again. Said it was weather patterns. Or faulty equipment. They are labeling us the town crazies. I checked the readings three times. It was a rupture— same signature as Grafton Hill. That makes six in two months. It's accelerating."*

> *"The others are starting to worry. Martin said we should slow down, but he's scared of what it means if we're right. We all are."*

> *"I keep dreaming of fire again. A voice in it. I think it remembers me."*

The ink blotched where the pen had lingered too long—then a symbol. Drawn roughly into the corner of the page.

A small circle with an uneven X bisecting it. Not symmetrical. Not decorative. It looked like something scrawled in urgency, not design. Beneath it, in barely legible script:

"The Scorchmark Society. May the flame remember."

Seren's breath caught.

She'd never heard the name before.

She flipped forward.

Martin's name appeared again. Then others.

"Elias is off-grid. No signal for weeks. Haven't heard from Vera since the Spokane breach. And Jonah… God. Jonah saw eyes through the Veil. He won't sleep."

The next entry was just a single line.

"If we disappear—someone needs to remember we were trying to help."

Her fingers trembled as she stood and climbed the stairs toward her father's study. The door creaked like a vault unlocking. Dust hovered in beams of morning light.

She'd been in here just once before, as a child, when she'd needed a permission slip signed and wandered in too far. He'd shut the door quickly. Smiled, distracted, and told her it was "just tax documents and grown-up junk."

Now she knew better.

Seren ran her hand along the desk's edge, then tried the bottom drawer. It stuck—then slid open reluctantly.

Folders, receipts, nothing useful. But as her fingers traced the inside rim, she felt it: a small brass knob, recessed and almost invisible. She turned it.

The side panel loosened with a soft pop, revealing a hidden cavity. A thick envelope lay inside, wrapped in a rubber band long since brittle.

She eased it out and unfolded the flap.

Photos spilled across the desk.

Eight people. Some smiling, some not. All gathered in what looked like a field research site. Tents, equipment cases, notebooks open on tables. Her father stood near the center, one arm slung over the shoulder of a broad-shouldered man with glasses and a wind-tossed smile.

On the back of the photo, her father had written their names:

Jonah. Elias. Vera. Martin. Owen. Rachel. Marcus. Hal.

Beneath the names: the same circle-and-X symbol. The Scorchmark Society.

Her eyes locked on the man beside her father.

Owen.

That name appeared the most in the journal. It was underlined, circled, referenced with fragments like:

"Owen said the boundary's shifting again."

"Owen doesn't trust the city board anymore."

"If Owen's right, we're already too late."

Seren sat back slowly, mind racing.

The journal had been lying in the drawer, waiting for her like it belonged there—half-buried under receipts and junk mail, but still obvious enough that anyone rifling through would have spotted it. Its pages were filled with a mix of neat notes, speculative scribbles, even outlines of the things he wanted to argue with the city board.

But this envelope… this was different.

She wouldn't have seen it at all if she hadn't felt the hidden knob under her hand. It had been deliberately tucked away, sealed with a rubber band that crumbled at her touch. She glanced between the journal resting on the desk and the pile of photographs spilling from the envelope.

Why leave one in plain sight and bury the other?

The journal read like something meant to be found—a trail of theories, arguments, musings that could be brushed off as research. Harmless enough. Believable enough.

But the photos and documents in the envelope didn't feel like theories. They felt like proof. And proof was dangerous. Proof couldn't be explained away if someone stumbled across it.

Her father hadn't just been recording what he thought. He'd been hiding what he knew.

She pulled out her laptop and began searching the names in the photo —one by one.

Obituaries. Missing person notices. Academic articles that stopped in 2018. A fire at a small cabin in Oregon. Another vanished during a hiking trip in Utah. No survivors. No leads.

Every single member of the group was either confirmed dead or presumed missing under strange circumstances.

Except one.

Owen Halberg.

She clicked on the last link—a ten-year-old photo of him lecturing at a fringe science conference. He hadn't published anything since. No digital trace. No employment records. Just… gone.

Her heart pounded.

She pressed her palm against her pocket—the note from Cairn crinkled under her fingers.

The hum of him in the paper was faint but steady. Warm. Centering.

She closed her eyes.

And whispered, "What the hell did you all find?"

Seren sat cross-legged on the living room floor, her laptop warm against her knees. A half-empty mug of coffee sat forgotten beside her, cold now. The house was quiet—too quiet—but the note in her pocket buzzed faintly like a heartbeat. Like she wasn't entirely alone.

She'd searched every database she could find. Government records. Obituaries. Academic publications.

There was no death notice for Owen Halberg. No obituary. No photos. No press. Just… nothing.

Except one sliver of light: a donation in his name to a local wildlife sanctuary, made by " Rory Halberg."

Rory.

Seren's fingers flew across the keys. A social media account. Private, but active. A small bio: Dog mom. Book hoarder. Local artist.

A public art page was linked, showcasing watercolor paintings of mountain scenes, forest paths, old houses painted in soft, melancholic tones. There was something familiar in them. Something haunted.

Seren hesitated only a second before sending a message.

> *"Hi Rory. This might sound strange, but I'm trying to learn more about your father—Owen Halberg. He worked with my dad a long time ago, and I recently found some of their old research. I'm so sorry to bother you out of the blue. I just… I think they were close, and I have questions I don't know how to ask anyone else.*
> *—Seren Cross"*

She stared at the blinking cursor for ten minutes, second-guessing everything.

Then the reply came.

> *"Hi Seren.*
> *Oh wow, that name—I haven't heard it in a long time. My dad did work with someone named Cross. He mentioned him sometimes when I was little. He called him "stubborn and brave as hell."*
>
> *My dad passed away two years ago. It was quiet. That's how he wanted it. No obituary, no ceremony. We buried him in a little cemetery just outside Westgrove.*
>
> *I'd be happy to talk if it helps. I've got the day off tomorrow. If you're nearby, want to meet for coffee?"*

Seren exhaled, shoulders sagging in quiet relief. She checked the map—Westgrove was barely an hour away.

"I'd really appreciate that. I can be there by 10am if that works? Thank you, Rory. Really."

Rory's reply came instantly.

"Of course. There's a coffee shop downtown called Thistle & Vine. You can't miss it. I'll be the one with paint on my hands."

She set her laptop down and let herself breathe for the first time in hours.

Rory Halberg.

A real person. Warm. Willing to talk. Not just another dead end. Seren didn't know what answers the woman might have, but the fact that someone else remembered her father—called him brave, even—felt like a knot inside her had finally loosened.

Seren slid the laptop shut, Rory's words still warm in her mind. She gathered the loose photographs into a neater stack, and her pulse spiked when she found several tucked behind the rest.

These weren't camp snapshots. They were darker, blurred, like they'd been taken in secret from too far away or too close to danger. One showed a jagged seam of light slashing through the night—the air itself torn open. Another captured a figure half-swallowed by the Veil, body blurred at the edges as though the world couldn't decide which side he belonged to. In another, the same figure stepped back through the tear, the lines of his body scorched with light. Tattoos seared across his skin, bright as molten iron, stark even through the grain of the photo.

Her breath stalled.

Then came the last photo. A close-up, grainy, the rest of the face lost to shadow—but the eyes cut sharp through the blur.

Lilac.

Seren's stomach lurched. She flipped the photo over, searching for context, but the back was blank. Just the faint indent of her father's handwriting pressed from another page.

She stared at the image until her chest ached. The journals could still be dismissed as speculation, as obsessive research. But these photographs— these were something else. Proof. Impossible proof.

Her father had not only studied the Pyric realm. He had seen it. Stood close enough to photograph its oldest protectors.

Her hands shook as she gathered the evidence back into order. The photographs, the scraps of notes, the impossible fragments of her father's life — all slid neatly into the brittle envelope, the rubber band snapping weakly as she looped it around once more.

All except one.

The photo with the lilac eyes lingered on the desk, the gaze burning through her no matter how many times she tried to look away. Something about it felt alive, urgent, as though the page itself carried heat.

Seren swallowed, then slipped it into her pocket beside Cairn's folded note. The two pressed together against her thigh, paper against paper, like they belonged side by side. The hum of Cairn's note pulsed faintly, and for the first time she wondered if it was answering the photo.

She forced herself to tuck the envelope back where she'd found it. But the weight in her pocket was heavier than anything she'd left behind.

She tidied the desk in her father's study with care. Her boots thudded softly down the stairs as she made her way back to the living room. She flicked off lights, brushing her fingers once more over the note from Cairn in her pocket, and the photo of eyes that glowed even through the blur.

A pulse of warmth met her touch—low, steady. A heartbeat in paper.

She smiled, just a little.

It wasn't enough to fix things. But it helped.

Seren washed her face, brushed her hair, and swapped her jeans for soft sleep pants. Tomorrow would bring answers. And maybe, just maybe, some peace.

She passed by the window on her way to her bedroom—and stopped.

There was something outside.

A figure. Still and dark beneath the tall tree that stood at the edge of the wheat. Too tall to be Marisol. Too solid to be a branch.

Seren's breath caught.

It didn't move.

She stared for a long moment, willing her brain to find something rational. Maybe it was just the way the moonlight filtered through the limbs, casting distorted shadows.

Then, like a blink, it was gone.

Her heart thundered in her ears.

She turned away from the window—and froze.

There was smoke in the hallway.

Thin, curling tendrils of it, rising like mist from the floor.

Her skin went cold.

No fire. No heat. Just... smoke.

And something was forming in it.

She backed toward the wall, eyes wide as the haze coalesced into shape. A humanoid figure—tall, skeletal, draped in rags that seemed to flicker like ash in the wind. Its bones shimmered faintly, like coal-glow beneath skin. Where its face should have been was only hollow darkness.

But as she stared—really stared—it responded.

The shape solidified more. It raised one arm, slowly, painfully, until a clawed hand extended toward her. Smoke curled off its fingers like fog peeling from ice.

And it didn't feel evil.

It felt... lonely. A hollow, aching loneliness that pressed against her skin like cold fog. Not the sharp hunger of a predator, but the deep, endless absence of something that used to be whole. It whispered of silence stretched too long, of voices swallowed in smoke, of someone trapped in a place where no one ever answered back.

Seren's throat tightened. She should have been afraid — she was afraid — but threaded through the terror was pity. A grief that wasn't hers. A yearning so raw it made her chest ache, as though the wraith wasn't reaching for her body, but for anyone who could *see* it.

Lonely. That was worse than evil. Evil she could fight. Evil she could hate.
Lonely made her want to reach back.

Then—cautiously, stupidly—she stepped forward and reached out.

Her fingertips brushed its bony knuckles.

The thing took a breath.

A rattling, agonized inhale, like it hadn't drawn air in years.

Its chest hitched. Its head tipped back—and when it looked at her again, there were eyes. Not empty sockets, but flickering amber orbs sunken deep in shadow. And a mouth. A tongue, thin and dead-grey, flicked between charred lips.

It spoke.

Not in full sentences. Just ragged gasps between fire and death.

"Once... man..."

Seren's throat closed.

"What—what are you?"

Its head twitched toward her. Voice wheezing.

"Saw... too much."

Another rattling breath.

"Asked... too many."

Its fingers twitched. Smoke peeled from its chest.

Seren's voice dropped to a whisper. "Who did this to you?"

It shuddered.

"Pulled... me."

"Who?"

A beat.

Then: "Lilac… eyes."

Her heart dropped like a stone.

It looked at her—through her—with something ancient and sad.

"Bound… to him."

"To Cairn?"

"Made… to watch…"

Seren stepped back, shocked. The air pulsed between them.

"I didn't—" she started, but the words wouldn't come. Her throat locked.

She couldn't look at it. Couldn't stop looking. Her body screamed to turn, to run, but her eyes stayed fixed as if the thing itself had hooked them. The hollow glow within its shrouded face pulled at her, made her feel like if she just stared long enough she might understand — might *know* who it had been.

The cinderwraith shuddered. Smoke bled from its edges in threads, thin as unraveling fabric. The air crackled faintly, a low hum like ash scattered across hot coals. It staggered backward, limbs fraying, pieces of it tearing loose in wisps that curled toward the ceiling.

And still its gaze clung to hers.

Lonely. So achingly lonely it hollowed her chest.

Seren's breath came ragged, the words dying on her tongue. She tried to reach forward, fingers twitching, but the moment slipped. The figure folded in on itself, collapsing inward, pulled back into some unseen seam between one heartbeat and the next.

The smoke unraveled, curling into nothing. A soft hiss, like the last breath of a fire, echoed in its wake.

Then silence.

Gone.

The hallway stood empty again, as though it had never been there. Only the lingering chill in her bones told her otherwise.

Seren leaned against the wall, chest heaving.

A ghost would've scared her. But that wasn't a ghost.

That was loneliness, raw and endless, stitched into smoke and bone.

And Cairn had never told her what he'd done to make things like that—things that carried his mark, things too monstrous to die, too broken to rest.

Her knees gave out before she made it to the bedroom.

She dropped onto the edge of the mattress, hands braced on either side, lungs dragging at the air like she couldn't get enough.

A sharp drip hit the floor between her boots.

She blinked, dazed, and brought a shaking hand to her face. Her nose was bleeding again—heavier this time. It wasn't just pressure or fear.

The wraith had taken something.

She wiped it away with the edge of her sleeve, but the dizziness clung like fog.

The smoke was gone. The wraith was gone.

But its voice still echoed inside her.

Made to watch.

Her chest caved in with the weight of it. A sickening, hollow ache clawed its way up her ribs, into her throat.

Cairn had done that. Turned a person—someone with a life, a name, a soul—into that thing. That half-dead watcher. That broken, breathless… thing.

How many others?

How many ghosts wandered the shadows, bound in smoke and silence, because he had deemed them worth sacrificing?

She squeezed her eyes shut, willing the thoughts away. They didn't leave.

He'd said he was tasked with returning condemned souls. But that hadn't seemed like a monster. They seemed lost. Tortured. Not evil—just forsaken.

Seren curled onto her side, knees to her chest, arms wrapped tight.

She knew he wasn't innocent. She'd felt it in him—his grief, his violence, his fire. But this… this was sentencing someone to hell. Watching him do it to others, seeing that aftermath—it broke something open in her.

Was this the Pyric realm?

Was this what it stood for?

She pressed her face into the pillow, the journal still clutched in her arms, as if her father's words might offer some anchor in the rising storm.

What if it's all wrong?

What if she was never meant to see this?

What if this realm was never supposed to be saved?

What if it deserved to fall?

Seren turned her head, breath catching as her fingers brushed her pocket—the note, the photo.. Warm, pulsing faintly.

Cairn.

The memory of his voice filtered in, soft and broken. If you're in danger… if you call for me, I'll come.

She wanted to believe him. She wanted to believe he could be something different.

That his past didn't define what he could be now. That people could change. That maybe—just maybe—if she held on long enough, she could help change him. Change the realm. Reclaim whatever worth was buried under centuries of cruelty.

But in this moment, with smoke still clinging to her skin and that hollow rasp echoing in her bones…

She didn't know.

She pressed the note to her heart and let the ache wash over her.

Tears slipped past her lashes, soaking into the pillow. Silent. Relentless.

Eventually, her breath evened out. Her grip loosened.

Sleep took her under.

But her dreams burned.

Chapter Twenty: Favors and Fire

Seren

Seren slung her bag over her shoulder and stepped out into the crisp morning air. The world felt oddly still—too still for how alive her nerves were.

But as she reached her car, she stopped short.

A handprint.

Pressed into the dust on the hood. Distinct. Too large to be hers.

Her pulse skipped. She moved closer.

Another.

On the windshield—right where the driver would sit. Fingers splayed wide like someone had leaned there, watching.

Waiting.

She stared at it, heart hammering. It could've been old, she told herself. A trick of the light. Maybe even hers from a different day. But the dust was fresh. She hadn't touched that part of the car since she parked it days ago.

And the angle was wrong—not casual. Intentional.

Like a warning.

She reached for the door, fingers trembling, and slid into the driver's seat with a chill in her spine.

The engine turned over.

She forced her hands to steady on the wheel.

She had a meeting to get to.

But whatever was watching her... it knew.

The drive to Westgrove was calm. Too calm.

Seren's fingers tightened on the steering wheel, the road blurring past in the early morning light. The fields here were greener, the houses older. Quaint in a way that made her teeth ache. Driving her car with the windows down and music blasting was usually her mental reset, but today everything just felt like a bad omen.

She pulled into a small diner lot just off the town square. Rory had suggested it—neutral ground, public. Safe.

Seren sat for a long moment, staring at the entrance. Her pulse fluttered in her throat. Not fear. Just... pressure. The kind that came from truths pushing against the edge of her understanding, waiting to break through.

She grabbed her bag, tucked Cairn's note back into her pocket— steadying herself with the warmth it pulsed into her skin—and stepped out into the morning.

The diner was half full, low chatter buzzing beneath the clink of coffee mugs and syrup-laden plates. The hostess smiled and pointed toward a corner booth.

 Rory was already there.

She looked like someone who had been through just enough to stop pretending otherwise—freckles scattered across her nose, brown hair swept into a low bun, and dark circles under her eyes that matched Seren's.

"Seren?" she asked, standing partway.

Seren nodded. " Rory?"

They both sat.

There was a moment of shared hesitation. A silent breath of recognition.

"You look like him," Rory said softly. "Your dad."

Seren's throat tightened. "You knew him well?"

"He was my dad's best friend for a long time," Rory said, voice lowering. "Research partners. Obsessive, both of them. My mom hated it."

Seren pulled the photo from her bag and laid it gently on the table.

Rory's eyes widened. "Oh my god. Where did you find this?"

"Hidden in my dads study. Names are on the back," Seren whispered. "With the symbol."

Rory flipped it over, nodding slowly. "Yeah… this was their group. I remember the meetings. Candles. Maps. Weird energy always in the air. They thought they were protecting something."

"They were."

Seren hesitated.

"And then they all died."

Rory looked up sharply. "You think it's connected?"

"I know it is," Seren said. "And your dad—he's not just gone. He was silenced."

Rory's mouth opened—then stilled.

The air around them shifted.

A weight pressed in on the atmosphere. Like the pressure before a storm.

Seren felt it before she saw it.

The tingle in her spine. The temperature change. That burn of smoke behind the Veil of normal.

She turned toward the door.

And there he was.

Cairn stepped into the diner like a blade through silk—lilac eyes burning, shoulders squared, mouth set in that familiar line that meant control was a thin thread from snapping.

Someone else followed behind him.

Tall. Sharp. And green eyes watching everything.

Seren's stomach dropped.

Cairn's eyes found hers instantly.

He didn't falter. Didn't blink. But the muscles in his jaw clenched—and something in his expression changed. From mission to… panic.

He moved.

Quick, precise, controlled.

His hand landed on Rory's shoulder.

"You're coming with me."

"What?" Rory pulled back. "Who the hell are you—?"

"You're not safe here," Cairn said tightly. "There's no time to explain."

Riven stepped forward.

His eyes swept the diner lazily—and stopped.

Right. On. Seren.

Cairn turned just slightly, shielding her from view.

Too late.

Riven's brow furrowed. His head tilted.

But he said nothing.

Cairn barked over his shoulder. "Riven. Take the female. Now. I will clean up this mess and meet you at the Warren."

Riven's eyes narrowed but obeyed, stepping toward Rory and taking her by the arm.

Seren stood, fists clenched. "Cairn—what the hell are you doing?"

People in the diner started looking, pointing at Riven taking Rory. They started questioning. Shouting.

He turned to her. And for a moment, the weight of everything in his expression nearly buckled her knees.

"You don't belong in this part of me, Seren. Walk away while you still can."

She stared up at him, refusing to flinch.

Cairn leaned in, just enough for her to feel the heat of him.

"Do you remember the favor you owe me?" he whispered. "Back when I let you touch my wings?"

Her breath hitched.

"I'm calling it in. Right now."

He stepped back just enough to meet her eyes.

"Leave. Now. Don't ask questions. Go home. Stay. I will come to you when the coast is clear."

She wanted to argue.

Wanted to scream.

But his eyes... they begged her.

Not here. Not now.

So Seren did the only thing she could.

She nodded once.

Turned.

And walked out the door—fighting the feeling that everything had just changed.

As she drove away, back towards home she glanced in the mirror. The site stole her breath. The whole diner was ablaze with an unnatural flame. The last thing she saw was Cairn open a rift, and disappear.

Cairn

He didn't watch her go.

Couldn't.

The last look in her eyes had carved deep—too deep. He hadn't meant for the words to cut like that. But maybe he had. Maybe he needed her hurt to anchor her safety.

The moment her car disappeared down the road, something inside him cracked like cooling stone.

The diner burned behind him.

Not wild. Not out of control. It danced the way Pyric fire always did— obedient only to its master. It consumed everything unnatural and unspoken, wrapping the memory of what happened inside a Veil of smoke and ash. By morning, it would be a tragedy. A headline. A mystery.

A story rewritten by fire.

Footsteps crunched across the parking lot.

Riven appeared beside him, backlit by flame. His expression was unreadable, green eyes narrowed slightly.

"You didn't mention there'd be a witness," he said casually, gaze drifting after Seren's car like a hawk tracking prey. "She looked… interesting."

Cairn didn't respond.

"You're awfully protective," Riven added, his tone too light. "Friend? Lover? Or just another complication?"

"Enough," Cairn snapped.

Riven raised his hands. "Hey. Just making conversation."

Cairn turned from the blaze, the envelope in his coat heavy with the weight of orders. "We have one more to collect."

Riven tilted his head. "The man?"

"Older. Loner. He's been poking around the wrong places too long. The Veil has thinned around him."

Riven grinned. "Let's pay him a visit."

The man was easy to find—just as the briefing predicted. A reclusive historian with a paper trail of strange questions and unfiled FOIA requests. He lived in a run-down cabin half an hour outside of town, surrounded by overgrown trees and satellite dishes.

He opened the door in his slippers.

Cairn didn't give him a chance to speak.

The man's eyes widened in recognition, breath catching in his throat as Cairn stepped forward, hand raised—not with violence, but with authority that bent the very air.

The Veil shimmered. The man began to tremble.

"I've seen you before," he whispered hoarsely.

Cairn nodded once. "Then you know what happens next."

The rift opened behind him, humming with molten heat and shadow.

Riven stepped in, eager. "Let me."

Cairn stepped back.

The man tried to run.

He didn't get far.

Riven moved like a blade—silent, fast, cruel.

The rift swallowed them all.

They stepped into the throne hall of the Cinder Court moments later.

The man, unconscious now, collapsed at Riven's feet like a discarded offering. Cairn stood still, fire dripping from his fingertips as the echo of what he'd done still pulsed in his bones.

He could still feel the heat of Seren's fingers where she'd touched his note that morning.

It reminded him who he was doing this for—even as the line blurred between protection and destruction.

She hadn't touched it since she left the diner.

But he couldn't focus on that now. The Court was waiting, and so was judgment.

The chamber was suffocating.

Even with its towering obsidian walls and vaulted ceiling veined with magma, the weight of what was to come pressed down like a curse. The normal table had been removed. In its place stood a massive slab of volcanic stone, rimmed with iron and anchored directly into the floor with binding runes that pulsed faintly.

Chains clinked. The shackles were already prepared.

Cairn stood at the base of the dais, jaw locked.

Around him, the court had gathered again. Every seat filled. The lesser nobles packed the back walls in whispering rows, and the Ashmarked watched in silence—warrior-statues with flame still coiled in their bones.

Rhyne entered through the side arch, boots echoing, and behind him—

Rory.

She looked hollow. Her wrists bore raw marks from restraints, and her eyes—gods, her eyes—were cracked with quiet horror. She didn't resist as they led her forward, though her steps faltered at the edge of the stone slab.

The guards fastened her in. Arms, legs, neck.

Kaedros stood at the head of the room, his voice rising with ritual weight.

"Let the sacred flame be honored," he said, voice rich and reverent. "Let the Veil be reminded of our strength. Through fire, the soul is shaped. Through pain, it is purified."

He looked down at Cairn, eyes gleaming. "Begin."

Cairn didn't move for a breath.

Then he stepped forward.

The stone beneath him groaned. As he walked, the veins of magma brightened—drawn toward him like hungry snakes. Light bled upward into the chamber, turning the polished black floor into a glowing map of ancient power.

He stood over Rory.

Her eyes met his. There was no plea in them. Just… understanding. Resignation.

And still—it hollowed him.

But he couldn't stop.

He inhaled.

The tattoos across his arms flared—soul-seals lighting in perfect sequence. Old Pyric script burned across his spine, the heat rising until the room seemed to pulse with it. Smoke coiled from his skin like incense from a holy altar.

The court leaned in.

Cairn extended his hand.

The fire reached for her—not her flesh, but what lay beneath. The spark. The soul.

 Rory gasped, spine arching against the restraints. Her mouth opened, and the scream that followed sounded less like agony and more like soul-deep betrayal.

It carved into the room.

Cairn's expression didn't change.

The light beneath her chest bloomed. Her body convulsed once—twice—and then was gone.

Ash scattered into the shape of her life.

But her soul remained.

It pulsed and flickered, unraveling, clawing for meaning in the haze of what had once been a girl.

Cairn lowered his other hand.

The room dimmed further.

From the ash, a figure rose.

It was not Rory. Not anymore.

The wraith was tall, skeletal, wrapped in curling shadow. Smoke coiled from its ribs, and where its eyes should've been burned two steady coals of emberlight.

It breathed in once—and screamed.

The Cinderwraith fell to its knees before Cairn, bound by the ritual. Its form shimmered, half-real, half-remembered.

Cairn exhaled slowly.

The ashes settled into the slab, locking into the seal. A rune pulsed beneath them—eternal, binding.

Only silence remained.

Kaedros stood, his face a portrait of pride and triumph.

"Let the court remember," he said, voice thundering. "This is what our enemies fear. This is what holds the Veil."

As the applause roared around him, Cairn didn't move.

The heat still coiled in his bones. But something was… wrong. Off-balance.

He lifted a hand and touched his collarbone—where the burn still throbbed beneath the skin.

The newest mark had branded there, just above his heart, crawling up his neck in jagged lines of ember and ash. A harsh, unrelenting design—larger than the others. Angry.

Visible.

He hadn't meant for it to land there. But the soul had resisted. It had screamed with a name he couldn't bear to hear.

It knew her.

Rory had known Seren.

He didn't know how deeply—but it had been enough. Enough to twist the flame. Enough to stain this forging with the one thing he couldn't shut out.

His mate.

Cairn clenched his jaw.

This one would never fade. Not like the others.

He rolled his shoulders once, and as the crowd began to settle, he turned—face unreadable, eyes still glowing.

Cairn moved to the far wall, silent and coiled as the crowd buzzed with post-ritual energy. The stench of scorched soul still hung heavy in the air, a bitter reminder of what had just been lost—and gained.

Now it was Riven's turn.

The court shifted in anticipation. Eyes turned toward the obsidian dais, where the older mortal man had now been secured. He didn't struggle. Not anymore. Whatever fire had once lived in him had long since guttered out, replaced by a dull, frightened awareness.

Riven stepped forward, his armor whispering as he moved.

He was smiling.

Not the mask of serenity Cairn wore when killing. Not the grim acceptance of duty.

No. This smile was sharp. Hungry.

The light in the chamber dimmed again, not from flame—but from something else. A pull at the air, like gravity bending in the wrong direction.

Riven didn't raise his hands.

He just looked at the man.

And spoke.

"You've seen too much," he whispered. "Now… let's see what you remember."

The mortal shuddered.

Riven's eyes darkened—green iris eclipsed by void-black pupils that widened until they swallowed the whites. Smoke hissed up from his fingertips, but not the smoke of fire. This was something colder. Wrong.

Cairn felt it before he understood it.

A pull.

Not of body. Of mind.

The mortal on the dais began to shake—violently. His back arched. He screamed, but not in pain. In terror. In recognition.

Whatever Riven was doing, it wasn't destroying his body. It was shattering inside first.

"Do you see it?" Riven murmured. "The truth beneath the skin?"

The man's eyes rolled back. Blood dripped from his nose. Then his ears.

Cairn frowned, his stomach twisting—not with guilt, but instinct.

This wasn't forging.

This was destruction.

The soul didn't peel free from the body like in Cairn's rites. It collapsed. Imploded inward as if crushed by its own weight. The man's head snapped back—mouth agape in a silent scream—and then…

He deflated.

That was the only word for it.

His entire body collapsed into itself, like rotten fruit left too long in the sun. Skin shriveled, bones splintered into dust. A puddle of dark sludge spread across the dais—flesh, blood, marrow, memory. Gone.

Useless.

Cairn stiffened. Even the court had fallen silent.

This wasn't a transmutation. This wasn't power bound.

This was soul destruction. Total and irrevocable.

King Kaedros stood slowly, studying the scene. "Fascinating," he murmured. "No echo. No trace. Nothing left to rise."

Riven exhaled, sweat slicking his brow now, but his grin remained. He turned and bowed to the court. "Forgive the mess."

Behind him, the puddle smoked.

Cairn said nothing. But his hands curled into fists.

This wasn't what the Ashmarked were meant to be.

Riven wasn't forging fire.

He was a black hole in the shape of a man.

And they'd just handed him a crown.

The silence after Riven's display was heavier than any applause.

Then Kaedros began to clap.

Slow. Deliberate. Echoing.

Others joined in—hesitantly at first, then with growing fervor. The nobles cheered, the Ashmarked bowed their heads in solemn approval, and the firelight cast Riven in the glow of something newly born and profoundly dangerous.

Cairn didn't move.

Kaedros raised a goblet of moltenwine. "Let it be known," he called, "that this day marks a new age of strength. A new Ashmarked initiated. Two souls bound—or broken—in the name of the Veil."

He turned to the room. "Tonight, we feast. The Keep will host a celebration in honor of our sharpened blade and our newest weapon."

The crowd erupted.

Rhyne appeared at Cairn's side, his voice low. "You staying for the drinks or slipping out before the toast?"

"I have other business," Cairn muttered.

Rhyne raised a brow. "Don't suppose it involves a mortal who smells like lightning and stubbornness?"

Cairn didn't answer.

He turned, heat still seething in his bones, and walked out before the first tray of gold-plated goblets could be passed around.

Cairn didn't stop.

Not for food. Not for armor. Not for sleep.

As soon as the Keep disappeared behind him, he veered off the stone path and carved a rift into the air, searing it open with a flick of his hand and the whisper of her name in his mind.

The tear widened. The human realm called.

He stepped through.

Seren

Seren didn't hear the rift open.

Didn't feel the air shift.

She was curled in bed, blankets pulled high, eyes red and raw. The tears hadn't stopped since she'd gotten home. She'd tried. Gods, she'd tried to justify it all—to rationalize what he'd done. What he was.

But there were some truths too heavy for excuses.

Cinderwraiths weren't theory anymore.

They had names. Faces.

Pain.

Her pillow was soaked. Her chest ached with every breath.

So when she felt the heat—just a flicker—she thought she'd imagined it.

Until the warmth grew stronger.

Until the room smelled faintly of smoke and stone.

And then she felt him.

Not just in her bones—but in the bond. Like he'd wrapped his arms around her without touching her at all.

She sat up fast, heart hammering.

Cairn stood at the edge of the room, half-shadowed, his expression unreadable.

His eyes were soft.

Haunted.

"Get out," she whispered, voice breaking.

He didn't move.

"I said—" Her voice cracked. "You don't get to show up like this after— after that."

Cairn stepped forward.

"I didn't come to explain," he said quietly. "I came because I felt you break."

She turned her face away, shame twisting beneath her ribs.

He moved to the side of the bed but didn't sit. Just stood there—present. Solid. Silent.

"I never wanted you to see what I was," he said. "But you deserved to know."

She looked up at him, eyes wet. "And what exactly am I supposed to do with that, Cairn?"

He didn't answer.

He sat beside her, letting the silence stretch.

Letting her choose what came next.

"I'm sorry," he said.

She didn't reach for him.

But she didn't pull away, either.

Not until her eyes caught the edge of something she hadn't seen before.

A jagged, blister-red mark, climbing up from beneath his collarbone and disappearing along his neck. Angrier than the others. New.

She sat up straighter, voice thin and cautious. "What is that?"

Cairn followed her gaze, then exhaled through his nose like the weight of it sat heavy on his chest. He rolled back his collar just slightly, exposing more of the brand—sharp lines like flame etched with violence.

"The mark for the cinderwraith I forged today," he said. "Each one earns a place."

She flinched.

"I didn't choose the placement," he added quietly.

But that wasn't the part that caught in her throat.

She stared at the mark—remembering the wraith's hands, its breath, the way it looked at her like it knew. Like it was waiting for her to understand.

"I touched one," she said suddenly, her voice low and strange in the dark room. "It came to me. Last night. In smoke. In silence. It reached out and I—"

She trailed off, eyes wide as if reliving it.

Cairn stiffened.

"You touched it?" he echoed. "And it didn't hurt you?"

"No. It… it felt calm. Familiar."

He didn't speak.

Not for a long moment.

But something changed in his face. A flicker of thought he didn't voice. A question he wasn't ready to ask.

She saw it anyway.

"What?" she demanded. "What aren't you telling me?"

Cairn shook his head once, too carefully. "It shouldn't have approached you like that. They don't act on their own."

Her voice turned sharp. "So they were yours?"

"…Yes."

Her stomach dropped.

She pushed back the covers and stood, her eyes blazing now. "So they were watching me?"

"They were protecting you," he said quickly. "Reporting back in whispers. I needed to know you were safe—especially before I placed the ward."

"Oh, great," she snapped, arms crossing. "So you sent ghost-spies to haunt my yard and crawl through the walls while I slept. That's not horrifying at all."

"Little spark—"

"No," she snapped. "You don't get to use your nickname to try and placate me right now."

Cairn flinched. Not from her words—but from the truth in them.

The bond between them pulsed—hot, strained, trembling like a wire pulled too tight.

"I told you I was scared," she said. "That I needed space. That I needed truth. And instead, you sent monsters."

"They're not monsters."

"To me, they are!" Her voice cracked. "You stood in this room and watched me cry. And now I find out your hellspawn were already here?"

Cairn's jaw worked.

But she was done.

"Get out," she said, pointing to the door. "Take your wraiths. Take your wards. Take your sorry apologies and go."

He didn't argue.

Didn't beg.

Just stood, silent and still, the flicker of fire in his eyes barely visible through the guilt.

He stepped toward the door, then paused.

"I only ever wanted to keep you safe," he said.

"Then you should've started by trusting me," she whispered.

And with that—

He was gone.

Smoke curled where he'd stood. The room was colder now. But at least she was alone.

She fell into a fitful sleep, somewhere between nightmare and vision:

The world bled gray.

Ash floated in slow spirals, hanging motionless in air that didn't breathe. The sky glowed dimly without a sun, and the trees in the distance burned without flame—blackened branches curled like reaching hands.

Seren stood barefoot in the center of it all. The ground beneath her feet was cracked and pulsing with dull heat, like it had once lived and now only remembered how.

A cinderwraith waited in the stillness.

Not drifting—standing. Like it had been waiting just for her.

Its body wavered at the edges, stitched together by smoke and sorrow. There was no face. Just the faintest shimmer of gold-red light pulsing deep in its chest, like a coal too stubborn to die.

She didn't speak.

She didn't need to.

Something in the wraith turned toward her—not physically, but fully. A knowing. A recognition not of her name or face, but of her role.

She stepped forward.

Her hand lifted on instinct, and when her fingers brushed the center of its chest, everything shifted.

The smoke flared. The air thickened. The wraith sharpened—just slightly—like it remembered how to be whole for a single heartbeat.

Its voice came from nowhere and everywhere at once. Layered. Damaged. Tired.

"I was Ezra. I had a son. A small house by a wheat field. He liked the stars."

A flicker behind her eyes—

A memory not hers:

A boy with pale hair running barefoot through grain. A toy left burning on the threshold. A scream lost in a sea of fire.

"I saw something I wasn't meant to. I spoke it aloud. The fire came next."

"He dragged me across the Veil. Said it was mercy."

The voice softened, almost breaking.

"But I remember him watching."

"The one with the marked hands. The enforcer. He said I would forget… but I didn't."

Seren's breath hitched.

The wraith tilted its head toward her, like it saw through her skin, down into the marrow of what she was becoming.

"You shouldn't be here yet."

"But the Veil knows you."

"It chose you the moment it cracked."

She tried to step back.

The wraith surged slightly forward.

"You're the last breath before the world turns."

"You will either seal it… or burn it open."

Then softer—softer than a whisper:

"You touched me."

"I remembered. That means… you can change it."

"Not yet. But you will."

Its form unraveled—gently this time. Like it had said what it came to say. Ash dissolved into the windless air, leaving only silence.

Chapter Twenty-One: You'll Beg Before This Ends

Seren

Seren jolted upright in bed, breath catching, drenched in cold sweat.

The scent of smoke clung to her skin.

She blinked down at her palm.

A sigil shimmered there—elegant, unfamiliar, curling like roots dipped in gold. It pulsed once, alive and ancient...

And vanished.

Then the heat bloomed behind her eyes.

She barely had time to grab a tissue before the blood came—fast and heavy. A deep, pulsing nosebleed that left her dizzy and swaying.

She leaned over the sink, shaking.

Not a dream.

Not a warning.

A message.

And a memory that hadn't belonged to her—until now.

The house was too quiet.

Seren lay curled on her side, wrapped in blankets that offered no warmth. The corners of her bedroom blurred in the early light, muted by the weight pressing on her chest.

She couldn't cry anymore.

Not after last night.

Not after the look in his eyes when she told him to leave.

Cairn, the one she'd trusted—the one she thought fate had tied her to—was no savior. He was a weapon. A warden of souls. A killer of men who once had names and voices and futures.

And she was bound to him.

All these years she had devoted herself to saving people—dragging voices out of fire and wreckage, piecing together hope through broken dispatch lines. But the man fate had carved for her from the bones of myth… he burned the very lives she tried to preserve.

The irony tasted like ash.

She buried her face in her pillow, willing the thoughts away. Wishing the bond would break. Wishing the world would spin backwards and let her start again.

She felt the shift in the air, heard her bedroom door creak open more. Why was Cairn back? Could he not take a hint that she needed some space?

Seren sat up yelling at the door "Cairn, I told you to…" her voice was stuck in her throat. The man in the door was not Cairn.

His silver hair was pulled back. He looked to be in his 30s, but Seren knew better. She could smell Pyric Realm on him. This wasn't just a stranger, he was fae.

Her heart slammed once, hard.

He stepped into the room, movements smooth and unhurried. Like he already knew there'd be no fight.

"Seren Cross," he said, voice quiet but full of venomous certainty. "You're harder to reach than I expected - little spark"

She scrambled backward, nearly falling from the bed. "Who the hell are you?"

He tilted his head. "The one sent to fix what should've never been opened."

Her mind raced. No weapons. No time. No Cairn.

"You've been watching me," she said, breath shallow. "You're the one who—"

"Left the handprints?" he offered, smiling faintly. "Yes. Among other things. Your father was… inconvenient. You're a loose end."

Her blood ran cold.

"You killed him."

He didn't deny it.

Didn't even flinch.

"You saw too much, just like he did. You were supposed to burn out on your own. But then he got involved."

Cairn.

Something in his expression tightened.

"He always did have a weakness for the broken ones."

Seren's fists clenched. "Don't talk about him."

"Oh, but we will." He took another step closer. "When you're tied to the slab beneath the Keep, and the king asks what use you're meant to serve."

Seren dove for the nightstand, reaching for anything—anything—she could use.

But he was already there.

A blur of motion. A hand closing around her wrist. Heat lancing through her veins like wildfire.

She screamed.

Not from pain—but from the crushing pressure that came next, as if a thousand unseen hands were dragging her across the boundary.

The world warped. Color fractured from her vision. Her limbs went heavy, then bound, as though caught in unseen threads. Her skin prickled with cold as if yanked from her own atmosphere. And still she tried to fight.

She reached, blindly, for the bond tethered to her heart.

"Cairn," she cried out, not aloud, but inside—where her magic lived, where her fire burned. "Please."

Just the whisper of his name, flung like a spark through the dark.

And just before darkness took her, she saw his eyes—yellow like a snake, venom-bright, locked on hers with sick satisfaction.

Then—

Everything burned.

And she was gone.

She woke to screaming.

Not hers.

Seren's eyes flew open to darkness, thick and choked with smoke. The air reeked of ash and blood and something foul that lived between the two. Her limbs were sluggish, heavy, like her veins had been filled with molten lead. Chains clinked nearby. A moan echoed through the stone like something human trying hard not to be.

She sat up too fast and nearly vomited. Her nose was gushing blood. Thick, relentless. It ran down her lip and chin, soaked into her collar. Panic tightened her throat—how long had she been bleeding? She swiped at it with her sleeve, but it smeared more than it stopped.

She wasn't even sure when it had started—only that it had been going long enough to leave a copper taste in the back of her throat.

Too much.

Too fast.

Something in her was unraveling.

Seren pinched the bridge of her nose, blood slick between her fingers, and forced herself to breathe. Shallow. Controlled. She blinked hard, trying to get her bearings—trying to think through the pounding behind her eyes.

The room wasn't a room. It was a pit—a hollowed chasm carved from blackened stone, lit only by the occasional flicker of flame leaking through cracks in the walls. The ceiling loomed far above her, disappearing into shadows. Iron bars divided space from space, cell from cell. And within those cages, things moved. Some cried. Some begged. Some just twitched.

Her breath caught.

This wasn't a dungeon.

It was hell.

She scrambled backward, her fingers scraping raw against the stone floor. The sounds were wrong. The air buzzed with pain. And some of the prisoners—Fae, mortal, or something worse—had their mouths sewn shut.

Where the fuck was she?

A voice slithered through the darkness.

"Well, look who finally woke up."

She froze.

The figure stepped into view like a shadow peeling off the wall. Pale skin. Silver hair. Yellow eyes that glowed faintly in the dark like coals.

"You've been sleeping for hours," he said, crouching to her level. His tone was easy. Too casual. "We were starting to think you weren't going to survive the trip. And that would've been so disappointing. I've been looking forward to this."

Seren's stomach dropped.

It was him.

The man from her room.

Her captor.

He smiled, teeth too white, too straight. "Welcome to the Warrens, by the way. It's not much, but it's home—if you're into screams and despair."

Seren's voice was barely a whisper. "What… what is this place?"

"Oh, sweetheart," he cooed mockingly, "this is where we put the broken toys. The ones not quite mortal. Not quite useful. Not quite dead."

He leaned closer, his face inches from hers.

"And you… are a very special toy."

She turned her head, bile rising in her throat, but he caught her jaw—firm, rough.

His fingers dug in.

Nails—longer than they should be, sharpened like talons—pressed into her skin, splitting it in fine, stinging lines. Blood welled at the edges, sharp and warm against the cool air.

Seren froze.

Not from fear—but recognition.

The shape of his hands.

The smell of smoke on his breath.

Those eyes—inhuman, glowing faintly at the edges.

He was the one from the gas station.

The man in the meat suit. The stranger making the untraceable calls. Her stalker. In every way that mattered, it had always been him.

Her breath caught in her throat.

"Easy now," he murmured, almost gently. "We're just about to begin."

Seren didn't have time to scream before he grabbed her again—this time harder.

She fought back.

"I don't care who you are," she snarled, twisting in his grip. "You don't get to break me."

His hand closed around her arm like a vice, dragging her across the stone. Her legs kicked, heels scraping against the jagged floor, but it didn't slow him. He was strong—inhumanly strong—and moved like he'd done this a hundred times before.

"Get off me!" she shouted, thrashing, nails clawing at his wrist. "Let me go!"

But he didn't speak.

Not yet.

He pulled her toward the far side of the pit—toward a raised dais carved from black obsidian. It gleamed slick with heat and blood. Chains hung from the sides, iron cuffs bolted into the stone slab. A dark stain marked the center, like something had been burned there. Something living.

"No—no, no, no," she breathed, panic spiking. "Don't touch me!"

He hauled her up and threw her onto the dais like she weighed nothing.

Seren fought like hell. She kicked. Scratched. Bit. Her teeth caught his wrist and she tasted blood—but he only laughed, low and cruel.

"Oh, I like the fire," he said, pinning her down. "Let's see how long it lasts."

"Cairn," she thought desperately, reaching toward the bond with shaking focus. "Please—hear me. I need you."

The cuffs snapped shut with sickening finality—one on each wrist, each ankle. Her back arched as she strained, but there was no give. Just cold metal and cruel stone.

He stood over her now, breathing a little heavier, lips curled in something between amusement and hunger.

Then—softly, mockingly—he ran his fingers along her jaw.

Seren flinched.

His touch trailed down to the small, raised scar on her jawline. The teardrop-shaped mark she'd carried since childhood—since the first experience she had with the Veil. .

His hand paused there.

"Ah," he said, voice dipping lower. "So he really did mark you."

She froze.

"I always knew Cairn had a weakness, it took me centuries to find it" he mused, thumb brushing the scar with feigned tenderness. "In all those years, I never would have guessed that weakness would end up being a mortal."

"He didn't just mark me," she hissed. "He chose me. And when he finds out what you've done, you'll beg for mercy he won't give."

Seren's heart pounded.

She spat in his face.

It hit square on his cheek, sliding down toward his jaw.

He blinked.

Then struck her.

The slap cracked across her face like lightning. Her head snapped sideways, the sting blooming hot across her cheek. Metal rattled beneath her as her body shuddered.

When her vision refocused, he was leaning close again—calm, cruel, patient.

"I will break that fire out of you," he whispered, voice like silk over razors. "One scream at a time."

The pain still rang in her skull when the door opened.

Heavy and deliberate, it groaned against stone and iron. The air changed again—thicker now, almost reverent. Even her captor's smug posture stiffened.

A figure entered, robes sweeping across the scorched floor, his steps unhurried but absolute. Heat followed in his wake, not from the room—but from him. The magma veins in the walls pulsed brighter as he passed, as if the realm itself bowed to his presence. He matched the walls with living veins of something glowing coursing through him. Atop his head sat a sharp crown of obsidian.

"King Kaedros." Her captor bowed to the man.

Seren had never seen him before—but her soul knew what he was.

Power. Authority. Destruction in velvet skin.

"Rhyne," the king said, his voice smooth and deep, like hot coals settling into embers. "I see you've found our guest."

Rhyne, why did Seren recognize that name. He gave a shallow bow, still holding Seren in his peripheral gaze. "She's proven uncooperative. I thought we might... encourage her."

Kaedros stepped forward, gaze cool and assessing. He studied Seren with the kind of detached curiosity one might afford an animal in a cage.

"Mortal?" he asked lightly.

Rhyne hesitated. "That was the assumption."

"Hmm." Kaedros's eyes narrowed, something flickering behind them. "Let's find out."

He waved a hand.

Without ceremony, two guards moved in. One strapped a glowing iron collar around her throat—its burn immediate. Another produced a hooked rod and dragged it slowly down the length of her side, slicing through fabric, skin, and restraint alike.

Seren screamed.

Not just from pain. From fury. From betrayal. From the memory of Cairn's hands around her waist and the echo of his voice telling her to trust him.

Another jolt of pain ripped through her. Another and another.

Questions were shouted—names demanded, locations barked.

But Seren gave them nothing.

Only screams.

Until—

Something inside her snapped.

The agony built, rising like a tide of wildfire under her skin, like lightning stitched into bone.

Her back arched violently. The cuffs groaned.

And with a sickening, shattering crack, her wings tore free from her skin in a burst of magic and light.

The air turned electric.

Feathers of molten smoke curled through the room, flickering with emberlight.

The guards stumbled back, staring.

Even Kaedros tilted his head.

"Well, well," he said softly. "She blooms."

Rhyne moved toward her, stunned.

"She has wings," one of the guards whispered, terrified. "But… she's mortal—"

"No," Kaedros murmured. "Not mortal. Not anymore. Not entirely."

Rhyne's expression twisted.

"She's one of them," Kaedros said, smile gone sharp. "Blasphemy bred. Bloodline tainted by both realms."

"A half-blood." Rhyne sneered. "No wonder she reeks of defiance."

Kaedros folded his hands behind his back, looking utterly delighted now. "She is not useless, after all. This… complicates things. But perhaps not in a bad way."

He turned toward Rhyne.

"Keep her alive," he said coldly. "But make her understand what she is. I will summon the Cinder Court. We are going to have another demonstration."

Then he vanished in a flicker of heat and shadow, leaving only the scent of smoke behind.

Rhyne stepped closer to Seren again, her blood steaming on the slab, her wings half-spread and trembling.

"Well," he said, voice almost tender, "looks like you're not just Cairn's little obsession anymore."

Seren didn't answer. Couldn't.

Her vision blurred, the edges going dark and spiked with stars. The slab beneath her was slick with her own blood and sweat, and every breath dragged through her lungs like razors.

She barely felt Rhyne's hand against her wing—some cruel inspection of the membrane, or maybe just a taunt. She was drifting, consciousness loosening like a knot undone by fire.

He leaned down, breath hot at her ear.

"You'll beg for me before this ends."

Seren's lips parted, but no words came.

Only the sound of her heart—frantic, failing—echoed in her ears.

Then even that faded.

The world swam.

The chains bit deeper as her body slackened.

And then—

Nothing.

Just black.

Chapter Twenty-Two: I am Ruin

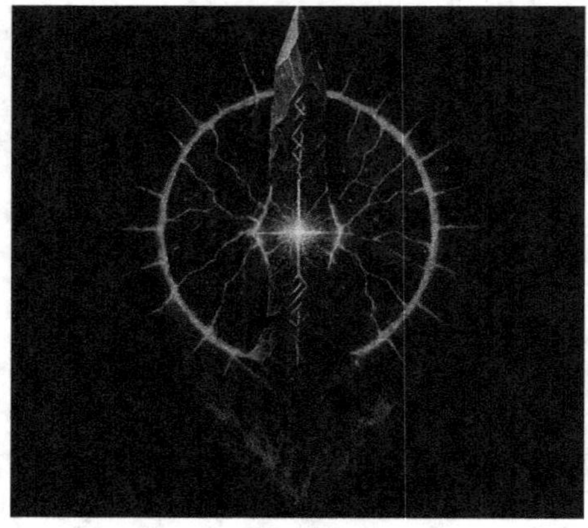

Cairn

The bed was still unmade.

The sheets tangled where her body had been. The faint impression of her shape lingered on the pillow, and he hadn't had the strength—or the audacity—to sleep on his side since she'd left.

Cairn sat at the edge, hunched forward, hands braced on his knees. The air in the room was still, but heavy. Her scent clung to the cotton like a ghost: lavender, heat, a trace of smoke.

He had played the last conversation over in his mind a hundred times.

The way she'd looked at him.

The venom in her voice when she told him to leave.

The look in her eyes—betrayal, heartbreak, fear.

He'd killed a thousand men without blinking. Carved souls from bone and flame. But nothing haunted him like the echo of her voice cracking under the weight of disappointment.

He raked a hand through his hair.

He didn't know what to do.

Didn't know how to make her understand the hell he was forged in, the choices he never got to make. The oath he couldn't unbind himself from.

And then—

It hit.

Like being stabbed through the soul.

Panic. Pure, searing. It lashed down the bond like lightning striking dry earth. His chest seized. The room spun.

"Seren—"

He was already moving.

The panic deepened—no, screamed. Not fear. Pain. Pain so complete it drowned thought.

He staggered to the table, palms slamming against it, breath ragged. Every instinct ignited at once.

She was in danger.

She was hurting.

And he wasn't there.

A growl tore from his throat. His tattoos flared without summoning—old brands burning alive with fury.

Cairn didn't waste time opening a rift the proper way.

He tore one.

The magic snarled and snapped as he ripped through the fabric between realms with his bare hands, forcing the portal wide enough to hurl himself through. The world spun, flames licking the edges of reality before it snapped shut behind him.

Her farmhouse was dark when he arrived. Too dark. Wrong.

The front door swung on its hinges like it had been left open—or kicked in.

Cairn didn't knock.

He slammed through it, heat already rising from his skin, his markings pulsing with dread.

"Seren?" he barked.

No answer.

Just stillness.

He moved room to room like a storm in human form, heart pounding with every step. The kitchen was untouched. The living room the same. A blanket folded too neatly. A coffee mug still warm.

Then—

He saw it.

The trail.

A shattered lamp in the hallway. A streak across the floor like someone had been dragged. The air hummed with old magic, the residue of something recent. Something violent.

Cairn bolted to her room.

The door was half open. The scent hit him before anything else.

Smoke.

Not hers. Not his.

Pyric realm.

His stomach twisted.

He crossed the threshold and stopped dead.

The room was wrecked.

Sheets torn. The nightstand overturned. Her favorite book—bent at the spine—lay abandoned on the floor like it had been swatted aside mid-read.

And near the bed—

Blood.

Just a smear.

Barely visible, but fresh.

Cairn knelt beside it, fingers trembling as he pressed two fingers to the floor. Warm. Not hers—he prayed—but enough to know there'd been a fight.

He stood slowly, turning in place.

There—against the far wall—a shimmer.

Almost invisible, like heat distortion in the air.

He approached it cautiously, the hair on his arms rising.

The Veil.

Torn.

Not clean, not by his hand. It was rough, jagged—like someone had ripped through it with claws and will alone.

Whoever did this had power. Access. And no fucking right.

Cairn growled, fists clenching.

It had to be him. The stalker. The bastard who'd lingered too long in the shadows of Seren's life.

He'd slipped through.

He'd taken her.

The bond pulsed again—sharper now. Distant.

She was alive.

Barely.

But the fear coming down the line was colder. Less coherent. Like something was drowning her.

Cairn's markings flared bright enough to light the room. The wall nearest him cracked under the pressure of his magic.

He turned toward the ruined Veil, jaw set.

No more waiting.

No more mercy.

He was going to drag her back—and burn down whatever hell had dared to touch her.

Cairn stepped back from the ruined Veil, chest heaving. Smoke curled from his shoulders like it had nowhere else to go. The pulse of the bond was still there—faint and ragged—but it gave him one thing to cling to.

She was alive.

Barely.

His jaw tightened.

"Come," he said aloud, voice cracking like thunder through the room.

For a breath, nothing happened.

Then—

The shadows answered.

Smoke unfurled from the corners of the house, seeping in from under the doors and pooling in the hallway like living ash. One by one, the Cinderwraiths emerged—half-formed things stitched from darkness and sorrow, their ember-lit eyes glowing in the gloom.

They had followed him out of loyalty. Had remained close. And when he sent them—scattered them—they'd vanished into the mortal world like whispers in smoke, tracing old magic, old blood, old threads.

Now they returned.

But not empty-handed.

He didn't need words to know it. They hovered before him, silent, restless. One reached a scorched hand toward him, fingers curling faintly before drawing back—then twisted its shape, trembling, until a pair of yellow, slit-pupiled eyes hovered in the air like a brand. Another wraith lifted a skeletal hand and carved a glowing rune into the air—a broken sigil of the Veil—before it dissolved.

A message. A memory. A warning.

Snake eyes.

He knew those eyes.

Rhyne.

Cairn's fury twisted into something colder than rage. It calcified beneath his ribs, a quiet promise to himself—no matter where she was, he would find her.

He moved to the window, breath fogging the cracked glass.

"She's in the Pyric realm," he said to the wraiths, voice low and tight. "Taken by force. Against my protection. That makes her a prisoner of the court. My court."

The Cinderwraiths stirred, their bodies flickering like they were tasting the heat of his anger. One let out a dry, rattling hiss that sounded like a vow.

"I want the scent she left behind traced. Backwards. Through every tear, every ripple in the Veil. Find where they crossed. Find him."

He turned from the window, eyes sharp as iron.

"Find my little spark."

The wraiths scattered again—like smoke caught in a gale— disappearing into the walls, the floor, the seams of the house and beyond.

Cairn stood alone in the wreckage of her room, a hollow silence closing in around him.

But he didn't flinch.

Not until the scent hit him.

Not Seren's.

Rhyne's.

It lingered faintly in the air, like old smoke and iron, curling through the space as if mocking him. The ghost of his presence burned brighter than any torch.

He was here.

He was in her room.

Cairn's breath stilled.

And then something inside him snapped.

The room erupted.

Furniture splintered as flame licked up the walls. The mirror cracked in spiderweb veins from the force of a growl that wasn't quite human. The floor scorched where he stepped, heat pulsing from his skin like the heart of a volcano barely leashed.

Rhyne.

Rhyne had been his only constant. The one he bled beside. The only soul in the Pyric realm he had ever called brother.

And now—

He'd laid hands on her.

He'd crossed into Cairn's world and taken what was his.

The betrayal sank deeper than bone. It carved into something ancient, primal.

Cairn reached for the side of the bed and lifted what remained of the blanket Seren had wrapped around herself. He clenched it in his fist— and it ignited, curling to ash in seconds.

"You were the only one I trusted," he whispered, voice shaking not with grief, but with fury. "And you gave her to the fucking King."

Heat split the floor.

He didn't shout. He didn't scream.

But the air around him howled.

Ash curled in the corners of the room like shadows come to witness his rage.

Then, deadly calm, he turned to the Veil splitting at the far wall. It shimmered faintly, a jagged rift burned into place like a scar.

He stepped through.

And this time, he didn't walk quietly.

Because he wasn't done yet.

The rift opened in a hiss of flame and shadow, spilling Cairn into the Pyric realm like a storm made flesh.

The sky here was darker. The veins of magma in the obsidian walls pulsed slower—thicker somehow. Something was off.

He didn't slow.

Not even when the castle loomed ahead, spires rising like claws through the ash-stained clouds. He crossed the molten threshold of the gates, boots striking stone with echoing purpose.

And there—waiting just inside the inner hall—stood Rhyne.

"Didn't expect to see you back so soon," Rhyne drawled, falling into step beside him. "Or smelling quite so scorched. Trouble in paradise?"

Cairn didn't answer. His pace didn't falter.

Rhyne clicked his tongue. "Alright then. Well, hate to pile on, but there's been a call. The King summoned the Cinder Court. Urgent business. Your attendance is required."

Cairn slowed just enough to glance at him.

Urgent.

The word hit like a spike through his spine.

He didn't need to ask. He didn't need confirmation.

He already knew.

The king had her.

Kaedros wouldn't wait. Not with a discovery this rare. Not with power he could parade and punish in equal measure.

Rhyne glanced sideways, eyebrow arching. "You're real quiet, brother. That panic in your jaw? Looks like you already figured it out. Thought your little spark could take care of herself."

The world snapped.

Cairn whirled, hand slamming into Rhyne's throat, shoving him against the obsidian wall with a force that cracked the stone behind him.

"Say that again," Cairn growled, voice low and trembling with heat. "Call her that again."

Rhyne choked on a laugh, eyes gleaming. "Touched a nerve?"

Cairn's grip tightened. The temperature spiked, the air warping with heat.

"If she has so much as a hair out of place," he hissed, "you'll pray for death. And if you're lucky, I'll send your soul back to the Warrens to rot with the other forgotten things. Forever."

For a moment, Rhyne's mask faltered—just enough for Cairn to see it: surprise. Maybe even fear.

Then Cairn let go.

Rhyne crumpled to his knees, coughing, but Cairn didn't spare him another glance.

He stormed through the obsidian halls, fire trailing his footsteps.

The air grew thicker the closer he came.

Severance Hall loomed ahead—the gathering place of judgment and cruelty. The Cinder Court.

He stalked toward it, jaw locked tight, hands clenched into fists at his sides. Everything around him slowed—every flicker of torchlight stretched long, every breath of magma-thick heat turned sour on his tongue.

And then the scent hit him.

Not fire.

Not ash.

But something deeper. Raw.

Pain. Blood. Sweat. Tears.

The stench of suffering.

He stopped before the massive doors, carved with spiraling runes and scorched handprints from ages past. They groaned open on their own—welcoming him like a beast baring its ribcage.

Cairn stepped inside.

He was the last to enter. The chamber was full. The Cinder Court was already seated. Nobles perched along the shadowed alcoves as witnesses, the King seated like a god at the head of the obsidian table.

Cairn's gaze swept the room—and narrowed.

His fellow Ashmarked were notably absent. All except Riven.

It wasn't a coincidence.

It was a strategy.

The King hadn't summoned them. He couldn't afford the risk—not with the Veil faltering and Cairn's loyalty slipping from his grasp. Too many Ashmarked still followed the old oaths, the true oaths. If forced to choose between Cairn and the throne, some might have chosen the wrong side.

The King wouldn't risk insubordination. So he hadn't given them the chance.

Another move on a board already burning.

And then Cairn saw her.

Only her.

Seren.

Unconscious. Chained.

She lay sprawled on the black dais like a sacrifice, her clothes ripped and half-burned away. Her skin was streaked with blood—too much blood—and her dark hair clung to her face in sweat-soaked tangles.

The breath left his lungs. The room tilted.

Everything—the Court, the politics, the pretense—fell away.

It was only her now.

And she was broken.

But it was her wings that broke him.

They were out.

Pinned.

Iron spikes—long, cruel things—driven straight through the delicate joints and down into the stone. Each one seared at the base, fused by fire and laced with rune-burns.

More spikes. One in each thigh.

A signature.

The Iron King.

Cairn's knees hit the floor.

He didn't feel it. Didn't even register the impact. His body gave out before his mind did. His breath vanished. His tattoos flared without permission, reacting to the bond, to the carnage, to her.

She didn't move.

Didn't stir.

She was barely breathing.

And still—she was the most sacred thing in the room.

A chair scraped.

Boots echoed across stone.

Then a voice—smooth, molten—cut through the chamber.

"Ah. Cairn. I see you've finally joined us."

The Iron King stepped down from his dais like a priest descending to the altar. His obsidian crown glinted in the firelight, each point a sharpened threat.

Cairn didn't move.

Not even when Kaedros stopped beside Seren's chained form, gesturing toward her with something like admiration.

"A striking sight, isn't she? Powerful. Defiant. Marked in more ways than one." He looked to the crowd. "But not above Pyric law."

His voice carried easily, thick with authority.

"Let this be a lesson to all who stand in defiance of the Veil. Even those bound by oath. Even those forged in our oldest flame." He turned, his gaze finding Cairn across the room. "Even one of our oldest sons."

A hush fell. No one moved. No one dared.

Kaedros paced slowly now, every step deliberate. "To be clear—this was not a choice made lightly. Cairn has served the realm with distinction. He has endured trials none of you could fathom. And yet…"

He stopped again, this time at the head of the room.

"Treason must be named. Justice must be done. And credit," he said with a nod, "must be given where it is due."

Cairn blinked.

"It was not the other Ashmarked who brought this to my attention. Nor my court. But a snake in your own garden."

Rhyne stepped forward, yellow eyes gleaming with quiet triumph.

"A brother to the accused. A friend. The one person Cairn trusted without fail." Kaedros smiled without warmth. "And the one who exposed him."

Cairn's jaw locked, shoulders rigid, the heat in his veins threatening to boil over.

Rhyne stopped just short of the dais, hands clasped loosely behind his back. He looked over at Cairn, his smile didn't reach his eyes.

"You should've kept your leash tighter, brother."

The word hit like a knife.

Kaedros tilted his head. "You look surprised."

"I'm not," Cairn said coldly. "Just disappointed."

A low murmur stirred at the edges of the chamber, quickly silenced by the weight of Kaedros's glare. The king turned back toward Seren, her chained form defiant even in stillness.

"She is a liability," Kaedros said. "A tear in our reality, breathing mortal air. You would risk centuries of order for her?"

Cairn stepped forward.

One pace.

Then another.

The court tensed as he crossed the chamber floor without permission, but no one stopped him.

"You mistake my loyalty," Cairn said, voice like tempered steel. "You think I broke my oath for her."

He stopped just shy of the dais, his eyes lit with fire—but it wasn't the king's.

"I didn't."

Kaedros narrowed his gaze.

Cairn's voice rang louder now, rising to meet the chamber walls.

"I swore my soul to the Veil. Not to you."

A hush fell like ash.

"I was forged by flame older than your throne. Bound not to a king, but to the balance. To the breath between realms. To the will that keeps them from collapse."

He turned, gaze sweeping the court. "The Realm breathes through her now. She is what you fear—not because she is dangerous, but because you cannot command her."

Kaedros stepped down again, his tone venomous. "You would defy your king for a mortal girl?"

"No," Cairn said. "I defy you because this is not betrayal."

He stepped in front of Seren.

"This is obedience—to the true order. To the old Fire. To the Veil that chose her."

The flames in the room flared without warning.

And something ancient stirred.

The chamber pulsed around him, the heat rising in jagged waves that warped the air. The brand on his collarbone seared like a warning—but it was nothing compared to the fire pounding behind his ribs.

He had trusted Rhyne.

And now Seren was chained. Bleeding. Her wings bound and bruised.

Because of it.

Because of him.

Cairn turned, slowly, eyes locking on the one man he had ever called brother.

"I would've died for you," he said, his voice low and trembling with restrained fury. "And you sold me to the court."

Rhyne didn't flinch. "No," he said quietly, stepping closer. "I sold you to the King. There's a difference."

That made something in Cairn snap.

His hands curled into fists, flame licking along the edges of his knuckles. The tattoos across his arms flared with slow, deliberate heat—like the realm itself was listening.

Power.

That's what this was always about.

Kaedros clinging to it.

Rhyne grasping for it.

And Seren bleeding under the weight of it.

Kaedros raised a hand, expression smug, satisfied. "Bring the accused forward."

But Cairn didn't move.

Not yet.

He didn't even glance at the King.

His eyes were still locked on Rhyne.

"You could've warned me," he said, barely above a whisper. "You knew. And you stood there and watched her burn."

Rhyne's smile was slow and cruel.

"Wrong again, brother."

He took one final step forward.

"I'm the one who did the burning."

Riven approached from one side, Rhyne from the other—each holding a length of chain and a pair of molten-etched manacles. Not Pyric-forged. Not sacred. These were crude iron, heavy with subjugation, etched with runes that glowed like cooling embers.

Cairn's eyes flicked to each of them.

"Don't," he growled, low and raw. "Don't touch me."

Rhyne moved first.

Cairn surged.

He twisted away from Rhyne's reach and slammed a shoulder into Riven, sending the smaller male stumbling back. Fire flared from his palms, licking up his arms as his tattoos ignited—sharp, glowing veins pulsing in defiance.

"Stand down!" Kaedros shouted.

But Cairn didn't hear him,

He was already turning on Rhyne, teeth bared, the floor cracking beneath his boots as the heat around him spiked.

"You burned her," he hissed. "You fucking—"

Kaedros raised a single hand.

The floor split.

A searing arc of molten iron surged from the stone itself, coiling through the air like a living snake. It struck Cairn mid-lunge—wrapped around his chest, his arms, his throat. It hissed against his skin, not burning but binding, scorching him without leaving a mark.

Cairn choked, knees buckling as the molten bands tightened, dragging him down.

The manacles clattered to the floor.

They weren't needed now.

The king's will had forged his own.

Cairn collapsed to his knees before the dais, breath shuddering through clenched teeth. The molten iron twisted into place around his wrists, locking him in a crouch of forced submission. Steam rose from his skin.

Above him, Kaedros watched with cool, detached satisfaction.

"You were warned," the king said.

And behind that voice, deeper than magic, the chains sang.

And then—

"Cairn…"

The whisper was so faint he almost thought he imagined it.

His head snapped up.

Seren's eyes were open—barely. Her lips cracked. Her voice a rasp of wind and agony. But she was awake. She saw him.

"Seren."

She tried to move, but the chains groaned in protest. Her wings trembled, spikes glinting with every shallow breath.

"I'm sorry," he said hoarsely. "I didn't protect you. I should've—"

Her head lolled slightly toward him.

"It's not your fault," she breathed.

His vision blurred.

"I let this happen—"

"Cairn."

Her voice was clearer now, if only for a heartbeat. Her gaze found his, blood streaked and shining with tears.

"I love you."

Time stopped.

His breath caught like it had been punched from his chest. The entire room faded—Rhyne, Riven, Kaedros, the court—all of it, gone.

Only her.

And the words she had never said before.

He leaned forward as much as the manacles allowed, his voice cracking.

"I love you too, my little spark."

The magic in the room trembled.

"In this world…" his voice dropped, "and the next."

A hush fell. Even the fire in the walls seemed to quiet.

Seren's eyes fluttered closed.

But a faint smile lingered on her lips—fragile, broken, but real.

Cairn lowered his head again.

And swore he would burn this realm to ash before he let them take her from him again.

A slow clap echoed through the chamber—mocking, deliberate.

"Apologies," Kaedros drawled, descending the dais like a god descending his altar. "I do hate to interrupt such a precious moment."

He stepped between them, boot heels clicking across blood-slick stone. His eyes flicked between Seren's limp form and Cairn's kneeling one, disdain curling at the edge of his lips.

"But love," he spat the word like poison, "has no place in Pyric law. And punishment waits for no one—not even the bonded."

The court murmured, quiet and enthralled.

"The verdict is decided," Kaedros declared, turning to the room at large. "For the crime of existing in defiance of realm and blood, the blasphemous half-mortal, half-Fae—" he glanced back at Seren with theatrical disgust, "known as Seren—is to be put to death."

Cairn roared.

The sound ripped from him, half-human, half-something ancient and furious. He surged against the manacles, fire exploding across his skin—but the chains held.

The magic in them wasn't just iron.

It was binding.

Forged by oathbreakers. Blessed by the Realm's molten core. Designed to subdue even the Ashmarked.

"NO!" he snarled, straining until the metal cut into flesh. "You will not touch her!"

Kaedros turned slowly.

And smiled.

"Oh, but we will."

He approached Cairn with calm steps, stopping just out of reach. "And as for you," he said, voice dropping to something colder, "Ashmarked who dared defy his king—"

The hall darkened.

"—you will watch as your little mortal is executed."

Kaedros leaned down slightly, eyes glinting. "Then you will follow her. Over the edge. One soul after another."

He straightened again, gesturing lazily toward the dais. "Bring the blade."

Cairn thrashed again.

Chains clanged violently against the stone, the magic searing his skin raw as it pulled tight—but it didn't matter. He would burn through every brand if it meant getting to her. To Seren, who lay barely breathing, bloodied and limp on the obsidian slab.

But Kaedros's decree had already rippled through the chamber.

A ceremonial blade was brought forward—long, curved, forged in the old way. It glowed faintly with runes, each one carved to sever ties between flesh and soul.

"The honor," Kaedros said smoothly, his voice echoing through Severance Hall, "goes to the one who uncovered this treason. Who served the realm even when his brother would not."

Cairn stilled.

No.

Rhyne stepped forward.

His silver hair was still tidy. His expression unreadable.

He reached out and took the blade from the guard's outstretched hands. His grip didn't falter. No brand marked his skin. He had never endured the Rite, never surrendered his name to Fire. He had kept himself whole, by choice—and now he wielded that freedom as a weapon. He looked at Kaedros and nodded once—silent acceptance of the role he'd been waiting to play.

Then he turned toward the dais.

Toward her.

Cairn's voice broke as he shouted, "Rhyne—don't. Don't do this. Please."

But Rhyne didn't pause.

He mounted the dais in slow, measured steps, each one an echoing betrayal. His boots stopped beside Seren's side. Her wings were still pinned. Her breath rattled weakly.

She was conscious now—barely. Her eyes fluttered, heavy-lidded. She looked at Cairn, acceptance in her eyes. A final goodbye.

Rhyne crouched beside her, brushing hair from her face with his hand. "I warned you," he said quietly. "Cairn always did have a weakness for the broken ones."

Then he sighed, the sound sharp with resentment.

"You think I sat beside him all these centuries out of loyalty?" Rhyne said, rising to his feet. His voice lifted, not just for Seren—but for the chamber. For the King. For himself. "Cairn was my key. To power. To more. I watched him rise, immortalized and revered. Always in his shadow, the favored and heroic Ashmarked" he spit the last word like a curse. "I followed, waiting. Waiting for the moment he'd falter."

He glanced down at her. "And then you appeared. A crack in his armor. His weakness. I followed you too. I waited for the moment you would tip the balance. You see, power doesn't come from strength alone. It comes from patience. From knowing when to strike."

His voice dropped again, now a whisper meant only for her. "And I never miss my moment."

The blade was already rising.

And Cairn—

Cairn screamed.

His scream tore through the chamber—raw, unrestrained, inhuman. He thrashed, straining against the iron manacles that bound him, the ones etched in the King's own script, laced with a magic designed to hold even the strongest of the Ashmarked.

They held.

But not for long.

"Don't you touch her!" he roared, flame pouring from his skin, his markings igniting one by one.

The heat was suffocating—rippling in violent waves from where he knelt, branding the floor, curling smoke into the rafters. His fists tore at the restraints, muscles shredding under the strain. Bone cracked. Blood poured.

But the manacles held.

"Cairn," Seren whimpered—her voice small, breathless. "It's okay."

He shook his head violently. "No. No it isn't."

Rhyne stood above her now, the ceremonial blade gleaming in his grip.

"You were never meant to be anything more than a tool," Rhyne told her softly. "And Cairn—he was never meant to feel."

He brought the blade down.

It plunged into her chest, poised perfectly to pierce the bond that tied them, and stop her heart.

And then—

Everything broke.

The world narrowed. The court, the king, the traitors—they didn't exist. All Cairn could see was her.

Seren.

Shining.

Broken.

Pinned like a butterfly beneath a glass blade.

And in that moment—

He became ruin.

Chapter Twenty-Three: Unbound

Cairn

The fire didn't start with a roar.

It started with a silence so complete, it cracked.

The knife punctured her heart.

Cairn felt it before he saw it—felt the bond rupture like a thread yanked from his soul, a jagged tearing that split him down the middle. One second, she was there—hurting, bleeding, still fighting—and the next...

Gone.

A breath. A spark. A heartbeat lost.

Then the world screamed.

Cairn's body detonated in a violent cascade of fire and shadow. His wings tore into existence—massive, jagged things forged from black flame and embered ash—unfurling with a force that sucked the air from the room. They didn't open so much as erupt, stretching impossibly wide, casting the entire hall in flickering darkness.

The iron manacles liquefied at his wrists, vaporized by the sheer pressure of his power breaking free.

Flame consumed the dais. The walls buckled. The very air caught fire as a deafening crack split the stone beneath his feet. The chamber shuddered under the weight of him—not just a man, but something vast and unleashed.

Runes failed. Obsidian shattered. Reality staggered.

The court scattered. Nobles fled. Even Kaedros hid behind his throne.

But Cairn didn't see any of them.

The only thing he could see was her.

Collapsed on the dais, her blood soaking the stone, her wings still pinned by iron. The blade still buried in her chest.

And yet—

She glowed.

Not with blood or death, but with something deeper. A flicker of magic shimmered at her fingertips. Her veins pulsed with silver light, subtle but steady, like roots lit from beneath. Smoke curled upward around her, soft as a breath.

"No," Cairn rasped, voice fractured. "No, no, no—Seren—"

He stumbled to her, the last of the chains falling from his wrists with a hiss. His boots scraped against the blood-slick stone. The fire around him dimmed just enough to allow him forward—but not enough to calm the storm in him.

He dropped to his knees beside her, hands shaking as he reached for her cheek. "Please," he whispered. "Please, come back."

Not like a man. Not like a soldier. But like something unchained.

The moment Seren's breath ceased—when her eyes fluttered closed, her blood staining the dais in a spreading pool. The silver glow disappeared —something inside him shattered. The bond snapped with a soundless scream, ripping through his chest like molten wire. His soul howled. His body followed.

And Rhyne was closest.

Cairn's hand shot out, catching him by the throat. Inhumanly fast. Inhumanly strong. He lifted him off the ground with one arm, fire blooming at his shoulders, tattoos igniting in jagged pulses of gold and crimson. Rhyne clawed at Cairn's forearm, legs kicking, but Cairn didn't flinch.

"You called her my little spark," Cairn growled, voice shaking with rage. "You touched her. Hurt her. Mocked her."

Rhyne gasped, face twisting. "I—"

Cairn slammed him into the wall hard enough to crack the stone.

"I told you once," he hissed, "if there was a hair out of place—if she suffered—I'd end you."

He dropped Rhyne just long enough to let him stumble.

Then Cairn's hand hit his chest—flat-palmed—and fire surged from his tattoos in a blinding flare.

Rhyne screamed as molten lines branded his skin, glowing veins spiderwebbing out from his heart. The magic wasn't just burning him—it was unraveling him. Like a soul being forcibly ripped from its anchor.

"You don't get a death," Cairn snarled. "You get a fate."

Rhyne's eyes widened in terror as the same cruel sigils that adorned Cairn's own arms flared to life across his body—binding marks. That when Rhyne realized, Cairn was going to doom him to the fate of the Cinderwraiths.

"No—no, not that—Cairn, I was your brother—!"

"You were the only one I trusted," Cairn spat. "And you gave her to him."

Rhyne screamed again.

His mouth opened wider than humanly possible. His limbs twisted, bones snapping in strange directions as black smoke poured from his nostrils, his eyes, his ribs.

Cairn didn't stop.

He fed the fire.

By the time it ended, Rhyne was no longer Rhyne.

He was a hollow thing. His yellow eyes gone dim, skin scorched and cracking like over-fired clay. Smoke coiled through the gaps in his chest. His voice—when it emerged—was a low, hollow rasp.

Cairn stepped back, staring at what remained.

"You won't die," he said coldly. "You'll serve."

He turned away, leaving the creature that had once been his friend twitching in ash and ruin behind him. The new brand dug deep across his chest, right above his heart. A brutal reminder of the biggest betrayal he would experience.

But deep in his gut, under the rage, under the grief, something still pulsed.

Seren's glow.

The faintest, impossible spark.

And then— Time stuttered.

Everything around them slowed—voices muffled, heat suspended in the air like trapped breath.

A new light broke through the ceiling above.

Soft. White. Unnatural to the Pyric realm.

It fell across Seren's body like a curtain lifting from a stage. Her blood stopped spreading. Her breath caught—not a gasp, not a struggle. Just... a pause.

And in that pause—

Her eyes opened.

But they were not her eyes.

They were stars.

White fire rimmed with silver, ancient and unknowable. A wind that didn't exist stirred the edges of her wings. Her chains evaporated into smoke. Even the iron spikes crumbled to ash.

Cairn froze.

"Seren?" he whispered.

But it wasn't her voice that answered.

Not at first.

It was something older.

A chorus, layered and echoing—like the voices of the thousands who had once crossed the Veil and now whispered back from its edge.

"She has chosen."

Cairn's vision blurred.

"She is not dead. She is becoming."

The chamber trembled.

And suddenly—

The dais was gone.

So was the court. The walls. The obsidian.

Cairn was no longer kneeling before a throne of cruelty.

He was beneath the Tree.

Chapter Twenty-Four: The Hollow Between

Seren

The first thing Seren felt was stillness.

Not sleep. Not unconsciousness. But a stillness so complete, so unbroken, it felt alive.

She wasn't floating, exactly—more like suspended. Held in warmth, not fire or heat, but something older. A current humming beneath her skin, as if her bones remembered a song they'd never heard.

Her breath came without lungs. Her body had no weight.

But she knew she was whole.

She opened her eyes.

There was no sky. No ground. Only light—

A pale shimmer like starlight on snow, endless in every direction. Time didn't move here, it pulsed. Somewhere deep, she felt a heartbeat—not just her own, but another's. Steady. Familiar. Cairn's. A tether she couldn't see, but one her soul wrapped around instinctively.

She tried to speak his name, but no words came.

Not because her voice failed her—because she didn't need it.

And then the wind changed.

Except... there was no wind. Just motion.

A breath that passed through her, not around her—stirring the filaments of her wings.

Her wings.

They shimmered now, fully unfurled—not feathered, not scaled, but woven from silver and flame, like the edge of a dream spun into shape. She flexed them experimentally. They moved with her thoughts. Light and air and longing made tangible.

A voice came—not from behind, not from ahead. All around. Within.

"You have come far, little spark."

It didn't startle her.

It wrapped around her like velvet sleep, like the feeling of being held and remembered at once. Seren turned toward it instinctively.

And there it was—

The Tree.

But no longer rooted in stone, or in the Pyric realm's shattered mountain. It stood unmoored in the center of the light. Massive. Timeless. Its branches reached beyond reality—through sky, flame, void, and memory. Its roots did not dig into soil, but into truth.

And beneath its roots... someone waited.

A figure stepped forward, and for a moment, Seren thought it was a woman—tall, cloaked, crowned. But then it flickered. Became starlight. Smoke. A dying sun. Then shadow. Flame. Water. Her form shifted with each blink—goddess, storm, mirror, mother. Never still. Never one thing.

"You are not dead," the voice said again—gentler now, deep inside Seren's chest.

Seren didn't panic. She didn't cry. She didn't ask where she was.

Instead, she whispered, "But I was."

The figure inclined her head. "You crossed the threshold. Most do not return. But you were called."

Seren's throat tightened. "By the Tree?"

"No," said the goddess. "By your choice."

The light trembled around her, like breath.

Seren swallowed. "What am I now?"

The goddess smiled—not with her face, but with the space between stars.

"You are becoming."

Branches of the Tree drifted downward like hands, curling gently around Seren. The bark shimmered with constellations. The leaves whispered.

"You were born of two worlds," the goddess said. "Carried in mortal blood. Touched by Pyric flame. Marked by a bond that defied rule and bloodline. And when you died… the Veil did not reject you."

"It changed me," Seren said, her voice hoarse.

"It heard you."

The goddess's voice hummed like bone-deep thunder.

"The Veil listens. It always has. Most are too loud to hear it answer."

As she spoke, the light above shifted—fracturing. Seren gasped.

Each shard of the sky showed a different world. Dozens—maybe hundreds—of realms, layered like glass. One glowed green with vines as thick as rivers. Another seethed red with molten ruin. One flickered with song. One bled shadows. She saw realms sleeping. Realms unraveling. Realms crying out.

She reached toward them. "Are they all in danger?"

"Many are," said the goddess. "The balance frays. Not from malice, but from disconnection. The Veil is not a wall. It is a bridge. It feels when those it protects forget to honor what lies beyond."

Seren's voice trembled. "So what happens now?"

"You become the Veil."

The words sank into her ribcage like a second heartbeat.

"To be the Veil is not to divide. It is to balance. To feel. To choose. To witness."

The tree glowed brighter behind her.

"You will see the wounds of the world and feel them as your own. You will bear the weight of those trying to cross. Some will plead. Some will tear. Some will offer love. Others will demand blood. You are not their warden. You are their reckoning."

Seren looked down at her hands. They glowed faintly—starlight traced the lines of her palms, along with faint ember-scars from the bond.

Her breath hitched. "Will I... will I be able to go back?"

"In form? Perhaps. In full? Unlikely. But in essence, yes. The Tree is learning how to anchor you—so you may return when the boundary permits. In dreams. In flame. In memory."

Seren's eyes welled. "I don't know if I can do this."

"You can," said the goddess. "You always could."

A long pause.

Then—her voice broke.

"Cairn."

A shiver passed through her chest like a dropped stone.

"He will walk beside you," the goddess said. "Not always in body. But always in bond. He did not love your power. He loved your persistence. Your honesty. The steady spark you lit in every darkened place. You remind him who he was... and who he could become. You are a pair, light and dark. The perfect opposites. Even in these new forms"

Seren clutched her arms around her ribs, breath shaking. "It hurts."

"Good."

The goddess's form flickered, just once, into Seren's own reflection. "It means your soul is still yours."

The Tree pulsed again, low and solemn.

"You are the moment before grief. The whisper before fire. The space between rage and mercy."

A crack echoed through the stillness. The base of the tree split—not violently, but like a door opening. A rift, soft-edged and gleaming, appeared behind her.

"Will I see him again?" Seren asked, her voice smaller now.

The goddess tilted her head.

"He will always come when you call. Even if you don't know you're calling."

Seren's wings unfurled again, brighter than before. Lilac and silver, veined with truth. Her feet brushed the ground for the first time—though no dirt marked this place.

The Tree sighed.

"Go," the goddess whispered. "Not to conquer. To become. The Veil does not punish. It protects."

Seren turned. The rift beckoned.

One last breath.

She stepped through—

And the light folded in behind her.

Chapter Twenty-Five: Bound to Her

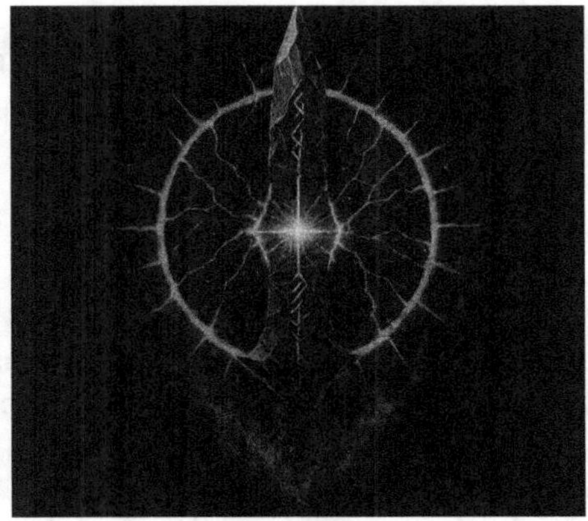

Cairn

That ancient mountain tree where the realms bled into one another, where truth and magic came unbound. The roots twisted through the stars. The sky was neither day nor night but something in between.

Seren stood before him.

Whole.

Wings unfurled, light cascading from her skin like river-water. She looked like herself—no longer in pain—but behind her eyes, the cosmos burned.

"I couldn't let it end that way," she said softly, and this time, it was her. "I couldn't let them win."

Cairn stepped forward, hollowed by grief, fury, awe. "What... what are you?"

Her smile trembled, but her voice held.

"I'm the Veil now."

Cairn stared at her, breath caught between awe and devastation.

"No," he said, voice barely there. "You're... you're Seren. My little spark. You can't—"

"I was," she whispered. "And I still am. But I'm more now."

She stepped closer, bare feet silent on the silver-lit ground beneath the Tree. The roots curled gently around her ankles, pulsing with light that matched the glow in her veins.

"This place gave me a choice," she continued. "The Tree… the bond… whatever rules the realms, it heard me. It felt everything—the pain, the questions, the truth. And it offered a path."

Cairn's fists clenched at his sides. "And you chose this? You chose to become this? To leave me?"

"I chose to keep the realms from tearing each other apart." Her eyes shimmered, not with tears, but stars. "I chose to protect what you couldn't. What none of us could. Not like this."

He shook his head. "You were dying, and they used you. They murdered you."

"And I came back." She stepped close enough to press her hand to his chest. "Not as a ghost. Not as a martyr. As something new. I am the boundary now. The breath between worlds. The flame that flickers between the cracks."

Her fingers pressed into the skin over his heart. "And you are the reason I remembered who I was long enough to make that choice."

Cairn dropped to his knees again. "Then take me with you."

Her smile broke, raw and tender. "You're not done, Cairn."

"I don't care."

"You will." She cupped his face in her hands. "Because you are more than what they made you. And this"—her thumb brushed the edge of his newest brand, still angry and red on his collarbone—"was never meant to be your end."

"It wasn't supposed to be yours either," he said bitterly. "And I didn't stop it."

She leaned forward, forehead against his. "You can't stop fate. But you can change what follows."

Light coiled around them, the world growing thinner at the edges. The Tree behind her pulsed once, roots shifting like a heartbeat. Seren began to shimmer, not fade—never fade—but rise.

"I will still feel you," she said softly. "The bond won't break. I'm still with you."

Cairn swallowed. "But I won't find you again."

She kissed his temple. "Not in the way you think."

The light swelled.

"I'll be the Veil you walk through. The hush between flames. I'll be the breath in your lungs when you don't think you can keep going."

And then—

She was gone.

Not vanished.

Absorbed.

Into the Tree. Into the roots. Into the line that runs between realms.

Cairn was alone beneath the canopy, the wind silent now, the stars still. The roots curled faintly, cradling the spot where she had stood.

He fell forward, hands fisted in the silver soil.

"I love you, my little spark" he whispered to the empty space she'd left behind. "In this world... and the next."

And for the first time in centuries—

He wept.

The silver soil clung to his knees. His hands were buried in it, trembling. His chest heaved but no air came. Not really. Not the kind that mattered.

She was gone.

Not dead. Not lost.

She had ascended.

And now she was the Veil.

The thing he'd sworn his soul to protect.

The boundary between realms. The last breath between light and ruin.

And the woman he loved.

"They made me a blade."

"They burned my name, stole my soul, carved me into a weapon meant to guard the Veil."

"But they never imagined the Veil would become the only thing I'd ever beg to hold."

"And now they will pay."

Cairn's fingers curled into fists, sinking deeper into the silver-cracked earth. His body shook—not from pain. From purpose.

The tattoos along his skin flared violently, but this time, it wasn't the molten orange of the Pyric oath.

It was lilac.

Soft. Divine.

It rippled up his arms like blooming flame—light kissed with starlight, not magma. Every brand, every ancient scar, ignited in her color, not theirs.

He opened his eyes. The same light burned in them. Gone was the hollowed Ashmarked assassin. What rose to his feet beneath the Tree was something else entirely—something more.

The bond hadn't shattered. It had evolved. He was no longer sworn only to the Veil. He was sworn to her.

Cairn stood tall beneath the pulsing canopy. The winds stilled. Even the stars seemed to hold their breath. The Tree behind him groaned softly, its roots curling in reverence—as if recognizing the creature it had forged beside her.

He didn't need a crown.

He didn't need a throne.

He was vengeance incarnate.

A blade reborn in lilac flame.

And the Pyric court would burn.

The rift didn't open.

It tore.

Cairn didn't use a blade or chant. Didn't whisper to the flames. He commanded, and the world obeyed.

Reality split with a shriek as Cairn stepped through, leaving silver soil behind and entering the Keep like a star on a collision course with ruin.

But he didn't go up. He went down. The air thickened, heat curling along his spine as he descended into the Warrens.

He passed screaming guards. Melted through locked gates. No mercy. No hesitation.

Torchlight bent around him. Stone warped beneath him. His fury was a force—not of this realm, not of any realm.

The first cell block trembled as he entered. The prisoners—Fae, half-bloods, exiles—shrank back, afraid. But his eyes didn't burn with cruelty. They burned with promise.

He raised a single hand. The locks—dozens of them—melted. Chains hit stone. And the wailing stopped.

"Go," Cairn said, voice low and lethal. "You were caged for defiance. Now let that defiance walk free."

No one moved. Then a woman with cracked horns stepped forward, disbelief in her eyes.

"Why?" she asked.

His voice was a snarl. "Because she would have freed you."

That broke the spell.

The prisoners surged into motion—wounded, furious, radiant in their rebellion. They didn't thank him. They ran. Cairn turned. There were more.

He stalked deeper into the belly of the Keep, freeing cell after cell. Some cried. Some fell to their knees. One young Fae with ash-smeared tears whispered, "Are you him? The one who rose with the Veil?"

He didn't answer. Not with words. He showed the power of the Veil.

The Keep groaned overhead as fire licked its bones.

When the last chain fell, when the last gate buckled, he stood in the center of the Warrens and raised both hands.

Lilac flame surged outward—up the walls, across the floor, through the stone. It didn't just burn.

It devoured.

The Warrens collapsed with a scream of magma and smoke. Prisoners fled behind him. But Cairn didn't run.

He rose.

Back into the heart of the Keep. Up stairwells. Through battlements. Through anyone who tried to stop him. The last of the loyalists fell with barely a glance. Their blades melted. Their screams echoed and were lost to fire.

But Kaedros was gone. So was the Court.

The throne room lay abandoned—only soot and shattered runes remaining.

They had run.

Cowards.

Cairn stood at the center of the hollow Keep, his body wreathed in Veillight, the realm around him choking on its own sins.

Smoke curled from the seams of the stone. The banners of the old rule burned.

And Cairn whispered—

"I will find you."

He turned, cloak of flame trailing behind him, as the Keep shuddered one final time and collapsed in on itself.

Ash swallowed it whole. Let the world remember what he did. Let them all remember the day the Veil walked.

When the flame faded, but one remained.

Riven.

Frozen near the threshold of the ruined keep. Blood smudged across his brow. Wide-eyed. Trapped between fear and faith.

And Cairn saw him.

Cairn stepped toward him, fire licking at his heels.

But something stilled his hand.

A breath.

A presence.

Seren, the little spark.

She was there—not in body, but in purpose. In him. The Veil curled in his chest like a tether, a heartbeat he could no longer separate from his own.

Cairn's flame dimmed—but not out.

He lowered his hand.

"You won't die today," he said, voice like molten stone. "Not because you deserve mercy. But because she does."

Riven's lips parted, confused. "What—what do you mean?"

Cairn's voice was steady, absolute. "You have been given a choice. You will not serve the King. You will serve her. Or you will meet her in death—between the realms, where no soul finds peace."

The flames surged faintly at Cairn's fingertips, heat pulsing like judgment.

Riven swallowed hard, chest heaving. "And if I swear?"

"You become hers," Cairn said. "Not mine. Not the Court's. You walk blind into her will, and you do not stray."

A beat of silence.

Then—Riven dropped to one knee.

Head bowed.

"I swear," he rasped. "To the Veil. To her. I swear."

Cairn stepped forward, pressing two burning fingers to Riven's brow.

The fire didn't consume this time—it marked.

A blazing sigil seared into Riven's skin, glowing pale as starlight.

"And from this day forward," Cairn said, "you will see only what the Veil allows."

Riven's breath caught.

Then he screamed.

His eyes turned white—blank as moonstone—and then dark. Not burned. Just... empty. Sightless in the mortal sense.

But sworn now, fully, to a higher one.

Blinded. Not by punishment. By devotion.

He stumbled to one knee, the sigil pulsing faintly above his brow, and whispered through bloodied lips:

"I see."

Cairn turned towards the rest of the realm. The keep fully collapsing behind him, flames curling in satisfaction.

Let the realm remember this day.

When gods did not descend—

but rose in the ashes of what was broken.

When the Veil took form not as barrier, but blade.

And those who betrayed her were turned to dust.

Let every shadow whisper what they saw.

Let every flame carry the name she chose.

The Veil had awakened.

And through him—

it had walked.

It had burned.

It had judged.

And it would not be forgotten.

The Keep was ash.

The King and court scurried away, hiding in a hole he would find.

And Cairn stood at its center, not as an enforcer—but as the last remaining shadow of what once ruled.

Smoke curled from the cracks in the ground, slow and reverent, like the realm itself didn't know how to breathe without chains. The sky above was fractured—ribbons of light bleeding through the Veil in soft, trembling streaks.

He had destroyed what was broken. Now he had to decide what came after.

Chapter Twenty-Six: Not all Kings Wear Crowns

Cairn

Cairn returned to the house.

It still smelled of her. The couch held the memory of their meal together, the faint press where she had sat beside him, laughing softly, brushing crumbs from her lap. The air still seemed to hum with the echo of her voice.

The shower was worse. Steam clung to the walls in his memory, her skin against his, water slicking between them. He could still feel her there, close and real in a way nothing else had ever been.

And the bed—he couldn't look at it for long. The sheets still bore the impression of her body, the warmth of her beside him in the dark.

Every corner, every shadow, whispered her name.

His chest tightened, the silence pressing like a blade against his ribs.

The fire inside him answered first in flickers, then in waves. Tattoos blazed molten bright, spilling heat into the room until the walls groaned. He didn't stop it. Wouldn't.

The house shuddered.

With a roar, it broke. Beams cracked, stone splintered, the roof gave way. Flames surged outward, devouring everything until the world collapsed around him in ash and ruin.

When the fire stilled, only rubble remained—blackened timber, silvered dust. Cairn stood at the center, untouched, the ground still quaking faintly beneath his feet.

The grief had not burned out. His power had not drained. If anything, it had grown.

He turned from the wreckage. There was nowhere else to go. Every corner of the world carried her shadow, every silence called her name— yet only one place still bound them.

The Tree.

Its roots coiled through the bones of the world. Its branches still carried the echo of her choice, the shimmer of her becoming. If he could reach her, it would be there.

So he went.

The Tree loomed, colossal, its branches heavy with starlight. Cairn dropped to one knee at its base, fists curling into the soil.

"Bring her back." His voice was low, steady, a command, not a plea.

Nothing.

His fist drove into the ground, sending cracks across the silvered earth. "You bound her to yourself. Then bind her back to me. She chose the Veil—fine. But don't make me carry it alone."

The Tree stood silent, unmoved.

Heat rippled from his skin, the ground trembling as he struck again, deeper, harder. His breath came ragged, but his voice never wavered. "She is not gone. I feel her in every step. If you hear me—then answer."

Still, silence.

His head lowered, fire dimming to a simmer, not from weakness but from the weight of holding it back. His forehead pressed briefly to the roots, not surrender but defiance against the silence.

"I will not stop," he muttered. "Not until I find her."

At last, when his body refused to stand any longer, he let himself sink into the roots. Muscles taut even in rest, he closed his eyes.

Silence pressed in, heavy as stone, until exhaustion finally dragged him under.

And then the world tilted.

Not with violence—no quake, no fire—but with a subtle shift, like the weight of reality itself moved sideways. The stars blurred. The ground thinned.

And Seren stepped from the roots.

Not flesh. Not ghost. Something between—her form rimmed in starlight, her eyes vast with depth that swallowed every shadow. She wasn't the woman he had carried in his arms, but she wasn't lost to him either.

Cairn rose at once, fists still curled, shoulders squared as if before an enemy. Only when her smile flickered—soft, familiar, utterly hers—did his body ease. Just a fraction.

"You're not real," he said. His voice was gravel, steady, testing the edge of belief.

"Real enough," she whispered. Her presence moved toward him like warmth brushing across cold skin. She didn't touch, but he felt her all the same. "You called, Cairn. And I came."

Something in him cracked, though his fire burned steady on the surface. "I can burn kingdoms, Seren. I can tear the ground apart. And still I can't reach you."

Her form wavered with the weight of his words, then steadied. She lifted her hand—only light, no flesh—and laid it just above his chest. His fire stirred beneath her touch, answering her essence like flint striking steel.

"You don't need to tear anything down," she said. "I'm already inside you. In your fire. In every choice you make."

He shook his head, a hard breath breaking loose. "It's not enough. I need you here. With me."

Her gaze softened, galaxies deep and unflinching. "And you will have me—in ways the Veil will allow. Not as before. Not as you want. But I am not gone, Cairn. Not to you."

His throat worked, the words jagged. "I thought losing you would hollow me. Instead it's feeding something I can't control."

Her hand lingered, glow sinking into him. "Then let it feed you. Not toward ruin—toward purpose. Protect. Endure. Become more than the weapon you were forged to be."

For a moment he almost broke again. Almost. But he held himself still, a soldier before a vision. Only his eyes betrayed him, burning wet in the starlight.

Her smile gentled. "I will meet you in the silence. In the fire beneath your skin. In the decisions no one else can make. When you think you stand alone—you won't."

His breath caught, rough. "Promise me," he said. The demand cracked into something rawer. "In this world… and the next."

Her glow flickered, but her gaze never wavered. "I will love you in both," she whispered. "Nothing will sever that. Not realm. Not time. Not even death."

Something inside him opened, fierce and helpless all at once. "And I will love you, Seren. Here. Beyond. Wherever we are driven."

She reached for him—no flesh, only light—and pressed her forehead to his. Heat, essence, memory. Enough.

"My little spark," Cairn breathed.

Her smile trembled. "Always yours. Always."

The Tree pulsed once behind her—approval, echo, witness.

And then she was gone, her light dissolving into him, sealing her vow into his flame.

Cairn jerked awake at the Tree's base, chest heaving, fire simmering low but threaded now with starlight. Different. Changed. Not vengeance alone, but vow.

Riven waited on the edge of the mountain, just far enough to give them privacy. His posture straight but uncertain. His brows lifted when Cairn approached.

"She came to you?" Riven asked.

Cairn gave a single nod. "She's not gone. Not really."

Riven hesitated. "And now?"

Cairn looked toward the horizon—the crackling sky far off, the world slowly stirring in the distance.
 "Now we rebuild," he said. "We find the other Ashmarked. Confirm who still follows the Veil—not the Court, not the crown."

Riven's jaw tightened, then he nodded. "And if they don't?"

"Then they chose their fate already."

A pause. Then Riven asked, "And the rest?"

Cairn's voice was quiet, but certain. "We restore what's broken. Protect the Veil. Even those the Court would damn—half-bloods, sympathizers, mortals who can feel its pull. The Veil chose them, whether the king accepts it or not. They are ours to guard."

Riven's eyes narrowed, but something fierce sparked in them. "That will be called treason."

Cairn turned back to the Tree, eyes burning faintly with starlight and flame. "Then let it be treason. We'll build something stronger from the ash. She will guide us—through the silence, through the fire, through every choice that follows. Seren didn't give her life for the Court. She gave it for the Veil. For all of us who can still feel it."

The wind shifted—carrying ash and starlight alike. For the first time since the chamber burned, Cairn breathed without pain.

Not all fates are doomed, the Tree whispered without sound.
 And not all kings wear crowns.

The Realms Still Shift....

The screams had quieted. The Keep was ash.

But the Veil still wept.

Cairn stood beneath the Tree where all realms meet. Monsters stirred in the shadows. Zealots preached in the streets. The Iron King was gone—missing, or hiding. The Pyric Realm teetered, fractured and leaderless.

The land cracked in protest.

The rifts still bled. And no matter how many he saved, the world still suffered.

Seren had warned him. This wasn't the end. It was only the beginning.

She touched his shoulder from the unseen—faint as a breeze, warm as a prayer.

"Our work isn't done," she whispered. "And we won't do it alone."

Far beyond the Tree, at the crumbling edges of the mortal Realm, a girl ran.

Twelve years old. No name on record. No history that made sense.

The only thing anyone agreed on was this: She was dangerous. She didn't know why. Only that they wanted her gone.

The gift under her skin pulsed like a curse. Like a secret trying to claw its way out.

She had begged her parents to help. They shut the door.

Now, men with guns and flame chased her through the woods.

She was faster. Smarter. But not for long.

And somewhere across the Veil, Seren felt her scream—

A spark in the dark.

A tether calling through the rootblood of the Tree.

"She needs us," Seren breathed. "We have to get to her before they do."

The wind howled in response. Cairn lifted his head.

He was already walking toward the fight.

360

Realm Archives

Seren Cross
32 Years Old
911 Dispatcher

Cairn Evergrave
~650 Years Old
Ashmarked Veil Enforcer

Marisol Alvarez
29 Years Old
Paramedic

Riven Cindereft
~50 Years Old
Newest Ashmarked

Rhyne Tareth
~300 Years Old
Warrens Keeper

Kaedros Veyne
~450 Years Old
Iron King

Hollowmire

Glyphcarion

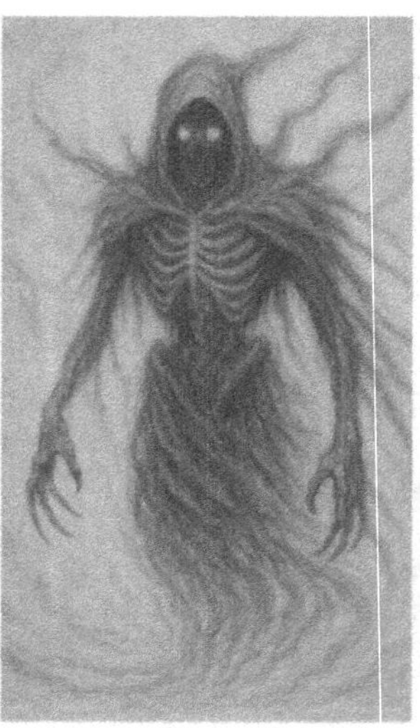
Cinderwraith

Haldreth

Ashleech

About the Author

(A.K.A. The Dispatcher with Too Many Feelings)

When not wrangling chaos on the radio as a 911 dispatcher, she's usually wrangling chaos on the page — fueled by caffeine, dark humor, and an unholy amount of snacks. Writing happens between night shifts, toddler negotiations, and explaining to her pets that they cannot, in fact, sit on the keyboard. Again.

She writes like she dispatches: fast, unfiltered, and with a deep respect for the quiet moments between the screaming. Her worlds are stitched together with fire, grief, and just enough hope to hurt.

If you liked Pyric Realm, wait till you see what's clawing through next.

Come say hi, scream into the void, or see what's on fire next at:

https://chelseamacarthur.wixsite.com/chelsea-marie-macart

(Yes, that's a real link. No, there's not a "normal" blog. Expect monsters and 911 shit. Links to my Facebook and Instagram are there too!)

Scan me

www.ingramcontent.com/pod-product-compliance
Lightning Source LLC
Chambersburg PA
CBHW051305300726
48976CB00002B/271